A Time to Die

★ NUMBER TWO IN THE AMERICAN ODYSSEY SERIES ★

A Time to Die

GILBERT MORRIS

Fleming H. Revell

A Division of Baker Book House Co
Grand Rapids, Michigan 49516

© 1994 by Gilbert Morris

Published by Fleming H. Revell
a division of Baker Book House Company
P.O. Box 6287, Grand Rapids, MI 49516-6287

Third printing, June 1995

Printed in the United States of America

Library of Congress Cataloging-in-Publication Data

Morris, Gilbert.
    A time to die / Gilbert Morris.
       p. cm. — (The American odyssey ; no. 2)
    ISBN 0-8007-5521-9
      1. Family—United States—Fiction. I. Title. II. Series.
PS3563.08742T563   1994
813'.54—dc20   93-36519

To Johnny Wink—my friend

Every writer needs someone to give him a start
—and you gave me that first push.
Thanks for that, and for the times you made
me laugh with your nutty poetry.
Thanks for the time you stood by me
when I needed a stander-by.
Thanks for being my friend.

CONTENTS

PART FOUR Action of the Tiger

THE STUART FAMILY

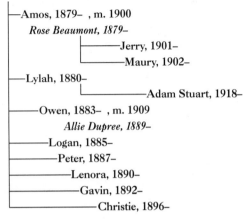

William Stuart, 1852– , m. 1878, remarried 1905
    Marian Edwards, 1860–1905   *Agnes Barr, 1875–*
        Amos, 1879– , m. 1900
        Rose Beaumont, 1879–
                Jerry, 1901–
                Maury, 1902–
        Lylah, 1880–
                Adam Stuart, 1918–
        Owen, 1883– , m. 1909
        Allie Dupree, 1889–
        Logan, 1885–
        Peter, 1887–
        Lenora, 1890–
        Gavin, 1892–
        Christie, 1896–

A Time to Be Born   A Time to Die

1900	1910	1920	1930	1940
Spanish-American War	Woodrow Wilson elected president	Lindbergh makes solo flight across Atlantic	The Great Depression	Polio epidemic ravages countr
Boxer Rebellion in China	World War I	Stock Market crash	Franklin Roosevelt elected president	Japanese attac Pearl Harbor

Part 1

STORM CLOUDS GATHER

1960	1970	1980	1990	2000
Billy Graham launches major campaigns	Vietnam War	Jesus People revival among youth	Ronald Reagan elected president	Bill Clinton elected president
racial segregation schools declared unconstitutional	Martin Luther King Jr. assassinated	Watergate scandal causes Nixon's downfall	Scandals involving TV evangelists	AIDS crisis worsens

1

REUNION

L ylah Stuart waited until the conductor placed the small steel platform in place, then smiled brilliantly at him as he took her hand to assist her from the train.

"It's been a lovely trip, Robert," she said, giving his hand a warm squeeze. It amused her to see his blink of astonishment, but she was accustomed to men being speechless in her presence. "Tell your wife and son I'd love to meet them sometime."

Robert Symington had been a conductor on the MoPac— the Missouri-Pacific railroad—for eight years. Before that he had served both as an engineer and a fireman, but he had never met anyone on the train as beautiful as Lylah Stuart. She had learned his name almost immediately, and somehow he had found himself telling her all about himself. All the way from Chicago, he had made it a point to see that the actress got the best treatment, and now he said eagerly, "I'll do that, Miss Stuart! Sure do hope to see you in a play someday."

"If you ever have a chance, send me word, Robert. I'll see that you get free tickets." Lylah smiled at him again, then turned and walked away.

Tim Malloy, the brakeman, sidled up to Symington. "Hey, Bob, you're in pretty fast company there," he remarked slyly. "Who was that dame?"

Symington shot a scornful glance toward the diminutive brakeman. "That was no dame, you hick! That was Lylah Stuart, the famous actress!" His eyes followed Lylah's progress as she made her way to the ticket office, then he shook his head. "Boy, she is really something, ain't she now?"

"Better not tell your wife about her, Bob." Tim grinned. "None of the wives I know would like their husbands getting close to a dish like that."

Lylah was aware of the admiring glances of the two men, but had become so accustomed to them that she paid no attention. Entering the small station, she walked at once to the ticket agent, a heavyset man of fifty with thinning white hair, and asked, "Is there any way I could get someone to drive me to my parents' home?"

The ticket agent blinked rapidly, then shook his head. "Well now, ma'am," he said, "there ain't but one what you might call a taxi in town. Belongs to Ed Jennings . . . but he's sick. Tell you what, though, I got a friend who's got a car. He usually drops in sometime a little later in the morning to play checkers. If you'd like to wait around, I reckon he might be willing to drive you where you want to go."

Lylah flashed him a dazzling smile, nodded, and said, "I'll go get something to eat. Then I'll come back and check with you later." She turned and left the station, walking slowly, tracing her way along the dimly remembered streets of Fort Smith, Arkansas. A soft smile played on her lips at the thought of how enormous this small Arkansas town had appeared to her during her youth. Now it seemed that it had shrunk to the size of a miniature village. The Grand Hotel on Oak Street with its majestic height of six stories had seemed to her a mammoth structure when she had come as a child of five to see the rodeo parade. But after the skyscrapers of New York and Chicago, the Grand now had for her the appearance of a small and pathetic warehouse. As she wandered the old streets, she thought, *Time does that to things, I guess. Everything changes . . . and most everything loses something. But I wouldn't go back to those days.*

A whim seized her and turning impulsively, she made her way across town to the stellar tourist attraction of Fort Smith—

a recreation of Judge Isaac Parker's gallows. During the late 1800s almost a hundred outlaws operating out of Indian Territory had been sentenced to execution by the famous "Hanging Judge."

A family of four, obviously tourists, were standing in front of the structure, staring up open-mouthed at the six ropes with their neat hangman's nooses, stirring with a ghostly motion in the spring breeze. The oldest of the children, a whey-faced fat boy of ten, suddenly reached over and took his sister by the throat, crying, "I'm the Hanging Judge . . . and I'm gonna string you up!" The father, a slight man wearing a suit that would have been fitting in New York society, said sharply, "Wallace! Leave your sister alone!" Whereupon, the mother, a leather-faced woman with a sour expression, snapped, "You always take Lucy's side! Come along, Wallace!" And she stalked away, her head high in the air.

Amos teased me that way when I was seven. Closing her eyes, Lylah allowed the strong memory of time past to flow over her spirit. *We'd come for the County Fair, and when we came to the gallows, Amos told me I was bad and would be hanged one day. I was scared—but didn't let him know it—and anyway, Owen whipped him for scaring me.*

Standing in front of the gallows, she was transported back to those days. Pigeons cooed softly and reverently, and from the river echoed the muted blast of a tug shoving its way up the Arkansas River. The sweet smell of cottonseed oil from the plants came to her, reminding her how it had always been her favorite smell as a child. *Let's go to Fort Smith so Lylah can smell the cottonseed,* her father had always called out when they were ready to go to town.

She closed her eyes and suddenly a saying that her Uncle Pete had been fond of leapt into her mind: *You can't step in the same river twice.* Once she'd asked her father about it. "Why can't you step in the same river twice, Pa?"

Will Stuart had been whittling on a stick of red cedar, not carving anything—just making beautiful curls of the fragrant wood, letting them fall to the ground. Carefully and deftly as a surgeon, he'd completed his stroke with the razor-sharp Buck pocket knife, then looked at her and smiled. "You can go back to the same spot on a river, honey, but the water that was there last time you went . . . why, it's moved on."

He'd snapped the knife shut, slipped it in the pocket of his faded overalls, then putting his hand on her head, he'd added almost sadly, "That old river over there won't stay still for nobody! Whut Pete meant was that the river keeps on goin' . . . and that's the way time is. Can't nobody stop it. And when you try to go back, it ain't there anymore. It's a brand new river—and that one will be gone as soon as you turn your back."

The memory disturbed her and when the mellow announcement from the clock in the tower of City Hall came echoing through the hot, still air, she started slightly. She opened her eyes and turned away from the gallows, thinking, *Hope I don't have nightmares about that blasted thing like I did the first time I saw it.*

As she moved along the street, a sharp sense of dissatisfaction stabbed at her, triggered by the disappointment the sight of Fort Smith had brought. It was a small shabby town hidden away in the backwoods of Arkansas, but during her years of trooping as an actress, she had kept some sort of dream: When she tired of the theater, she could always go back and pick up the life she'd left as a young woman.

"I couldn't abide living in this burg for two days!" she muttered, and abruptly hurried to the area where Bethany Bible Institute was located. She had hated it fervently during her days as a student there, but years had dimmed that part for her, so that she had now come to regard that time as an edenic period. It had been the last time she'd known anything that resembled tranquility.

Turning down Laurel Avenue, she was pleased at the sight of the huge elms shading the broad street. Long fingers of amber light from the burning sun overhead passing through the leaves made a filigree pattern on the pavement. All the houses were set far back from the street, unlike those in New York and Philadelphia and other eastern cities. Each one had a broad porch with a swing, and in one of them an old woman with a crown of silver hair rocked with a rhythmic cadence that matched the movement of the earth itself.

Meandering down the broad streets that led to the school, Lylah passed an ice wagon driven by a huge black man. He wore a leather cloak to keep dry, and she stopped to watch as he drew up to a big white house with three gables. A covey of children fluttered down the walk, crying in shrill voices, "Ice, Dorsey! Ice!" The large man laughed, the fragmented sunlight gleaming on a gold tooth. He stepped to the ground and chipped pieces of ice for them. They walked back toward the house, sucking on the clear crystal pieces as the iceman shouldered a massive block of shimmering ice. It looked like a huge diamond glittering in the sunlight, Lylah thought as she watched him carry it into the house.

Slowly she moved along the shaded street, drinking in the peace of it. Her world was loud and hectic and frantic, and she had a sudden weariness, thinking of the years that had passed since she had walked this street as a seventeen-year-old girl.

And then she turned the corner and there it was—Bethany Bible Institute. Stopping abruptly, she was shocked at how the sight of it affected her, for it was like stepping into the past. Years and months and days had passed, but time had left little mark on the school. She noticed one new building, but the mossy brick structures, dressed neatly in ivy, that made up the two main edifices of the college squatted lazily in the mottled shade just as they had years ago. Staring at the classroom buildings, she thought of those days, of the students she had made friends with, and wondered if the faculty were still there . . . and if they still remembered the wayward girl, Lylah Stuart, who had run away from school to become an actress.

Slowly she turned to walk along the sidewalk toward the chapel that rose beneath huge oak trees. As she stepped up to the door, the thought came to her of how she had hated chapel with a passion! She had missed so many times that the president himself had had to call her in and warn her about it. She had thought about those chapels many times in her travels, sometimes lying awake in a third-rate rooming house, touring with a play that was slowly going broke. She had remembered those chapels and the men who had preached the long fiery sermons. *If I had to do it again, I might listen to them a little more closely.*

Abruptly she shook her head and stepped inside. It was like stepping into the past. The chapel had not changed. The familiar smell of the old wood took her back. Looking up at the high ceiling, Lylah saw the stained glass windows portraying David killing Goliath, Daniel sitting among the group of lions as if they were big tabby cats, Joshua marching around the walls of Jericho. The past rolled over her, bringing a taste of sadness for days long gone. Slowly she walked down the aisle and sat down on the pew that had been her seat in those days.

The silence of the building surrounded her. She sat there thinking about her life—what it had been and what it had become. Then suddenly she became conscious of another presence. A tall man had come through the front door and was proceeding along the aisle. He came almost even with her before he lifted his eyes and then stopped abruptly.

"Oh!" he said. "I'm sorry . . . I didn't know anyone was here."

The light in the chapel was dim, but Lylah recognized him instantly. She smiled and said, "Donald? Don't you know me?"

Leaning forward, the tall man peered through his wire-rim glasses and his eyes went wide as recognition came. "Lylah!" he gasped. "Is it really you?"

Lylah stood to her feet and put out her hand. "Yes, it's really me. I suppose you couldn't have been more surprised to find the Kaiser himself in church here, could you, Donald?"

Donald Satterfield was a tall man in his mid-thirties with sandy hair and bright blue eyes behind the lenses of his glasses. He was homely enough, but Lylah thought he always had been. Still, there was that kindly look in his eyes she remembered fondly. As she stared at him, she also remembered how he had been in love with her seventeen years ago. She had known it then, but her sights had been fixed on much more than marrying a preacher and trying to satisfy the ladies of a congregation for the rest of her life.

"Lylah, what in the world—"

"I've just gotten off the train, Donald. We're having a family reunion and I'm on my way home. I'm waiting now for someone to come to the station and take me."

Donald Satterfield straightened up. "Why, you don't have to do that," he said eagerly. "I've got a car. I'll be glad to take you."

"That would be wonderful! We could talk about old times, couldn't we?"

Satterfield nodded vigorously. "Come along. I want you to meet my wife and children. Then we'll go right on out to your place."

He led her into the parsonage that had been the president's home and there introduced her to his wife, a plump, pretty woman of about twenty-eight, and his two boys, Henry and Charles, ages two and five. When he told his wife about Lylah's profession, Lylah did not miss the flash of apprehension that came into Mrs. Satterfield's eyes.

She's heard about me, I see, Lylah thought. *And she's afraid to let her husband go with one of those loose actresses from the big city.*

Perhaps that was the case, but Mrs. Satterfield, when her husband had explained the problem, was gracious. "Why, of course you must take Miss Stuart to her home, Donald." She turned to Lylah then and asked, "Would you let me fix you something to eat before you go?"

"No, thank you. I ate on the train, and I'm anxious to get home. I haven't seen my family in five years."

Donald bustled about, getting ready, and ten minutes later the two of them were headed out of Fort Smith in his Model T Ford. She waited in the seat until he cranked the engine. It fired, and he ran back to adjust the spark.

"It's got a few miles on it, but she runs fine," he said. There was a proud note in his voice as he spoke of the car. "Didn't like that black paint, so I put the red paint on myself."

"It's beautiful, Donald. I know you're very proud of it. Not everyone has a car."

As the old Ford chugged out of Fort Smith, Donald shouted above the racket. "It must be exciting, being an actress. We read about you from time to time, and I always wished you'd come here to do one of your plays."

"I don't think you would be able to go, would you, Donald? I mean, we don't have many preachers in the audience. Most ministers think stage plays are of the devil."

Satterfield turned and gave her a smile. "I . . . I'd go to see you no matter *what* the congregation thought," he declared firmly. "Nothing you would do would be really wrong."

Lylah fell silent, disturbed by his words, and as Satterfield chattered on, she thought about some of the plays she had appeared in. Some were not fit to be seen because they were of poor artistic quality. Others glorified a lifestyle she herself did not fully agree with. She thought also of some of the shabby affairs she had had, mostly with actors, during the ten years she had been in the theater. She was glad that Donald did not know any of this, for she remembered him warmly, as part of a past that she was no longer in, but which she somehow treasured.

Lylah herself was a warmhearted, loving woman, but her desire to escape the poverty and the monotony of the Arkansas farm had been too much for her, and when the opportunity had come to join a traveling road show, she had grabbed it.

The years had been good to her financially. She had been in several good plays and had gained a reputation as a fine actress, though never had she achieved top billing. But now, as they traveled through the hills that were bursting with green, she knew that deep down, she'd missed this part of life. She felt a surge of longing for the serenity, the peace, the lack of pressure that went with living in this world.

Lylah removed her hat and let the warm morning breeze caress her hair. She listened as Donald spoke of the things that filled his life—Sunday school, revival meetings, church suppers—all the little details that made up the life of a small-town preacher.

He turned off the asphalt highway onto the narrow dirt road that wound through the hills and the valleys surrounding her old home. Somehow the closer Lylah got to the place where she had been born, the more nervous she became. For one thing, she was not at all certain of her welcome, for her professional status as an actress had not been accepted, at least by her stepmother. And even her father had been leery of it.

Suddenly they crested the hill overlooking the valley where Lylah had grown up, and she cried out, "Stop, Donald! Stop the car!"

He slammed on the brakes and the idle clacking motor jarred the silence of the morning air. He cast her an anxious glance. "Something wrong, Lylah?"

"No," she said quickly. "I—I just wanted to look for a moment. I haven't seen the place in such a long time." The house sat among a stand of hickory trees, with pecan trees out back. She'd gathered those pecans a thousand times during her youth. She thought of the pies and cakes and cookies her mother had made from them. She saw that a new barn had been built and a new pasture added. There were cattle with white faces grazing out there now instead of the wild scrub cows she remembered.

The tire swing—it's still there! Logan fell out of it on Easter morning and broke his arm. I was so mad I wanted to cut it down and burn the rope! Lylah smiled, letting her eyes run over the farm, every inch a receptacle for some memory from her childhood. She recalled the barn where she'd hidden her collection of racy novels and that she'd used as a shield when smoking corn-silk cigarettes. *I wonder if the younger kids tried out things like that?* An ancient milky-colored horse ambled across the pasture, and Lylah said, "Look, Don! Old Bing is still alive!"

"Remember the time he kicked you in the stomach, Lylah?" Satterfield smiled. "It was the first time I ever heard you cuss."

Lylah laughed and put her hand on his. "I gave you a hard time, didn't I, Donald?"

"No," he said quietly. "It wasn't all that bad." He was acutely aware of her hand pressing on his, and added, "You just weren't meant for life in the hills, I guess."

Something in her face changed, and she murmured, "Sometimes I wish I'd never left this farm." Then she blinked and said almost brusquely, "Let's go, Donald."

He revved up the engine and drove quickly along the rutted dirt road, pulling up at last in front of the house.

Before they even reached the door, the yard was flooded with the family coming out. As soon as Donald helped her down, Lylah was surrounded by her brothers and sisters. She was shocked at how old they seemed. In her mind, they had been mere children—but now they were all grown. They pulled at her, anxious to touch her, to hug her, and she went around hugging each one, speaking to them.

"Logan! Why, you good-looking thing! I can't believe you've gotten so old. How old are you now?"

Logan Stuart, twenty-nine and the oldest of the boys still at home, hugged her. "Good to see you, Sis." Logan grinned. "Never mind how old I am. You look great."

Lylah turned to face Lenora. "How pretty you are! Let me look at you!" She held the girl at arm's length, admiring the ash blond hair, the hazel eyes. "My, you are lovely! How old are you now? Twenty-four?" She shook her head. "And not married. What's the matter with the young men around here?"

"They don't have any sense, that's what's the matter." Gavin, twenty-two, shoved past Lenora and stood in front of Lylah. He had dark hair and eyes, much like his father's mother. "About time you got home, Sis," he said. "We thought you'd forgotten us."

"Not likely. Where's Christie?"

"Right here." Christie Stuart, age eighteen, pushed her way through the crowd and collected her hug from Lylah. With her very blond hair and dark blue eyes she was extremely pretty. "Oh, I'm so glad you're home, Lylah. We've waited so long for you to come."

They talked rapidly, babbling, everyone trying to catch Lylah's attention, and then as she lifted her head and saw her father come to stand on the porch, she quickly went to him.

"Hello, Pa," she said as he stepped down. He hesitated, then he put out his arms, and she went into them as she had when she was a little girl. He held her and she clung to him. When she stepped back, there were tears in her eyes. "You look fine, Pa," she whispered. "Real fine."

But in truth, William Stuart did not look at all well, and she was shocked at the changes in him. Instead of the muscular, athletic man she remembered, her father was bent and gaunt, and there were wrinkles around his eyes. His chestnut hair still had reddish glints, but it was streaked with gray with the familiar white streak running from front to back on the left side where a minie ball had plowed through his scalp at the Battle of Five Forks, the last battle of the Civil War. He had been only twelve when he had joined up after his own father had been killed at the Battle of Nashville.

"It's good to see you, Daughter," Will said quietly. He tried to smile, but she could see that he was deeply affected by the meeting. "Come on in the house and tell us what all you been doing."

He led the way in and the other children followed. When

they were inside, Lylah saw her stepmother standing in the door that led to the kitchen.

She walked over to greet the woman. "Hello, Agnes. It's good to see you again."

Agnes Barr Stuart made no move to welcome Lylah—no handshake, no hug. Agnes had been one of William Stuart's "lady friends" and had trapped him after his first wife had died. Agnes was still an attractive woman with lustrous sable hair, but her lush figure was beginning to run to fat, and there was an icy light in the green eyes. She had been a loose woman. Still was, according to gossip in the valley. What concerned Lylah most, though, was her treatment of the children. From their expressions, it was easy to see that they despised their stepmother.

She nodded slightly. "I'll fix you something to eat."

"Oh, that would be nice," Lylah said. "I really am hungry." Then she thought, "Oh, we left Donald out in the car! I forgot!" She ran to the door and called, "Donald, come in."

Donald got out of the Ford and ambled up to the porch, putting one foot on the bottom step. "No, I've got to be getting back, Lylah," he said with a warm smile. He shook his head when Will and the others insisted, saying, "No, this is a *family* reunion. But if you need any preaching done before it's over, give me a call." He grinned as he added, "I'll be sure to take up a collection after I get through."

Donald turned and went back to the car. Racing the engine, he waved and disappeared in a cloud of dust.

"That's a good young man," Will Stuart said. He glanced at his daughter and grinned, "You coulda had him, Lylah, if you'd wanted him."

Lylah grinned right back. She had been very close to her father and felt so even now. "And wouldn't I have been a bird as a preacher's wife, Pa!" She laughed freely, and the others joined in.

"Well, let's get some food on the table," Will said when the laughter had died down, "and start this here celebration!"

The babble of voices grew, and all the children began hustling around to put the meal on the table. But Lylah grabbed her father by the arm and said, "While they're putting it on the table, let's you and me walk down to the creek, Pa. I want to find out what you've been doing."

As they walked away, she caught a glimpse of Agnes's narrowed gaze and thought, *That woman has ground Pa to bits. I wish she'd drown in the creek!*

But she said nothing of her feelings to her father as the two of them strolled outside and down the shady lane, Lylah chattering happily and Will smiling fondly at his prodigal daughter.

That night, Lylah slept with her sisters, Lenora and Christie, although "sleeping" is not actually what went on. They shared a small bed in a tiny room up in the loft and the two girls kept her awake for most of the night, urging her to tell more stories about her travels, about her life on the road in the theater.

Finally, when she lapsed into unconsciousness, the girls gave up. She didn't know a thing until she heard a voice saying, "C'mon, Lylah, you've got to get up. Breakfast is almost ready."

"Wha—what is it?" Lylah opened her eyes to see Christie bending over her, her blond hair hanging around her shoulders.

"C'mon," she urged. "It's late."

"What time is it?" Lylah mumbled.

"Why, it's 'most six o'clock," Christie said. "Day's half gone. C'mon, now. Let's get down and eat breakfast. Amos'll be here pretty soon."

Lylah groaned, then crawled out of bed and began dressing. She brushed her hair as best she could and then went into the bathroom she and Amos had sent the money to add, only four years ago. Until then, there had been only washbasins and cold spring water. The hot water had been saved for her, she was glad to see, and she was able to take a quick bath, put on her makeup, and fix her hair.

When she came out, she heard Gavin shouting from the front yard. "They're comin'! They're comin'! Amos is comin'!"

Again there was a mad stampede with all the young people running out, and this time Lylah joined them. A large, copper-brown touring car pulled into the front yard, and there was Amos at the wheel, waving his hat and yelling as he slammed on the brakes. She ran out with the rest to meet him, and Amos got out of the car and fought his way through all of his siblings.

When he reached Lylah, he gave her a big hug. "Lylah! I haven't seen you in . . . how many years?"

"Too many!" Lylah cried and pulled his head down and kissed him full on the lips. He had always been her favorite, and now she said in mock anger, "I *hate* you, Amos Stuart. You don't look a day older than the last time I met you . . . and I'm an old woman now."

Amos grinned at her. At thirty-five, his five-foot-ten-inch frame still carried only one hundred and sixty pounds, very trim and athletic. He looked so much like their mother that it made Lylah want to weep. He had the same ash blond hair and startlingly dark blue eyes, the same oval face and determined features. In truth, he did not look one day older than when she had seen him five years before.

"You're just like all those other actresses, Sis, always putting a fellow on!" Amos complained. "Come see my family."

He scurried around and helped Rose to the ground, and Lylah saw that the woman was as striking as ever. At thirty-five, Rose's coal-black hair still had not a single trace of gray in it—the legacy of her Spanish mother. Her light bluish-green eyes still sparkled when she smiled.

Rose threw her arms around Lylah and greeted her emotionally as she always did. Then she turned and said, "Look at these two kids of ours, Lylah. I bet you wouldn't know them, would you?"

Lylah stared at the two. She had pictured them as small children, and now they were almost as tall as she was. "Is this Jerry?" she asked, walking up to the boy. "I can't believe it! Last time I saw you, you were begging for a sucker."

Jerry Stuart was a very handsome lad at fifteen. He had his mother's black hair and pale green eyes. He grinned and said, "I didn't get one, either, so you owe me one this time, don't you, Aunt Lylah?"

Lylah laughed. "You'll get it, and something better than that. And this is Maury? Look at that beautiful red hair! Have you got a temper to go with it?"

Maury, a year younger, glared at her brother, who laughed and said, "Yes, she has. If you don't believe it, just cross her."

Maury shook her head. "I do *not!* Well, not unless somebody makes me mad, anyhow."

Lylah laughed and hugged her niece. "I'm exactly the same way, people tell me."

"Well, Pa," Amos said, as his father came forward, "here I am. The bad penny turns up again."

Will Stuart shook his hand firmly. "Good to see you, Amos. I've missed you." He eyed this well-dressed son of his, scarcely able to believe he had fathered such a successful son.

Amos Stuart had risen rapidly in his newspaper career until he was now the star reporter for William Randolph Hearst's *New York Journal,* the biggest newspaper in the United States. Self-educated, Amos had achieved this position through sheer tenacity and determination. Now his name was mentioned along with the top newsmen of the country.

"I read that last story you wrote about the war," Will told him. "It was good, son." His eyes twinkled. "Why, I couldn't have done no better myself!"

Amos laughed and threw an arm around his father's thin

shoulders. "Sure you could, Pa. You always had a way with words."

They moved into the house where Amos and his family were greeted by Agnes in a rather cold fashion. For the rest of the morning, the house rang with talk. Everyone ate cookies, cake, and pies and drank gallons of coffee and sweet milk. The sweets had been baked by the girls for dessert, but they had been unsuccessful at keeping the men out of them.

Just before lunch, Lylah had time to get Amos off to one side. Down by the creek where she had fished and caught thumping bluegills as a girl, the two of them sat down and talked. Lylah was hungry for news of her brother. She was fiercely proud of him, as was the rest of the family, and she pried out of him the facts about his close communion with the famous people of the world, including Theodore Roosevelt!

Amos himself did not speak of this unless pressed. But he kept Lylah amused for a long time with his stories. Finally, they heard someone calling from the house, and Amos got to his feet.

"Hey . . . there's a car coming. I wonder if it could be Owen."

The two hurried back to the house to find their younger brother, Owen, and his wife, Allie, descending from their car. The ancient vehicle seemed to have barely made it there.

Lylah stood back, watching Owen and Allie as the others rushed forward. She admired her tall, strong brother tremendously. He was almost six feet tall and very strong. She finally forced her way through the milling group, grabbed Owen, and pulled his head down for her welcoming kiss. He held her and she felt the tremendous strength of his arms. When he lifted his head, she saw he was smiling at her in the same old way he used to, and memories flooded through her.

Then she turned to Allie and the two women embraced. Allie, at twenty-five, had the same dark blue eyes, the same honey-colored hair, and the same square, determined chin that Lylah remembered. As always she was very glad to see

Lylah. They had always gotten along well on the few occasions they were together.

For just a moment, the three of them stood looking at each other—Amos, the oldest son of the Stuart clan; Lylah, the oldest daughter; and Owen, the largest and strongest of them all. *We are strangers here,* Lylah thought. *The others have stayed, but we've gone out into the world.* She said with a roguish grin, "Well . . . the three prodigals are back again!"

Amos shook his head. "No . . . *two* prodigals. You and me, Lylah." He turned and smiled at his brother. "At least this one here isn't as worldly as you and I."

Owen broke the momentary silence that followed his older brother's declaration. A smile crossed his broad lips, and he glanced around at his younger brothers and sisters, then at his father, who had just stepped up to join the group. "Well, Pa, prodigals or not, we're all home." He looked around the valley and up to the mountains and said, "This place is good, isn't it?" And Amos knew what he meant.

Suddenly, both of them were glad to be back in the hills of Arkansas again. To be with their own flesh and blood. To see their family. To smell the fresh mountain air.

It was Lylah who said gently, "Yes, Owen, it is good to be home."

2

County Fair

The younger Stuarts begged their visitors to spend the night, offering to sleep on pallets or out in the barn, but Amos vetoed that idea. "No, we wouldn't want to put you out like that, and we city folks are too soft for that kind of living. We'll just go into Fort Smith to a hotel."

A noisy chorus of protests broke forth, but in the end, the visitors piled in the cars and drove into town, where they got accommodations at the Palace Hotel. After a good night's rest, they got up very early to meet in the hotel restaurant for breakfast. Over ham and eggs and pancakes, they reminisced about the early days.

Amos grinned at Lylah. "Sis, do you remember the day you left to go to Bible school?"

Lylah swallowed a sip of her coffee and nodded, recalling the incident well. "I sure do." She laughed quietly. "You caught me out behind the barn, smoking a cigarette."

Owen almost choked on a big bite of biscuit at the memory, then joined in the laughter. "Now wasn't that the way to leave home for Bible school? Smoking cigarettes out behind the barn!" He shook his head. "You made your mark on that place, sure enough. When I got there a few years later, they were still talking about your escapades."

Lylah nursed her cup, and a wry smile tugged at her lips. "I hated those days. I hated everything about that school, I guess—the chapels, the Bible studies, the professors, *and* the ministerial students. Talk about somebody being in the wrong place at the wrong time!"

Amos gave her a sidelong glance. "I always felt sorry for Don Satterfield," he said. "The way you went on that trip to Little Rock with the other students ... and just disappeared." He blinked then, sorry he'd said anything. He hadn't intended to bring up unpleasant memories.

The reference caused Lylah's brow to furrow, and she fell silent. She remembered those days, when she had made a trip to a Baptist State Convention in Little Rock. While she was there, she had encountered an actor, James K. Hackett. Fascinated by her first trip to a big city, Lylah had been wandering the streets when Hackett had noticed her outside the theater and invited her to see the play. *But that*, Lylah thought, as she sat, only half-listening to her brothers' conversation, *was the end of everything ... in some ways ... for me.*

She had left town that night with the troupe after scribbling Don a brief note. Since then, she had spent ten years as an actress. During the first years, she'd had high hopes and had found glamour and excitement in the world of the theater. But her beauty and verve and wit had not been enough to take her to the very thin air at the top. She had never gotten her one big break. Now, as she sat listening to the quiet hum of her brothers' voices, she knew that the restless spirit that had driven her from the rocky farm had not been stilled. Perhaps she would never find the peace she had begun to long for. The thought frightened her, for she was no longer a girl of eighteen, but was approaching her mid-thirties—an old age, in a way, for an actress.

She began to pay attention to what Owen was saying. He was speaking of their younger brothers and sisters and their hard lot at home. "I don't like to be judgmental," he said, stroking his chin thoughtfully, "but those kids don't have it easy. I can't see why they've stayed as long as they have."

Amos knew at once that Owen was referring to Agnes and agreed. "Yes, it's strange. Logan and Peter are both old enough to be out on their own, but they haven't gotten away. Maybe they just don't have enough get-up-and-go. I don't know. I've never understood it."

"Well, I'll tell you one thing," Owen said abruptly. "Gavin won't be around long. He's downright sick of farm life. Doesn't talk about anything but cars and motors and engines! He begged me to help him get away when I talked to him yesterday."

Amos nodded. "Yes, he talked to me, too, and I'd like to help him. He has real talent."

Rose, too, was concerned. "We've *all* got to help him."

Allie, Owen's wife, who had been quiet during breakfast, spoke up. "He's like my brother Joey. Doesn't care about anything but cars." At the age of twenty-two, Joey Dupree was traveling around the country, driving in races whenever he could and generally working as a mechanic for the other racers. "Maybe Joey will know of something Gavin could do."

"It's that Agnes!" Lylah said with a flash of anger. "She treats those kids like dirt!"

No one said anything for a moment, realizing their father would never put Agnes out of the house. It seemed hopeless.

Finally Owen said, "Well, let's make this a day to remember, anyway. The county fair's in town, I see. We'll take them out to the fairgrounds, treat them to a fine meal in a big restaurant. We'll show them the best time they ever had, okay?"

The rest of them took up on the idea immediately. They finished their meal, collected the children, and started back to the farm.

As soon as they got there, Amos informed them of the plan. At once everyone began getting ready—washing, combing their hair, putting on their best clothes. Gavin, however, took no pains at all with his personal dress. Instead, he came out to talk to Owen, who was standing by the cars.

"Wish you'd left your car with me so I coulda worked on it. Cleaned it up, got it all tuned up," he said wistfully. "That ol' heap of yours is in bad shape, Owen."

Owen glanced over at the 1908 Hupmobile. "Well, I got it cheap, but it had been wrecked. Pretty good car, though," he said, admiring the brass headlights and the square lantern that gleamed where he had polished them. The open two-seater boasted a steering wheel on the left side, a lever for a brake, and had wooden spokes and small tires.

Gavin walked over to the automobile and ran his hands over the chassis almost lovingly. "Hmm. Sliding gear transmission and magneto ignition," he murmured, and began to explain how it all worked.

Owen's strong face grew thoughtful as he listened to the boy. He knew how Gavin felt. He himself had been trapped on the farm as a young man, escaping only after Agnes came to rule the house. He longed to find some way to help Gavin and finally said, "You know, maybe we can get you a job as a mechanic's helper in town."

"Why, that'd be great, Owen!" Gavin exclaimed. "Do you really think I could?"

Owen studied the boy for a moment. "God can do anything, Gavin. If he can make a world, he can get you off this old farm." He smiled, went over, threw his arm around his brother, and gave him a squeeze. "We'll see what God can do, but we'll give him all the help we can."

Just then the door opened, and the clan boiled out, everyone jabbering excitedly. They piled into the cars and Amos led the way, followed by Owen's Hupmobile, and trailed by the old Model-A Gavin had found wrecked and had restored. All the way to town, Owen kept looking back to make sure the ancient car hadn't quit, as it usually did. But the small caravan rolled safely into Fort Smith and followed the traffic flowing toward the fairgrounds. Finally they pulled up, along with hundreds of cars that filled the huge lot.

Spilling out of the cars, the group joined the crowd moving toward the front gate, where Amos paid the twenty-five-cent admission fee for all of them. For the next two hours, they wandered around the carnival, taking in the sideshows, let-

ting Jerry and Maury ride the Ferris wheel. Soon Lenora and
Christie demanded their turn. With much squealing and clinging to one another, they took their first ride in outer space.

There were merry-go-rounds and other rides, and it did
Amos good to see how much fun they had. He whispered,
"Rose, I should have done this before. These kids don't have
anything. Just look how much a little carnival means to them."

"I know, Amos." Rose squeezed his hand warmly. "We'll
have to have the girls . . . the boys, too . . . come and visit us
in New York. Not all at once, of course, but one at a time. We
can show them around, find them jobs." Her dark eyes
glowed. She'd always been a compassionate person, and now
she cast a sympathetic eye at her young relations, saying
firmly, "You're right. We'll have to do more for them."

By noon, they were all hungry, despite having eaten popcorn and exploring the mystery of cotton candy. "Why, I'd as
soon eat *grass* as this stuff!" Logan sputtered. Lylah laughed
at him, and then Amos led them into a large tent where they
had hot dogs, heavily laced with mustard and chowchow, and
ice cream for dessert, all washed down with glass after glass
of lemonade.

"Probably make us all sick." Owen grinned. "But I guess
it's worth it."

That afternoon, they took in some of the agricultural exhibitions. "I see enough horses and cows and pigs when I'm
home," Pete complained. "Let's go back to the fairgrounds."

The others agreed, and they went back. This time, as they
entered the midway area, they heard a barker making his
spiel. "Step right up!" he cried out in a shrill tone, and everyone pressed forward to crowd around the platform.

Several men wearing robes were standing in front of the
tent. The painted canvas behind the barker read: BOXING
SHOW! GREATEST BOXERS IN AMERICA! WIN $100
IF YOU CAN STAY IN THE RING FOR 5 ROUNDS!

The barker was warming to his task. "Now, some of you
young men out there, hear this! Want to impress your sweet-

heart? No better way to do it than to demonstrate your skill in the manly art of self-defense." He waved a thin arm toward the robed men behind him. "We have here three of the finest proponents of the art of boxing to be found in this great country of ours. All of them have boxed in New York, Chicago, and other great cities of America. Now then, we are offering you a deal you can't refuse! We've got Jackie Smith," he gestured toward the smallest of the men. "One hundred twenty-six pounds for you lightweight fellows." He motioned to the next man, who was obviously larger. "At 160 pounds, we have Cole Kelly for you middleweights—" He paused, adding dramatically, "And we have Killer Morgan for those of you who've lived a full life!"

He let the titter of laughter ripple through the crowd, then said, "Killer weighs in at 210 pounds and doesn't get much work. Not many men want to get in the same ring with him. Now, which of you fellas will be first to make an easy hundred bucks?"

The shill continued his patter and, without too much trouble, found volunteers to fight the lightweight and the middleweight. While he talked on, a big man, tall and ponderous, made his way through the crowd. Coming up behind Owen, he tapped him on the shoulder. "Hello, Preacher. Didn't expect to see you in a place like this."

Owen turned and, recognizing the man who'd spoken, smiled. "Hello, Governor." A glint of humor sparked in his eyes. "Didn't expect to see *you* in a place like this, either."

Governor Al Benning laughed loudly, and some of the spectators who had recognized him turned to watch, listening avidly. "That's where you're wrong. Look at these votes around here, Preacher," he said. "Any time you get this many folks together, you'll find a politician right in the middle of them!"

A laugh went around the crowd, and someone yelled, "That's the way, Guv! We're for you!"

Al Benning was one of the most popular governors

Arkansas had ever had. Though the man had never seen the inside of a college, he was a shrewd, able politician and had learned to do the infighting necessary to rise to the top of the heap. He knew, it seemed, half the people in his home state. Everywhere he went, he could call hundreds—even thousands—of men and women by their first names.

Now, seeing Owen and remembering a story he had read about him—"Fighter Turned Preacher"—he saw an opportunity to make a little splash, perhaps sway a few votes in the upcoming election.

"Well, now, Preacher," he said, "I've been wondering for years when you were going to stop preaching and get back to your regular trade. I always thought you'd be the one to whup Jack Johnson." He shook his head sadly. "You was the one white hope that I had some confidence in."

Jack Johnson, the black heavyweight champion, had ruled the boxing world for years. The search for the Great White Hope had swept the country, but no white man had been found who could outbox the crafty champion until the previous April, when Jess Willard had knocked him out to regain the heavyweight championship of the world.

"I guess any fighting I do will be with the devil, Governor," Owen said with a smile and a shake of his head. Then he grinned. "I'm having a meeting in Little Rock next week. I'd sure like to see you there in the front row."

Benning grinned. "Get me up with the rest of the sinners where you can rake us with both guns?"

"Something like that. Will you come?"

Benning knew the crowd was listening, and a thought came to him. "Well, I'll tell you what, Preacher." He glanced up at the huge heavyweight fighter on the platform. "I know you're not a gambling man, so I'll just make you an offer." He waved his hands and shook his head to indicate his sincerity. "Not a bet, you understand, just an offer."

"An offer?" Owen asked. "What kind of offer?"

"You get up there and go five rounds with that fellow, and I'll come five straight nights to your meeting in Little Rock."

Owen hesitated. He glanced at Amos, whose lips formed the words, *Do it, Owen.* Recklessly, he agreed. "Why, I'll take you up on that offer. I'd do just about anything to get a man who needs God in hearing sound of the gospel."

A shout went up and the shill said, "Now, there's a sport for you! Do I understand, sir, that you're a minister of the gospel?"

Owen nodded. "That's right. I'm an evangelist."

A satisfied smile curved the barker's lips. "Well, we're always glad to entertain the ministry here, aren't we, Killer?"

The huge boxer looked the part—battered lips, scar tissue over his eyes, shoulders bulky under the robe. He grinned, exposing broken teeth. "I ain't had a preacher to whip in quite a while!" he said loudly. "Bring the reverend on back."

It was a barker's dream, for everyone within hearing distance clambered forward to buy a seat. "Well, ordinarily the price is fifty cents for admission," he said, seizing his opportunity. "But seeing as how we have the governor here, I'm afraid we're going to have to charge a dollar."

A cry of protest went up, but there was no shortage of takers. The ticket taker handed out tickets until he finally had to say, "No more room!" And still the people surged forward to get into the tent.

"I'll be your second," Amos told Owen. "Don't drink anything if they offer it to you. It'll probably be doped."

He gave his family the tickets he had bought for them, then he and Owen accompanied the barker back to a small dressing room, barely big enough for the boxers with the show. But they were already dressed, and Owen quickly stripped down and put on a pair of rather smelly trunks he found and shrugged on an equally ripe bathrobe.

"I'm not sure," he said uneasily, as he slipped the robe on, "that I'm doing the right thing."

"Well, I'm not either," Amos admitted. "That pug looks

pretty tough. Don't let him mess you up. If he gives you too much trouble, just go down for the count."

"Take a dive?" Owen smiled. "I never took one in my life, Amos, and I'm not going to start now."

In the large tent where the fight was to be held, Logan and Pete had used their considerable height and strength to muscle their way to good seats down at the front. The seats themselves consisted of rickety folding chairs that swayed dangerously when one sat on them. But the family found themselves places, and talked excitedly of the fight.

The men—Will, Logan, Peter, and Gavin—were all bright-eyed with anticipation. Will especially had taken great pride in his son's pugilistic career and now leaned forward, his face alive with excitement. "I bet he floors that gorilla in the first round," he muttered hopefully.

"I don't know, Pa," Gavin said, shaking his head. "Owen hasn't fought in a long time. That fighter looks pretty tough to me."

"We shouldn't have let him do this," Lylah said nervously, but she knew stopping Owen would have been a difficult task.

Behind the crowd, Governor Benning had drawn the manager to one side and was whispering in his ear. "I sure hate to think of having to sit in church five nights in a row," he said. Reaching into his pocket, he pulled out a folded bill and showed it to the thin entrepreneur. "There's a hundred here if your man puts the preacher away so I don't have to do that."

The barker grinned. "Don't worry about it, Guv," he said confidently. "I'll put a bug in Morgan's ear. He'll flatten the preacher so fast it'll make your head swim!"

The manager was a good showman, and he began the event with the lightweight and a smallish young man with no skill, but with great enthusiasm, who lasted four rounds with the fighter called Jackie Smith.

The second fight was shorter. A burly farm boy, stripped to the waist and bulging with muscles, plodded after Cole Kelly, who toyed with him for three rounds. Then the fighter

sent a thunderous right to catch the young farmer in the jaw
and put him out like a light.

Finally the barker stepped to the center of the ring.
"Ladies and gentlemen, we now have the feature presentation of the evening. In this corner, the Reverend Owen Stuart, weighing in at 183 pounds. And in this corner, we have a
contender for the heavyweight championship of the world,
at 210 pounds, Killer Morgan. Come out, gentlemen, and get
your instructions."

Owen slapped his gloves together and strode out into the
middle of the ring. He stared across at the beetle-browed
Morgan. "Good afternoon, Brother. I hope you are well."

Morgan grunted, and his thick lips curled into a snarl. "Better say your prayers, Preacher. I'm gonna tear your head off!"

The manager muttered the usual instructions. "Break
clean. Go to your neutral corner in case of a knockdown."
Then he sent the two men back. Owen shook off his robe,
and the bell sounded.

Morgan, with the hundred-dollar bonus in his mind, rushed
across the ring like an enraged bull and threw a right at Owen's
head that, had it landed, would have ended the fight right
then and there.

Owen simply moved his head to one side and allowed the
burly heavyweight to go rushing by him. He had such grace
that it was like a matador allowing the ponderous bull to go
by, following the motion of the cape.

The crowd yelled and Morgan turned, his face red with
anger. He'd been slow. This time he came in more carefully.
"Don't worry, Sweetie-pie," he taunted. "I'll catch up with
you yet. You can run but you can't hide."

Owen, up on the balls of his feet, moved backward, easily
catching the punches the big man threw at him on his gloves,
or else flipping them. His feet whispered sibilantly on the
canvas floor and he was aware that he was enjoying himself,
which was a little strange, he thought, considering he never
liked fighting all that much. However, he *was* pleased at the

opportunity to get the governor to one of his meetings, and
for the first round, he thought about what he might preach to
such an august member of his congregation.

The first round ended, and Morgan went back and slumped
down on his stool. "What's the matter with you!" the barker
hissed. "Quit playing around and put this guy away!"

"He's slippery," Morgan growled. He spat out a mouthful
of water and glared across the ring at Owen. "Pretty good,
too. But I'll get him this time."

But it was not that easy. In the second round, try as he
might, he could not land a clean blow on the weaving, dodg-
ing, shadowy form of Owen Stuart. Around and around the
ring they moved, Owen throwing light lefts that connected
sharply and effortlessly sidestepping Morgan's punches.

The crowd began to cheer, and by round four, the barker
was desperate. "You've gotta spike this guy, Killer!" he said.
"It's gonna make us look bad if you don't and, besides, we'll
be out a hundred bucks!"

"I'll get him this time," Morgan muttered. "I'll rough him
up and get him to lookin' down . . . then I'll nail him."

The bell sounded for the final round, and Amos was ec-
static. "Just three more minutes, Kid! Keep on dancing
around that big ape!"

"Okay, Brother, I'll do what I can."

Owen went out once again, but had barely reached the center of the ring before he was met by another mad bull rush,
Morgan throwing leather from every angle. Owen was caught
off guard, and a hard left caught him high on the head. It made
the stars dance before his eyes and put a metallic taste in his
mouth, a sensation he remembered clearly from the old days.
He was driven backwards, and for thirty seconds, the bully
Morgan threw every punch he had. Some of them were landing below the belt, which brought a sickness to Owen's mouth.

Owen, confused and half unconscious, forgot that he was
a minister, forgot everything. In that moment, instinct took
over.

His wide lips twisted in a snarl and he leapt forward, throwing a deadly right that caught Morgan squarely in the chest. The power of it sent the breath whooshing out of the fighter's body and drove him back across the ring. He had time only to set himself before Owen was on him again like a panther, throwing blows, one after the other. Morgan tried to ward them off, but one, delivered to the stomach, doubled him over. A second caught him across the bridge of the nose, sending a shower of blood down across his chest.

Morgan tried to get his guard up, but there was no hope. The smaller man was all over him, raining punches. And then, as he lunged to the left, Owen's powerful right cross caught him in the center of the forehead. The blow snapped his head back and he fell to the floor, completely unconscious.

Owen stood over the big man like an animal. Slowly, as reason returned, he took a deep breath, shook his head, and walked back to the corner. As the crowd yelled and screamed and stomped the floor, everyone standing, Owen waited for the count.

The barker counted as slowly as possible, giving Morgan a full extra five seconds. But when he saw it was no use, he motioned Owen to the center of the ring and lifted his hand. "The winner, Reverend Owen Stuart," he muttered in disgust. He shot one look at the fallen fighter, shook his head, and walked away.

Owen went at once to the center of the ring where Morgan lay still and called back, "Come on, Amos. Give me a hand with him." They lifted the heavy figure, carried him back to his corner, and propped him up on the stool. "Wash his face, will you Amos?" Owen said, then shook off his gloves and took the sponge from his brother, wiping the blood and sweat from the fighter's face himself.

After a few moments, the boxer came to and opened his eyes. "You put up a good fight," Owen said, relieved to see that he was conscious.

The battered face of Killer Morgan was a study. He had

been beaten before, but never so thoroughly in such a short time. He shook his head and muttered, "You ain't like no preacher I ever saw!", then got to his feet shakily.

Owen and Amos retired to the dressing room, and Owen changed clothes as quickly as he could. Outside, they found the family, along with the governor, who was speaking to a gathering of his constituents. "Well, Brother Stuart," said Benning, a weak smile on his face, "it looks like you've got me. You let me know when you're at the capitol, and I'll be in the front row. Take your best shots at me and all the rest of the sinners."

"I'll do that, Governor." Owen smiled and shook the big man's hand.

"Let's go celebrate your victory," Amos suggested.

Owen held up one hand. "Just a minute." He walked over to the barker and put out his hand to collect the prize money.

Grimly, the barker slapped a few bills into his outstretched palm. "Don't come back, Reverend. We don't need fellas like you in my business."

Owen grinned and went at once to where Lenora and Christie were standing. He counted out the money, putting half the bills in each of the girls' hands. "Now go do some shopping. Allie, you and Rose and Lylah take the girls to town. Buy them the best outfits to be found, and take them to a fancy place to eat. We'll catch up with you someplace."

Lenora and Christie, their eyes big as silver dollars, left with the others, as excited as children.

"Now, let's get out of here and have us a time," Amos said. "You all right, are you, Pa?"

Will Stuart had a broad smile on his lips. "I never was so proud," he said, looking at Owen, "except, of course, when you went into the ministry."

Owen laughed. "Oh, come on, Pa. You weren't all that happy about me becoming a preacher!"

Will Stuart looked at this big, broad-shouldered son of his, and spoke slowly, "Well, I may have been a little bit disappointed at first—" He paused, looked down at the ground, and a long silence ensued. When he lifted his eyes, they shone with pride. "But I want to tell you right now, son, I'm right proud of you . . . more'n I've ever said." He glanced at Amos and nodded. "You too, Amos. You been a good son."

To break the embarrassing silence that followed, Owen reached over and cuffed Logan and Peter on the shoulders. "Wait 'til these two get going. They'll put us both in the shade."

Amos, in turn, caught Gavin by the nape of the neck and gave him a little shake. "*This* is the one we've all got to watch. No telling *what* he'll wind up doing." There was a roar of laughter, and when it died down, Amos went on. "By the way, Gavin, I've got a surprise for you."

"A surprise? What is it, Amos?"

"I'll have to show you. But not until two o'clock. In the meanwhile, let's just wander around for a while. We'll see if we can knock over some of those milk bottles and win some Kewpie dolls for the ladies."

They went to the midway and paired off, Amos taking care to walk with his father. "Where's Agnes?"

Will shook his head. "I dunno. Gone off with some friends of hers, I reckon."

Amos said nothing, but thought to himself, *Pretty typical of Agnes to leave the family and go find her "friends."* He changed the subject at once. "Pa, I've never had so much fun. We ought to have a family reunion twice a year."

"I reckon that's right. It's been good for the young'uns," Will said. They walked around slowly, talking amiably, and finally Will asked, "Son, what's going to happen about this war business over in Europe?"

Amos paused and let his eyes roam around the crowd. The tinny song of the calliope sounded harsh in his ears and the cries of the barkers carried faintly on the afternoon breeze. There was a smell of popcorn and hot dogs and sawdust. Finally he shook his head. "It's coming, Pa," he said. "No way this country's going to stay out of it."

"Hate to hear that," Will said. He looked ahead to where the boys were walking along, watching the crowd, and said, "I guess maybe you and Owen might be too old. But Peter and Logan and Gavin, they'd be right in the middle of it. Couldn't keep them boys out, could you, Amos?"

Amos shook his head. "I don't think so, Pa. I don't like to think about it . . . what it would do to us, to all the families in this country."

They stopped and watched as the boys began to toss rings, trying to win the cheap dolls on the rack at one of the booths, laughing, shoving each other playfully.

"They act like a bunch of little kids, don't they, Amos?" Will said proudly. There was a wistful light in his eyes as he said, "I remember back when I was their age. Everything was fun. And later, too. Remember how we used to go to all the parties, me playin', and sometimes you singin'? You always could sing pretty, Amos. You ever sing anymore?"

Amos shook his head. "Not the kind of songs we sang back then, Pa. Just in church now. I get asked to sing a solo every once in a while."

"That's nice, Son. Real nice." A thought crossed his mind, and he frowned. "What about Lylah? You had a chance to talk to her since you been here?"

"No, but I'm going to find time tonight. She's not happy, is she, Pa?"

"No, she ain't. Never has been, since she was a girl." Will Stuart pulled off his hat and ran his hand through his hair, then put the hat back on. "I don't know what she wants," he said finally. "But whatever it is, she ain't found it yet. And I don't reckon she ever will, unless—"

"Unless she finds the Lord. I think you're right. But she seems a long way from God. The theater's not the place to find him, I don't think," Amos said soberly. "I'll try to talk to her tonight, Pa. Maybe she'll listen to me." Amos silently whispered a prayer of thankfulness that his father was finally beginning to see the importance of knowing God.

A faint light of humor touched Will Stuart's eyes. "If she does," he grinned slightly, "it'd be the first time she ever listened to anybody."

Amos laughed and slapped his father's thin shoulder. "You're right about that, Pa. But there's always a first time. C'mon, now, let's you and me see if we can show these young whippersnappers how to win a Kewpie doll!"

3

A RIDE FOR GAVIN

The Stuart clan left the fairground, the women disappearing into a large department store as soon as they reached Fort Smith.

"C'mon, fellas," Amos said. "They won't stop 'til they run out of money." He led his brothers to the Palace Hotel, saying, "I'm hungry. Let's get something to eat."

They entered the restaurant, and it was hard for Amos not to smile as he watched the response of Logan and Pete. Their eyes grew large, and they walked as if they were afraid a mine might go off under their feet at any moment. Gingerly they sat down at the table, gawking at the white tablecloth and the unfamiliar array of silverware. When Amos offered to order for all of them, he saw the look of relief on the faces of his younger brothers. "Bring us all a steak, a baked potato, and a lettuce salad."

As they ate, their talk turned to news of the war. It was Owen who asked, "Do you think we're going to get into this war over in Europe, Amos?"

Amos shook his head. "Well, Paris is safe since the Allies won at the Marne, but they took 250,000 casualties." When Logan gasped Amos turned to his younger brother. "That's just the beginning, Logan. There's never been a war like this one."

Owen looked down at his salad, pushed a piece of lettuce around with his fork, then turned his gaze back toward Amos. "Will America get into it?"

Amos shrugged. "Bound to. The Germans have ordered total submarine warfare. Last February they sank two ships—the *Carib*, and the *Evelyn*—and they haven't stopped since. Even President Wilson won't be able to keep us out now."

Gavin slapped the table with a force that made the glasses rattle and startled the people sitting at the next table. "We can whup 'em, Amos! Just like we whupped them Yankees in the Civil War!"

Amos grinned. "Well, we didn't exactly whip them, Gavin."

"Sure we did! We just sort of played at it."

All of them wolfed down their steaks and potatoes, and when it was time for dessert, the waiter asked each one what they wanted. By this time, Logan had gained some confidence.

"How about some apple pie a la mode?" the waiter suggested.

Logan nodded. "Yeah. And put some ice cream on top of it, too."

At that Amos, who had taken the last bite of his steak, almost choked on it. But he managed to save his brother from embarrassment. "I'll have the same," he said to the waiter. "Apple pie a la mode—with ice cream on top."

The waiter kept a straight face and nodded, "Yes, sir. That's just the way it'll be."

As they were eating their pie and ice cream, Owen asked, "What's this surprise you got for us, Amos?"

"Finish up and I'll show you. But I warn you, it's more for Gavin than it is for you fellas. Hurry up, now."

Gavin glanced up, a question in his dark eyes, but he said nothing.

They rose and pushed back their chairs, and Amos laid a tip down on the table. They were halfway to the door when Peter rushed after him. "Hey, Amos, you forgot some of your money! You left it back there on the table!"

Gavin turned red in the face and grabbed the money. "That's a tip, you idiot!" He retraced their steps and placed the coins on the table again, trying to ignore the giggles of the customers at adjacent tables.

They were all relieved to put the restaurant behind them. Rounding up the women, the men helped carry their packages to the cars. "You can show us your new clothes later," Amos said. "Now we've got to get back to the fairgrounds."

When they returned and parked, Amos jumped out and opened the doors. "All right. Time for your surprise, Gavin. You come with me. The rest of you go over to that field, where the crowd is gathering."

Owen glanced in the direction Amos indicated and said firmly, "Okay. Let's go, everyone. Amos is the boss."

"Now . . . when's the last time I gave you a birthday present, Gavin?" Amos asked as Owen led the others away.

Gavin stared at him and shrugged. "Well . . . I guess it was my last birthday. Why?"

"Because I'm giving you your next birthday present right now. Come along." Amos began to walk rapidly, and Gavin, mystified, followed alongside. He was a quiet young man, not given to much talk anyway, and Amos's mysterious behavior intrigued him.

Amos made his way through the crowd and suddenly Gavin stopped dead still.

"A plane!" he said, his eyes glowing. "A real airplane!"

Amos grinned at him. "I thought you'd like this. There's going to be a demonstration here, and I know the pilot. Come on, let's see if we can find him." He led Gavin over to the plane, and asked one of the men working on it, "Is Mr. Beachey around?"

The mechanic, an undersized young man with a sunburned face, gestured vaguely with a wrench. "Over there. At that hot dog stand."

"Thanks." Turning quickly, Amos made his way to the stand, with Gavin close on his heels. As they approached, Amos said, "There he is. Come on, let's talk to him."

Gavin hung back a little, as Amos walked right up to a man

eating a hot dog and holding a glass of what looked like iced tea in one hand. *He sure don't look like a flyer,* Gavin thought. *He looks more like a salesman of some kind.*

"Hello, Beachey," Amos said and stepped up to put his hand out. "You remember me? Amos Stuart, of the *New York Journal.*"

The man eating the hot dog paused before taking another bite and regarded Amos steadily through a set of steel gray eyes. He was a small man with a pugnacious jaw and was rather peculiarly dressed in an expensively tailored pin-stripe business suit with a high, starched collar, a two-carat diamond stickpin in his tie, and a checkered golfing cap, which he had on backwards.

"Why, sure. I remember you, Stuart," he said. "You did that story on me a few months ago." He carefully set down the glass and put out his hand. "What are you doing out here, Stuart?" he asked. "Come to see me loop-the-loop?"

"Back home for a family reunion," Amos explained. "I'd like for you to meet my brother, Gavin Stuart. Gavin, this is Lincoln Beachey, the world's greatest flyer." He waved toward Gavin, and the two men shook hands. "Tell you what, I'd like to make a deal with you, Beachey."

Beachey stared carefully at Amos. "What sort of a deal you got in mind?"

"You take my brother here for a ride, and I'll do a story on you that'll stir up interest all over the country. I think I can even get it reprinted in most of the other big papers. What do you say?"

Gavin's heart seemed to stop beating, and suddenly he could not breathe. To go up, up up in the clouds! Up in that blue sky! He had spent hours watching buzzards circle, smoothly gliding over the air currents, easily, with no effort at all. He'd watched the purple martins doing their acrobatics at sundown, twisting and turning in the air. Always, ever since he could remember, he'd kept his eyes turned upward, and he had read everything that had been printed about flying. And now, he stared at Lincoln Beachey and prayed that God would give him favor.

Beachey smiled and shrugged his shoulders. "Why, sure. That's a good deal. I got lots of offers after the last story you did. Let me do my act first, and soon as that's over—" here he paused and eyed Gavin—"you and I'll take a little ride. That be all right with you?"

"Oh, yes, Mr. Beachey!" Gavin gasped. He tried to say more, but the words wouldn't come out.

Beachey balled up his fist and gave him a light tap on the shoulder. "We'll have some fun, you and me." He took another bite of the hot dog, washed it down with the iced tea, and said, "Time to go now. Got to give the crowd their money's worth."

"C'mon, Amos!" Gavin urged. "Let's go get us a good seat!" He hauled Amos along, who was laughing at the boy's enthusiasm.

"So? Is that a pretty good birthday present or not?"

Gavin stopped and looked at his brother, his eyes warm and his whole face filled with simple gratitude. "Nothin' . . . I mean *nothin'* could have been as good as this, Amos. I'll never forget it, not ever!"

And then he started tugging on Amos again, and the two made their way to the edge of the crowd at the field and watched as Lincoln Beachey got into his plane and took off.

As the small craft was gaining altitude, Amos explained a little bit about Beachey to his brother. "There's nobody quite like that fellow. Not for flying airplanes, anyway," he said. "He's the best acrobatic flyer in the country. He had a slow start though." Remembering, Amos grinned. "Just couldn't seem to learn how to get a plane down and wrecked two or three of them in the process of finding out. But, when he finally learned how to bring one in without smashing it up, off he went. He's been all over the world. Everywhere he goes, people come out to see his show."

Gavin watched the plane, which looked almost as fragile

as the kites he himself had flown in the pasture back at the farm. "Have you seen him before, Amos?"

"Sure. He's done several exhibitions in New York. Of course, I saw him when I did the story on him. Look at him now."

At the far end of the field, Beachey had brought the plane down to an altitude of no more than a hundred feet from the ground. He gave it a turn that, one would have thought, might wrench the wings off, then turned back and roared straight along the ground. When he was even with the crowd, Gavin saw him pull back on the stick and the plane rose, making a circle until it looped-the-loop, then roared off down the field.

A roar went up from the crowd, and applause filled the air. Gavin's mouth dropped open. "I never thought I'd see anything like that."

Amos merely shrugged. "Well, the world's first loop was done by a Frenchman named Adolph Pegoud a couple of years ago. He did it the hard way—an outside loop. But as soon as Beachey heard about it, he was pretty upset. In fact, he was overheard to say, 'Here I am—the greatest aviator in the world—getting upstaged by a Frog!' He took a plane up and immediately started turning loops. Loop after loop. Now, loops are his specialty. But he does other things, too."

The crowd watched, spellbound, as Beachey executed perfect stalls, turns, loops. Then he flew along the runway upside down, seeming to hang by his toes, before making another turn, this time holding his hands free.

Gavin breathed, "Just like a bicycle. No hands!"

For an hour, Lincoln Beachey proved, at least to the satisfaction of the crowd, his claim that he was the world's greatest flyer. When he landed, he crawled out of the plane and walked away, waving his hand to acknowledge the cheers that greeted him.

He found Amos immediately. "Let's let this crowd thin out a little bit. After the mechanics service the plane, I'll take our young friend here for a ride."

Thirty minutes later, Gavin, his hands trembling and his knees so weak he could hardly stand, walked across the field to the plane and, at Beachey's direction, clambered into the seat.

"Be a little bit crowded with two of us." Beachey grinned. "But a one-seater is better for stunting." He looked at Gavin carefully and said, "You don't get sick easily, do you? From motion, I mean?"

Gavin shook his head. "No, sir. I've never been sick in my whole life."

"Good. Well, here we go."

The mechanics stepped forward and spun the propeller, and the engine fired off with a roar that almost deafened Gavin. Sitting inside the plane, the noise was so much greater. He gripped his knees until his knuckles were white, and Beachey advanced the throttle.

The plane moved across the rough field, gaining speed. The ride was bumpy, like a wagon going over broken ground, Gavin thought, and he bounced up and down, scarcely able to breathe.

And then—suddenly—the bumping stopped, and Gavin felt for the first time what the birds must feel. The plane rose in the air effortlessly, no bumping, only weaving slightly from side to side as the wings dipped. He looked down and saw the crowd growing smaller, individual faces shrinking to mere dots, the tents of the midway like handkerchiefs spread out on the ground. As they rose still higher, he saw the buildings of downtown Fort Smith, looking like toys in the distance.

Up and up and up they went. Finally the aviator banked the plane and yelled to Gavin. "That's what it looks like from up here. How do you like it?"

"Oh, Mr. Beachey. There ain't nothin' like it, is there!"

Beachey laughed and slapped the boy on the shoulder. "No, there really isn't. We'll look for a little while."

Cruising around the serene blue sky, he showed Gavin the river and the fields. Once he flew through a low cloud, and

Gavin was delighted with the moistness of it. *Like a fog,* he thought. *Like a white fog.*

After they had flown for perhaps twenty minutes, Beachey said, "Here. Put your hand on this stick." Startled, Gavin gave him a wild look. Beachey laughed, his lantern jaw wagging as he shook his head. "Come on. I'll give you your first flying lesson, Gavin. Take over."

Gavin never forgot the next fifteen minutes. The pilot showed him how to make the plane rise and fall, how to bank and turn. There was nothing in the young man's life to compare with the exhilaration of this experience. He made the plane dive slightly, then rise, and as they flew around the blue sky, Gavin turned and looked at the pilot, saying again, "There ain't nothin' like it, is there, Mr. Beachey?"

Beachey knew the boy's heart, for his own dreams had been the same. He patted Gavin again on the shoulder. "No. There's nothing like it. Nothing in the world."

"Could we do some of them tricks you did before?" Gavin asked hopefully.

"You sure you want to do that, young man? It can be a little bit scary." When he saw the boy nodding furiously, he relented. "All right. Fasten that belt. Gotta be sure we're locked in." First, he saw to it that Gavin's belt was fastened securely, then said. "Okay! Here we go!"

He pulled back on the stick and the plane roared upward. Suddenly Gavin found himself upside down, and then gliding back to a sitting position. He gave a wild cry of pure ecstasy as Beachey made the loop. "Do it again! Do it again!" he cried.

The pilot was enjoying himself, too, almost as much as his young friend. He loved to stunt, and he put the little plane through a series of rigorous exercises. Turns, banks, stalls, loops. Finally he said regretfully, "Well, we'd better go back. I know you hate to get back down to earth."

Gavin stared at him, startled. "How did you know that?"

"Because you're like me. I always hate to put my feet on

the ground again." A strange look crossed the aviator's face. "I wish there was some way a man could stay up here always and never have to go back to earth again."

He landed the plane skillfully, and the two got out. At one side of the field, the family was waiting to greet Gavin. They rushed toward him, their questions tumbling over one another.

"What was it like?" "Were you scared?" "Weren't you afraid you'd fall out?" The questions rained on him from right and left.

Finally, Gavin got a chance to answer. "It was fine!" he said, his face flushed, his eyes sparkling. "It was better than anything ever was." He stood there with a rapt expression on his face, then turned to Amos. His jaw tightened, and he said firmly, "Amos, I'm gonna be a flyer!"

Amos stared into the face of his younger brother and nodded. "I expect you will, Gavin. I expect you will."

The air show put on by Beachey was the climax of the trip to Fort Smith, and it was Will who said, "I guess we better get on back. I've had about enough excitement for one day."

Amos glanced at Owen and a mischievous light sparkled in his eyes. "Oh, come on now, Pa. I'd planned on taking us all to one of those moving pictures that's so popular now."

Christie glanced at Amos and saw the fun in his expression, and how he was watching Owen, and caught on at once. "Why, sure," she said, "we've got to see one of those! C'mon, Pa. I've heard so much about them. Besides, we never get to do anything out on that old farm!"

The brothers all joined in, and finally Will Stuart gave in. "Well, might as well go whole hog, I reckon. What kind of a picture is it down there at that place?"

"I saw it in the paper," Amos said. "Tilly's Punctured Romance." He thought for a minute. "Fellow named Charlie Chaplin's in it. And a woman named Marie Dressler. I've heard it's pretty hot stuff!" He cocked an eyebrow and stared at Owen. "But I guess we'll be all right as long as the parson's along."

Owen flushed. He knew he was being teased, and said lamely, "Well, I guess the parson won't be there this time. Doesn't seem right for a minister to be seen in a place like that."

"Oh, come on, don't be an old woman, Owen!" Pete Stuart said. He turned his light blue eyes on his older brother. "Tell you what. I'll sit behind you, and if anything comes on that there screen that you hadn't oughta be lookin' at, I'll put my hands over your eyes. Okay?"

Owen laughed in spite of himself and glanced over at Allie, who smiled back. "All right. I guess that'll answer. Let's go do it, then."

They piled into the cars, drove to the Apollo Theater on Main Street in Fort Smith, and saw what was for some of them, their first motion picture. They came out of the theater, shaking their heads.

William Stuart said, "I've been to three county fairs and two snake stompin's . . . but I ain't never seen nothin' like that!"

Getting into the cars again, they made their way out of town, wound around the highway, and finally turned off on the old dirt road. By ten o'clock, they were pulling up in front of the house.

"C'mon in," Will said. "We can have a little more fun before we go to bed."

Amos began to protest, but Peter pulled him inside, saying, "Put them kids of yours to sleep over on a pallet. I want to hear Pa play that fiddle some. Owen, I ain't heard *you* play and sing in a long time, neither. Let's get at it and have us a party."

Soon every lantern and lamp was lit, and the house echoed with the sounds of the fiddle and the guitar and the voices, singing the old songs. Once, Owen glanced around at his father, wondering what he thought about his wife not being there, but Will seemed completely content. So, Owen shrugged and merely whispered to Allie, "I guess Pa's learned to put up with her ways after all these years."

Finally at midnight, Amos shook his head, saying, "We've got to get out of here. I won't be worth a dime in the morning. And those kids will be up, bright-eyed and bushy-tailed."

He started getting the kids together and, when they were ready, he thought of something. Reaching into his pocket, he said, "Pa, I got you a present while I was in the drugstore. Thought you might enjoy reading it." He handed Will a small book.

His father stood there for a moment, then pulled his glasses out of his pocket and put them on the end of his nose. Staring at the book, he read aloud: "*Tarzan of the Apes.*" He looked up at his son and cocked one eyebrow in a familiar expression. "What in tarnation is this, Amos?"

"Book by a fellow named Edgar Rice Burroughs." Amos grinned. "Look at the picture on the inside. You girls might be interested, too."

Will opened the book, and the girls all crowded around as he held it at arm's length.

Lenora said in a shocked fashion, "Why, that man don't have nothin' on but a little ol' piece of underwear!" Christie giggled, and Gavin whooped with laughter. Then the other men crowded around and they all stared at the picture.

"It's a popular book in New York," Amos explained. "All about an English nobleman who gets lost in the jungle as a baby and is raised by the great apes."

They pored over the book, studying the illustrations of the mighty ape-man in the company of huge gorillas, fighting lions, and sitting astride an elephant.

Will Stuart shook his head. "I don't believe a blamed word of this stuff," he snorted. "Them apes ain't got sense enough to raise no human baby. And if they could, what'd he be like? He'd talk gorilla talk, wouldn't he?"

"Naw," Logan denied. "He'd talk just like we do. It'd be born in him."

Amos and Owen laughed, and the others joined in. Owen asked, "You think if a Chinese took one of our American babies and raised him, when he grew up, he'd speak English, Logan?"

Logan nodded stubbornly. "Yep. It's born in us," he stated firmly.

Amos laughed loudly and slapped his brother on the shoulder. "Maybe you're right at that."

The visitors left the house, got into their cars once again, and drove back to the hotel. All the way, they talked about the family and the changes that had taken place since their last visit. When they reached the hotel, they went to bed at once without any further conversation.

Lylah slept like a log and got up and dressed the next morning with her eyes feeling gritty. When she went into the hotel restaurant, she saw that the others were already seated. "Good morning," she mumbled as cheerfully as she could.

When none of them answered, she looked around with a puzzled look in her eyes. "What's wrong with all of you?" she asked. "Somebody die?"

Amos tossed a newspaper onto the table, turning it so she could see the headlines. "*That's* what's wrong," he said.

Lylah read the heavy black print: *LUSITANIA SUNK BY GERMAN U-BOAT*. Looking up, she asked quietly, "What does this mean, Amos?"

"The Germans have been sinking English boats with Americans on board, but so far, Wilson's been able to keep us out of war. But the *Lusitania* was an American ship, carrying passengers, not munitions." Amos's face was set and stern, and he tapped the newspaper with his fist and shook his head. "It's too late now. Wilson will have to declare war on Germany."

Lylah sank into a chair.

No one was hungry, and they ate very little. The news seemed to have cast a pall over everyone in the dining room. Others were staring at the headlines, and conversation seemed either strained or slightly hysterical.

When breakfast was over, some of the family prepared to leave, and Amos and Lylah were left alone. "I've got to get back to New York right away, Lylah," he said. "I think Mr. Hearst will probably send me to Europe. I know he'll want me to go interview Teddy Roosevelt."

Lylah had remained very quiet. Now she said, "Amos, do you have room for me to go back to New York with you? In the car, I mean?"

"Why, sure, Lylah. I didn't know you wanted to go."

Looking down, Lylah traced the design of the tablecloth with her finger. There was a pained look on her face, and Amos knew her well enough to recognize that something was bothering her. "What is it? What's wrong, Sis?"

She lifted her eyes and said, "I'm going to Europe, Amos."

"Europe!" Amos blinked his eyes in startled amazement, then shook his head and began talking rapidly. "Why, you can't do that, Lylah! I'm telling you, this thing is going to blow up! You'd be caught over there, right in the middle of a war!" Lylah just sat there, watching him. Finally he asked, "What do you want to go to Europe for?"

She took a deep breath and looked straight at Amos. Lylah was still a beautiful woman, who looked much younger than her years, he thought. Fatigue had dulled her eyes, and her lips thinned as she pressed them together, a sure sign she was troubled.

"Amos, I've *got* to get away from America. I have a chance to go to England with a company that will be doing a repertoire of American plays. I'll be the starring actress—" She hesitated, then said, "It's James Hackett's company."

"James Hackett!" Amos stared at her and his forehead creased in a frown. "I would've thought you'd had enough of him, Lylah."

Lylah shook her head, knowing what he was thinking. Hackett was the man she'd run away with ten years earlier. He'd taken her out of Arkansas, and they'd carried on a torrid romance for two years, before he had turned to another woman. He had also led Rose into a bad life before she found the Lord in a New York mission.

"There's nothing but business this time, Amos," she said quietly. "I'm getting older. If I'm going to make it as an actress, I've got to do it *now*. If I can make a name for myself in England and maybe some other parts of Europe, I can come back in triumph. Then some of the big producers here will listen to me. I've got to do it, Amos. I've got to do it."

Amos drew a deep breath and said, "You'll do what you say you'll do, Lylah. You always have."

"Don't hate me, Amos," she said. "You can't hate me. I won't let you."

Amos smiled. "No, I'll never hate you, Lylah. We Stuarts have to stick together." He reached over and clasped her hand warmly. "This country . . . no, this *world* . . . is never going to be the same again. But you and I and all the rest of the Stuarts have got to stick together!"

4

"THE LIGHTS ARE GOING OUT!"

The dock at New York Harbor was packed with hustling, bustling people, and as Amos and Lylah stood at the rail looking down, the huge British liner, *Hartford*, uttered three short, raucous blasts.

"Well," Amos said reluctantly, looking at Lylah, "that means I've got to go." He threw his arms around her, and she clung to him almost fiercely, then stepped back.

"I'll be all right, Amos," she said, trying to smile. "Don't worry about me." They had made the trip back from Arkansas to New York in record time, but now that she was ready to leave America, somehow it didn't seem right. But Lylah was a woman who had determination to the bone, and now with all her skills at acting, found it possible to smile and say, "I'll come back the toast of Europe. You'll have to have an appointment to interview me, Amos!"

A smile pulled at Amos's lips, but he was worried. "You know," he said finally, "the Germans are torpedoing passenger ships, and this is an English ship at that. I wish you'd wait and go on an American ship at least. You can meet your troupe over there later."

"No, I'll travel with the others. We'll be all right." She felt her throat constrict and knew that if he didn't go soon, she wouldn't be able to control the tears that welled up in her. She leaned forward, kissed him, then slapped him on the chest. "Get out of here, you old newshound, you! I'll be back before you know it!"

Amos said quietly, "I pray that God will watch over you, Lylah." Then he turned and squeezed between the throngs lining the deck of the *Hartford*.

When he had made his way down the gangplank, he turned and looked up to find her watching him. She lifted her hand and waved. He waved back. Somehow, even though she was surrounded by other passengers, and even though she was traveling with a troupe of her fellow actors, his sister looked very lonely, very isolated, almost alien, standing there on the crowded deck of the huge ship. He waited until the ship began to move and then watched Lylah's figure grow smaller as the liner picked up speed and finally disappeared.

Amos threaded his way through the crowd moving toward the parking lot. He drove at once to downtown New York, weaving expertly through traffic composed of horse-drawn cabs and loud automobiles, finally arriving at the offices of the *New York Journal*, the creation of William Randolph Hearst. Amos parked the car, entered the building, and walked rapidly to the office of the editor.

"Hey, Amos! You're late. Better get in there," said one of his fellow reporters—a tall, gangly man named Stevens. "The old man's having a genuine fit. I think you're his raw meat for the day."

Amos grinned, waved his hand at Stevens, and entered Hearst's outer office. The receptionist, a short woman with gray hair, stared at him with obvious disapproval. "It's about time. He said for you to come in as soon as you got here."

As Amos went in, he heard the secretary announcing him on the intercom: "Mr. Stuart is here, Mr. Hearst."

Amos entered the office of William Randolph Hearst and found the editor crouched over a large table littered with maps. Hearst, who had made journalism in America more like a bullfighting sport than anything else—shedding literary blood right and left, espousing every cause that caught his fancy, and developing yellow journalism to almost a fine art— looked up and frowned. "Come in, Amos. Look at this map."

Amos walked over to examine the map as Hearst began pointing out the positions of the European countries and informing Amos didactically where the battles would be fought. He had this quality, almost clairvoyant, of being able to predict when news would come, where it would come from, and who would be involved. Because of this, Hearst was always first on the scene. He and the *Journal* had the jump on every other paper in the country as a rule.

"Sit down, Amos," he said gruffly. "On second thought—" he changed his mind—*"don't* sit down. You've got a job."

"Yes, sir?" Amos asked curiously.

"Go find Teddy Roosevelt and find out what he's got to say, although we already know." Hearst grinned sharkishly. "He'd like to raise a new corps of Rough Riders like he did in the Spanish-American war. Remember that?"

"Yes, I remember it very well." Vivid images of the charge behind Teddy at San Juan Hill flashed through Amos's mind. He'd been there that day, and the fact was a matter of pride to him.

"Then go talk to the president," Hearst broke into his thoughts.

Amos blinked in surprise. "Well, sir, I think I can see Teddy without any problem. We've been pretty close for years, but I don't know about the president. They say since the *Lusitania* was torpedoed, he's not seeing anyone."

"That's *your* problem!" Hearst snapped. "That, and hanging onto your job. So, get out there, get those interviews, and get back as quickly as you can." He dismissed Amos with a wave of his hand and went back to studying his maps.

Amos left the office, so engrossed with the problem Hearst had tossed out to him that he didn't even hear the greetings his fellow workers called out to him as he left.

At least, he said to himself as he got into his car, *I can see Teddy. That won't be any problem.* He left the inner city, headed for the home of Teddy Roosevelt.

★   ★   ★

"You may wait in here, sir. Mr. Roosevelt will be with you shortly."

"Thank you very much." Amos nodded at the tall servant who had ushered him into the fabulous North Room at Sagamore Hill, the home of Theodore Roosevelt, located at Oyster Bay on Long Island.

He walked around the North Room and thought how much a room could reflect the life of a man. There were elephant tusks, a gift, he knew, from the Emperor of Abyssinia. The carpet, thick and lush, had come from the Shah of Persia. Over to one side was a glass case containing a suit of Japanese armor presented by Admiral Togo. One wall was decorated with the head of a magnificent elk staring down at him. On another was a St. Goudens bronze, "The Puritan." Somehow it contrasted with the hunting trophies. The presidential flag hung high on the wall over a blue couch.

"Well, well . . . here you are! Good to see you again, my boy."

Amos turned as Teddy Roosevelt entered the room, striding purposefully toward him, and put out his hand. "Good to see you, sir. You're looking well."

"Oh, not bad for an old man." Roosevelt grinned, exposing huge teeth, easy to caricature by his political enemies.

He *did* look fit. Although blind in one eye from a boxing accident, he still had the glow of good health that had taken him all over the world—from the jungles of Africa hunting big game, across the American prairie, to the Panama Canal, where he had operated one of the huge earth-moving machines. He was—and had been for a long time—the symbol of American energy and dynamic willingness to dare all things. He had even taken on the crooked and corrupt monopolies and smashed them to bits, gaining the title of "The Trust-Buster."

"Sit down! Sit down! Tell me what you've been doing,"

Roosevelt boomed. His voice seemed to echo, filling the room, as if he were speaking in a large arena.

Amos sat down and said at once, "Well, sir, if you'll let me off, I'd much rather hear what *you've* been doing."

Roosevelt stared at him, a sharp light in his eyes. "You're here to find out what I think about this European war. Isn't that so, Stuart?"

Amos shrugged and smiled slightly. "Sir, I *think* I know how you feel. I've been listening to you for a long time. But, if you don't mind, I'd like to hear it directly."

"Mind? Of course I don't mind," Roosevelt said, shaking his head. He looked around the room at the many trophies; at the trophies of a lifetime, really, spent fighting for this country he loved so dearly. "We'll have to fight, Stuart," he said without hesitation. "No way out now. It's got to be. Everyone seems to know that, pretty much . . ." he paused, then shrugged his husky shoulders. "That is, everyone except President Wilson and Secretary of State Bryan."

Amos took out his pencil and made notes rapidly as Roosevelt restated all that had gone on in the past few months. He pointed out that the German decision to sink without warning any Allied ships found in waters around the British Isles was in itself an act of war. "How," he said, "are those U-boat commanders going to be able to tell the difference between a ship full of munitions and a ship full of passengers?" He got up and began to pace the floor, voicing his opinions loudly and defiantly as he always did.

"Wilson is a good man," he said finally, "and Bryan's a good man." He turned to Amos and smiled suddenly, baring his huge teeth again. "Both of them elders in the Presbyterian Church. They have a lot in common. But this is war," he said vehemently. "The longer we stay out of it, the longer it will last. The French and the English will fight with all they've got, but Germany has built up a magnificent war machine, and it's time to smash it!" He pounded his fist into his palm.

"Smash them once and for all! And make this world a fit place to live again!"

He continued for nearly an hour, Amos taking notes now and then, not really needing to, for he had heard it all before from Teddy Roosevelt. He knew that if Roosevelt, who had lost narrowly to Woodrow Wilson in the last election, were President of the United States, there would be men on the way to France and elsewhere in Europe right now. *Probably,* he thought with a grim smile, *with Teddy leading the way, waving his sword and his pistol as he did when he charged up San Juan Hill.*

When Mr. Roosevelt wound down, he took on an apologetic tone. "I'm sorry to have dumped all this on you, Stuart. But you've always been wise in the ways of politics, and you've always had a good feel for what's going on in America." He took off his pince-nez and asked in a low voice, "What do you think the president will do?"

Amos sighed. "He won't declare war until he's tried every other way out. That's what I think, Mr. Roosevelt."

Roosevelt grunted and got to his feet. "You're probably right, my boy. Probably right."

Later, as Amos left the grounds, he looked back and spotted Teddy Roosevelt playing in the yard with his granddaughter and wondered if anyone would listen to the old lion.

The country watched Woodrow Wilson closely. What would he do about the Germans? Would he go to war with them? Or would he build a moat around this country and declare, "It's America for Americans"?

Along with everyone else, Amos had read the harsh letter the president had sent to Germany. And, like most others, he was not surprised when Germany paid almost no attention to it.

But he could not think of a way to get in to see Woodrow Wilson. Every reporter and every writer in town—in the country, for that matter—would have given their right arm to speak to the president. But Wilson had disappeared . . . at least, he had refused to see any reporters, and rumor had it, he was not even talking to his fellow politicians.

"He's gone into hiding," Amos said to Rose one morning as they ate breakfast. Then, seeing the kids outside, their voices resounding on the May air, his tone grew wistful. "I wish I didn't have any more problems than those two."

Rose came around the table and put her hands on his shoulders. She ran her hand across his hair, then said, "Isn't there any way you can get in to see the president?"

"Can't think of one."

Rose hesitated, then said, "Well, I thought of something while you were gone yesterday. But it may be just a foolish idea."

He reached up, took her hands and kissed one soft palm, then turned around to gaze up at her fondly. "I like your ideas, even when they're foolish. What is it?"

"Well, you were always close to Mr. Bryan, the secretary of state," she began. "Why don't you go see him? He might be able to get you an appointment with the president."

Amos blinked in surprise. Then he jumped to his feet, threw his arms around Rose and swung her in a wide circle.

"Put me down!" she gasped.

Amos obliged, but not before kissing her soundly on the lips. "I'm going to raise your salary!" Giving her an appreciative look, he added, "Why didn't I think of that?" He stopped and took her in his arms again and looked into her eyes. "You're definitely the smart one in this family." With one last kiss, he was gone.

She went to the window and watched him jump into the car and roar off. *I married the right man all right. Marriage with anybody else would be so dull.*

Amos had no trouble at all seeing the secretary of state. He had always been good friends with William Jennings Bryan, had supported him on all of his futile tries for the presidency.

Besides, Bryan had an open door policy. Almost anyone could simply walk in and often did.

However, when he did get in to see Secretary Bryan, he saw at once that the man had aged visibly. His face was lined, and his hands had a slight tremble that had not been there before.

"Come in, come in, Amos," the secretary said in a friendly way. "Sit down, and let's hear what's on your mind."

Amos shook Bryan's hand, took a chair, and the two of them began to talk. "I'd like to see the president," Amos said, "but I don't suppose that's possible. I know he's not talking to anybody."

Bryan shook his head. "No, I don't think he'd see you, my boy. He's not even seeing me very often these days."

"Well, he's got a hard decision to make. What do you think he'll do about the German submarine problem?"

"I don't know," Bryan answered, heaving a sigh, "but I'm afraid of what he might decide. He's against war, but he's got lots of warhawks in this country yelling for it . . . screaming, as a matter of fact."

Bryan talked on about the situation. After a while he said, "I can't get you in to see the president, but I may be seeing him myself fairly soon." He hesitated, then confided, "I'm afraid I'm going to have to resign as secretary of state."

Shock ran along Amos Stuart's spine, and he knew he was on top of a big story. "Resign? You can't do that, Mr. Secretary. Mr. Wilson needs you."

"I had hoped so, but we seem to be going in different directions. I've urged him to take some firm measures without declaring war. For example, I asked him to encourage, even *command* Americans to stop traveling on ships belligerent to the Germans. But he said, 'That's impossible in a democracy.' I tried to get him to issue a warning to the British to observe the neutral zones, but he has even refused to do that." Bryan regarded Amos sadly. "Now I'm afraid of what's going to happen."

"I'd appreciate it if you'd let me go with you to talk to the president... if you have to, that is," Amos said. He knew that by being with Bryan, he would absorb some of the things that were coming out of the White House.

Bryan smiled genially, if a little sadly. "Of course, of course, my boy. Be glad to have you."

For the next three days, Amos stayed very close to William Jennings Bryan. And each day, it became more evident that things were not going well. Finally on Wednesday, Bryan spoke to him just before the office closed, and said in an unsteady voice, "I've decided to see the president. If you'd care to go along, I'd be glad to have you, Amos."

"Certainly, Mr. Secretary," Amos said quickly.

He did not question Bryan, but got into the automobile with him, and the two of them went to the White House. On Pennsylvania Avenue, they got out of the car and went inside.

When they handed their hats to the servant, Bryan turned to Amos. "You'll have to wait in the sitting room. I'll see you after I've talked with the president."

"I'll be waiting. And I'll be praying for you, Mr. Bryan."

Bryan looked at Amos gratefully, a warm light in his eyes. "I appreciate that, more than you know. And I know you mean it, Amos."

He turned and left. The servant showed Amos into a large sitting room filled with uncomfortable chairs. He sat there for nearly an hour, wondering about the meeting between these two stalwart Presbyterian elders. Finally, when Bryan came back, one look gave him the answer.

"He would not see it my way," Bryan said brokenly. There were tears in his eyes. He stared at Amos and said, "We will have war . . . although you mustn't print that. That's not my announcement to make. But I wanted you to know. Maybe you can say some things in your paper that will prepare the country for it."

"I'll do the best I can, and of course I wouldn't print anything without your permission."

William Jennings Bryan dropped his head. He seemed almost to be praying. Then he looked up at Amos. "A British duke—Lord Gray, I think it was—said something the other day. . . ." He hesitated, then dropped his voice to a near whisper. "Gray said, 'The lights are going out all over the world. . . . We won't see a light again in our lifetime!'"

5

A Visitor for Lylah

The audience at the Palace Theatre came to their feet as the curtain fell, the fine old building reverberating with their applause. Lylah, her eyes gleaming with excitement, grasped her friend, Helen Ulric, by the arm and whispered, "Listen to that! Isn't it wonderful!"

Helen, after three months, was still surprised at the effect an audience had on Lylah Stuart. She smiled and shook her head. "Go on and take your bow. It's you they want . . . not me."

Helen watched as Lylah moved to the front of the stage, smiled, and waved gracefully at the audience. As Helen looked on, the thought came to her: *I'll never feel as strongly about the theater as she does. She loves it better than she loves air!*

Helen thought back over the run of the play which had been a hit beyond the expectations of the backers. She remembered the first time she had met Lylah Stuart, how a hot streak of jealousy had run through her over Lylah's fresh beauty. She had quickly learned, however, that, unlike most actresses, Lylah had a gentle, sweet side to her nature. The two of them had agreed to take an apartment together in London, close to the theater, and it had worked out very well indeed.

Helen waited until Lylah took her bows, and then blew a kiss at the audience. *They'd laugh me off the stage if I tried a thing like that*, she thought.

When Lylah came back to the wings, she tossed Helen a bright smile. "C'mon. I'm starved to death. Let's get changed."

They made their way to the small dressing room they shared, and they met up with a stage hand who was frankly admiring. "Good performance, Lylah."

"Thanks, Harry," Lylah replied, and Helen could not help thinking that the American actress really *was* a democrat, that her familiarity with those men was no act.

Inside, Helen began undressing. "Good job tonight, Lylah, as always." She slipped out of her dress and reached for a robe. "But tonight was something extra."

Lylah's eyes were still bright with excitement from the applause of the audience. As she changed, she talked about the play—reliving it, regretting her single miscue, laughing when she remembered the leading man tripping and falling over a chair. She came alive any time she was onstage . . . or even now, just talking about it.

As they removed their stage makeup, Helen brought up the war. Wiping the cold cream from her face, she turned a troubled gaze on Lylah. "This war is bad. I plan to leave for Germany soon."

Helen was an attractive woman with blond hair and blue eyes—a true Nordic specimen. She came, Lylah knew, from an aristocratic family, although she had said very little about them. Now Lylah glanced at her with a puzzled expression. "Why would you have to do that, Helen?"

"Too much anti-German feeling." Wiping her face with a clean cloth, she began carefully applying her regular makeup. "It won't be safe for any German here soon."

Lylah fell silent and, caught up in their own reflections, the two women said no more. Lylah was aware of the truth of Helen's statement, but had hoped that the escalating war in Europe would not mean she would lose her friend.

When they were nearly dressed, someone knocked at the door, and one of the managers stuck his head inside and asked, "Will you see some of your admirers?"

"Send them in," Helen said. "I could use a little admiration."

The two women received the guests—two gentlemen and a lady. Both saw it as part of their profession. These were important visitors, they knew, wealthy people from Bristol who were prospective backers for their next play. They smiled and chatted, making themselves agreeable, and finally when the visitors left, Helen said with satisfaction, "I think they're hooked, Lylah. They've got more money than they know what to do with anyway. So they can pay us for the next play."

"Oh, I hope this one runs a long time," Lylah said quickly. "I love it!"

The two women were putting away their cosmetics when there was another knock at the door. A look of irritation swept across Helen's even features. "Another stage door Johnny," she fumed. "I'll get rid of him."

She went to the door and opened it barely enough to look outside. "Sorry. No more visitors tonight," she said brusquely. "Come back tomorrow night." She closed the door firmly, but she had no sooner settled again in her chair in front of the mirror than the knock came again.

"I'll get it," Lylah said. She had been in the theater for ten years, but she had never tired of receiving those who came backstage—a trait which puzzled the rest of the troupe, who considered these devoted fans little more than pests. She opened the door, opened her mouth to say something . . . then froze where she was.

"Lylah! It's really you!" Gavin burst out. He stood there, a broad smile on his face, then stepped in and took her in his arms.

Lylah, too surprised to speak, could do nothing but cling to him. Finally she drew back and looked up at him. "Gavin," she gasped, "what in the world—?"

"Surprised you this time, didn't I? Well, it took a lot of doing to work out this surprise, I can tell you for sure." Gavin was dressed in a shapeless suit that looked as though it had come from a third-rate pawn shop. He grinned at her. "Aren't you going to ask me in, Sis?"

"Oh, come in, come in!" Lylah grabbed his arm, pulled him inside, and looked over at her friend. "Helen, this is my brother Gavin. Gavin, this is Helen Ulric." Then she turned again and shook his arm almost fiercely. "What in the world are you doing? I just got a letter a week ago, saying you'd run away from home!"

Gavin stood there, looking pleased with himself. "Well," he admitted, "reckon I'm a little bit old to be running away from home . . . at twenty-two. What I did was run away to New York and beg enough money from Amos to get me to England."

"But . . . but what are you doing here?" Lylah stammered. She had not realized until this moment how much she missed her family, and now she held on to his arm firmly.

Gavin glanced at Helen Ulric, then decided he could speak freely. "You remember that pilot, Lincoln Beachey? I pestered him until he finally taught me to fly. I've come over here to join the French Air Force."

The world seemed to stop for Lylah. It was all she had dreaded, and she had hoped it would never happen. She had seen the releases of the casualty lists and knew how men were dying like flies at the Marne and other awful places. "You can't, Gavin, you can't do it! This isn't your war!"

Helen got up quickly. "Well, I'll leave you two alone. I know you want to talk." She put out her hand to Gavin and said, "I'm glad to meet you. This is some sister you have here, you know."

Gavin took her hand and squeezed it so hard she winced. "Yes, ma'am. Reckon I know that."

Helen left the room and Lylah said to her brother, "C'mon. Let's go somewhere else. We can't talk here."

They left the theater, walked to a small restaurant only four blocks away and sat down at a table for two.

"You'll have to pay for it, Sis," Gavin said with chagrin. "I just barely had enough money to get here."

"All right now, tell me all about it," Lylah said after they had ordered.

She listened as Gavin poured out his heart. He told her how miserable life at the farm had been—not just recently, but for years—and how he couldn't stand his stepmother another minute. He finally wound up by saying, "You ought to know, Lylah. You couldn't stand it even when Mom was alive. I just couldn't take any more of Agnes!"

Lylah shook her head and searched for the words that would make him change his mind. But she really knew that it was hopeless. Gavin was stubborn, she knew, with that same adamant quality that had driven her from the farm. As she sat looking at him, so youthful and handsome, she wanted to cry. But she willed back the tears. *What's done is done, and I'll have to do the best I can for him.* "All right, Gavin. I won't fuss at you anymore. Now, tell me about the family."

They talked all through the meal, then sat drinking coffee for hours, until finally the owner of the restaurant approached, coughing slightly as he placed the bill on the table. Lylah looked up, startled, then turned to Gavin with a laugh. "We always could talk all night, couldn't we?" She paid the bill, and the two walked outside into the night air.

"I'll get you a room at my hotel," Lylah said.

"Fine, Sis, but it'll just be for one night. Tomorrow I join the Foreign Legion."

Lylah stopped dead still, her mouth agape. "You'll do *what?* Join the Foreign Legion?"

Gavin looked chagrined. "Well, I didn't know 'til I got here that the French Air Force doesn't accept anyone except Frenchmen. So, I've got to join the Foreign Legion so I'll be a Frenchman. They take volunteers with no questions asked."

Holding onto Gavin's arm, Lylah began walking again, and when they reached the hotel, she said quietly, "All right,

Gavin. If you've got to do it, I guess you've got to do it. Besides, I can't talk, can I? Look what I've done with my life."

Gavin said quickly, "Aw, Sis, you haven't done so bad. You're a famous actress! Everybody back home is proud of you."

Tears stung Lylah's eyes, and she shook her head without answering. At the desk, she registered Gavin for the night, saying no more than was necessary.

Upstairs, he walked her to her room, then said, "I'll be gone when you get up in the morning, Sis. But you'll be hearing from me. You'll see my name in the newspapers one of these days—'Yankee Ace Shoots Down 10 Aircraft in One Day!'"

Lylah kissed him and whispered, "Good night, my dear, good night. Don't forget to write." Then she went inside, fell across her bed, and wept as she had not wept since she was a child.

When Gavin walked into the room, he was startled to see that it was full of tough-looking specimens of every race under the sun. There were even a couple of dark-skinned Negroes and one or two whose real color was nearly indistinguishable, so colored were they with plain ordinary dirt.

Feeling very small and more than a little afraid, he backed up against the wall to wait until his name was called. But he had come this far, and he wouldn't back out now.

Finally his name was called and Gavin moved across the room, entering a small office. It was occupied largely by various charts and a much-harassed, beetle-browed individual with a booming voice. He had the caduceus of the Medical Corps on the deep red velvet tabs of his uniform collar.

"Strip," he ordered, and Gavin immediately pulled off his clothes and dropped them to the floor.

Impersonally, as if Gavin were a horse, the doctor gave him a brief once-over and, seeing that he had the regulation torso—arms and legs—he grunted, and Gavin knew the first hurdle had been surmounted.

Then the doctor picked up a dirty, grease-spotted towel

and laid it on Gavin's chest. Gavin shuddered at the thought of how many chests like those in the anteroom that same towel had already covered.

"Breathe deeply," the doctor grunted.

Gavin breathed, his heart beating like a trip-hammer. With his ear to Gavin's chest, protected by the towel from contamination, the doctor listened for something—waterfalls? volcanic upheavals?—but didn't seem to hear anything alarming. Briskly he nodded approval, and Gavin drew a sigh of relief.

He stood Gavin in front of a chart, the letters of which looked as large as one of the signs in Times Square and commanded him to read. "The second line," he said. "I see there a 'B.' What do you see?"

"Uhh . . . I see a 'B'."

"*Bon!*" he exploded enthusiastically.

The doctor continued to read the chart, allowing Gavin to read it after him, never once trying to confuse him by calling the wrong letter. He wasn't taking any chances that Gavin would be wrong, and his '*Bon!*' grew even more enthusiastic with every answer.

They went on to the color chart, where the process was repeated.

"I see red. What do you see?"

"I see red, Major."

"*Bon.* I see green. What do you see?"

"Oh, I see green, Major."

Finally the major gave Gavin a friendly pat on the bare back, which sent him staggering across the room, signed his name to the papers with an official flourish, and congratulated him on being a perfect physical specimen. He said—as far as Gavin could make out—that Gavin was well qualified to get himself killed for France at any time.

Gavin dressed and went back to the outer office, where he signed his name to a paper that gave the French Foreign Legion permission to send him anywhere they saw fit.

"Wonderful!" the sergeant said, beaming. "Now, you can go to war for France!"

With his instructors and twenty-nine other pupils in his class watching from a safe distance, Lieutenant Manfred von Richthofen, lately of the Supply Corps, determined to appear as if what was about to take place was the most natural thing in the world. But when the engine of the ancient two-seater started, his look of composure slipped away in a blast of smoke and air. His safety helmet, strapped loosely under his chin, blew off and pulled taut against his neck. His partly unbuttoned jacket filled with air until it looked like an inflated brown sausage. His scarf unwound and disappeared. As the noise and the vibrations intensified, he touched the controls and the old biplane started to move.

As it bounced over the field and rapidly gained speed, von Richthofen squeezed the controls as tightly as he could and promised God that if he would let him complete his solo in safety, he would never do anything wrong again. When the tail lifted off the ground, he felt a little sick at his stomach. But suddenly the jouncing stopped. Although the ground seemed as close as before, now he was airborne, and he pulled back on the stick, bringing the nose up, and into the blue corridors of the open sky.

At the exact moment that Gavin Stuart was taking the eye test in the office of the Foreign Legion, Baron Manfred von Richthofen was making his solo flight. He had been a soldier in the German army for several years, but had quickly decided that the Cavalry, where he was assigned, was not going to win this war. He had been intrigued with the idea of airplanes and asked for a transfer to the Air Service. Instead, he had been transferred to the Supply Corps, whereupon he had written a haughty letter, beginning: "My Dear Excellency, I have not gone to war to collect cheese and eggs, but for another purpose...." He had ended with another request for transfer to the Air Service and, to his complete astonishment, had been assigned to the air station at Cologne.

At this moment, however, von Richthofen was trying to remember a few of the instructions he had been given by his teacher—a man called Zeumer—who had consumption and was determined to find an early grave by being shot down in the air. At least Manfred remembered enough to put the old plane through its paces and did so with some satisfaction.

What happened next was completely unexpected. Having cut his engine for the long ride that was supposed to end in a smooth landing, he felt his airplane move unexpectedly to one side. He overcorrected with the stick and pedals, and the biplane hit the ground hard, bounced, and nosed over.

As Zeumer pulled him out of the cockpit of the crumpled airplane, von Richthofen rushed to explain. "I lost my balance." He was afraid that was the end of his career as a pilot, but crashes by beginners were common at Cologne. Two days later, with the laughter and sarcasm of his companions still ringing in his ears, he made a series of successful landings.

Zeumer met him after the last one and said grumpily, "Well, I guess you're not going to kill anybody. Any of *us*, anyway. Now, let's see if we can make a pilot out of you so you can kill the French and the English."

6

LYLAH AND THE KNIGHT

O h, Helen, it looks like a fairyland!"
Lylah turned from the window of her large bedroom to face Helen Ulric, her eyes bright with excitement. "I've always loved snow," she confessed. "We never got much of it back home in Arkansas. But every time we had any at all, my father had to make me come in. I wanted to be out in it every minute of the day and night."

Helen smiled and shrugged. "Well, you'll get enough of it here in Germany. It's already over a foot deep, and there's likely to be more by morning. Come along. We'll go outside and watch it fall, since you like it so much."

The two had reached Helen's home at Schweivnitz, about forty miles southwest of Breslau, on December 22. They had arrived in a flurry of snow and for the next two days, Lylah went for long walks with her friend and sampled the rather dull German-style cooking served by Helen's mother. It was a placid setting and Lylah gradually unwound from the pressures of the nightly performances.

"We have a treat," Helen said one day soon after their arrival. "At least, I *think* it's a treat. We're going to stay over Christmas with my relatives, the von Richthofens. Their place is only a half hour from here. I think you'll enjoy meeting them."

The two women packed a few things and left later in the day. It was a thrill for Lylah to ride in the sleigh driven by Helen's family servant. The runners hissed sibilantly across the snow which still drifted in lazy flakes from a wintry sky.

By the time they arrived at the von Richthofen estate, the watery sun was out again, but it gave no heat. Hurrying inside out of the cold, Helen said, "I think the whole family's here . . . even Manfred."

As they entered, a tall, attractive woman came to greet them. "We're so glad to have you," she told Lylah warmly.

She put out her hand, and when Lylah shook it, she found it firm and strong. Indeed, everything about Kunigunde von Richthofen was strong. She had a strong full-bodied figure. Large bright blue eyes dominated an aristocratic face, offset only by her wealth of auburn hair, carefully done up.

"The boys have gone out hunting with their father," she said, "so that will give us time to get acquainted."

She took the two young ladies into the study, where they had coffee so thick that Lylah could hardly drink it. Mrs. von Richthofen plied her American guest with questions. She was interested, Lylah saw at once, in America's position on the war. All of Germany was interested, as were France and England. It was obvious that, sooner or later, the Allies would be drained dry of the machinery of war, while across the sea were strong young men by the millions and factories by the hundreds to turn out the guns and tanks needed to crush the German armies. The Germans looked with apprehension to America, while the Allies hungered for her entrance into the war. Carefully Frau von Richthofen steered the conversation, getting the information she wanted without being demanding in the least.

Later that afternoon, the men came in from hunting. The head of the family, Albrecht von Richthofen, stood erect, with a soldierly stance and clicked his heels as he took Lylah's hand, bowed low and kissed it, welcoming her to his house. He introduced her to his two sons. "This is my younger son, Lothar," he said, "and this is the eldest son of my house, Manfred."

Both young men acknowledged the introduction with a slight bow, and then Albrecht von Richthofen took over, as was the custom of a Prussian father. In that time and in that place, the father was almost omnipotent in his own household.

As the visit passed, Lylah learned that these von Richthofens were Teutonic primitives, given to strength and muscle and keenness of eye, with no doubt about their skill or their proper place in the world.

Lylah observed that Manfred's mother was of the same stock—rigid, conservative, getting the most out of the land, worshipful of order, and expected rights of small country nobility.

The von Richthofen estate was orderly and ran with precision and efficiency. Lylah had found the family home rather tasteless and grim, but clean. Since hunting was a way of life, the decor sported elk and deer horns in the hallways. Among the trophies of successful hunts hung portraits of solid thick faces, stern and unsmiling, turning black under old varnish, with not a masterpiece among them.

Manfred's father, half godhead of the family, followed the traditions established by these solemn ancestors and gave the code as a lover of order in the Schweivnitz tradition in which they lived.

On the second day of her visit, Lylah was surprised when Manfred approached her with an invitation to accompany him on a hunting trip just outside the estate.

Lylah beamed. "Why, thank you! That would be exciting."

She put on her warmest clothes—a wool dress, heavy overcoat, and hat that pulled down over her ears—and met Manfred in the study. Pulling down a gun from the gunrack on the wall, he handed it to her. "This should be light enough for you," he said, smiling. "Do you shoot?"

"When I was a girl I did," Lylah said. She returned his smile, adding, "But I may need some lessons to bring me up to date."

"Of course."

The two left the house, bearing their weapons, and walked across the top of the snow, now frozen solid enough to support their weight. Manfred led her away from the manor, around the side, following a trail that went directly into the huge evergreens, rising up against the laden winter sky. Their feet made a grinding noise, for the snow was gritty beneath, and Manfred kept her entertained with stories of his past hunts.

Lylah had already been informed by Helen that Lothar was a womanizer, whereas Manfred took little interest in girls. He was, she knew, only twenty-three years old, and she felt a hundred years older than he. So as they walked along, enjoying the crisp, cold air and the wintry landscape, she was surprised to find him far more outgoing than she had expected.

"Quiet now," he said when they reached a spot deep in the forest. "I think we may find something around that bend."

He showed her how to load the gun, then carefully instructed her on the safety features that must be observed. Then the two of them moved slowly ahead as quietly as possible.

As they stepped into a clearing, there was a sudden whirring that startled Lylah, and she saw birds rising from the ground.

"Shoot!" Manfred cried.

Lylah raised the single-shot shotgun, followed the flight of the birds, and pulled the trigger. She heard the roar of Manfred's gun in her ear and then she felt his hand on her shoulder.

"Wonderful!" he cried. "You got him!"

Lylah turned, not knowing what a beautiful picture she made—eyes shining, hair down around her shoulders, red lips parted in delight. "I haven't done that in a long time!" she exclaimed.

"You shoot very well," Manfred gave an approving smile. "How did you learn?"

"Oh, my brothers taught me. We grew up on a farm, and everybody hunted. Most of the meat we had on the table we had to shoot—deer, birds of all kinds. My whole family loved to hunt . . . all the boys, anyway."

Manfred walked over, picked up the birds, and shoved

them into the game bag at his side. "Come," he said, "we will try another place."

As they walked, he asked about her family and what she was doing in England. "My cousin tells me you are a wonderful actress," he said. "I've known no other actresses besides my cousin. Tell me, how does one get into that world?"

Continuing over the crystalline white snow, Lylah spoke cautiously of her past life, leaving out parts and editing others. When she was finished, Manfred shook his head. "It is strange for a woman to be on the stage. I am worried about my cousin Helen."

Lylah said quickly, "She's a wonderful girl, Baron. You must not worry about her. Helen is well able to take care of herself." Then she smiled and changed the subject. "Now, tell me about yourself. You're in the army?"

"Yes, of course," von Richthofen said. He began to tell her of his life, relating how he had gone through school preparing to be a soldier, and how he had joined the Cavalry. "But," he said, "this war will not be won by horses. It will take more than that. So I put in for a transfer into the aviation branch of our service."

"It must be wonderful to fly," Lylah said wistfully. "I saw my brother go up in an airplane just before I left America. I think I'd be frightened."

"No, I think you would not be frightened of anything," Manfred said seriously. "You are not the kind of woman given to fear."

Lylah was curious. "How do you know that?" she asked. "You haven't spent much time observing women, or so I hear."

Manfred smiled. "You heard that from my cousin. Or perhaps from my mother. And it is true enough. I've been too busy preparing myself for my destiny."

The words sounded pompous to Lylah, but she ignored them saying, "Tell me about it, Baron von Richthofen."

"Please," he said, "call me Manfred. And I may call you Lylah?"

"Of course. Now, tell me about yourself."

As they walked along, Lylah quickly discovered that to Manfred von Richthofen, the game of the hunt was the thing, with the kill the prize of skill and knowledge. Winning and losing. He had spent his life hunting the animals that filled the forest around his home. He had traveled with an uncle to Africa to hunt big game and, for him, the hunt had become a way of life. Finally, as they walked back toward the house, he said simply, "It is my life, Lylah. I am a hunter. There is in me, as there is in many of my people, a pure love of the hunt. Sometimes I think it's the only emotion I have—the love of conquering some other living thing."

Lylah was silent. She had watched his face—a handsome face, yet somehow cold—and had wondered what he was really like on the inside. Now she felt that she knew something about him. "Isn't that dangerous?" she asked quietly. "I mean, there's so much more to life than hunting and killing."

He listened to her question and seemed to consider it. With eyes constantly scanning the horizon, unconsciously seeking for gain, some movement that would betray an animal or a bird that would fall beneath his gun, he finally replied, "Perhaps you're right. There *is* more than hunting. There's my mother," he said warmly, turning to face Lylah. She saw that for the first time there was a genuine light in his eyes. "I love my mother very dearly."

Lylah thought that a little odd and yet, remembering the stern face of Albrecht von Richthofen, Manfred's father, she could see how difficult it would be to love such a man. He was no doubt generous and upright, but he was not a man one could easily love. On the other hand, Manfred's mother was a handsome woman with an unexpected tenderness a boy might admire, failing to find it in his father.

"Your mother is lovely," she said. "And I'm glad you do have a love for her. I hope you always will."

They continued walking until Manfred said suddenly, "You are a very beautiful woman, Lylah."

His observation startled her, and she stopped on the path, turning to face him. She could not resist flirting a little. "Will you make me the object of one of your hunts?" Her smile softened her features, and there was a dimple in her right cheek that intrigued him.

"If I did," he said, "I would catch you. I always get my quarry."

Lylah laughed and, without thinking, reached up and touched his cheek. "I'm afraid you might at that," she said, "so I'd better go in at once, lest I be brought down by your Teutonic charm."

The days passed quickly. Christmas came and went, and still Lylah lingered. Several times Helen had mentioned going home, and once she had even said, "I think you're paying too much attention to Manfred."

"Oh, he's just a boy," Lylah had quickly replied. "But I do so enjoy the hunting. Let's stay one more day."

And so they had stayed. Each day Manfred took Lylah out, and each day they brought back proof of their hunting prowess. If the senior von Richthofens noticed anything strange about their companionship, they kept it to themselves.

Finally the day came when Lylah knew she must return to England, and she mentioned it to Manfred as they were getting ready for a hunt.

He was quiet for a moment, then said, "That will be a sad day, but I, too, must return to my unit, so we will both be busy."

They went into the woods once again, and this time he took her farther than ever before. Another heavy snow had fallen. The trees were draped with heavy loads and sparkled like diamonds under the sun. They walked quietly, and Lylah realized that Manfred had taught her much about stalking animals. They spoke in normal tones until they got close to a small creek, where he said, "Quiet now. A stag may come to drink."

They waited silently under the trees, under the blue sky that scrolled over them, dotted now and then by flights of wild geese. The only sound was the sound of the branches as they groaned beneath their loads and the far-off cry of some sort of animal—a wolf, perhaps.

"It's been wonderful to be here," she whispered. "I'll remember it always."

He started to answer her, then suddenly froze. Slowly he nodded, and Lylah followed his line of vision to see a beautiful doe stepping out of the woods and approaching the creek. The animal was nervous, sensing their presence, perhaps, yet unable to see them from its vantage point. The doe continued to the creek, delicately bent over and pawed at the thin skim of ice, breaking it, then taking a look around before dipping its head to drink.

As the deer's head lowered, Lylah felt Manfred's elbow nudging her. Slowly she turned her eyes toward him and saw him urging her to take the shot. She lifted her rifle and drew a bead on the animal, but she could not do it.

Manfred looked at her with surprise, and then with a shrug, swept his rifle to his shoulder and the shot rang out. The deer leapt into the air, took two staggering steps, and fell dead.

"Come!" Manfred shouted.

"No," she replied, "I'll wait here."

Lylah watched as he put his gun down, ran along the side of the creek until he got to the deer and then pulled out a knife and slit the animal's throat.

He returned to Lylah with blood on his hands, wiping it off with his handkerchief. His eyes were bright, and he was alive with the excitement of the kill. "A fine specimen." He nodded in satisfaction. Then he asked curiously, "Why didn't you shoot?"

Lylah shrugged. "Oh, I don't know. She was so beautiful."

The thought seemed to trouble von Richthofen. "Yes, she is beautiful. But deer are put here by God for us to use, are they not? Man has always hunted for his food."

Lylah, half ashamed of her squeamishness, laughed. "Yes, you're right, of course. I'm just too fainthearted, I suppose."

"Well, let's go home now," he said. "I'll send a servant out to bring the animal in."

They turned and walked back beside the creek for a long time. Finally Manfred said, "Let's stop and rest. You must be tired."

They stood beside a huge fir tree, savoring the silence. Then Manfred began to speak. Lylah could tell he was troubled. Finally he came out with it. "What about the war? Do you hate all of us Germans?"

Lylah was startled. "No, of course not! Why would you say that?"

"It's a terrible war. Men on both sides are going to get killed."

"I *am* afraid," she confessed. "I have a brother in the French army and other brothers at home. They will probably enlist if America enters the war."

They talked about the war, and Lylah could see that Manfred felt differently. And yet, he was not what she had expected a typical German soldier to be. She had seen the propaganda of the bull-throated Prussians with their bayonets drawn on women and children. But the days she had spent with him had revealed a side of Manfred von Richthofen that most people never saw. Deep down, in the heart of this hunter was a gentle spirit. She saw this in his obvious affection for his mother and for his brother, Lothar.

"I don't hate you," she said. "How could I ever hate you?"

Manfred did not know what to say. During her visit, he had gone through some strange and traumatic experience. He was tremendously drawn to this woman, although she was older than he. He had never seen a woman so beautiful, yet so dynamic. She was not like German women, who were totally submissive and obedient to their husbands. This woman would be herself. She would maintain that flamelike spirit he admired in her. But he was confused.

Finally he said, "We cannot be lovers. We are on different sides."

At his words, Lylah was shocked to find that she had even considered taking Manfred as a lover. Impulsively, she put her arms around him and kissed him passionately. He responded at once. Her hands clasped behind his head and the softness of her lips seemed to stir him, more than he had ever been stirred. He held her even closer, inhaling the sweet scent of her hair.

Finally he lifted his lips, and she drew back, whispering, "Love isn't a matter of politics, Manfred."

He had not been drawn to the young women who swarmed around him from time to time. But there was something of his mother in this woman that moved him. He knew he would never find another like this one.

He put his arms around her once again and simply held her. Finally he said, "I have a feeling for things, Lylah. I always have. One thing I've always known is that I would be a great soldier. I know that, but I don't know *how* I know it."

They clung to each other, and Lylah felt herself filled with a longing she had seldom known.

"Lylah, we're making a mistake to let ourselves be drawn together," he whispered hoarsely.

Lylah drew back and gazed up into his eyes, tears gathering in her own. She had seen the yearning beneath the proud military bearing. "I know, my dear." And then, with a shake of her head, she said, "I've been making mistakes all my life . . . and I just can't seem to help it." She drew his head down and pressed her lips to his.

As they kissed, a hawk flew over, surveying the scene before swooping down forty yards away to sink his talons into the quivering flesh of a small rabbit. But the German soldier and the American actress did not hear. They clung to one another, oblivious to the world about them, knowing only that something had come to them, and they would never be the same again.

Part 2

THE LAFAYETTE ESCADRILLE

7

A YANK IN THE MUD

A lmost at the same instant his sister was embracing Manfred von Richthofen in Germany, Gavin Stuart was standing in a trench somewhere in France, up to his ankles in thick yellow mud. The shrimpy smell of the sea was in the air. It was raining again, a soft rain that tapped on his helmet, looking for a chance to trickle down inside his poncho. The duck boards along the bottom of the trench were awash in the fetid, mustard-colored water, and all but one of the men in the Third Platoon section of the Zig-Zag had pulled their boots up onto the fire step.

The only one who didn't mind was a rather plump farm boy from Nancy that somebody had nicknamed 'Girly.' His smooth, girlish face wasn't really as pretty as all that. Sitting on the fire step with his feet in the water, his eyes fixed blearily on the other side of the trench, his mouth hanging open, he bore little resemblance to any girl or anyone else—alive.

He'd been dead for some time, and the smell would have been noticeable by now if the water lapping at his puttees hadn't smelled far worse. Besides, Gavin and the others had learned to deaden their nostrils to all smells—all except the warning odors of scorched garlic, crushed uranium leaves, or a sickeningly sweet version of the smell of new-mown hay. All this was very much like the poison gas the other side kept sending their way.

A star shell hissed into the rain-swept sky and became a

brilliant ball of frozen lightning, dangling from a little paper parachute.

Down the line, a British infield cleared its throat nervously and was answered by the irritated woodpecker rattle of a German machine gun. As the gun fell silent, Gavin stood up straighter and gingerly raised the brim of his helmet about an inch above the sandbags of the parapet.

"See anything, Yank?" Sergeant Albert Moritz demanded. He was a thick man, in body and in face, almost like a cave man. "The Neanderthal," they called him behind his back. Tough and crude, he'd been a dockworker in civilian life, and, some suspected, a petty criminal. Since Gavin had come to the Legion, Moritz had been the bane of his existence.

Gavin didn't answer for a moment, but continued to scan the eerily lit landscape between the opposing armies. There were six lines of rusted and badly tangled concertina wire between the sandbags in no-man's-land. A country inn and a tracked forest had once occupied part of that lunar landscape. The inn had been flattened in the first drum fire, but the stump of a fieldstone chimney still stood above the tortured earth a little to Gavin's right. Directly in front of his position, standing Pisa-like in defiance, was a single miraculously preserved toilet bowl. Its white porcelain was washed clean by the rain and, like the chimney, the porcelain commode was an important landmark to the Third Platoon. Everything else out there looked pretty much the same.

"Well!" Moritz demanded, his voice rising. "Do you see anything, you booby, or not?"

Startled, Gavin shook his head. "Not a thing, Sarge. Not nothing moving out there."

He looked back again, peering into the darkness illuminated, from time to time, by shell fire, and by a moon that seemed cleaner in its pristine whiteness than anything Gavin had seen for a long time.

Mostly the landscaping of no-man's-land consisted of shell holes, all kinds of shell holes—from the convenient shelters excavated by Allied 75s and German Whiz-Bangs to the dangerously deep water-filled craters left by Howitzers, or the awesome house-swallowing pits torn out of the earth by the occasional big stuff hurled by railroad guns. Most of the area had been hit over and over again. Crater walls overlapped in a bewildering pattern of rain-soaked earth, shattered tree trunks, abandoned packs, rifles, helmets, and all the other trash the war had dropped in the long months since the balmy summer of 1914.

Then . . . there were the men. Soggy figures sprawled here and there in the chalky magnesium light. They were scattered across the wet mud like the discarded rag dolls of a very untidy little girl who didn't like to take care of her toys.

Gavin felt a movement and turned to see that Sergeant Moritz had stepped up beside him and was also peering into the darkness. "Go get some grub from the kitchen, Yank," he said. His face looked blunt and lumpy, unlike most of the rest of them who had lost weight during the long siege. "And be sure you get something fit to eat. Don't let that swine of a cook give you any of that garbage like last time."

"Right, Sarge," Gavin said and jumped back into the sucking yellow mud with a squelching sound.

"Take somebody with you," Moritz added. "Bring it back hot."

"I'll go." Marcel DeSpain got to his feet and looked around for a dry spot. Finding none, he placed the butt of his rifle in the middle of the trench. There was no way to keep anything clean in the trenches, and most of them had long ago given up, all except DeSpain and Gavin. "Let's go," he said. "Maybe they'll have something fit to eat this time."

DeSpain, a young man of twenty-five, was of medium height and very thin, with high cheekbones and fine gray eyes, sunken deep into his skull. His dark brown hair was lank and uncut, like the rest of them. He would have been a handsome young man if he had not been whittled to the bone by trench warfare.

"Let's go," he shrugged. "Not that we'll do any good."

The two soldiers made their way along the trench. Gavin thought how different war was than what he had imagined. Like most young men, he had envisioned racing across the field with the sun overhead, flags waving, drums beating, bugles blowing. But since the Battle of the Marne and especially since the first Battle of Ypres, the war on the Western Front had settled down to a system of trenches that stretched all the way from the Alps in Switzerland to the North Sea close to Dunkirk.

Dug into deep ditches four hundred miles long the two armies faced each other. These trenches had become almost like little cities. Each trench line had an alternate fire bay with bulkheads so that it twisted into zig-zag formations. Support trenches, one hundred or more yards back of the front line, were less pretentious.

Every conveniently sighted knob along the front was made a strong point, usually a thick-walled bunker or a concrete turret, housing weapons. Machine guns replaced the fire diagonally across the front so that one bullet swarm interlocked with another, splintering an attack with crossfire. Outposts were pushed forward into no-man's land to warn of night attacks or to ambush enemy patrols.

All too often, the front line rested on a marshy flat, and wherever the trench fell, it was shielded by a thicket of barbed wire strung in broad aprons, sometimes a hundred and fifty feet or more in depth. Soldiers called "Pioneers" trimmed the barricades by night, and enemy artillery tried to blast them apart by day. At times, the distance between the trenches was so close that the Germans and the Frenchmen fought within hearing range, often screaming at one another. At other times, the lines were more than a mile apart. The pattern followed no sensible plan that Gavin could see, but then nothing about this war made any sense.

Great gun duels would go on for hours, often, he knew, arising from nothing more significant than a nose-thumbing incident from a soldier. First, the small weapons would be put into play, followed by the complete orchestration. Where the opposing trenches were close, the soldiers were mutually immune to the big guns, but were vulnerable to grenades, mortars, automatic fires, and trench raids.

All this ran through Gavin's mind as he and his comrade made their way back through a diagonal trench until they reached the field kitchen. The cooks occupied a space underneath what was called a bomb-proof—which was nothing more than a hole in the ground, covered by sandbags. Inside, the half-naked cooks had their stoves going, and one of them looked up grumpily and asked a question in French. Marcel replied sharply, and the two men fell into some sort of argument. Finally, DeSpain seemed to have won the argument, for the cook began slamming pots and pans about. Ultimately, the two soldiers left the cookshack with four iron pots of food, enough for the whole squad.

When they made their way back through the trenches and reached their own sector, they called out, "Sarge! Here's the grub!"

Moritz nodded. "I'll keep watch. See that all the men are fed."

Gavin and Marcel carried the food down the line. Each man had his own pan, and when they were all served, they found themselves a place and sat down to eat.

DeSpain stared into his tin plate and shook his head. "I wouldn't eat this slop if someone brought it to me in a restaurant," he said moodily. "What is it, anyway?"

Gavin stared into his own plate and said, "Better not to know, I reckon. Just eat it and be glad it's hot."

The two soldiers ate the tasteless stew slowly, pausing from time to time when a flare went off, waiting to see if a bigger shell would follow or if the sergeant would call out that an attack was forming out of the trenches. They finished and Gavin cleaned his plate as best he could with his filthy handkerchief, then stuck it back into his knapsack.

"Well, no dessert," he said, and grinned at DeSpain. "If I was home, I'd be having apple pie or blackberry cobbler."

"Blackberry what?" Marcel demanded.

"Cobbler! You pick blackberries, you make crust, and you put the blackberries in the crust with their juice, and when they're all bubbling up, you eat it! Gosh, I wish I had some right now!"

DeSpain stared with sunken eyes at his friend and shook his head sadly. "You're not likely to get any *coobler* around here," he grunted. He was a gloomy young man, given to writing poetry which he was careful never to show to anyone . . . except once or twice to Gavin. Gavin had no literary taste at all, so he bragged on it enthusiastically.

DeSpain had been in the army since a week after war broke out in 1914. He had come in with high hopes, but like many others, he had seen so many men killed and so little accomplished that now he was completely stripped of any hope of victory, or even of an end to the hostilities.

As they sat there, he began explaining again his theories of war to Gavin. "You see, as long as armies are mobile," he said, waving his hand around, "they can change positions. One can catch another from the flank, sneak around, and come in behind them."

He glared around at the trench and continued, "But in a hole like this—these trenches—the enemy never moves and we never move. Nobody can catch anybody else by surprise."

"Well, sometimes there's a surprise attack," Gavin argued.

"Yes, there is." Marcel laughed bitterly. "And what happens? Either they rush across into our machine gun fire and *they* all get killed, or we rush across into theirs and *we* all get killed. And the bodies pile up in no-man's-land out there."

Gavin was still young enough and green enough to have some hope. "Well," he said, "it'll have to end sometime, won't it? I mean, we can't keep on killing each other forever."

"That's right, my friend," Marcel nodded, disillusionment scarring his face. "It will end when everybody is dead. When the Germans are all dead and we Frenchmen are all dead and the English are all dead . . . when you are dead and I am dead . . . then it will all be over."

The two young men went on arguing and finally Sergeant Moritz said, "All right, you two. Get up on the step. I want you to watch. I think I saw something moving out there."

But there was nothing moving. Nor for the next two weeks did anything seem to move. By day, the artillery blasted the barbed wire, and by night the Pioneers laid it back, but nothing happened.

The only thing that gave Gavin any relief in the filthy trench was that from time to time during the day, he would look up and watch the planes fly over. Just by observation he had learned to tell the Allied planes from the German planes, and twice there had been a dogfight in the air over him, when he had almost been able to see the faces of the pilots. Unfortunately, the Germans had won both times, and the French planes went down somewhere behind his line. Once the victorious German had flown his plane over the trenches, waggling his wings. He was so close Gavin could see his goggled face.

Gavin dreamed about those planes. It was why he'd come to France in the first place. He would have sold his soul to be a pilot. But no matter how much he protested or attempted to transfer, his pleas were met with ridicule.

"You're a trench bug, Yank," Sergeant Moritz would say with a short laugh. "You'll stay here 'til you're buried in the mud like all the rest of us. Now, get back to your place."

Nevertheless, Gavin hoped that someday, something would change. This was no life at all; rather, it was like a living death. The new year came and went and still nothing changed. Twice his unit was called on to go over the top to charge the German machine guns. But the first time, the attack was called off before they got ten yards from their own trench.

The second time was not the same. Gavin crouched on the fire step, waiting for the signal. When it came, he threw himself over the top and ran clumsily toward the hole in the barbed wire that had been blown by their artillery. He looked around to see Marcel DeSpain running beside him, behind the rest of the squad.

Suddenly it became like a mad race to Gavin. He had to get to that trench, where those Germans poked their spiked helmets up, and kill them. *If I could do that*, somehow he reasoned, *the war would be over. And I could go home.*

The tremendous rattle of the machine guns addled his senses, and the jarring sounds of grenades exploding on both sides of him added to the nightmare. Still he ran forward, aware that others were falling like limp bundles into the mud. Some were caught on the barbed wire and began screaming at once. Sometimes the scream would be cut off abruptly as machine gun fire raked the body.

Finally, hearing a soft cry to his right, he turned and saw Marcel standing rigidly, his eyes wide with disbelief. He merely looked at Gavin, saying something Gavin could not understand. Then he grabbed his chest, and blood spurted from his mouth in a crimson fountain. He fell forward into the mud, his face burying itself, and lay still.

Gavin dropped his rifle and ran to him, but then he heard Moritz shouting, "Leave him! Leave him! Get going, Yank!" Gavin grabbed his rifle and started once again across the field.

Once more the charge was halted short of their goal. And one of the noncoms shouted, "Retreat! Retreat!"

Gavin, mad with battle lust, would have gone on, but Moritz grabbed him, turned him around, and gave him a kick. "Back to the trench, you stupid idiot!"

Gavin stumbled back to the line along with the rest. As the bullets crisscrossed the area, he somehow found himself sitting back in the water at the bottom of the trench. Then a thought occurred to him. As the others came stumbling in, he tried to climb back up on the fire step.

But it was the sergeant again who grabbed him, demanding, "Where do you think you're going!"

"It's . . . Marcel!" Gavin gasped, his eyes wild. "I've got to go back and get him! He's been shot!"

Moritz shook his head. He was a tough, crude soldier, but he had developed a liking for this young man. "Too late, boy," he muttered in a kindly tone. "I saw him go down. Three bullets right in the chest. He's gone."

Gavin stared at him. Slowly the meaning sunk in. Without a word, he stumbled away, sat down with his back against the bulkhead, put his head in his hands, and began to weep.

After the death of Marcel DeSpain, Gavin Stuart was careful to form no new friendships. He could not afford to go through that kind of grief again. He saw the men go down from time to time, and each time he had to tell himself they were just numbers. At night, he would sometimes dream of Marcel, but he never told anyone.

The year wore on, and one day early in May—the sixth, it was—Gavin was awakened from a nap by a shout. "Look! Look! He's coming down!"

Gavin rose with a start, looking around in confusion. Focusing on the noises coming from above him, he looked up to see a plane coming down directly in front of his position. It was, he knew instantly, an Allied plane, but there was no enemy aircraft in sight. The plane was belching white vapor, which Gavin guessed to be gasoline. He expected to see the frail aircraft explode at any moment, but it did not. It came down almost at full speed, it seemed, and Gavin could see that the pilot was still alive, though the plane seemed to be shot to pieces.

The aircraft touched down, miraculously kept going past crater after crater, until it dropped its wheels in a very small one. Then it bucked up into the air, performed a small flip, and landed on its back.

"Poor beggar," Moritz said. "He ain't got a chance! Them gunners have him spotted."

It was true, Gavin knew. German machine guns had al-

ready begun to rattle and several rifles as well—all aimed at
the hapless airman. Fortunately the craft itself was hidden
behind a huge mound, and the gunners could not get a clear
shot at the victim, who was struggling in his harness.

It was one of those moments Gavin would never forget—
the sight of that airman trying to get loose, the sound of the
crackling gunfire. Afterward, he could never remember what
went on in his mind. Everything seemed to have been blot-
ted out. All he knew was that he was racing across the cratered
field without a gun, and the sergeant was screaming at him
to stop. He heard the whistle of a slug as it went past his ear.
He dodged, fell down, and saw the dirt where he had been
standing blow up into fine dust. Somehow he managed to
stay concealed behind the raised mountains of the craters
until he reached the plane. When he had made it, he scrambled underneath.

The smell of gas was strong and, looking inside, he saw
that the pilot was covered with blood. *Probably dead*, he
thought.

But at that moment the goggled face turned to him and
said, "Get me out of this, will ya, fella?"

Gavin used his pocketknife to sever the straps. The pilot,
a big heavy man, fell on top of him and the two rolled in the
mud.

"Can you walk?" Gavin asked, jumping to his feet.

The pilot put up his goggles and glanced down at his
bloody leg. "I don't think so," he said. "But I can crawl. Let's
get out of this place."

The airman did his best, but halfway across, he fainted
from the loss of blood. With bullets striking all around, Gavin
managed to drag him to safety, using what cover he could
find. The machine guns on his own side, he was aware, were
crackling to cover him as much as possible. He fell halfway
into the trench, wrestling the body of the heavy man over
with him, and the two of them were at once pulled inside to
safety.

"Here! Put him on this stretcher!" Sergeant Moritz barked. "He's bleedin' like a fountain!"

"Lemme go with him to the hospital, Sarge," Gavin pleaded.

Sergeant Moritz grinned at him. "You bloody beggar! Ain't got the sense of a flea!" He shook his head. "Okay, you can go with him. But get back as soon as you can."

"Right, Sarge." Four of them lifted the stretcher and began the trip through the maze of trenches. They staggered into the field hospital and Gavin said with more authority than he felt, "You fellas go on back. I'll stay with the pilot." To his surprise, they nodded and left at once.

Gavin hovered nearby while doctors stripped the pilot of his uniform and began working on him. When they were through, Gavin edged close enough to peer down at the wounded man.

The pilot's eyes were open and he said, "Hey, you're the joker who brought me in, aren't you?"

Gavin grinned, for the accent was unmistakably American. "Sure did," he said. "How you feelin'?"

The aviator said, "Well, from the sound of your talk, you must be from the good ol' U.S.A."

Gavin nodded. "Way back in the hills of Arkansas. Are you all right?"

The pilot shrugged. "No, I think they're going to ship me to a hospital in Paris." A light flashed in his eyes, and he said, "Listen. I want you to come with me, Bud. I ain't said thank you yet, and we got some talking to do."

Gavin shook his head. "I can't do that. I'd be a deserter."

The big man grinned at him. His face was pale from loss of blood, but there was something authoritative in every line of his body. "I'll take care of that," he said. He called one of the French doctors over and rattled off something in French. The two talked for a moment, and at last the doctor nodded in agreement.

"He'll get word back to your unit. Tell him your name and

your outfit. Then you can stay with me 'til I get out of that bloody hospital."

Ten minutes later Gavin was climbing into the ambulance beside the wounded aviator.

"My name's Bill Thaw," he said before he drifted off to sleep. "When we get to the hospital, you stay close to me. I'll tell them you're my body servant or wing man or something. I need somebody close to me besides these Frogs, okay?"

"Sure, Lieutenant," Gavin assured him and patted the beefy shoulder. "Don't worry none. I'll stay right with you from now on."

8

TWO KINDS OF PILOTS

Gavin could not tear himself away from the shower. He had been admitted to the hospital as Bill Thaw's roommate or wing man and had been given a bed in one of the wards. Adjoining the ward was a bath, and the first thing Gavin did was to strip off his clothes and plunge under the cool water. Over and over again he let the soothing liquid run over his head, trying to wash away the filth that had accumulated during months in the trenches.

When he finally got out, he stared at the dirty clothes he had thrown on the floor. Determined not to wear them in that state, he washed them with laundry soap scrounged from one of the ward attendants. With no change of clothes until his wet ones dried, he crawled between the clean sheets and fell asleep instantly.

He awoke with a start. The familiar stench of the trenches and the sounds of cannon booming and machine guns rattling were missing. The silence seemed to sweep over him and startled him more than the explosion of a mine or a bomb falling from an airplane. He lay there, luxuriating in the feel of the clean sheets next to his equally clean body. He finally got up, put on his freshly washed uniform, and made his way out of the ward.

The other patients appeared to be sleeping, so Gavin left quietly. Going at once to the desk at the end of the hall, he found an attendant, a tall Frenchman, who spoke only broken English. After a struggle with the language, Gavin learned where Lieutenant Thaw was quartered. He made his way through the hospital, getting lost more than once. He finally found the room he was seeking.

Pausing outside the door of a hospital room, Gavin heard a very English voice behind him. "Are you looking for Lieutenant Thaw, Private?"

Gavin wheeled around and found himself looking into the face of one of the most attractive women he'd ever seen in his life. She was obviously a nurse, wearing a white uniform that reached to the toes of her polished black shoes, and some type of a fitted cap on her head.

"Why . . . I . . . yes, ma'am, I am." He stared at her. "You're . . . uh . . . not French, are you?"

The young woman smiled at him. "No, I am English," she said. "I'm Nurse Spencer." She was rather tall—about five-eight, he guessed—and no more than twenty-two or twenty-three. Her ash blond hair and blue-gray eyes made a perfect match for her oval face. *But*, Gavin reasoned, *I haven't seen a woman in so long that even a female gorilla might look good to me!*

"Yes, Nurse, I'm here to take care of Lieutenant Thaw until he gets out of the hospital."

Nurse Spencer nodded her approval. "That's fine, Private. What's your name?"

"Gavin Stuart."

"American, aren't you?" The nurse gave him an appraising look. "Well, I'm glad you're here. We're packed and jammed with the casualties from the big push. Have you had any experience nursing?"

Gavin scratched his head and stared at her. "Well, ma'am . . . I mean Nurse . . . not really, just tendin' horses and cows and dogs, I guess."

Nurse Spencer laughed out loud, making a delightful sound. He had read somewhere in a book that certain women laughed with a tinkling sound, like music, but he'd never expected to hear it. "It's all about the same, I suppose," she said quickly. "Come inside and I'll give you instructions."

She half turned to go inside, but Gavin put a hand on her arm. "How is he, Nurse? Is he hurt bad?"

"Oh, no. The wound in his leg is healing nicely. It didn't break any bones. I think he can go home in a couple of days. The main thing is to see that an infection doesn't get started. Of course, he lost quite a bit of blood so we need to build his strength up. Come along. He was awake a few moments ago."

She led him into the room, and there, sitting up in bed, staring at them was Lieutenant Thaw.

"Well, it's you again, Nursie. I think it's about time I had another bath."

A slight touch of crimson colored the nurse's cheeks, and she shook her head, saying firmly, "One bath is all you get, I'm afraid. But if you want another, here's your new nurse."

Thaw grinned beneath his bushy mustache. "Well, that's a fine kettle of fish! Good things don't last very long, do they? When do I get out of here, Nursie?"

"In two days, if you behave yourself. Now, I've got work to do."

When she left the room, Thaw turned to Gavin. "What's your name again? I'm a little fuzzy about what happened."

"My name's Gavin Stuart, Lieutenant."

"Well, Gavin, I owe you my life, so I guess I'm going to let you take care of me to make sure you did a good job. Here, why don't you sit down and tell me all about yourself. What are you doing over here, anyway, all the way from America?"

Gavin sat down and began to answer Thaw's questions. Soon Gavin found he had told the aviator more than he'd intended to.

"So," Thaw said with interest in his dark eyes, "you say you came over to fly airplanes, but you haven't done any flying. Is that right?"

Gavin nodded sadly. "Well, that's about it. I've tried everything I can think of."

Thaw winked at him. "No, not everything. You haven't tried Bill Thaw yet. How about giving me a shot at it?"

"You mean . . . I . . . you could get me into the Air Force?"

"I can do better than that," Thaw grinned. "Have you ever heard of the Lafayette Escadrille?"

Gavin shook his head. "I know an 'escadrille' is a name for a French flying unit, but I never heard of the 'Lafayette Escadrille'."

"Well, you're going to be happy to hear it now. The Lafayette Escadrille," he said, "is a new unit composed entirely of Americans. There aren't many of us yet, but our numbers are growing all the time."

"Americans? I didn't know there were that many Americans over here."

"Quite a few of them joined the Legion like you did. Others who could fly got into the regular Flying Corps. A man called Bill Prince put together the Escadrille. He got some bigwigs back in the States interested, but the French wouldn't listen to him at first. They were too afraid of spies to let any Americans into their forces. But Prince kept at it. And now, as of March 14, 1916, the Lafayette Escadrille has become an official unit of the French Flying Service."

"Do you really think I could get in?" Gavin demanded, his eyes bright. "I wouldn't want to mislead you, Lieutenant. I'm not a very good flyer."

Thaw laughed. "None of us were when we started. But we're going to have a fine training program, and we've got some good men. Of course," he said, shrugging his burly shoulders, "a man learns best by watching what the good flyers do and trying to imitate them. But I figure I owe you a few lessons, so when you get me out of this place, we'll see what we can do."

For the next two days, Gavin hardly moved from Bill Thaw's side. Consequently, he got well acquainted with Nurse Heather Spencer, who, he found out, was not a regular nurse but a volunteer who had come over from England to help care for the wounded. She had told him this about herself over a cup of tea when he caught her between rounds.

"I came over to serve God, Private Stuart," she said simply. "I could've gone as a mission volunteer to Africa, where some of my friends went, but I found that I have just as good an opportunity to share the gospel here as over in the Dark Continent."

Gavin was dumbfounded. He'd had the notion that all missionaries and most Christians, for that matter, were dour-faced and determined to put an end to all fun wherever they found it. "Well, my brother's a preacher," he said blankly. "An evangelist over in the States. But I guess it hasn't rubbed off on me yet. I don't have any more religion than our horse back home."

Heather Spencer was an astute young woman. Already she had learned that she could not force men to believe in God, and she wasn't about to begin now. She simply said, "The time will come, Private Stuart, when you will know God. Every man has that time, I think." She put her hand on her cheek, bracing her elbow on the table. "I think God is on some sort of manhunt . . . or womanhunt. He wants everybody to know his love, so he sends hundreds out to find them. His scouts are chasing after us, and every one of us has some sort of bloodhound hot on his trail. Sooner or later he will find us."

Gavin was entranced. He shook his head in wonder. "I never heard anything like that before. What would God want with a guy like me?"

The nurse said gently, "He wants us all, every one of us. From the savage in Africa to the Eskimo eating frozen blubber to the King and Queen in Buckingham Palace, God loves us, one and all."

The conversation was then abruptly broken off by the arrival of others, but Gavin never forgot what she said. It burned through his head, and he repeated it to Thaw.

The pilot was now able to sit in a chair. A burly brute with a splendid physique, he had thick black hair, and snapping black eyes. His flowing mustachios were the pride of his heart. "Better watch out for that kind," he said. "They mean marriage."

On the third day the pair prepared to leave the hospital. Thaw was on crutches but able to maneuver fairly well. As they left the hospital, Gavin spotted the blond nurse and said, "Excuse me, Lieutenant. I'll go say good-bye to Nurse Spencer." He ran over quickly and pulled off his hat, cradling it in his hands. "We're leaving now. I want to thank you for all the kindness you've shown to the Lieutenant . . . and to me, too."

Heather put out her hand and took his in a surprisingly firm grip. "I'll remember you in my prayers," she said. "You, and the lieutenant as well." She smiled and added, "Come back and see me if you're ever in Paris again. We can talk."

"I'll . . . I'll do that, miss," Gavin said and backed away awkwardly, turning with a wide grin for Lieutenant Thaw.

As the two got into the cab that was to take them back to their unit, Thaw said, "That's a good-lookin' woman. But she's too religious for me. She wouldn't even let a fella chew tobacco, would she?"

Gavin quickly changed the subject. "Well, I guess we'll be parting company, Lieutenant. It's back to the trenches for me."

A delighted grin crossed Thaw's lips beneath the black mustache. He reached into his pocket and pulled out a paper. "Nope. That's where you're wrong. You're going to be a pilot in the Lafayette Escadrille." He handed the paper to Gavin, who read it, his eyes almost bugging out as he learned that he was now assigned to the Lafayette Escadrille and was to report for active duty immediately.

Gavin, like most of the Stuart clan, was not one to show his emotions much. But he had to blink the tears back as he stared at the paper, not daring to look up. "Lieutenant Thaw, I'll never forget this," he said when he could manage to speak, "Never!"

Thaw glanced at the boy and frowned. "Not sure you ought to thank me, Gavin. The losses are going to be terrible. The

Germans have the best planes and more of them. Until we catch up, we're like clay pigeons up there."

"I'll never forget it," Gavin repeated. Then he looked up and smiled. "That nurse said one time that God does strange things to people. She told me that. And now I sort of believe it, from the way things are working out."

Without further conversation, they rattled along over the rough streets of Paris, out into the countryside. As they headed toward the Lafayette Escadrille Air Station, Gavin was thinking, *This is what I came for . . . to fly. This is what it's all about.* Then he added a little prayer. *God, if you are there, thank you . . . thank you a lot.*

With a carefree heart, Gavin Stuart drew on black leather pants, jacket, goggles, gloves, and crash helmet. He discovered that from the moment he first slung his leg over the edge of a cockpit and a gold-braided, high-ranking brass hat clapped him on the back, saying, "*Mon enfant,* you are a pilot!", he never had anyone with him. There was no dual control in the ships. He was strictly on his own.

Of course, there were instructors—the older pilots. Bill Thaw, especially, kept his eyes on Gavin throughout the first days and weeks. Nothing seemed to escape him, and by easy stages, Gavin absorbed enough fundamentals to keep from killing himself.

The school at Buc, near Versailles, was a training center for pilots who would eventually go into pursuit squadrons. If a man didn't make a good showing, he was eliminated and sent back to his regiment or to some other duty. But nearly everyone who got to Buc finished with honors. Of the sixteen candidates in Gavin's class, fifteen got their brevets.

The training was no bed of roses, Gavin learned. He was shaken out of sleep at dawn every morning with only a cup of lukewarm chicory, masquerading as coffee, to sustain him until the first meal at eleven o'clock. Then the class members went out, shivering, to one of the fields, each awaiting his turn on the wonderful and fearful contraption known as the Blériot model plane.

The Blériot was a source of never-ceasing wonder. It seemed to be constructed of odds and ends of wood, discarded matchsticks, and the like, which were wired together in catch-as-catch-can fashion with baling wire to form the fuselage. Old handkerchiefs were sewn together to cover the rings in the part of the fuselage around the pilot's seat. The remainder of the fuselage was left naked, which gave the ship a kind of half-finished appearance.

When Gavin asked why they weren't covered, Thaw shrugged. "Easier to replace than brace wires when they get hit by a bullet or when they get a little strain on them."

To make things more complicated, the planes' engines were not identical and ranged from a three-cylinder Anzani Italian radio motor to the sixty-horsepower LeRhone rotary motor.

In addition, the stick in the Blériot had an odd feature—a triangular-shaped grip on top with a contact button on one side so the motor could be blipped on and off. Instead of grasping the stick like a broom handle, the pilot curled his fingers around the top bar of the triangle. There were no ailerons; the wings, owing to their light construction, warped quite easily. It was an out-moded system, of course, for the Wright brothers' first plane had used this system.

On that first flight, Gavin found himself sitting with half his body projecting above the fuselage giving no protection against the full blast of the propeller stream. The whirling stick was only a couple of feet in front of his nose.

He took off, rising about ten or twenty feet, then blipped the motor on and off, bringing the ship down almost flat, hardly peaking at all. Again and again he repeated the procedure, his landings improving gradually.

But by the end of the day's training, partially wrecked Blériots lay all over the field. Bad landings that even the tough little Blériot wouldn't take, motor failures in very embarrassing spots, and the general uncertainty of the new pilots themselves spread the little ships all over the surrounding landscape.

"You know," Gavin once said to Thaw, "it's a wonder we don't have more broken backs after all these crack-ups."

Thaw glanced around the field and nodded. "I've thought about that myself. Look there, those planes themselves dissolved in splinters—simply disintegrated—but most of us just get out of the wreckage and walk away. We're tougher than that airplane, I guess."

For two weeks, the Americans were drilled daily in the techniques of flying at the front. And in their off hours, the older pilots spent much time discussing an important problem—the choice of an official insignia to designate their squadron. Dozens of different ideas were proposed. They finally settled on the painting of the head of an American Indian wearing a war bonnet of red, white, and blue feathers.

Almost as soon as that decision was made, Captain Thenault announced that the squadron would make its first patrol over the German lines on May 14. Takeoff was scheduled for six o'clock in the morning.

At dawn, Gavin climbed into his own sleek new plane, a speedy little Nieuport single-seater pursuit ship, powered by a ninety-horsepower LeRhone rotary motor and equipped with a single forty-seven-shot Lewis machine gun mounted on the top wing. The synchronized gun that fired through the propeller had not made its appearance on the Allied side to any great extent. But the Nieuports were the last word in speed and maneuverability, with a ground speed in excess of one hundred miles per hour.

Gavin's hands were trembling when he took off from the airfield as dawn flooded the runway, and he stayed carefully on Bill Thaw's left wing. Thaw had said just before takeoff, "We won't do any shooting today. Just watch."

They cleared the ground easily, nosed up before leveling off, and soon were heading over the moon-like surface of no-man's-land. It did look like the moon—still, blasted craters—

but Gavin had no time for sightseeing. He was attempting to stay as close as possible to Bill Thaw—right on his tail. They flew a long circle, slightly over the German lines, but saw no German planes in the sky.

The mission lasted two hours and, when they came back and landed, Gavin got out of his Nieuport, feeling deflated.

Thaw drifted over to where the young man stood, pulled off his helmet, and grinned at him. "Wanted to shoot down a Jerry, did you?"

"Well, I thought we might at least *see* some," Gavin said.

Thaw squinted upward at the sky. "Don't worry. You're going to see plenty, if what I hear is true. The Germans have got themselves a new airplane called the Fokker and a whole stable of hotshot pilots under their ace, Boelcke. We got some information that they're going to be coming at us with every-thing they've got. So, in the meantime, we're going to drill the socks off of you pups!"

And so it was for the next three weeks. Gavin went up every day. They drilled, they trained, they simulated dog-fights, but they kept far back of the German lines. Then one day Thaw came by, saying to his young friend, "You know what I've been telling you about these new airplanes made by this man called Fokker? Well, the word down the line is they've hit. They're shooting our men down like they were sparrows." The lieutenant's face was grim and his mouth a thin line. "I wish we had some of those new Camels they're building in the factories here. But we won't get 'em for a while. Meanwhile, just stay under Daddy's wing."

Gavin dreamed that night of a blue sky filled with air-planes—some, with the red, white, and blue target on the side denoting America; others, with the Iron Cross of Ger-many. He could almost hear the staccato sound of machine guns and the whistling of air through the wires of his ship. He woke up just as his craft seemed ready to burst into flame.

He wiped the cold sweat off his face, his hands shaking. *Got to do better than this*, he thought. *Can't let the other fellows down.*

★   ★   ★

Germany had been fighting a two-front war for more than a year. Since it was winning on the Eastern Front, but was in a stalemate in the West, the German High Command had decided to pull out more of the men who were chasing the Russians and send them to France.

Manfred von Richthofen boarded a train heading for a large airfield. Halfway to his destination, he walked to the dining car. Seeing an empty seat, he asked the lieutenant sitting on the other side of the table if he might join him. The man's face looked familiar—squarish, with neatly parted blond hair, wide nose, thick lips, large boyish eyes. It was a shy face. Von Richthofen thought he had seen it in the newspapers.

"Lieutenant von Richthofen," he introduced himself.

"Lieutenant Boelcke," came the equally formal reply.

Von Richthofen blinked, for he was staring at his country's most famous ace. Oswalt Boelcke had already been awarded the Iron Cross, and had shot down fifteen French fighters. But Boelcke was more than a fighter; he was a student of planes and a teacher of flyers. Manfred had read everything he could about the man, which was not a great deal, and now he carefully approached the famous pilot and, during that train ride, got to know him fairly well. Von Richthofen, before he left the table, resolved to cultivate Boelcke's friendship.

During the following weeks, Manfred von Richthofen continued to learn his trade, but all the time he had but one thought—to become the best fighter pilot in Europe.

One afternoon, on his way back to Germany from a tour of air groups in Turkey, Oswalt Boelcke appeared at his air station. The trip had been arranged by the High Command with the double purpose of giving Boelcke a rest after his nineteenth kill and showing the German and Turkish forces how to fight. Boelcke had shot down more enemy airplanes than any other German and was now being touted by Berlin as the world's greatest combat pilot.

Now, Boelcke was looking for talent. Von Richthofen was one of the pilots sitting around the dining table that afternoon and he smiled at Boelcke whenever their eyes met. After the meal, he followed Boelcke to a lounge and listened attentively while the pilot described conditions in France and some of the outstanding Allied pilots the Germans were encountering there. Finally the officers began to leave, and Boelcke explained to von Richthofen why he had come.

"I must have the best fighter pilots in the world," he said, "and you have come to mind as a likely candidate."

"I?" von Richthofen asked in astonishment.

"Oh, yes." Boelcke knew all about von Richthofen's background—his wealthy family, his renowned passion for hunting, his apparent indifference to women and alcohol. As he sat there, Boelcke asked himself, *But what about his temperament? Would he fit into a hunting squadron? Can he stalk in the air, with patience, as he does on the ground? Does he have the eyes and reflexes to be a successful pilot?*

Boelcke had talked to his brother, who had told him that von Richthofen had had a difficult start and tended to be ham-fisted, but he was working to improve. He told him also that the young pilot knew almost nothing about how an airplane works or about machine guns, and showed little inclination to learn.

"Ah," Boelcke said to his brother, "that is a trait that will have to be watched. It is the sure sign of a glory-seeker, one who does not wish to be bothered with details." Then he added with a shrug, "But if the man is eager, hungry for fame— even *too* hungry—that may not be a bad thing." He grinned at his brother's surprise. "If fundamentals can be beaten into his thick skull before he gets himself killed, he may make a good record. I must try him."

Later in the day Boelcke asked von Richthofen, "Would you care to come with me to the Somme?"

The young man snapped back, "Indeed I will!"

On the train carrying him to the battlefield, von Richthofen

glowed with pride and hope. The Somme! This colorful battle was talked about as one long journey to hell. The stubborn, mutton-headed British generals were threatening to destroy the youth of England in headlong attacks launched
directly into the German machine guns. Thousands had died
within a few yards of some broken section of trench. Back
and forth swayed the two weary armies. Nothing was gained,
yet the staggering casualty list mounted. On the train, moving west of the Somme's slaughter, Manfred von Richthofen
was thinking, *Now begin the finest hours of my life.*

Early on the afternoon of November 9, Major Lanoe
Hawker, the leader of Number 24 Squadron, walked slowly
to his airplane. He was concerned about the wind, the mud,
and the frail and inadequate biplane he was about to fly into
combat. Hawker was a slender man who sported a neatly
clipped brown mustache . . . and the Victoria Cross. He was
the product of an unbroken line of Army and Navy officers
who went back to the reign of Elizabeth I, and, like others of
his caste, carried himself with a dignity and the firm gentil-
ity that did credit to his school.

Hawker was the Allies' premier fighter pilot. He had grad-
uated from the Royal Engineers, but was posted to France
with a Scout Squadron. Within a year, having shot down more
airplanes than any other Englishman, he had become the
first Royal Air Corps pilot to win the Victoria Cross. The
twenty-five-year-old officer now looked like a good prospect
for general.

He stood in front of his airplane and felt the Channel wind
blowing gently against his face, knowing it would not be gentle high in the sky. Their mission would demand that they
face a stiff headwind to make it back home. The wind was
no friend, often giving the German scouts enough time to
plunge into and maul their lumbering formations.

It was one o'clock, and the rain had stopped several hours
before, but the sun was just breaking through the dark tow-

ering clouds that slid eastward on a fast breeze. Hawker hesitated, then climbed into the DH2 that squatted obstinately in front of him. A year and a half earlier, the sleek new German Albatros had made this plane a dangerous antique. The pilots called it a "spinning incinerator." Constructed of wood and canvas, the craft was basically a ten-foot-long, coffin-shaped box, rounded on top. It could do a bare ninety-three miles an hour and was delicate, like a huge kite.

Now, behind his machine gun, Hawker huddled in his woolen underwear, uniform, fur-lined flying coat and fly boots, and flipped the switch that sent the electricity to the engine behind him. When the current and the gas in the engine cylinders touched, there was a loud sneeze that sent a shudder through the wooden box along the intricate network of crisscrossing cables and out over the large cloth-covered wings. The little engine caught and settled into what was more or less an even roar. Blue smoke came out of the cylinders in thin streams and was drawn back into the propeller, where it was chewed up and sent tumbling into the mud and the wet grass behind the airplane.

Hawker released the brake, and the plane jumped forward and began to roll through the mud, gaining speed. After a short roll into the wind, the plane rose from the tarmac and climbed steeply into the dark clouds. Banking, Hawker turned northeastward and was soon joined by three other scouts. They formed a squat diamond and proceeded to their destination.

Twenty minutes later, a couple of two-seaters were seen flying low, slightly to the west. Hawker hesitated, considering, then decided to take them. He waved the group forward into the attack, but suddenly he knew the truth. The two-seaters were bait for a trap. *Get out of there*, he thought. He kicked the rudder bar, moved his stick to the right, and brought his scout into a wide right turn.

The others, seeing their leader attempting to leave for home, moved to follow him. But one of the planes was shot to pieces before he could get away. Hawker looked up to see a bullet-nosed Albatros, following him around a tight circle at 3,000 feet near Bapaume. Hawker realized immediately that he was not up against a nervous type. This German pilot was doing all the right things. He was not going to let his hunger for a victory force him into a mistake.

The German and the Englishman flew across the sky, sometimes like fluttering moths, sometimes with winds screaming at full speed over a hundred miles an hour. Then the German came within sixty yards of the Englishman, firing almost continuously. Suddenly the English plane straightened, hung limply in the air for a second, and then began to fall. Around and around it went until it smashed, nose first, into the ground, burying its machine gun in the mud, spinning and crunching wood and tearing fabric. The wreckage bounced once, then came to rest in a waterlogged shell hole five hundred yards inside the German forward lines. Its pilot lay somewhere in the debris with a bullet in his head.

Baron Manfred von Richthofen did not know, at that moment, that he had become the most famous ace in the German Air Force, having earned the honor by shooting down Lanoe Hawker, the leading British ace. He looked around for other victims and, seeing none, allowed himself to look down at the fallen plane. His heart was pounding with excitement as it always did. There was no other feeling like it. He felt potency surging through his body, and waiting in his fingers to be used again.

Two of them had fought for the sky. One was the victor. He, Manfred von Richthofen, was the victor. Therefore, he owned the sky for as far as he could see and as far as his gun could reach.

He pulled gently back on the stick and aimed his Albatros toward a higher altitude where he could catch the wonderful wind that always carried him home. He thought the wind could carry him to heaven.

It was the eleventh time Baron Manfred von Richthofen had felt that way.

9

FIRST KILL

1 916—perhaps the bloodiest year Planet Earth had ever known. And it had all begun when General Erich von Falkenhayn, leader of Germany's armies, made the rash and unsound decision to attack his country's enemies full force. Germany, he pointed out to the Kaiser, could not win a long, drawn-out war because its manpower sources were too thin. Germany must launch a battle that would "bleed France white," compel her to capitulation, and collapse the Alliance.

This was Falkenhayn's brief for staging the greatest battle in world history and doing it in the dead of winter, ignoring every lesson that had ever been taught about military strategy. Falkenhayn was convinced that if Germany would stage one battle so terrible in its dimensions, so shattering in its impact on both camps, then governments and peoples would be shocked into making peace with Germany, on terms barely short of ruin. This operation was given the code name *Gericht*—meaning, the place of execution. As Falkenhayn penned this in Berlin, carolers abroad were singing "peace on Earth."

On February 21, 1916, the battle began—two days of full-scale bombardment—before the Shock Divisions were to reap the harvest of chaos. The German guns spoke until the crews dropped from exhaustion, expecting to create a zone of death where no Frenchman drew breath.

Early the next morning over a six-mile front, two million shells were thrown at that narrow triangle containing Verdun.

There were ingenious fires, mixed shrapnel, high explosives, poison gas, and blockbusting projectiles that ripped the earth, shaking it. Ravines, forests, trenches were all worked over. Shells came down at the rate of 100,000 rounds per hour, and the French forward trenches were obliterated.

Just before dusk of the first day, the German infantry came forward. They expected to cross a passive field of mangled corpses and crazed derelicts. Instead, Frenchmen black as stokers, uniforms torn off, looking more like scarecrows than soldiers, stirred amid the desolation and pumped away with their rifles. The Germans should have known that artillery alone can never saturate and silence an entrenched resistance.

Before the month was out, the German army had advanced to a position within four miles of the city. During that time they captured 10,000 French prisoners and many machine guns and cannon. On February 24 they stormed the French secondary system of trenches. Always the bombardment moved ahead of them.

The one thing that the German leadership did not correctly estimate was the reckoning of the French will to resist. To stem the German tide at Verdun, France sent an unending column of men, youths of twenty going into the fiery furnace of battle. The real hero of Verdun was the *poilu*—the self-reliant veterans of the French army.

The war at Verdun came as close to hell as earth can get. One German soldier wrote: "Verdun transformed men's souls. Whoever floundered through the morass full of the shrieking and dying had passed the last frontier of life, and henceforth bore deep within him the leaden memory of a place that lies between life and death."

Across the lines, a Jesuit priest echoed the grim sentiment: "Having despaired of living amid such horrors, we begged God to let us be dead."

For ten months the soldiers of the two nations were locked in mortal combat, fighting with a savage intensity that made victory or defeat hollow terms. It seemed as if the battle would continue, one German predicted, "until the last German and the last Frenchman hobbled out of the trenches on crutches to exterminate each other with pocketknives or teeth or fingernails."

The flawed planning and mistakes were not only in the German camp. General Douglas Haig, called "Whiskey Doug" by his troops because his family founded the Haig whiskey empire, made a blunder every bit as terrifying. He led the British army into the Somme.

The German line had been made impregnably strong overlooking the Allied trenches. Massively timbered dugouts, rebutted with concrete and equipped with electric lighting, were serviced with an underground reticulation of laundries, aid stations, repair shops, and arsenals. Life was relatively good there. The Germans didn't wish to be disturbed and felt it would be folly for the Allies to try.

It was.

But Haig set his jaw, convinced that the Somme was an open sesame to final victory. He would cut the German army in two, and do it in one day. He would have the Cavalry Corps under bit and ready to charge through the shell-cratered gap into the blue as proof of his intent to crush the enemy.

Britain's army for the attack on the Somme was shaped largely of new conscripts—half-formed soldiers who, never having seen action, truly believed in their first go over the top. They were bound for Berlin. But the more seasoned fighters noted that the earth-shaking bombardment that opened at dawn on June 24 still hadn't cut most of the enemy wire. There were some shrewd soldiers eyeing the preparations for the Somme.

There was also a muster of poets—Robert Graves, Siegfried Sassoon, John Macefield, Edmund Blunden, and Mark Plowman. For what they heard and saw, there were no new songs to sing. "Armageddon is too immense for my solitary understanding!" cried Sassoon.

Haig ordered the opening of the battle and the earth

churned, the landscape shriveled, the noise deafened, the fumes stifled. In that vast barrage, 1,508,000 artillery rounds were spent, and at the end of it the German works and wire were still intact.

At 7:28 A.M. on July 1, the French and British infantry climbed up from their trenches and jumped off into the exploding unknown. Sir Douglas Haig, far to the rear, sent in encouraging reports; but all along the lines his soldiers were falling in droves to zeroed-in machine gun fire. It was a catastrophe. By day's end more than 60,000 soldiers of the British Empire were corpses littering the field, and dying men were trapped in the beaten zone. And not one plot of ground had been won.

Haig should have called off the Somme that night and cut his losses. But having failed, he was too bulldoggish to quit. In consequence, this hideous turmoil must be recorded as the most soulless battle in British annals.

America understood very little of how Europe bled and suffered during 1916. The shore was too distant. President Wilson ran again and was re-elected on the party slogan "He Kept Us Out of War." But many of the more pugnacious sons of America were training in earnest in Plattsburg and other camps for command jobs in the conflict they knew lay ahead. A popular song took hold: "I Didn't Raise My Boy to Be a Soldier."

A song—"There's a Long, Long Trail," written by a Yale student for a college production—fired the imagination of the nation, and the British Infantry sang it while moving up to the trenches because it eased the pain in the hearts of men. For soldiers who had the luck to survive, there was no worse year in a war, nor one in a wretched memory.

But from the perspective of the years, 1916 was the nadir in the ordeal of men and nations. There were no electrifying changes. There was only slaughter, grim and great. The war looked so far from being won that, in their misery, people high and low despaired that any termination was possible.

Toward the end of that horrible year, Germany sent out peace feelers through various embassies. These preliminary overtures came to nothing because it was apparent that the Kaiser wanted peace on his own terms. This was rejected by the Allies, but neither set of generals had the foggiest idea of how the war could be won.

By now Gavin Stuart had become a good pilot. He had acclimated himself to the aerodrome, which had grown from a haphazard collection of tents and vans into a more permanent arrangement. The flying area was a smoothed-out field, rectangular in shape. Dugouts, topped by heavy timbers and sandbags, served as rain shelters.

Gavin had learned that there was a difference between nationalities even so far as food was concerned. Food in his own mess was poor unless they had a French cook, so they scoured the countryside for them. One Frenchman remembered the British cuisine as "everything boiled to death in live steam, then covered with a white sauce made of wallpaper paste."

The French always ate well and usually looked the best. They were always impressive in their dress parades, and their fighting spirit was excellent. Everyone was aware that the Americans who joined the British and French Air Forces were the most reckless and innocent, spendthrifts with life. Gavin tried to explain it once to a French flyer: "We all grew up on Buffalo Bill's Wild West Show," he said. "Then the early Bronco Billy films. We came from the frontier tradition where a man is a man. He walks right up and shoots it out. We saw this in our movies and read it in our books over and over again," Gavin said. "Now we fight the same way in the air."

It was true enough. Most Americans flew, ignoring science and advice, and their casualties were fearful until they simmered down. Some of them were college men or students living abroad—upper-middle-class sons, full of pictures of planes, confident it would be fun and romantic to fly in a war. Some of them were race car drivers, and it took time and tragedy before they became as accomplished as many flyers in the war. Gavin, on the other hand, seemed to be one of the more steady flyers. Perhaps because of this trait, he was selected to be one of three men to fly some bombers back to England, across the Channel.

His friend Bill Thaw came to him with the news one day after he had returned from a routine flight over the trenches. Thaw grinned broadly and slapped him on the back saying, "Well, believe it or not, some *good* news for a change."

Gavin had flown missions every day for over a month and was worn thin. "Did the Kaiser drop dead?" he asked wearily.

"Not that good." Thaw shrugged. "But you and I and Smith are going to get a little vacation over in England."

Gavin listened as Thaw explained that three of the bombers that had been sent recently to fly missions into the enemy territory had developed problems. "We're flying them back so the factories can test them and work the bugs out. Then we'll bring them back." He smiled gleefully. "It'll probably take at least a week! London, here we come!"

The American production of *Tonight's the Night* took London by storm. After the terrible battles of Verdun and the Somme, with their tragic casualty lists, the city needed some light comedy. They were also taken with the star of the show, Lylah Stuart. She did not have the raw colonial character seasoned theatergoers had become accustomed to in American actresses, but played her role in the more refined English manner.

Lylah had taken her final bow, smiling graciously at the audience. As soon as she left the stage and started for her dressing room, the smile left her face. She said nothing to Helen, who was waiting for her and accompanied her to the dressing room. But when the two women were inside and were taking off their stage makeup, Lylah said, "I asked that we not have any visitors tonight, Helen. I'm tired."

Helen paused and looked over at Lylah, noting the lines

of worry. There was compassion on her face as she replied, "You've been working too hard. You need some rest."

Lylah shrugged wearily. "That's the trouble with being in a successful play. There *is* no rest. You have to keep going." She ran her hand across her hair, then smiled up at Helen. "Here I am, complaining about success after working all my life to become a star. Now I'm jaded."

"Maybe for Christmas you can go home with me again," Helen suggested. "The manager said we might take a week off then, maybe two."

A strange expression crossed Lylah's face as she thought of last Christmas, of her time in Germany at the home of Manfred von Richthofen. Shaking off the nostalgia that swept over her, she said, "Well, I'm not sure of—"

She was interrupted by a knock at the door. "I'll get it," Helen said and opened the door. "Lylah, look who's here! I can't believe it!"

Lylah turned from the mirror, and, seeing Gavin standing there in his natty uniform with a broad smile on his face, jumped to her feet. Crying out his name, she ran and threw herself into his arms. She could not stop the tears that came, for almost daily she had expected a letter saying he had been killed.

"Hey, hey! Turn off the waterworks, will you, Sis?" Gavin protested, yet his voice was a little unsteady. He had not passed many days that year without thinking that each one might be his last. Now, as he stood there holding Lylah, he found himself unable to speak for a few moments. When he stepped back, the grin was back. "Well, now. This is like deja-vu, all over again, isn't it?" He grinned at Helen. "Picked up a little French since I've been here."

Helen laughed and stepped forward. "I'm afraid you'll have to hug this old woman, too, Lieutenant. I've heard lots of good things about you since you became a famous flyer." She pulled his head down, kissed him, and stepped back.

"What in the world are you doing here, Gavin?" Lylah

asked, her hands fluttering over his shoulders. "How did you get here?"

Gavin explained briefly his mission, then said, "Enough of this. I don't want to waste a single minute. What I want to do is take two gorgeous women out to the best restaurant in London. Let's go."

An hour later they were sitting together at the Hotel Elite, eating steaks. Gavin was in rare form, laughing and telling his experiences, making light of his own part in the air war over the trenches. But the two women knew better.

"I read in the paper that you've shot down four airplanes," Lylah said. She glanced at Helen across the table, knowing they shared the same fear: Each time Gavin went up, there was a possibility that he would kill Helen's relative . . . or Lylah's lover.

"Oh, nothing big about that," Gavin shrugged. "They were all observation planes. I haven't even been in a fight yet." He shook his head sadly. "It's a shame we have to do it—shoot down those observation planes, I mean." An odd look flashed into his eyes, and he added, "It's like shooting fish in a barrel. They have no chance at all. They've got a gun up in the top rear cockpit, most of them, but if you come in behind, they can't shoot at you because they'd blow their own tail off. So you just come in behind them, low, and hose 'em down with bullets."

His talk of killing in the air made Helen uncomfortable. Shortly after that speech, she rose, saying, "We did this once before, didn't we, a year ago? I'll see you before you leave, won't I, Gavin?"

"Every night, right out in the audience," Gavin replied as he stood. He reached over and took Helen's hand firmly. "You're not going to get rid of me."

"Well," Helen said, running an appraising eye over his strong young physique, "you won't have any trouble finding young ladies to fit on your arm. But if you need help, let me know. I've got some ideas about that. Good-bye."

When she had gone, the two—brother and sister—sat back down and talked for hours. Finally, it grew late and Gavin said, "Let's take a walk. I need some fresh air."

He paid the bill and they left the restaurant and began walking along the streets of London. Gavin talked quietly, mostly of little things—the men he flew with, the food he had missed . . . home. Lylah listened, saying little in reply. She clung to his arm as they walked in the cold air along streets that were newly cleared of snow.

She was wondering what Gavin would think if he knew that Baron von Richthofen had been her lover, and that for nearly a year they had been writing one another, the mail taking devious routes, but always arriving sooner or later. It had been a strange relationship. She had had lovers before, but always she had either tired of them quickly, or they had left her. But in the months that had passed since Manfred had held her in his arms, something was different. She did not know what it was, could not explain it to herself. When she read newspaper accounts of the exploits of the young German flying ace shooting down British and French planes, killing her countrymen, she could not reconcile it with the gentleness of the man she had known back in Germany.

Finally the two turned toward her apartment. "It's getting late," she said. "I have to get some rest. You can't imagine how much acting takes out—"

Suddenly there was a series of loud thumps, almost as if someone were beating a carpet. Puzzled by the sound, they noticed that other pedestrians were hurrying away. Lylah looked up. "Zeppelins!" she cried out. "They're here again!"

Gavin looked up to see searchlight shafts moving across the sky, their long fingers picking out the silvery cigar-like crafts floating quietly overhead. Little winks of red began appearing around the zeppelins. "We've got to get out of here!" he said. "That antiaircraft fire won't stop them!"

Instantly, there was a series of loud explosions as the bombs from the zeppelins fell. Not half a block away, a bus exploded, sending orange flames high in the air as the two stumbled toward a doorway.

"Let's get under that archway!" Gavin shouted to Lylah. "It's safer!"

They ran and ducked inside one of the brownstone buildings, and Gavin held his sister in his arms as the bombs went off all around them. There was a high-pitched scream of agony from someone so badly hurt they could not tell whether it was a man or a woman.

They crouched in the doorway, expecting at any moment to be blown apart. Finally the explosions stopped, and the sounds of the rescue efforts began to be heard. "Let's get out of here," Lylah said nervously.

Back at her apartment, she begged Gavin to come in for a while. "I don't want to be alone," she said.

"All right. Just for a while."

They went inside and she made tea, and he sat on the couch, trying to relax. They drank the soothing brew slowly, and Lylah's jangled nerves began to unwind.

Finally she felt something within compelling her to say, "Gavin, I have no one to talk to. But something has happened to me that I need to tell someone about."

Gavin's face registered surprise. His sister had never been a woman to express herself. She kept her own secrets. But he saw that her fists were tightly clenched, and now she got up and began to pace in agitation. He listened as she began to tell about her visit to Germany the previous Christmas, and about her meeting with a German fighter pilot.

Lylah felt somehow she was doing the wrong thing but she could not help herself. Finally she turned and said, "We were lovers, Gavin." Her face was tense as she added, "He's a *German* fighter pilot, and yet I love him. I know we were taught that this is wrong, but I just can't help myself."

Gavin stared at her. "What's his name, Sis?"

Lylah hesitated, then came to him and put her hands in his. "If I tell you, will you not hate me? Will you not tell Owen

or Amos—or anyone?" She was like a little girl as she stood
before him, her face vulnerable, tears glistening in her eyes.
"Will you never tell anyone?" she repeated. "And, please . . .
will you not hate me, Gavin?"

"How could I hate you, Sis?" he said gently. "Tell me. Who
is it?"

Lylah licked her lips and said in a very small voice, "Baron
Manfred von Richthofen."

The room was silent. Gavin heard only the ticking of a
small clock up on the mantelpiece. Lylah, waiting, quivered
before him. Shock ran along his nerves. *The worst enemy we
have is my sister's lover*, he thought incredulously. Forcing aside
his revulsion, he put his arms around her, drew her close, and
held her as she trembled and wept on his shoulder.

Neither of them said another word. They clung to each
other like two children trapped in a dark place.

10

A NEW KIND OF WAR

Amos Stuart disembarked from the crowded troop ship at Dunkirk, joining the mass of milling soldiers that poured ashore. His face was pale, for he had always had difficulty with sea travel. But he recovered quickly and, by the time he had found transportation to the airfield at Luxeuil, located near the eastern boundary of France, he felt better.

Amos spoke no French whatsoever, but quickly discovered that most of the Frenchmen he encountered spoke enough broken English to give him a semblance of instructions. Following those instructions, and getting lost only twice, he found his way to the Commanding Officer of the Lafayette Escadrille, Captain Georges Thenault.

Thenault was surprised to see an American newspaperman and said so. He was a slight man with a thin, Gaelic face and a pencil-fine mustache.

"Well, *Monsieur*," he said, "we are glad to see you. When will the million men from America arrive to help us win this war?"

Amos grinned back at the officer and replied, "We'll have to declare war first, Captain."

"And when do you think that will be?"

"Not long, not long," Amos replied quickly. "It's just a matter of time." He did not want to talk about America's lack of response.

He remembered the interview he had had with President Wilson when Wilson, drawn and haggard, had obviously shown

129

every inclination to keep America out of the war. "After all," he had said, "the platform that won me the presidency this term was: 'He Kept America Out of War.'"

Amos remembered his own daring when he had said to the President of the United States, "Yes, sir, it may have gotten you elected, Mr. President. But we must enter the war. If America doesn't go in, France is lost; and if Germany wins, we then have an enemy we can never rest with."

He had gulped, expecting Wilson to throw him out of his office, but the wan president had merely sighed and said, "I'm afraid, sir, you are right. But we shall wait as long as possible."

"What can we do for you, Monsieur Stuart?" Captain Thenault inquired.

"I am here to see my brother, Gavin Stuart."

"Ahh . . . of course! Lieutenant Stuart! I did not put the names together. Come, let me take you to his quarters."

Amos followed the dapper officer across the fields to a barrack. When they stepped inside, someone called out, "Attention!" The men who were lounging on their bunks leapt to their feet, while the cardplayers over at a table by the far window followed suit.

"At ease," Captain Thenault said. "We have a distinguished visitor." His eyes swept the room. Spotting Gavin, he called out, "Your brother is here, Lieutenant Stuart."

Gavin had been lying on his bunk, thinking about a meal of fried okra, fresh tomatoes, and pork chops, like his mother had fixed when he was a boy. When the captain entered, Gavin had not noticed the man with him. Now, as he came to his feet and Captain Thenault mentioned Amos's name, he stood transfixed, scarcely able to believe his eyes.

"I will leave you here to visit with your brother," Captain Thenault said to Amos. "Afterwards you will have dinner with me in the Officer's Mess." He nodded warmly, turned and left, and then and only then did Gavin rush across the room to throw his arm around Amos's shoulders, hugging him.

"Why, you no-account scoundrel!" he cried, squeezing

Amos so hard the smaller man almost gasped. "Why in the world didn't you let me know you were coming?"

Amos fought loose from the strangling embrace and struck Gavin a sharp rap on the chest with his closed fist. "Because I didn't know it myself. Besides, I wanted to surprise you." He looked at the suitcase he had in his hand. "Got enough goodies in here to last you for the duration." He grinned. "The women packed every kind of cake and cookie they could cram into this thing."

"Hey, you guys!" Gavin called out. "Groceries from home! Come and get it!"

For the next half hour Amos looked on as the pilots fell on the sweets like ravening wolves. They could not seem to eat fast enough and one of them, a short man that the others called Luf, said warmly in a broken accent, "You are velcome here always if you bring such good tings."

"Is your name Raoul Lufbery?"

"Ja. Dat is my name."

"I'd like to talk to you when you have some time, Lieutenant," Amos said. "We've been hearing great things about what you've been doing over here." He studied Luf and was filled with awe. "I've never met a real ace before."

Luf said genially, "Keep your eye on dat brudder of yours. He vill shoot down more Jerries dan all da rest of us."

Hearing this and the laugh that went up from the other pilots, Gavin shook his head. "Don't pay any attention to him, or the rest of these yokels either. C'mon, let's get away from here, Amos. I want to hear all about home."

The two men left the barracks and began walking around the airfield. The air was cold and the sky was a leaden gray overhead. As Amos spoke of home, he saw how thin Gavin had gotten, but said nothing. The war had worn his brother down to a fine edge, washing away, it seemed, all signs of the immaturity that he remembered. But he said nothing of this; instead he cheerfully spoke of Owen and his own family and soon the two men had made a complete circle of the airfield.

Amos grew quiet for a while, then asked, "How are you, Gavin? Really?"

Gavin smiled. "Why, I'm all right, Amos." Then he bit his lip and gazed off into the distance. "But this war is not like I thought it would be." He hesitated, grateful that Amos, good reporter that he was, was not rushing him. He continued quietly, "I still kind of go to pieces every time I shoot down a plane. And it's worse when I see the pilots. I wish I didn't have to see them up close . . . their faces, I mean." They walked along silently and, after a while, he added, "I dream about them, Amos, sometimes. I see their faces and their chests ripped into bloody messes where my bullets tear them to pieces, and . . . and . . ."

Amos could think of nothing to say, and finally muttered, "Well, all soldiers worth their salt probably feel that way."

"No they don't," Gavin snapped quickly. "Some of them *like* it! They like the killing. They see the whole thing as sort of a game. We've got some in the Lafayette Escadrille. So it's not only Germans who think like that."

The two men walked on a little farther, and eventually Gavin gave a short laugh. "Well, I didn't mean to lay all this on you, Amos. You didn't come over here to listen to me gripe and bellyache about doing my job."

Amos bit his lip, trying to sort through his thoughts. He was a man with an ability in analysis, making him a great reporter. He had always been able to look at a situation on the outside and somehow know what it was like on the inside. And now, looking at his younger brother, he tried to find the boy he had hunted with, the boy with the carefree face, the laughing eyes. But he could not find that boy. He saw instead the hardness of a man who was going out daily to kill other men. He finally said, "No, you're wrong, Gavin. That's exactly why I've come over here. Let the other reporters talk about the big battles and the big pushes, what's going on in the whole theater here on the eastern front." He paused and then said softly, "I'm interested in one man. One man at a time. How does the war affect Gavin Stuart? How does the war affect Captain Thenault? How about Raoul Lufbery? What's happening to him on the inside? That's what I've come over to see and to hear and to try to take back to the United States."

Gavin stared at him. "Do you think America will come into the war? Because if they don't, France is a dead duck, Amos. They're bled dry, and the Germans seem as strong as ever."

"I think they'll come in. But when they do, what will it do to the boys who come over? To live in the trenches and to die in no-man's-land?" He looked up then and added, "Or to those who die in the air?"

Gavin said hurriedly, "Well, if anybody can do the job, it'll be you, Amos." He slapped his brother on the back and said more cheerfully, "You always were a guy who could get inside a fella's skin. C'mon, let's go see if we can find something to drink."

Oswalt Boelcke led his group into a rain-scrubbed sky under a lead bowl ceiling. There were no cloud formations low enough to hide in or to use for ambushing the enemy. This was the fifth patrol that the commander of the squadron had flown. A deep exhaustion had been so evident in his face that his mechanics had timidly suggested he wait for another day. He had refused.

After his fourth mission that day, a call had come from the infantry, pinpointing two British scouts overhead. "Come along, you fellows," Boelcke said to Boehme and von Richthofen, along with three others. They climbed into their Albatrosses and flew west until the light began to fade and the cold air grew heavy with moisture.

"There they are!" Boelcke said aloud and waved to his fellow flyers, gesturing toward the British planes silhouetted against the dark clouds. He set up an ambush and pounced.

The British were outnumbered three to one, but decided to fight anyway and turned to meet the attack. Boelcke, with

Boehme next to him, dropped on one. Von Richthofen, racing ahead of his wing man, went after the other. The British pilots changed their minds and dove away from the Germans. Von Richthofen, the wind whistling through the crosswires on his wings and a pleasant blast of warm air rushing back from the engine over him, caught up with his intended victim and began firing.

Boelcke and Boehme, a couple of hundred yards away and slightly higher, zeroed in on the other British airplane and opened fire. Von Richthofen's Englishman suddenly swerved, pulled out of his dive, and cut across Boelcke's and Boehme's path. Both rose sharply to avoid a collision. Boehme felt a dull thud beneath him. Evidently Boelcke had turned a little more tightly than his comrade, and Boehme's landing gear had struck the upper left wing of his leader's Albatros.

Boehme, forgetting the fleeing Englishman, looked down at Boelcke's wing. Its tip had broken off, exposing shattered spars and making the fabric flap. Von Richthofen broke off from the Englishman who had caused the accident and began circling Boelcke's falling Albatros.

He and Boehme, now horrified, saw the crippled scout disappear into a dark cloud and followed him. When they came out it seemed as if Boelcke still had some control over his fluttering airplane. They watched, slightly relieved, as the Albatros appeared to respond to Boelcke's manipulations. Then they saw its upper wing tear off and float away, half tumbling in another direction. Boelcke fell straight down and landed in a heap near the infantrymen who had summoned him.

Von Richthofen and Boehme circled the wreckage and headed back to Lagnicourt. The two British pilots were forgotten. Boehme swore all the way back that he would commit suicide if Boelcke were dead.

But Boelcke *was* dead. The man who had put the German Air Force together, the leader to whom they all looked for counsel, was dead. As Manfred von Richthofen landed his plane, he suddenly was aware that things would never be the same again. Somehow the war would go on, and he would go on, and the others would go on, but without Boelcke, things would never be quite like they had been.

The next few days were like a bad dream for Manfred von Richthofen. The elaborate funeral, which would have done justice to a reigning prince, was held in Cambrai Cathedral on November 3. Von Richthofen carried a pillow with Boelcke's decorations resting on it.

Flowers had arrived from all over the country and beyond. A Royal Flying Corps airplane flew over Lagnicourt to drop a wreath. The attached note read: "To the Memory of Captain Boelcke, Our Brave and Chivalrous Foe." Another wreath was dropped later: "To the Officers of the German Flying Corps in Service on This Front: We hope that you will find this wreath, but are sorry it is so late in coming. The weather has prevented us from sending it earlier. We mourn with his relatives and friends. We all recognize his bravery."

But all of this pomp and pageantry meant nothing to Manfred. He missed Boelcke. He felt that part of his inner life had been torn away. One night while walking around the airfield, he had what amounted to a vision. Von Richthofen had had these before. He himself put little stock in spiritual things, but more than once, he had been visited with a premonition, a foreseeing some might have called it, that he could not ignore.

He paused beneath the November sky, the stars glittering overhead. He looked up at them as if to find some answer, then shook his head. But the feeling persisted. It was nothing he could put into words, just a sudden wave of certainty that he, Baron Manfred von Richthofen, was a man marked for destiny. That his name would not go unnoticed and unrecorded in the annals of history. He stood there, letting the cold wind bathe his face, knowing that he walked a fine line between life and death. And somehow he knew as well that his name would be remembered long after he himself was gone.

11

A TIME OF PEACE

The men who fight and die in wars are very seldom aware of the forces that thrust them incessantly toward death. Before every big push that sends thousands of soldiers over the top, somewhere far back of the front lines, there is a small room where generals sit and study the maps on the wall. These maps are covered with thousands of tacks, red and blue. Occasionally one of the generals will move a tack three inches. Only three inches, with almost no effort demanded of the general who makes that slight move. But the next day or the next week, a whistle blows, and forty thousand men come crashing into the barbed wire of no-man's-land. They die, bleeding in the ditches or blown apart, and fifty miles of battlefield is filled with sound and fury—all because a general moved a pin only three inches.

The unseen force that directed the destiny of Baron Manfred von Richthofen was not so much a group of generals staring at a map as it was a meeting of the German High Command. Far from the guns of war and the men dying in the trenches, General Erich von Falkenhayn was surrounded by a small group of his leading advisors. The tension in the room was thick, and von Falkenhayn—an erect, handsome Prussian—glared angrily at his officers.

"I am a soldier," he said in a raspy tone, "not a journalist. I have no time to devote myself to pleasing the press."

"Ah, you must not think of it like that, my General," said a tall man with a crop of white hair and a fiercely bristling mustache. This was Karl Mundt, who alone, of the general officers, had the courage to stand up to General Falkenhayn. "This is a matter of war no less than the training of men and the moving of materials," he insisted. "The British naval blockade is strangling the fatherland. It has reduced the flow of war materials like Chilean nitrates, which are used to make explosives, to dangerously low levels. It has also cut off consumer goods, and you yourself have seen, General Falkenhayn, the long lines in front of the shops and the raised prices."

Falkenhayn glared at his chief advisor. "Mundt, what does that have to do with winning the war for the fatherland?"

Mundt sighed heavily and shrugged his massive shoulders. "General, in the old days workers in the factory could be ignored. Not any longer. This war has settled into a massive stalemate—a siege—and it feeds on hundreds of thousands of men in order to stay alive. These men have to be supplied with mountains of guns and biscuits."

Another general, a short thick-set man, nodded and spoke tersely, his eyes glittering with anger, "Yes. And not only that, General Falkenhayn, but these Communists are everywhere, haranguing the people, using words like *exploitation* and *bloody revolution*."

"Nonsense. A good German worker knows better than to listen to those wild lunatics."

Mundt hesitated, then said slowly, "I wish that were true, General Falkenhayn, but times are changing. The first heady days of the war," he shook his head sadly, "they're only a fading memory. It is now an old war, and we must keep in mind that this war has chewed up and digested the sons of the fatherland, and it has put the fathers and the mothers in an ugly mood."

Von Falkenhayn argued steadily, vehemently, his face turning red with anger. But he saw, finally, that his staff was in agreement that he must modify his views. "Well," he said stiffly, "what do you suggest?"

General Mundt answered, "The Information Department of the general's staff has agreed that what we need are heroes—visible heroes—that the people can see, that the soldiers themselves can see."

"Heroes?" Von Falkenhayn grunted. "Why, every soldier that gets up out of a trench and charges across no-man's-land is a hero!"

"Yes, indeed, I agree. We are soldiers, and we understand that that is how the war will be won. However, finding heroes among ground troops is never easy. They always fight in groups, and groups can be heroic, sir, only in the most general of ways."

"Very true," the commanding general conceded grudgingly. "Also, foot soldiers are seldom heroic more than once."

"Exactly." Mundt nodded enthusiastically. "What we need are individual, Wagnerian heroes who will keep on doing the brave things when needed. And the Information Department has suggested that there's no better place to find them," he paused, looking upward toward the ceiling as if he could see through it, "than in the sky. All the elements are there, General von Falkenhayn."

Encouraged, Mundt pointed out that flying itself was still new enough that most people considered the very idea of going up in an airplane to be death-defying. Since the aviators thought so, too, they respected each other and were even chivalrous to their enemies, provided their lives did not depend upon it.

At this point, Mundt threw himself into the presentation with a dramatic flair. "Why," he said, "our airmen are like knights! Their airplanes are steeds! The ground crewmen who repair the steeds are their squires, and the clumsy insulating flying garb which makes walking awkward is reminiscent of armor! And best of all," Mundt said, "aerial combat—man against man—is jousting! And the flyers choose to joust until . . . well, until they are killed."

The meeting went on for quite some time, and General

von Falkenhayn was finally persuaded to see the need of the creation of heroes in the Air Force.

With his permission, the machinery that would make Manfred von Richthofen the premier hero of all of Germany was set in motion. The newspapers began recounting epic battles in the air. The Information Department had them photograph the postcards called "Sanke" after the company that printed them, and these were sold all over Germany. The German aviators were also filmed "climbing confidently into their steeds which were pointed toward the Western sky" for segments of short movies that circulated to theaters in the larger cities and towns.

These were the seeds, strategically planted, of the power that would elevate Richthofen from an unknown pilot into the gallant hero Germany was seeking. The General Staff took a particular interest in Lanoe Hawker's death and of the newcomer who killed him. Lieutenant Manfred von Richthofen, a young baron from a good Prussian family, was the man to watch.

The decision of the General Staff to create heroes in the German Air Force changed the tactics of the day. Up until this time, Germans in the trenches rarely saw their own airmen or airplanes. The German strategy was to keep scouts and fighter planes in defensive positions, well behind the lines. This helped draw Allied airplanes deep over German-held territory until their fuel ran low and they were forced to turn and run the gauntlet of wind and German interceptors. Secondly, it helped prevent one of the new scouts from falling behind Allied lines, where the improvements on them could be stolen and copied.

For some time, however, the German soldiers daily watched French and British formations passing over in waves, apparently unchallenged, and suffered the indignities of being photographed in the aftermath of bombing and strafing by what seemed like any Allied airplane that cared to do so. They wanted to know where their aviators were and began coining such sayings as, "God punished the English, our artillery, and our air force."

So the decision being made, the machinery began to roll, and German fighter planes were sent to the front lines to put on a show of strength for the men on the ground. The month of December furnished little opportunity, for the weather was bad. Nevertheless, on December 11, von Richthofen demonstrated his skill for soldiers on both sides of the barbed wire when he shot down his twelfth victim, a British DH2.

Five days before Christmas, he led his flag to a near-massacre of a third of the Royal Flying Corps' Number 29 Squadron. Flying in front, and slightly below in a V-formation, he led the attack against five British planes. All five were shot up. Von Richthofen claimed his second daily double—his fourteenth victory.

Sitting alone in his quarters that night, Manfred looked at the little silver cups, each representing a kill, and felt good. He would soon be his country's leading war pilot. Ace of aces. Furthermore, he had great hopes that this would be the last Christmas he would spend without a *Pour le Mérite*—the Blue Max, as the premier medal of Germany was called. He promised himself that he would either wear the Blue Max or die the next year.

He slept well that night and for the next few nights, although he shot down no more planes. However, he did achieve one thing that had long-ranging consequences: He painted his airplane. Toward the end of 1916, German airplane manufacturers began to paint their products in standardized camouflage color schemes. Early Albatrosses had the upper sides of their wings and tail painted in irregular patches of khaki and dark olive green. Undersides were light sky blue, and fuselages were varnished over their natural plywood color.

The pilots, in their never-ending search for individuality, wanted their own trademarks and therefore modified parts of their scouts—usually the engine cowling and tail—painting them with varying colors. Boelcke had had his scout painted red, and members of the squadron began to associate that color with their group.

Now, von Richthofen stood looking at his fighter plane. It was due for a paint job, and the men who were to do the job stood waiting silently for his instructions. Von Richthofen's face was still, but his eyes moved over the fragile body of the airplane and he pictured in his mind what he wanted. He turned to the sergeant, a smile turning the corners of his lips upward. "Red," he said finally.

"Red?" the sergeant asked in surprise, his eyes flying open. "Which part, sir? The cowling?"

"The whole aircraft," von Richthofen said firmly.

"But . . . but . . . uh, sir! Isn't that—"

"And not a dull red, Sergeant," von Richthofen said, his voice growing eager. "Find the most brilliant red you have in stock. Fiery red! And paint everything that will take paint! You understand me?"

The sergeant wanted to object, but one look at the flyer's face convinced him that would be unwise, so he said, "Ja. Red. Bright red. Ja, it shall be so, sir."

Two days later, von Richthofen's superiors watched as the red airplane took off from the field with a roar. One of them shook his head. "Bad. Bad for discipline, I think. Perhaps we ought to have him tone it down a bit."

"No," the other said thoughtfully. "If von Richthofen keeps shooting down Englishmen, and if he's proud enough of his work to want the whole world to know about it, let him go. He might get shot down once they learn to look for him, but a gaudy, conspicuous airplane is a small price to pay for making one a hero."

Christmas day came, and Manfred von Richthofen showed his father Albrecht and his brother Lothar around the aerodrome. They were impressed, especially Lothar, who had transferred recently out of the Cavalry into the Air Force.

Lothar was lean like Manfred, but three inches taller, with

a more angular face and a totally different personality. Where Manfred was quiet and often brooding, Lothar was boisterous and forward. Where Manfred was fond of sitting by himself for hours, Lothar was prankish, impudent, very much like one of the boys. Manfred, who stayed away from women—saying that he had no time for them or that he did not want to make some girl a widow—was in stark contrast to Lothar, who had plenty of time and didn't intend to get married anyway, at least not until after the war.

The three men walked around the field and spoke of the situation. "Will you be going to the front right away, my son?" Manfred's father asked.

"Well, no, not right away. I do have a week's leave."

"Will you go to Berlin and do some partying?" Lothar asked, eyes gleaming.

"No. I am flying this new red ship of mine home. I'll get in a bit of hunting, and then in one week I'll be back to fight the enemies of the fatherland."

"Too bad," Lothar said. "You've become headline news." He clapped his brother on the shoulder. "I see those Sanke cards everywhere. You must hear from plenty of the girls, ja?"

Manfred barely smiled and shrugged. But Lothar was right. Mail had been coming in by the bagful. Perfumed letters, proposing everything from marriage to less formal arrangements, had come in. In fact, he had shared them with his squadron mates, who delightedly read them aloud by turn, laughing at the mushiest.

"I'll let you do the Berlin party," Manfred said to Lothar. "Me, I need time away. I leave in the morning for home."

"I think that is wise, my son," Albrecht von Richthofen said. "The family is proud; the whole nation is proud!" he cried. Then in a rare gesture of emotion, he put his arm around Manfred's shoulders and said huskily, "You have made me very proud."

"Thank you, Father," Manfred whispered. "I hope to do more yet."

★   ★   ★

"I did not expect to see you here."

On his second day home, Manfred entered the sitting room to find Lylah waiting for him. She was wearing a beautifully designed green dress that highlighted her eyes, and she looked far more beautiful than he had remembered.

"I didn't know you would be here," Lylah said. She felt strangely out of place and hastened to explain. "You've heard about Helen?" When he shook his head, she continued quickly, "She had to leave England. The anti-German feeling was growing. It got so bad she almost grew ill."

Manfred stared at Lylah. "I tried to get her to come home long ago, but she would not. How is she?"

"Not well, I'm afraid. She caught a cold and it got worse, so when she decided to come home after the play closed, she needed someone with her on the trip. It's not easy getting to Germany from England these days."

Manfred nodded earnestly. "I should think not, but what about you? How did *you* cross the lines?"

"Oh, Americans aren't bothered much. Germany is very respectful of America, hoping we won't get into the war, I suppose." She did not move, but stood there remembering their intimacy and wondering what was behind the silence he was manifesting. Finally she said quietly, "I've missed you, Manfred."

Von Richthofen looked at her, taking in the classic beauty of her face and the slimness of her figure, and once again, as he had done hundreds of times before, he let his mind dwell on those golden days they had known. The days of love that he had never thought would come to him.

"I have never forgotten," he said quickly and stepped forward and took her in his arms. He kissed her hungrily, and she responded, pressing close to him, holding him tightly. So caught up were they in one another that neither gave a thought to the possibility someone might enter through the door and find them kissing.

Finally Lylah broke away, putting her hands on his chest. "Oh, Manfred, I've been so afraid! Every day I would read the newspapers, dreading to find your name there!"

Manfred shook his head. "No, you will not find my name there. Not yet, anyway. I know it."

Lylah stared at him, her eyes large and moist. "I pray not. How long will you be here?"

"For a week. And you?"

A smile softened Lylah's lips, and she whispered, "For as long as you're here." Then she hesitated. "It isn't right; it's mad, you know! What can we possibly gain from this, with things the way they are? My country and yours will be at war soon! What then? It's madness!" she repeated.

Manfred von Richthofen was a man of iron will. By sheer determination he had brought himself into a place of prominence. But he had discovered that, if there was one area of his life that did not seem to be in keeping with his rigid discipline, it was where Lylah Stuart was concerned.

Night after night he had lain on his bed and thought of the softness of her lips, the eagerness of her love, and had marveled that a man such as himself could be stirred by these feelings. He was, in a way, ashamed of them, seeing them as a weakness, and wondered why he alone of all the men in his squadron did not take advantage of the many adoring young women who pressed themselves forward, offering nights of love to the German airmen. He had kept himself aloof, saying that he did not have time for such things, but that was not the reason. He knew it now.

"I could not forget you, Lylah," he said. "And I do not understand it. When the others are grabbing at any woman that comes by, I find myself thinking of you. And I have not been able to put you out of my mind."

"Have you tried? Do you want to forget me?" Lylah whispered.

"No . . . yes . . . oh, I don't know." He rubbed his forehead with a nervous gesture and looked at Lylah in confusion. "I worry about you. I've said that I don't want to get married because I might make some girl a widow."

He turned to her, took her hand and traced with one finger the fine blue veins on the back, then raised it to his lips and kissed it. He put his arms around her and held her close. "Yes," he said, his voice almost harsh, "it is madness. We both know it, but whatever this madness is that's drawn us together, I cannot pull away from it, my dear. I never will."

The two stood there, holding one another, wanting each other more than either had thought possible and knowing that there was no way happiness could come out of it.

All week they tried to forget about the war. Manfred was already sick of it and, even though he was the hero of the hour, he had confided to Lylah that Germany could not win, in his opinion.

"There are too many of them," he said grimly. "And when the Americans come in, it'll all be over."

But they did not talk of the war very much. They spent their days hunting, or at least roaming the woods. More often than not, when it came time to make the kill, Lylah would hold his arm and whisper, "Let them go," and he did.

On the last night, he came to her room, as he had every other night. They held on to each other with a sense of loss. Lylah finally broke into tears, something that had never happened to her before. "This may be the last time we'll be together," she whispered miserably. "I can't bear the thought of it."

Baron Manfred von Richthofen had the same fear, but he could not stand to see her weep. So he held her and tried to bring some cheer into the moment. "This isn't the last time," he said. "Not for us. It can't end like this. I feel it too strongly." He reached up and brushed the hair back from her forehead and then traced her cheek with his finger. "I've told you I see things. I know, somehow, that I am going on to greater things than I've already known." He laughed lightly, saying, "You've fallen in love with a fortune-teller." Lylah laughed with him, but there was no real joy in her.

The next day, he put her on the train. They stood stiffly, shaking hands as his mother and the servants looked on.

Manfred's mother kissed Lylah on the cheek. Something in her expression told Lylah she knew what had been going on. She was a very wise woman, Lylah knew, and although she had not said a word, Lylah suddenly understood that she had been aware of their love from the beginning. The baroness said nothing now, but held Lylah close. "You must come back . . . you and Manfred."

Then Lylah turned away, tears filling her eyes, and found her seat on the train. As the train pulled away, a darkness fell across her spirit—a heaviness that seemed to weigh upon her more than anything she had ever known. All the way across Germany to the coast, where she boarded a neutral ship bound for England, she felt it.

And when she set foot on English soil once again, she knew that things would never again be the same.

12

"Bloody April!"

When Manfred von Richthofen returned to his base at Douai and assumed command of Jasta 11, he announced that a competition would begin at once. The Boelcke squadron, Jasta 2, was ahead of his group by one hundred kills, and von Richthofen coldly put it to his pilots that they would have to try harder.

Manfred embraced the war, chasing Englishmen and immortality in his scarlet scout, wearing his country's highest military decorations even under his flying suit, ordering more silver cups, sending serial numbers and other souvenirs back to Schweidnitz as he molded Jasta 11 into his own image.

But while he himself was successful, the General Staff was smarting under the massive beatings at Verdun and the Somme and were beginning to wonder if the war could ever be won on land. The final answer was given by Admiral von Holtzendorff, Chief of the Naval Staff, who maintained that five months of unrestricted U-boat attacks would finish Britain. Hindenburg telegraphed an ultimatum to the Kaiser, who signed a formal order on January 31 for his U-boats to be launched the following day, despite warnings that such a thing would bring the United States into the war. Immediately 111 U-boats put to sea in search of almost anything to torpedo.

In addition to the U-boat warfare, the Germans pulled back to what was called "the Hindenburg position," a zone between the existing and proposed front lines, twenty feet deep and sixty-five miles long. So far as possible, it was to be made into a wasteland—every village destroyed, every well polluted or filled in, every tree and other obstacle cut down, and every resident removed. The area was to be turned into a flat exposed belt of devastation that could be easily watched and heavily bombarded.

But although the army might be on the defensive, von Richthofen was not. During the first two weeks of February, 1917, while he was developing Jasta 11, he became a tyrant. His pale face was frozen into a mask as he commanded that any pilot returning with holes in his tail must have a good explanation. They had begun to call him "Der Rote Kampfflieger," or "The Red Battle Flyer," sometimes shortened to simply "The Red Baron." He scored his twentieth and twenty-first kills on February 14, and that night ordered a regular trophy cup and a second double-sized one.

More than two weeks passed before he scored again, but when he did, on March 3, it was the beginning of his greatest string of victories. Kills that were largely responsible for the Royal Flying Corps' term for the following month— "Bloody April." It was the happiest, and by air war standards, the most productive month of von Richthofen's life.

In spite of unusually heavy rains and even a late snowfall, the British kept coming, and von Richthofen shot down twenty-one of them, including four in one day. Around Easter, he was promoted to *Rittmeister*, or Cavalry Captain, and by the end of the month, had surpassed Boelcke's forty victories to become the leading ace of the war and his country's paramount hero. General Ludendorff was to proclaim that The Red Battle Flyer was worth two whole divisions, and while the effect of the remark on the infantry can only be imagined, it did wonders for the morale of the Air Service.

As he strolled down the streets of Paris on a sunny April afternoon, Gavin Stuart was blissfully unaware of the fiery trial into which the Royal Air Force was about to be plunged. He could not know that 151 Allied planes would soon be shot down in flames, while the German Air Force would lose only thirty.

But Gavin had left behind at the base all thoughts of the patrols he had been making almost daily and was concerned primarily with having a good time and seeing the city. Already, on his first day in Paris, he had walked the streets until his legs were tired. Pausing to rest, he watched the passing parade of people and thought, with a streak of wry humor, *I should have been in the infantry. I've forgotten how to walk!*

He had been given an unexpected reprieve in the form of a three-day leave when an epidemic of problems developed among the aircraft. So many were backed up for repairs that there was simply nothing for him to fly.

But when Captain Thenault had told him to take a three-day leave, Gavin had been ribbed by his fellow pilots. "Stay away from those girlies, young fella," Bill Thaw had warned. "They'll do you in!"

Now as he stood there he suddenly realized that he had three days and nothing to do. He knew no one in Paris. His whole life had been taken up with his squadron, and now, as he looked up at the tall buildings and ambled down the wide streets, he wondered just what to do with himself. He knew full well what the other members of the squadron would do. They would head for the saloons and bars, where, according to their reports, plenty of women were available for all sorts of entertainment. But Gavin did not feel inclined to throw himself into the fleshpots of the great city.

As early as it was, several ladies of the evening had already approached him with bright phony smiles, speaking one sentence in the only English they knew, as far as he could tell: "You vant to have a good time, soldier?" He had been embarrassed by these encounters, for his time in the army had not yet been sufficient to free him from the inhibitions he had brought with him all the way from his childhood in Arkansas.

The city amazed him, and all morning and most of the

afternoon he walked down side streets, stopping to taste the wares at the fruit stands and to listen to the music of strolling accordion players that evoked memories of home. He recognized one of the songs—"There's a Long, Long Trail A-Winding." He had heard it sung in English. The song had a sad, plaintive melody and a rather macabre message that, sooner or later, we're all going to die. But this time a short, stocky Frenchman was singing it with a happy lilt, pumping at the accordion with all of his might.

Gavin took a note out of his pocket and gave it to the street singer, who smiled and began singing it again. But Gavin had heard enough and, with a wave, he moved on down the street.

At noon he went into a café and ordered a sandwich. He was joined at the table by the proprietor, Louis Cerdan, a veteran of Verdun, with one arm missing and three medals pinned to his shirt.

"Tell me about that war up in the sky," Louis said. "What's it like up there away from the mud and the blood?" His Gaelic face grew stern. "All I saw was the trenches."

Gavin nodded in acknowledgment. "I was in a few of those myself in the Legion. Transferred to the air war, though." He leaned back and sipped the wine the proprietor kept pouring into his glass and thought about it. "Well, it's better up there. There are no rats to nibble at a man's face while he's asleep, and it doesn't smell bad either."

He looked off into the distance, recalling the rush of air, humming through the struts and the wires, that turned into a scream when one went into a dive. He thought about the moistness of the clouds as one dived through them, and how he had occasionally flown out of a cloud to find himself right in the middle of a German formation, dropping suddenly to avoid their fighter planes.

"It's . . . clean up there, too. And one thing about it, you either get them or they get you. It's a quick death, anyway."

After a while Gavin looked out the window. "Well, it's getting dark. I think I'll take another little stroll."

Louis glanced keenly at the young man. "You have no one in Paris? No friends?"

"No, I don't know anybody."

Louis said quickly, "Then you must join our family for the evening. Our house is small, *mon ami*, but we will be happy to have you stay with us."

Gavin was touched by the offer. "I'll take you up on it . . . and thanks."

He took his meal that night in Louis's home. Gavin enjoyed being with the four children ranging in ages from three to ten. They were amazed when he got down on the floor and played games with them just as if he were one of them. Louis and his wife looked on, beaming, and finally when the children were sent to bed, Louis said, "You Americans are odd people. Odd people, indeed."

Gavin laughed. "I guess everybody thinks everybody else is odd, Louis."

He went to bed and slept well, except for once when he was startled awake by a nightmare. In the dream, Gavin was being machine-gunned by a huge fighter plane, spewing bullets at him by the thousands. He was burning up—his gas tank exploding, throwing fire into his face—when he woke up in a cold sweat.

Gavin sat up in bed and wiped his forehead. He sat there until the tremors running through him began to subside. Then he laughed and said out loud, "You're going crackers, Gavin Stuart! You can fly right through real bullets and never flinch, but go to sleep in a bed and nearly die of a heart attack over a bad dream!"

He slept fitfully the rest of the night, got up early the next morning, and had breakfast with his host. Insistent on leaving, Gavin tried to pay for his night's lodging, but saw that it would be in poor taste. He left with Louis's invitation ringing in his ears: "Come back, come back anytime! Our house is yours!"

Once again Gavin roamed the streets, enjoying the relative quiet of the morning air and the stillness of the city, which seemed to be much like a giant, barely stirring as he struggled to wake up.

By noon, however, Gavin was tired of just watching and was seriously considering finding some sort of female companionship. The thought displeased him, however. He had seen some of the women his fellow pilots had met—hard-eyed women with bright but artificial smiles, hanging on to the flyers. It appeared to Gavin that as soon as those men were out of the way, the predatory females would once again be looking for new victims. *Victims*, he thought. *That's how they see us. I don't think I need that.*

He had stopped for a glass of cool juice at a stand when he looked up and saw, to his surprise, a building that looked familiar. At first he thought he had walked by it in his wanderings of the previous day, but then he realized that it was the hospital where he and Bill Thaw had been taken after Thaw had been shot down and wounded.

At once he thought of the nurse—Heather Spencer—and the memories came flooding back of the last time he had seen her, of the gentle smile that had been on her lips. He had thought of her often, sometimes in the middle of the night after a terrifying dream of conflict in the air, when his nerves had been jangled and shaken. Knowing he would lie awake for hours, reliving the combat, he had sought desperately to distract his mind, usually going back in his memory to the farm in Arkansas, thinking of the innocent days he had spent there a long time ago, halcyon days. But more than once his thoughts had strayed to times he had talked to the English nurse. Something about her manner had been different from other young women—a calmness and quietness and certainty about her, and a gentleness that he found attractive. And now as he stood looking at the hospital, he suddenly decided he had to see her again.

He walked across the street to the graystone building and found a sour-faced woman in a nurse's uniform seated at a desk in the foyer. "I'd like to see Nurse Spencer, please."

Looking up at him, the dour nurse asked sharply, "Why do you wish to see her?"

"Why . . . uh . . . she was kind to a friend of mine," Gavin stammered. "And I got to know her a little bit while I was here with him. Can't I see her?"

"No, you cannot."

Her manner irritated Gavin and he snapped, "Why not? We're on the same side in this war, aren't we? Do you think I'm a German spy?"

The nurse had eyes like steel marbles. "No, you're not a spy, I can see that. But she's not here. She's off duty for the week."

Her answer deflated Gavin. "Oh, well, I guess in that case—"

He had turned and was walking away when a voice behind him spoke up, "You'd like to see Heather?"

Gavin turned and found one of the nurses had come up to walk beside him. She was a short woman with black eyes and black hair peeping out from under her cap. "I can tell you where she lives," she went on. "She's a friend of mine."

"I'd appreciate it," Gavin said quickly, and then added honestly, "We don't know each other very well. A friend of mine was brought in wounded, and I came with him. But I got to know her a little while I was here."

"You're the American, aren't you? Heather's mentioned you several times."

"She has?" Gavin was amazed that the aristocratic Englishwoman would even remember him, much less speak of him. "I—I didn't think she would even remember me," he said.

"Oh, yes. She remembers you very well. I'll give you her address. I think she'd be very put out with me if I didn't." She got a pencil from one of her pockets, found a scrap of paper and scrawled something on it, then handed it to Gavin. "You'll have to hire a taxi; it's too far to walk." Her eyes crinkled. "Tell her if she doesn't want you, that I'll take you."

Gavin blinked in astonishment, and then he grinned at the

nurse. She was very plain, but she had merry eyes. "Hey, I may take you up on that," he grinned. "Thanks a lot."

He left the hospital, hailed a cab, and looked at the writing. "Do you know where this is?" he asked, and handed the slip to the driver, a tall thin man with a sallow complexion and a pair of muddy brown eyes.

The driver glanced at the paper and said, "*Certainement!*" in an insulted tone. He tossed the paper aside and sent the cab careening away from the curb with a display of carefree and rather hazardous driving manners. Weaving a path through the streets of Paris, he managed to avoid the horses, the carriages, and the loud cabs. The journey took so long that Gavin began to think he was being cheated. He'd heard of taxi drivers who would drive people all over the city to get to an address that was only one block away, but he had put himself in the man's care and said nothing.

Passing through downtown Paris, they came at last to a less populous area where residential neighborhoods on the edge of the city gave way to greening fields studded with trees. The trees were blossoming, tinged pink and white, and Gavin relaxed as the pastoral scenery flowed by him.

Eventually the cab turned down a side road and Gavin straightened. *We're out in the country*, he thought. *She didn't seem like a country girl to me.*

The driver pulled alongside a stone fence and waved his hand toward a house that was set back some distance from the main road. "*Voila!*" he cried. "I take you now to front door."

Gavin was shocked at the size of the house as they moved into a circular drive by way of an access road. It was not at all what he had expected. The imposing residence, flanked by massive oak trees, reminded him of some type of manor house he had seen in pictures. Built primarily of stone, the side walls were, nevertheless, timbered with heavy beams, and there were at least a dozen chimneys.

Gavin got out of the cab and paid the bill, adding ten francs for a tip. The cab driver looked at his uniform, then at the imposing house and said, "You want me to wait, perhaps?"

"Maybe you'd better," Gavin said. "Gimme a minute." He turned and walked up the steps, lifted the large door knocker, and let it fall.

Almost at once the door opened, and he found himself facing Heather Spencer.

"I . . . uh . . . guess you're surprised to see me," he said lamely.

"I saw you from my bedroom window," she confessed with a smile. "It's good to see you again, Lieutenant." She looked over his shoulder and saw the cab and said, "Send the taxi away. We'll see that you get back to Paris."

Gavin turned, waved at the cab driver, and shouted, "Thanks a lot!" Then he turned back to Heather and began apologetically, "I feel like a fool, Nurse Spencer."

"Come in, Lieutenant," she said warmly. "I want you to meet my parents."

Gavin felt her hand on his arm as she pulled him inside, intimidated at once by the tall ceilings, the expensive furniture of gleaming walnut and rosewood, and the ornate antiques that filled the foyer.

"Come along," she said. "They'll be in the study."

Gavin followed her, wondering what in the world he would say to such people, and entered the study to find a couple who looked up curiously at him. The woman rose and came forward as Heather introduced him. "This is my mother, Mary Spencer," she said, "and this is my father, Leo."

Gavin shook the woman's hand, noting that Heather was a later edition of Mary Spencer. Mrs. Spencer was very much as he had imagined an English lady should look; that is, she looked like Heather with the same blond hair and blue eyes. He turned to Leo and saw with a slight shock that he was in a wheelchair. Stepping forward, he took the man's hand that was very hard, firm, and strong, saying, "Sorry to come busting in on you folks, but . . ."

"Not a bit of it," Leo Spencer said. A well-tended mustache covered his upper lip and a pair of steady, very dark blue eyes smiled warmly into Gavin's. "Here, sit down. Mary, have Alice bring some tea and some of those good cakes she made yesterday. Sit down, sit down."

Awkwardly Gavin sat on a fragile-looking chair, half expecting it to break beneath his weight. As he did so, he cast a look at Heather. She was smiling at him as she sat down near her mother in another impossibly fragile chair.

Leo Spencer stared at Gavin steadily. "You are in the Lafayette Escadrille?" he inquired.

"Yes, sir."

"We are proud to have you. France needs all the men she can get these days, especially flyers."

Gavin stared at the three, then blurted out, "Sorry, but I don't understand! I thought you were English! You live *here* . . . in France?"

Mary Spencer came to his aid. "This is a summer home. It really isn't ours; we exchange with a family who is presently living in our home in England. But we've been spending more time here, now that Heather's nursing in a Paris hospital."

At that moment a servant came in. "Lady Spencer, shall we have crumpets with the tea?" she asked. "And Sir Leo, would you like some cucumber sandwiches?"

Gavin tried to rearrange his thoughts. *Sir* Leo? *Lady* Spencer?

He darted a desperate glance at Heather, who saw his dilemma, but said only, "Bring some of those for all of us, Alice. I think you would like some, wouldn't you, Lieutenant?"

"Oh . . . uh . . . oh yes," Gavin stammered.

When the maid left, Leo Spencer began to question Gavin about his family and his home in America. Thirty minutes later, when the maid brought the refreshments in, Gavin had told them pretty much everything about himself, though he still knew very little about the Spencers.

Lady Spencer said, "Heather told us about you and your friend. Is he all right?"

"Oh, Bill Thaw? Yes, he is doing fine. Shot down his twenty-sixth last week. A real fine fellow and a great pilot."

"And you, have you seen action since you joined the Escadrille?" Leo asked. He nibbled at a small sandwich, waved his hand to indicate Gavin should do the same, and continued before Gavin could answer his question. "There weren't many airplanes on the front. . . ." Catching an inquiring glance from Gavin, Leo Spencer explained, "I was a career officer in the British Fusiliers. I caught a bad one at Marne during the first big battle. It put me in this chair. But, of course, I still keep up with what's going on."

Gavin never knew what to say to handicapped people. He didn't know whether to express sorrow over the disability or to ignore it. He finally chose the latter. Quickly he began explaining his own role. "Well, I've had a bit of luck. Had some good teachers, and so far I've managed to stay alive."

"I understand you got your ninth kill last week," Heather broke in. She smiled at his surprise. "It was in the French newspaper here. They keep up with the Escadrille very closely. I know quite a bit about it—more than you might think."

Gavin showed his surprise, then shrugged. "Well, there aren't many of us. But we all try to do the best we can."

They proceeded with tea, and by the time it was over, a strange sense of belonging had crept over Gavin. He liked Leo Spencer very much, but was careful, however, to call him by his title. Afterwards he accompanied his host to a side of the room where maps were laid out, showing the battlefields, and for the next hour, the two men spoke of the war and military strategy.

Finally Heather came over, interrupting with a light laugh. "You've had him long enough, Father. I'm going to show him around the estate."

"Oh, all right." Leo smiled. "Take him then, but bring him back. You're staying overnight, I take it?"

"Why . . . why . . . I didn't—"

"We'd like very much to have you," Heather said. "There's plenty of room in this house." Then, not giving him time to argue, she said, "I'll tell Alice to make up the big room in the East Wing."

Taking possession of Gavin's arm, she walked with him out of the house and soon the two were strolling around the grounds, enjoying the aroma of the flowers and the sound of birds chattering in the trees. There was a duck pond in the back, and they stood for a long time, watching a family of ducklings paddling after their mother.

"Reminds me of home," Gavin said with a raw pang of nostalgia. "We always liked to keep ducks . . . well, my mother did, anyway. Made featherbeds out of them, and pillows— and we ate them." He laughed at his own remark. "Guess we used up those ducks pretty good. But I suppose that's what ducks are for."

Heather's hair captured the glints of the April sun and gave off a reddish tint. Her skin looked as fresh and rich as new cream, the smoothest Gavin had ever seen. She laughed and said, "I suppose so. Every time I eat a steak, I have to remind myself that a cow had to die in order for me to have that meal."

Gavin laughed and the two of them walked over the estate, looking at the cows, talking to two of the gardeners who were glad to stop and meet the American visitor. Finally, as they walked back, Gavin said, "You didn't have to ask me to stay. I can find a place in Paris."

"No," she said, "I want you to stay here." There was a determination about her that Gavin recognized. Something about her told him that here was a woman who knew her own mind and usually got her own way.

"You sound like my top sergeant when I first joined the Legion," he said with a grin.

Heather laughed, making that delightful sound he liked

so much. "I suppose nurses get that way. We get to boss everyone, even generals. It's delightful—but I suppose when I
marry, I'll have to be retrained."

Gavin grinned again. "Unless you marry a milksop. But on
the other hand, most of us who've been in the army are used
to high command, so maybe you can find someone to boss
who won't mind it."

They walked back into the house, and Heather showed
Gavin to his room on the second floor. A pair of large windows
gave him a view of the grounds. The bed was enormous and
he thought with a smile on his face, *This bed's about the size of
our whole house back home.*

She had turned to the door but stopped and smiled back
at him. "You can refresh yourself, Lieutenant, and we'll have
dinner later. Lie down and rest if you wish."

"Not a chance," he said. "I might wash up a little, but I'm
not wasting any of this leave. I'll be down pretty soon."

"How long can you stay?"

"Just through tomorrow, I'm afraid. By the way, do you
think you could call me something besides 'Lieutenant'? My
name's Gavin."

"Of course. It's a lovely name. English, I think."

"I thought it was Arkansan," he quipped. "And what do
I call you? Nursie? Or are you Lady Heather? Or Lady
Spencer?"

"That's much too formal. Why don't you just call me
Heather." With that, she pulled the door to behind her, and
he walked to the window to look out on the expansive
grounds. This serene estate was far from the war, but he
scanned the sky as if expecting to see fighter planes that could
so quickly become cockpits of death. But here there were
only blue skies and fleecy white clouds like sheep on a huge
blue pasture. He breathed deeply, inhaling the sweetness of
the first flowers, the smell of loamy earth where it was being
broken in a field, and he said to himself, *Gavin, old boy, don't
you wish you never had to leave this place!*

★ ★ ★

Heather stood watching the tall young flyer as they waited in the train station. She had enjoyed her time with him immensely, and now, as they waited for the train that would take him back, she was sorry to see it end. "It's been delightful, Gavin," she said. "I don't know when I have had more fun." A mischievous light sparkled in her eyes. "Americans are fun, I think. We English are so stodgy and so confounded *rigid*." A thought came to her. "You've been good for my father. He needs someone to talk to. He feels so useless and left out of things. I think sometimes that if he didn't know God, he would kill himself."

Gavin was startled, but he knew she was speaking truth. He had come to know Leo Spencer very well. The Englishman had taught him to play chess, for which Gavin had shown an almost spectacular flair. Spencer could not believe it when Gavin had beaten him after only four games, and he had laughed and said, "If you can fly an airplane the way you can play chess, my boy, I pity the poor German flyers!"

Heather had encouraged Gavin to spend time with her father and now, as they stood on the train platform, she thanked him for it. "It was good of you to spend so much time with my father. He needed it."

"Why, it was fun," he said, then shyly, "I like your parents, both of them. They're not what I thought nobility would be."

"Oh, we're *poor* nobility," she said lightly. "A good name and no money. Our home in England isn't like this at all. It's really a very small place."

"I'd like to see it sometime," he said. "Maybe I . . ." He broke off, fearing that she might consider him forward.

"Come to see us anytime, Gavin," she said.

As they talked, Gavin was thinking how strange that he, an Arkansas plowboy, should be carrying on a conversation with an English lady, daughter of a titled nobleman. But he had learned that although there was some rigid pride in the

Spencers, there was also a very warm streak. They were, he knew, very religious. He had known this about Heather before; she had told him the last time they had met, and now he brought it up himself. "I wish I had more time. Maybe I could go to church with you."

Heather regarded him with surprise. He had been rather adamant about that the last time. "I thought you'd given up on church and God."

Gavin was embarrassed. "No, I hope not . . . or at least I hope he doesn't give up on me."

"Do you ever think about God when you go into a fight?" she asked curiously.

"Yes, I do. I don't know about the others. But, of course, my brother's a preacher, and my other brother, Amos . . . well, he's a fine Christian."

"What about you, Gavin? Don't you believe in God?"

Gavin shook his head. "I don't know, Heather. I really don't. I'd like to, but there's something in me that says no. I look at all this death and dying and I wonder, if there's really a God, why does he let all this happen?"

He talked for a few moments about his beliefs, something he had never done with anyone else, and finally he said, "I wish we had more time, but the train's coming."

Heather put out her hands, and he took them in his. Her hands were soft, but very firm and very strong. She squeezed Gavin's hands, smiled up at him, and asked, "Will you come to see me the next time you're in Paris?"

"Sure I will. But why don't you come out to the aerodrome and visit with us? You'd be a hit there. C'mon," he urged. "It'll drive the rest of them crazy when they find out I've got an English girlfriend, I mean lady friend, who's a duchess or something."

Heather laughed with delight. "Well, I'm no duchess, but I will come and see you. That's a promise."

"All right," he said. "All right!" When the train squealed to a stop, he had the urge to kiss her, but did not. He took a step toward the train, then shyly turned again in her direction, reluctant to leave. "Come on out, as soon as you can! This week! Or next!"

"It'll have to be next, I'm afraid. Next weekend, if I can manage it."

She watched him as he boarded the train, smiling at him as he leaned out the window. She waved as she thought, *What a fine young man! I'll have to go out to that aerodrome. Maybe I can take Father with me. It would be good for him.*

13

SHOT DOWN!

ey, Gavin! Wake up! Wake up!"

Gavin Stuart, deep in a coma-like sleep after a late mission, pulled himself up out of the darkness and forced his eyes open, staring at the burly figure in front of him. "Go away, Thaw," he mumbled. "Leave me alone."

Bill Thaw's big hands gripped Stuart, ripping the blanket down, and jerking him out of bed as if he were a child. "C'mon, crawl out of there! Try to get some life into yourself, boy." Thaw's face broke into a wide grin as he added, "You got yourself a visitor. A real pippin! It's that nurse from the hospital, Heather Spencer."

All sleepiness fell away from Gavin instantly. He shoved Thaw away and grabbed his pants from a nearby chair. Pulling them on, he threatened, "If you're kidding me, I'll break your nose!"

Thaw laughed. "No kidding! She came in about an hour ago. Been looking for you." He tried to assume a virtuous expression and failed completely. "Being a good friend of yours, old boy, I tried to keep the rest of these lechers away from her. But you'd better hurry up! You know how they are with women! I'll just go watch out for your interests."

Gavin scrambled frantically into his uniform, gave his hair a few licks with a brush, then hurried out of the barracks toward the long frame building that served as a combination mess hall and officers quarters. As soon as he entered, he saw Heather surrounded by the flyers.

She looked up as he came in and waved. "There he is now. Hello, Gavin."

As Gavin drew near, the flyers began throwing insults his way. Norman Prince, the most popular man in the squadron, looked at Gavin and then back at Heather. "I don't know what you want with a tadpole like this, Lady Spencer," he said. "He has no manners whatsoever." Prince was a slight and comparatively short man, but he had broad, powerful shoulders, blond hair, blue eyes, and a flowing straw-colored mustache. His expressive face was rarely without a genial smile, and he fairly oozed personality. His energy and enthusiasm were unbounded. He added smoothly, "Now, I, on the other hand, have learned how to treat an English lady. If you would just allow me to show you around the aerodrome . . ."

"Pay no attention to him, ma'am," Victor Chapman spoke up. He was six feet tall with a finely shaped head, crowned by an unruly thatch of thick black hair. His deep-set eyes shone beneath bushy brows. He had a generous mouth where white teeth flashed in a frequent friendly smile. "I'm the official greeter of nobility around here. Don't pay any attention to these other chaps."

Not to be outdone, Raoul Lufbery shoved his way to the front and said in his atrocious accent, "Why, dese are all babies! You deserve de ace of the Lafayette Escadrille, which iss *me!*"

Luf had a broad forehead and deep-set eyes. His squat figure was just a trifle over 5'6", but he had muscles of steel and had cleared a path through the men as if they were weightless.

"Wait a minute! Wait a minute!" Gavin shouted. "Lady Spencer didn't come to see *you!* She came to see *me!*" He tried to elbow his way forward, but Lufbery simply picked him up and set him to one side as if he were a doll.

Heather laughed and said, "Gentlemen, please! I'll be here for several days, and I expect to get to know all of you better."

"You heard her, you birds," Bill Thaw said. "Now, let the pup here have some time with Lady Spencer." He herded the rest of them away, some of them catcalling back with risqué advice to Gavin on how to treat a woman.

When they were gone, Gavin turned to face Heather. "They mean well," he said, shrugging. "They just don't have many manners."

"They're a fine group of men. I read about them all the time in the newspapers." She smiled at him, asking, "Do you think me impertinent, taking you up on your invitation to come to the aerodrome?"

"Oh, no!" Gavin shook his head violently. "I didn't think you'd do it . . . but I'm glad you did. How are your parents?"

"Oh, very well. They instructed me to give you a strict invitation—a summons, really—to come back." Her generous lips turned up in a smile, her eyes sparkling. She was like a breath of fresh air in the gloomy room, he thought. "They like you very much, Gavin."

"Well, I don't understand that. I'm just a poor hillbilly from the hills of Arkansas." He bit his lip cautiously, trying to phrase his thoughts. "I don't know what nobility—knights and ladies and all that—would be interested in me for."

Heather took his arm saying, "Come on. Take me for a walk. Forget about Lady Heather. That's not really my title yet, anyway. Show me your airplane."

For the next two hours, Gavin showed Heather around the aerodrome. When they came to his own ship, she insisted on getting into the cockpit. Looking at the machine guns, she asked innocently, "But wouldn't they shoot your propeller off?"

Gavin explained how the synchronizer gear had been stolen from a crashed German aircraft, enabling the French aviators to copy the assembly that allowed bullets to go between the propeller as it turned. "I'd like to take you up for a ride," he said. "Would you like to go?"

Heather's eyes opened wide with surprise. "Is that permitted?"

Gavin grinned and ducked his head sheepishly. "No, it's not. But this outfit seems to find a way to do whatever it wants to do. It's not like the regular Air Force." He tried hard to explain to her. "You see, all of us came from America—the Wild West, I guess you'd call it. We don't have a lot of discipline. The captain . . . he tries to keep us in line enough to prevent us getting thrown out of the French Air Force, and I guess as long as Luf keeps shooting down Germans, they'll let us stay. So I'll have a two-seater warmed up and we'll take a spin."

Heather never forgot that flight. She found herself in the backseat of Gavin's aircraft, her hair hidden under a helmet, wearing a bulky flying suit. Everyone knew what was going on, but Captain Thenault merely turned his face the other way, whispering to Thaw, "If Lady Heather gets killed, we'll probably all be shot."

"Aww, don't worry about it. Gavin's got a little sense; he won't take her near the front," Thaw said.

And so they flew around the countryside, now low, now high. Gavin would turn and shout something to Heather and she would shout back. He could see she was having the time of her life.

When they landed and he helped her down, he said, "You'd better get out of that flying outfit. If anybody saw you, we'd all be thrown out."

She put her hand on his arm. "Oh, Gavin, it was such fun! How wonderful to be a flyer!" Then her eyes darkened, and she bit her lip. "But this isn't what you do, is it? Your missions aren't joyrides like this." The thought troubled her, and she dropped her hand, saying briefly, "I'll go change."

He took her to the room where she had donned the flying gear and left her there. As he waited, he spoke to one of the mechanics about his aircraft for the next mission. He was so intense in his instructions that when the scream came—a woman's high-pitched scream—it ran up his back as if he had been raked with a bayonet. Wheeling, he saw that Heather had come out of the dressing room and was plastered against the wall, her eyes wide with fear, her hand over her mouth.

There, right in front of her, was a lion! His ears were back, his yellowed fangs wide open, and he looked like a giant cat who had cornered a mouse.

"Whiskey!" Gavin shouted and plunged toward Heather. He dropped to one knee and put his arms around the lion, grasping the ruff of his neck in one fist. "Don't be afraid! He's just a pet!"

To one side, Bill Thaw was choking back his laughter.

"It's not very funny, Bill!" Gavin snapped angrily. "It's all right to scare some poor mechanic to death, but you ought not to treat a lady like that!"

Repentant, Thaw came at once to stand before Heather, blinking in the fading light and spreading his hands apart. "I'm sorry, Lady Spencer. But he's just a big pussycat, wouldn't hurt a soul."

Heather took a deep breath and put her hand over her breast, feeling her heart slow its frantic beating. She summoned up a smile. "Well," she said breathlessly, "he did give me quite a start, you know."

Gavin got to his feet. "Bill got him from a zoo in Paris when he was just a month or two old. Bill's right . . . Whiskey wouldn't hurt a soul, but he scares the daylights out of people. Would you like to pet him?"

Heather looked at the huge cub that was now yawning, exposing a mouthful of pointed teeth. "Thank you, no. I believe I'll stick to my cat at home."

"Here, let me take him." Thaw picked up the lion as if he weighed two pounds and carried him off, chastising him. "You shoulda known better than to scare a lady like that. . . ."

Gavin was embarrassed by the whole thing. "I'm sorry. But Bill thinks it's funny. Are you all right?"

Heather had regained her sense of proportion now and, to Gavin's surprise, giggled slightly. "Yes, I'm all right. And it was funny," she said. "Wait'll I tell Father. He'll love it." She hesitated and asked, "Do you think it would be all right if I brought my parents sometime to visit? Father, especially, would love to see all of this."

"I don't see why not. Everybody else comes. There's prac-
tically no security at all on this base." He grinned. "Well, what
shall we do now? No more flights for you today. How about
mess with all the flyers? Think you could take that?"

Heather was a good sport and, of all the meals the flyers
ate in that mess hall, it was that one that stuck in their minds.
April had been a bad month. They had lost many friends to
German guns. Later that night, when dinner was over and
the humor had turned to seriousness, Kevin Rockwell
brought up the fact that they were losing men more quickly
than they could be replaced. "Most of it can be blamed on
von Richthofen," he said glumly. "That fellow is becoming
a real pest."

Prince said, "I'd like to get him one-on-one somewhere. I
think I can take him."

"From what I hear he's quite a scavenger," Thaw said
thoughtfully. "It's said that he lays back and lets his flag go
in until somebody gets in trouble. Then he goes in for the
kill. Got no respect for a bird like that!"

"Pay no attention to dat," Luf said suddenly. "I have seen
dis man. He is a killer and de best flyer dose fellows have."
He paused solemnly, looking around the group. "Never get
yourselfs involved wid him one-on-one." He smiled slightly
and added, "Leave dat to me. I vill take care of him . . . dot
Red Baron!"

The talk ran around the table, and Heather listened quietly, saying little. After the meal she and Gavin went for a
walk. The stars shone brightly in a clear sky. A full moon rode
high in the sky, and a soft April breeze touched Heather's
cheeks, blowing the tendrils of hair about her face. They
strolled around the airfield, and she noticed that Gavin was
intensely aware of her—but was just as aware of the sounds
of aircraft that came occasionally.

Gavin couldn't help but remain aware of Heather. She was
wearing a scent that was somehow elusive, almost impossible
to identify, and yet it was there, very mild, very sweet . . . and

very feminine. By the light of the full moon he admired the brightness of her eyes and the smoothness of her cheeks and once again found himself wondering what there was about this woman that made her so different from all others he had met.

"Tell me about your family," Heather said. "I'm fascinated by them. Do you want to go back to the farm when the war is over?"

"I guess not." He shrugged. "It was a good place to grow up, for the most part, but I want to fly for the rest of my life." He looked up, hearing the sound of an airplane limping back to base. "One of ours," he said, then turned his attention back to her. "I've told you about all my family, I guess." He hesitated. "Except for my sister Lylah. She's . . . she's . . . an actress."

Heather laughed. "You say that like you might say, 'She's an ax murderer.' There's nothing wrong with being an actress, Gavin, is there?"

"No, I guess not." They walked on, their steps making little noise against the bare earth. Then he spoke even more hesitantly. "I never told anybody this . . . but she's in love with a German."

Heather waited for a few moments, then said with gentle understanding, "I'm sorry about that. It makes for a bad situation, doesn't it?"

"Yes, it does. And what makes it even worse, he's . . ." Gavin was about to mention von Richthofen's name, but something held him back and he only said, "He's a flyer. Like I am."

Heather grasped the situation immediately. "Oh, how terrible! For your sister, I mean. She loves both of you, and one day you two may meet. That is a terrible, terrible thing! I'll pray for her. And for you, too, of course," she added.

"And for him too? The *German?*" Gavin demanded. "How could you pray for him? How can you pray for any of those people over there? They're the ones who started this war."

"I can't explain that, Gavin," Heather said softly. She looked up at the bright April moon and tried to put into words the struggle that had been hers, as it was his now. "I can't hate the Germans. I think, really, they're just like us except for very bad leadership. If I were a German girl, I'd probably have been exactly like they are. You know, the German soldiers go into battle with 'Gott Mit Uns' on their belt buckles, which means 'God With Us.' They think they're doing God's will just as we do."

She stopped walking and turned to face him, putting her hand lightly on his chest. "I do know one thing. The Germans are God's creation. And anything God created is worth something. So I will pray for him just as I pray for you, Gavin."

As he stood there for a moment, he had an impulse that he could not resist. "Would you mind if I kissed you?"

Her lips turned upward, and she asked, "If I were an American girl, would you ask? Or would you just do it?"

Gavin saw the light of humor in her eyes and without further hesitation reached out, took her in his arms and held her very gently. There was no roughness in him, and she marveled at this, for she had heard the other nurses talk about soldiers and their needs. But he held her as if she were a piece of fragile china and slowly lowered his head until his lips were on hers. Still, though there was hunger in the caress, there was a lightness and a gentleness that amazed her. She had been kissed before, but not like this. She held to him lightly and returned the kiss. When he stepped back, she said, "That was a nice kiss."

"I guess I don't know what I feel. I–I don't understand you. You're different from anyone I've ever known, any other woman."

"Well, don't think too much of this. You're a long way from home and from all of the girlfriends you had there. And I'm *here*."

Gavin took her arm and turned her back toward the base. "I don't think that's it, Heather."

★   ★   ★

Heather's visit at the aerodrome was a complete success. She had become the sweetheart of the Lafayette Escadrille in short order, although several of the men had been a little put off by her unusual questions, such as, "Have you ever been born again?" However, she was always cheerful, never pressured them, and was quick to learn their interests and provide a sisterly shoulder to lean on.

On the third day, she got up early, dressed, and went to meet the men in the mess hall.

They all rose when she arrived, and Thaw pulled a chair out for her. "We have to leave early, Lady Spencer. We have a little business to take care of."

Heather looked across the table at Gavin and saw the watchfulness in his eyes. "A mission today?" she asked.

"Oh, nothing to worry about," Gavin said quickly. "Just a little routine flight."

Something about the way he answered her bothered Heather, and after breakfast she sought out Captain Thenault. "May I ask what sort of mission this is, Captain?"

Thenault made a dismissing gesture. "No more dangerous than usual. But . . . no less either, I suppose. Every time these lads go up, they stand a chance of running into the Germans. But I think it'll be all right."

Heather watched later as the flyers took off—six of them, including Gavin—and for some reason she could not fathom, was uneasy. Although she was scheduled to leave at noon, she decided to wait until the flyers returned from the mission. Long after the six planes had disappeared over the blue horizon, she continued to peer into the sky. Then, pacing the field aimlessly, she found herself wondering what it was about this young man, Gavin Stuart, that so drew her. At length she said to herself, *He's just a fine young man. That's all there is to it. There couldn't be anything else.*

Gavin forced all thoughts of Heather out of his mind and followed as Thaw led the flight. By eight o'clock, they were on the other side of the line. It was a clear morning, except that the sun's glow from the east held the promise of hot weather.

He had been keeping a very keen lookout. So had Thaw, up ahead, and both of them saw the fighters at the same time. Thaw waved them into close formation, but not before the fighters slipped in among them, beginning to shoot as they flew by. What had been a nice neat formation, with all the planes in the inverted "V," broke up into a wild melee.

Suddenly Gavin saw a red triplane flash by him, and before he could think, the triplane had flipped over in an incredibly short turning space and was on his tail. He had heard about this plane—an imitation of a Sopwith triplane—but much more maneuverable. It was not particularly fast, but he had heard it could turn on a dime and now he had proof of it.

Immediately Gavin threw his plane into a sideslip, having learned that usually he could get away from his pursuers in the Pup that he flew. But this time it did not happen. He made a steep turn, expecting to lose his pursuer, and suddenly found out that he could not. He did get one quick look at the plane as they whirled and the thought came to him instantly: *That's von Richthofen! He flies an all-red plane!*

Suddenly the report of machine guns cracked in his ears, and he realized that this was no ordinary pilot behind him. He couldn't shake the killer loose.

Holding the stick between his knees, Gavin threw his plane all across the sky, but to no avail. He was at the mercy of the red aircraft behind him, and he suspected there would be no quarter. Slug after slug crashed around his head and into his instrument panel. He felt a tug at his right arm and saw that the fabric of his flying suit had been ripped by one of the bullets. Before he could turn, there was a pinging sound as a bullet severed the metal aileron control on the right side, a foot from his head. Aileron flopping, half out of control, the plane started to spin. Gavin fought it with everything he had, but nothing he did could pull the plane out. He had thought, many times, of what he would do if his plane lost control and was about to crash. Some had said it would be better to jump, hopefully landing in a tree or a stream, than to risk burning to death or crashing directly into the ground.

Glancing back he saw the red triplane still hard behind him and, even as he turned, the sparkle of von Richthofen's guns twinkled and the tracers punched holes in his left wing. *I'm not going to jump*, Gavin thought grimly. *If I go out, it'll be in my plane.*

The plane hurtled toward the ground, and Gavin heard more machine gun fire. But this time it was Bill Thaw, who had found the red triplane in his sights and was sending a stream of tracers toward it. The red airplane broke away, flipped over, and slipped past Thaw's slower aircraft.

Oh, God! Please get me out of this! Gavin prayed as the earth rushed up to meet him. Desperately he yanked on the controls. Then, with only a few hundred feet separating him from the ground, he came out of the stall, pulled the nose of the aircraft upward, and had just enough time to pick out a fairly level spot on the field below.

He landed roughly, breaking the undercarriage and hitting a shellhole that flipped the airplane over completely. This maneuver succeeded in demolishing the aircraft. But Gavin himself was miraculously unhurt.

Still, with the noxious fumes in the air, he knew what could happen. Flames could envelop the fragile piece of wood and fabric instantly. Desperately Gavin scrambled out of the airplane and jumped, falling to the ground and scrabbling along. Getting to his feet at last, he ran perhaps fifty yards before he felt the whoosh and the heat and the sound struck him, knocking him back off his feet. He looked back to see the fireball that had been his airplane. Shielding his eyes, he climbed to his feet and staggered away.

He had not gone more than twenty yards, however, when he heard a voice calling, "Halt!"

Gavin stopped immediately and whirled to see a squad of

German soldiers forming a semicircle behind him, each of them pointing a rifle in his direction. Instantly he threw up his hands. "I surrender!"

Evidently the German sergeant understood him. He came at once and searched Gavin for weapons, then nodded in satisfaction. "Come mit uns!" he commanded.

Gavin followed across the broken field. He looked up as he walked along, seeing the dogfight still in progress. Just before reaching the trench, he saw the Americans retreat for home and was relieved to count five aircraft.

Well, they only got me, Gavin thought. *The rest of the fellas have gotten away.* He stepped down into the trench and for the next few hours was kept in a respectably clean bunker, no worse than he had seen on their own side. He was given something to eat and was interrogated by a Lieutenant of Artillery, informing him that he must state his name and the airfield from which he had flown. The men gathering around seemed friendly enough, but he realized that if he had been an artillerist and had been bombing and shelling them for days, they might not have been so kindly disposed toward him.

Looking up, Gavin was surprised to see a man wearing the uniform of the German Flying Service enter the room. He was a rather short man with a pale face and bright eyes peering out from beneath the bill of his officer's cap. Gavin stood up at once.

"What is your name?" the officer asked.

"Lieutenant Gavin Stuart."

Instantly he saw something in the German's eyes change. The officer stood there watching him, Gavin wondering why his name should have been so significant, and the German said, "I am Baron Manfred von Richthofen."

Time seemed to stand still for Gavin. He studied the erect form of his enemy, and suddenly the two men seemed to be alone in the universe. A silence, thick and palpable, descended on the room. Each man stood there, filled with his own thoughts, waiting for the other to speak. Both of them were thinking of the same woman—Lylah Stuart. One thought as a brother, the other as a lover.

Finally von Richthofen said, "I will see to it that you have good treatment."

"Thank you," Gavin said stiffly. He wanted to say more, but could not.

Von Richthofen hesitated, then said quietly, "I am glad you were not killed."

Gavin realized that von Richthofen knew who he was. "So am I," he replied curtly. Again he struggled to speak, but nothing came. All he could think was, *This is the man my sister loves, and he's the enemy!*

The two men were a contrast in every way. American and German, enemies by the very nature of the uniforms they wore and what life had molded them to be, and now enemies more surely than ever. For in that moment, seeds of hatred were planted deep in the heart of Gavin Stuart. It was an alien emotion for Gavin, who all his life had been good-natured and easygoing. But now, staring into the eyes of his sister's lover, he could only think of the damage this man had done to his sister. He thought of the disaster that lay ahead if she did not break off with him, and right then, right there, he began to form a resolution.

I will kill this man, Gavin vowed silently. *I will break out of whatever prison they put me in, get into an airplane, and I will hunt him down and kill him if it's the last thing I ever do.*

Von Richthofen bowed in a mockery of civility and said briefly, "Again, if you are not treated well, get word to me and I will see to it."

He waited, but Gavin kept his expression carefully shuttered. His gaze remained steady and Manfred von Richthofen, without further ado, turned and left the room. On the ground in a prison camp, Gavin knew, his captor might abide by the Articles of War. But if they were ever to meet in the air again, neither man would rest until he had killed the other.

Part 3
OVER THERE

14

THE END OF SOMETHING

T he United States was, in the beginning, an innocent by-
stander. She was, however, inexorably drawn into the European conflict as surely as fallen leaves are drawn into
whirlpools.

Americans watched the madness from a distance, thank-
ful to be on the far shore of the Atlantic. Neutrality was the
policy of the nation, for ever since George Washington had
warned against "entangling alliances," no president had made
an alliance with a foreign country. America wanted nothing
more than to stay out of other people's scrapes.

With the outbreak of the war, President Wilson pledged
neutrality. But the American people were more outspoken
than their president and when the *Lusitania* went down, sunk
by German U-boats, they discovered they had a monstrous
enemy on the other side of the Atlantic. If the Kaiser could
get away with such an act, what was to keep him from the
very shores of America?

A storm of outrage had swept the United States after the
sinking of the *Lusitania*. Cartoons portrayed U-boat captains
as sadistic killers, enjoying their victims' pain. Ghosts of
drowned children were shown, pointing to the Kaiser and asking, "Why did you kill us?" All eyes turned to the president
during the crisis. What would Woodrow Wilson do now? The
nation waited and wondered.

Those who expected him to plunge the nation straight into
war didn't know their man. Wilson hated war with all his soul.

179

He always had. The first thing he could remember concerned war—the Civil War. At the age of three, he had stood at the door of the family home in Augusta, Georgia, as passersby yelled, "Mr. Lincoln's elected! There'll be war!"

Puzzled, young Wilson had toddled into his father's study to ask, "What is war?"

He had found out soon enough. Georgia became a blistering battleground. General Sherman's Union army burned and blasted their way across the state on their march to the sea. Lines of retreating Confederate soldiers, whipped and miserable, trudged wearily past the Wilson house. That boy, now grown to a man of 59, was haunted by visions of war. His visions, however, didn't make him cowardly—only cautious. It might be necessary to fight Germany one day, he knew, and if that day came, the president was prepared to lead the nation through the terrible time. But he didn't have to like it. And in 1915, he had tried to keep peace with honor.

On May 10, three days after the sinking of the *Lusitania*, Wilson had addressed a gathering of citizens, reminding them that the nation was neutral. He ended with a memorable phrase: "There is such a thing as a man being too proud to fight."

Opponents gasped. *Why, a man—a real man—would be too proud* not *to fight!* Theodore Roosevelt sputtered and fumed. A former president, hero of the Spanish-American War, he had never forgiven Wilson for that speech. "Flubdubs and mollycoddle!" he thundered. Wilson and his followers were "bunglers and sissies," not fit to lead a proud people!

Germany took a hint from Wilson, who made it clear that American ships had a right to go wherever they pleased. In April 1916, the German High Command had ordered its U-boats not to sink merchantmen without warning. This was, of course, a victory for Wilson. In November he was elected to a second term as president on the slogan: "He Kept Us Out of War." And so he had—for the moment.

The problem was that the Germans couldn't keep their

submarines on a leash forever. The subs were the most potent weapon possessed by the Germans, and every day they restrained them gave the Allies an edge. The German military put its case to the Kaiser simply: "Either use the U-boats to the fullest or risk losing the war." The diplomats warned that such an act would bring the United States into the war, but the Kaiser's admirals and generals weren't worried. The United States, they knew, was unprepared for European-style warfare. The military won the debate, and this single act did more than anything else to draw America into World War I.

On January 31, 1917, a note to American officials from Ambassador von Dernstorff had stated that Germany would begin unrestricted submarine warfare. It was to be sea warfare without limit or pity. Kaiser Wilhelm II made only one concession: One American ship per week—only one—could sail for England if it obeyed certain rules. It had to arrive on a Sunday and leave on a Wednesday. It must be decorated appropriately—red and white stripes painted on the hull, a large checkered flag displayed on each mast, an American flag flown at the stern. In addition, the United States must guarantee that the ship carried no war material.

An outcry arose the moment the note appeared in the newspapers. *Sabotage the Lusitania, and now this! The nerve of them!* One writer said the Germans were demanding that our ships be "striped like a barber's pole"! And to fly "a rag, resembling a kitchen tablecloth"!

President Wilson read the message, then read it again, hardly believing his eyes. Putting the paper aside, he said in a half-whisper, "This means war!"

And then, in the first two weeks of March, the *Algonquin*—American-built, American-owned, American-manned—met a submarine on the surface off the English coast. Forced to stop, she was shelled by a deck gun while her crew scrambled to safety. A few days later, the *City of Memphis*, the *Illinois*, and the *Vigiliancia* were torpedoed, with some crewmen killed.

It was the last straw. Grimly President Wilson broke diplomatic relations with Germany and called Congress into a special session. The man of peace would ask for a declaration of war. It was the hardest thing he would ever have to do, but he could see no way out. The president had no doubt that the Senate and the House of Representatives would agree to his request; indeed, they would welcome it eagerly.

After his tour of the European battlefields, the ace reporter for the *New York Journal*, Amos Stuart, had returned to America. Now on the early morning of Monday, April 2, he was standing outside the White House as President Wilson set out for Capitol Hill. It was a bad day, damp and dreary, a fitting setting for what was to take place. President Wilson looked haggard as he sat next to Mrs. Wilson in the big limousine.

"Why all the police guards?" Amos asked Fred Hargrove, one of his friends in the police department. "What are those soldiers doing here, Fred?"

Hargrove stared at the troop of mounted officers surrounding the presidential vehicle, their horses' hooves clattering on the wet pavement shimmering under the streetlights. As the troopers spurred their mounts, making them dance to throw off the rain, as well as any would-be assassins in the crowd, he muttered, "There's a lot to be afraid of tonight. The crowds were ten-deep, jamming the sidewalks either side of Pennsylvania Avenue. A lot of them shouting, 'No War!' There's no telling how these folks might react, Amos. Why, I heard that Senator Henry Cabot Lodge and a demonstrator have already gotten into a fistfight!"

Amos nodded. "I heard the Secret Service was afraid for the president's safety. They're probably remembering that bomb that went off in the senate wing back in July. But nothing like that will happen tonight, do you think?"

"Uhh . . . I ain't saying. All I know is, a crowd like this can turn mean."

The procession moved away and Amos followed the entourage and headed toward Capitol Hill. As he approached, he saw a startling sight. For the first time in history, floodlights lit the white dome of the Capitol, giving the impression that it might sail off into space at any moment.

When Amos got out of his car, he ran into another friend who asked, "Have you seen all those guns up on the roof?" He waved at the top of the building. "Machine guns. Positioned to sweep the street."

Discouraged and disturbed, Amos entered the House of Representatives. As he left the street, the rain began to fall harder, lightning streaked the sky, and there was a rumbling of distant thunder. He found a place in the crowded gallery, where Mrs. Wilson sat, looking down on a sea of American flags.

Only the German diplomats were absent, Amos noted, taking inventory. If he had but known, they were busy at the Embassy with last-minute packing and the burning of secret papers.

At 8:32 P.M., Uncle Joe Cannon, Speaker of the House, announced, "The President of the United States!" Cheers and applause rocked the room as Mr. Wilson walked to the rostrum, a thin figure in a black suit. The quiet was almost oppressive.

"Gentlemen of the Congress..." Wilson adjusted his steel-rimmed spectacles and began to speak, his words reaching into every corner of the great room. The war message was his own, picked out word by word on his battered portable typewriter. Calmly, sentence followed sentence in logical order as Wilson built the case against Germany. The warlords of Berlin were the enemies of freedom, warring against humanity, unleashing their U-boats to ravage the seas. The United States must resist such outrages.

"We must fight," he said, "for the ultimate peace of the world and the liberation of its peoples. The world must be made safe for democracy."

Ed White, the seventy-two-year-old Chief Justice of the Supreme Court, sat in the front row, his eyes fixed on the president's face. Snowy-haired and wrinkled with time, he was a Civil War veteran who had never lost his fighting spirit. At these words he tossed his hat away, leapt to his feet, and clapped his hands above his head, giving the Rebel Yell. Long ago that battle cry had chilled the blood of bluecoats at Shiloh, Chickamauga, and other Civil War battlefields. Now it stirred this audience, which unleashed a roar like a storm.

President Wilson finished his speech and was led through the crowds by Secret Service men for the ride back to the White House. There were congratulatory handshakes and smiles of happiness, as if he'd won some great victory.

Back at the White House, the Wilsons had dinner with friends. After they left, his wife went upstairs to bed, and the president wandered into the empty Cabinet room. Some time later his secretary, Joseph Tumulty, found him seated at a long table.

Wilson had just given the greatest speech of his life, yet he was not happy. As he and his secretary talked about the day's events, an overwhelming sadness came upon the president, and tears filled his eyes.

"Think of what it was they were applauding," he muttered. "My message was a message of death for our young men. How strange to applaud that!"

With those words, Woodrow Wilson laid his head on the table and cried.

"Which way to the revival?" Amos asked.

The clerk of the small grocery store took the bill Amos handed him, slipped it into a clanging cash register, and slammed the drawer shut. Handing Amos his change, he grinned. "Follow the crowd," he drawled in a deep Southern accent. "Don't reckon you'll have no trouble findin' Brother Stuart's meeting."

Amos returned the clerk's smile and walked out of the

store, noticing the long line of cars headed north. The proprietor ambled to the door, leaned against the frame, and called, "Out that way 'bout two miles. You cain't miss it. Everbody in the county'll be there."

"Thanks." Amos climbed into his car, slammed the door, and pulled away from the grocery store, easing into the steady stream of traffic. Fifteen minutes later, he saw what he had been looking for—a round wooden structure, set in the middle of a field and surrounded by what seemed to be thousands of automobiles.

Parking his car, he joined the crush of people and was soon jostled by eager revival-goers. When he finally stepped through one of the doors, he found himself inside a huge open structure, the smell of raw lumber and sawdust almost acrid in his nostrils. Approximately halfway down to the front, he located a seat, nothing more than a two-by-eight thrown on a clever arrangement of scaffolding. He held on gingerly as he clambered into his place, squeezing in between a farmer wearing bib overalls on his left, and a well-dressed woman of about thirty and her equally well-dressed husband on his right. There was a hum of conversation as the crowd filed in, filling the structure, and Amos waited eagerly for the meeting to begin.

Finally several men came out and mounted the platform that was situated at the far end. Amos felt a warm rush as he saw his brother Owen standing tall amidst the others. Amos had hurried from New York to get to this meeting just outside of Richmond, Virginia, and sat there as the choir—composed of several hundred people, probably from the various churches in the area—began to sing. The familiar melodies rang out—"Revive Us Again," "Are You Washed in the Blood?", "Amazing Grace"—and Amos joined in lustily.

There was a pause for a long prayer by the chaplain of the local Ministerial Alliance, followed by several announcements. Then the offering was collected efficiently by a group of men using woven straw plates for the purpose. Amos tossed in ten dollars and grinned as he thought, *Brother of mine, I can remember lots of times when ten bucks was all the offering you'd get for a meeting!*

A plain-looking young woman got up and sang a solo, then the visiting evangelist was introduced by the president of the Ministerial Alliance, a tall, rotund, bulky man with a red face and a booming voice. For several minutes he extolled the accomplishments of the evangelist, telling how thousands had come to know Jesus through his ministry, how the whole nation was being shaken, and that soon, no doubt, the world would be moved by the message of Reverend Owen Stuart. On and on he went, and Amos noted that Owen was shaking his head slightly and did not lift his eyes. *He never did like that kind of talk*, Amos thought, and he was glad when the speaker finally finished.

Owen rose and walked to the pulpit. Tall, strong, confident, he gave one glance at the departing minister who had introduced him. Then he looked out at the audience and grinned endearingly. "I wish my mother could have heard that. She would have agreed with every bit of it."

Laughter rippled through the crowd and Owen added, "I feel like a pancake that's just had syrup poured all over it. But I thank you, dear brother. I'll try to say something nice about you before I leave here." Again a pleasant laugh ran around the huge auditorium.

Owen spoke for a few moments, thanking those who had had a part in bringing him here. His gesture encompassed the huge auditorium that had been built especially for this meeting as he said, "I know some of you put hours of labor into this structure, and I appreciate that. When it's taken down, the lumber will be given to build an orphanage in a small town only a few miles from here, and God will certainly honor that."

Amos had never seen a building such as the one housing this revival crowd. His brother had begun his ministry in tents. But Owen's appeal had spread until finally the crowds grew too large for even the largest tent. He had then fallen on the idea of having the city where he would hold the revival erect a wooden tabernacle. It would be paid for out of the offerings, and the lumber would be donated to a worthy project.

Very soon he began speaking on the text, "Ye Must Be Born Again." Amos had heard that sermon many times during his youth, and not a few since. But he never heard a speech delivered with more passion and earnestness than on that April evening. He thought back over Owen's first awkward attempts to preach the gospel. He had matured since those days. He was sure in his movements and quoted Scripture after Scripture from memory. As he threw himself into his message, he moved from one side of the platform to the other, sometimes lifting his hand and clenching his fist. He was serious at times and he laughed at other times. *He's a fine preacher! I wonder how big he'll be before he gets through*, Amos thought.

When it was time for the invitation, the entire congregation stood together and began to sing "Just As I Am, Without One Plea." The farmer next to Amos turned to look at him and whispered hoarsely, "Are you saved, young man?"

Amos said quickly, "Yes, I sure am, and I take it you are, too."

"Bet your boots! Baptized two nights ago by that very preacher you see up on the platform, Brother Stuart." The farmer's leathery face and work-hardened hands spoke of a man who'd labored all of his life. He looked at Amos and there was a light of wonder in his eyes. "Been a member of a church for twenty years, and two nights ago I come and that young feller up there, he preached on the same thing he's preachin' on tonight—'Ye Must Be Born Again.' Told us all it wasn't church membership or bein' good or treatin' folks right that saves you. Only Jesus. And you know what?" His eyes grew moist and he slapped his meaty hands together. "I done 'er! I went up that aisle and I began to beller and call and that young feller, Brother Stuart, why he come right down and knelt right with me in them pretty white britches o' his, put his arm right 'round my shoulders, and began to pray jist like I done. And first thing you know, why the Lord, he come down and saved me."

Amos smiled warmly at the humble farmer. "That's Owen, all right. He's always been like that, ever since he started preaching."

The invitation stretched into the night, for many went down, and Owen stayed, along with the other ministers, to pray for the lost and backslidden.

As Owen was preparing to leave, Amos met him at the front. "Brother, I believe that's the finest sermon on that subject I ever heard!"

Owen wheeled and stared at Amos, then let out a whoop and grabbed him. "Why, you no-account something! Why didn't you tell me you were going to be here?" His strong arms wrapped Amos tightly, almost lifting him off his feet. Then he released him. "C'mon, let's you and me go get something to eat! This preaching's hungry work!"

It took a while to get out of the auditorium. Everyone wanted to speak to Owen, and he spent time with each one, shaking hands and smiling, telling people he would pray for them. Finally he and Amos made it to Amos's car and they drove away in the thinning traffic.

"There's a café down the road called Mom's Place," Owen said. "They make a good hamburger."

"Somebody named Mom run it?" Amos asked.

"No. A scruffy old fellow named Ike. But he said nobody would come in to eat at 'Ike's Place' so he named it 'Mom's Place.'"

Thirty minutes later they were pulling up in front of a small diner. They went inside and found a seat.

Ike himself, a tall, thin man wearing a white apron and a pair of silver spectacles, appeared to take their order. "Well, Preacher, did you get 'em saved tonight?"

"No, but the *Lord* saved a whole bunch, Ike," Owen said. "Now, this is my brother Amos and I've told him all about your hamburgers. I want you to prove I was telling the truth— that you make the best in the country."

"Why, sure, Preacher, you just sit right back there in that booth. You want a big red drank, too?"

"Sure. And bring one for Amos."

The two men relaxed in the booth and Amos said at once, "That was fine, Owen. Biggest crowd I've ever seen you preach to." Then he smiled. "But you preach as if there was a half a dozen there. I felt like you were talking right to me." He grew thoughtful and nodded. "I think that's the reason you've been so successful. You have a way of preaching that's very personal."

Owen disliked being praised and said, "Well, give God the glory. Thank God for what he's doing through me." And then he began to ask Amos about the family, and the two men sat there chatting until the burgers came. They ate hungrily.

Over coffee, Owen said, "I guess you were in Washington when the president declared war, weren't you, Amos?"

"I was there." Amos swallowed from the cup of scalding black liquid and shuddered. "That's the strongest coffee I've ever tasted. It'd take the paint off an automobile!" Then he grew sober. "Wilson's an unhappy man. He knows what's coming."

Owen nodded. "I guess we all do, don't we? It's going to be a terrible war."

"Well, you and I won't have to go," Amos put in, "but I can tell you right now there'll be a draft—Selective Service, you know. I predict there won't be enough men to volunteer to fill the ranks. They might get Peter, since he's only twenty-seven. But you're thirty-one, so they won't take you, and of course I'm an old man, so I'm not going . . . not to fight, anyway."

Owen did not reply, but began to trace the pattern on the tablecloth with his forefinger. He was so quiet and so still that Amos finally inquired anxiously, "What's the matter? Anything wrong at home? Anything wrong with Allie?"

"Oh, no. We're fine."

As he sat there in silence, Amos thought how much Owen looked like their father, Will Stuart—the same short nose, the chestnut hair, the cleft chin. And his brother appeared to be as strong and fit as when he was fighting in the ring. He was,

Amos decided, a handsome man who didn't know it, for there
was not an ounce of pride, that he could see, in Owen.

Finally Owen lifted his head and looked him in the eye.
"I've got something to tell you, Amos."

"What is it?"

"This may sound crazy to you. Fact is, I didn't know how
I was going to tell Allie, but . . ." He drew a deep breath and
then said quietly, "I've decided to enlist in the army."

"What?" Amos slammed down the cup and blinked in surprise. For a moment he thought he had not heard his brother
correctly. "What did you say? Enlist in the army?"

Owen shrugged a little. "I know. I know, Amos. I know everything you're going to say. I'm too old, I've got a family, I've got
a ministry, there are younger fellas to go . . . I know all that.
Don't you think I've told myself those things a hundred times?"

Amos was dumbfounded. "But why? Why in the world
would you do a thing like that?"

Owen sighed, and a faint smile touched his lips. "Don't
you hate it when people say 'God told me to do something'?
Sounds like they've got a private telephone line to God. But
that's as close as I can come," he said earnestly. He laced his
fingers together and shook his head stubbornly. "I've fought
God on this thing for days now, and still—I haven't heard any
voice, you understand—but I know that's what God wants
me to do. And I'm going to do it."

Amos began at once to try to persuade Owen that he had
misunderstood God. But the more he argued, the more Owen
just sat there, his jaw firmly set, saying, "I know it's what God
wants . . . and I'm going to do it."

Finally Amos saw that it was useless to argue. He took a
deep breath and asked, "When are you going in?"

"Right away."

"Have you told Allie?"

"Yes, of course. She didn't understand at first," Owen said
slowly. "But we prayed about it . . . and now we're one in this
thing."

"What about your ministry?"

"I don't know. I guess my ministry will be carrying a gun for a while." Owen leaned back and said thoughtfully, "You know, we're seeing hundreds get saved in these meetings, but maybe there's one man in that trench over there in Europe, and God's got his eye on him, and I'm the one man that could lead him to Jesus."

"You always were a stubborn cuss. Just like all the rest of us Stuarts," Amos said, leaning over to slap his brother's thick forearm. Then he grasped it, holding on for a moment longer. "I know you'll do what God tells you. Just be careful, will you?"

"Sure."

The two men got up, laid some bills on the table, and left the café. When they parted, Amos said, "I'll tell the family. We'll all pray for you every night."

"Good. I'm going to need it, I think," Owen admitted, adding softly, "God's downright peculiar, isn't he, Amos? Look what he's doing to me! But I know his hand's in it. And I know, somewhere out there in those trenches, I'll find out the reason why."

15

BIRTH OF AN ARMY

On the day America declared war in 1917, a songwriter named George M. Cohan, a writer of Broadway musicals, wrote a song that swept the Allied armies. It caught on almost at once and was played wherever British, French, and Belgian troops were serving. They sang it in the trenches, whistled it on the march, hummed it while at camp chores. The song was called "Over There," and it told the Europeans to prepare and say a prayer, for "the Yanks are coming."

Amos Stuart sat at his battered portable typewriter, banging out a story and humming the song under his breath unconsciously. Unlike the song, this story was destined to be *un*popular. It would say basically that President Wilson might declare war, but the United States was ill-prepared to enter such a conflict. It was, however, just the kind of story his publisher liked because it would hold up to display the sorry job the politicians had done preparing the country for the inevitable conflict. He was interrupted when the phone rang. Picking it up distractedly, he grunted, "Yeah."

"What do you mean, 'Yeah'?" came a familiar voice over the line. "Is that the way you newspaper guys talk?"

"Nick!" Amos exclaimed, recognizing his old friend. "Yeah, it's the way we newspaper guys talk! Better than you Italian guys, anyway! What's going on?"

"Gotta see you, Amos. What about we go out and eat lunch?"

"Can't do it, Nick," Amos said reluctantly. He had known Nick Castellano for a long time, ever since the days when, as a penniless youth fresh from the farm, he'd come to the big city and found a home with the Castellanos. "Gotta get a story out."

"Yeah, well, you gotta help me, Amos. I'm in a jam."

Amos paused, knowing that Castellano was not one to plead for help unless it was serious. "Okay. What say we meet at Frankie's for lunch?"

"Great! I'll see you there at noon."

Amos pounded out the rest of the story, but his mind was on Nick Castellano. He had kept in close touch with Nick's mother but had not heard from Nick in months. He did know, as most newspapermen did, that Nick Castellano was one of the rising stars in the world of mobsters and hood-lums who played such a large part in the life of New York City. He worried about Nick and had talked to him several times but had gotten nowhere. Nick had simply shrugged off his concern. "It's a way to make a living. Forget it, okay?"

Amos ripped the sheet out of the typewriter, took it in to one of the typists, and tossed it on her desk. "See if you can straighten this mess up, Helen. I gotta run." Without wait-ing for an answer, he left the building. All the way to Frankie's Restaurant, his mind tugged and pulled at Nick's strange request.

When he got there, the maitre d' met him. "Ah, Mr. Stu-art. Mr. Castellano is already at his table. Come with me, please." Amos followed the headwaiter and when he came to a choice table toward the back, set off by a series of pillars, he found Nick toying with his drink.

"Hello, Nick," Amos greeted him.

"Yeah, sit down, Amos." Castellano nodded. There was a glum look on his face, Amos noted as he took his seat, and the handsome features appeared downcast. He was not a big man, not over 140 pounds, very trim and quick. True to his Italian roots, Nick had a swarthy complexion and jet-black hair and eyes. He was a hot-tempered man, Amos knew, but generous and loyal to his friends. "What do you want to eat?" Nick asked now.

The two men ordered and, after their waiter had brought Amos his cup of hot coffee, they talked about their families. Finally Nick said, "I talked to Mama yesterday. She told me what you said about Owen."

"About his joining the army?" Amos inquired. He shrugged his shoulders. "Yes, I know it sounds crazy, but that's what he's doing, Nick. I wish he wouldn't. He's too old for that."

"Owen? No, he ain't too old . . . but he's pretty stupid! Musta got his brains scrambled worse than we thought when he was in the ring." Nick swallowed part of his drink, then put the glass down. "I like the guy, though, even if he is a preacher." His intense black eyes narrowed in speculation. "He really gonna do that? Join the army?"

"Sure. You know Owen. When he says he'll do something, he'll do it or die."

"Yeah. He's like that."

Amos waited, then asked curiously, "What's wrong, Nick? You in some kind of trouble?"

"Me? No, I'm okay. It's Eddy."

Amos thought about Nick's twenty-five-year-old brother Eddy. He'd been a wild young man, even by mob standards. Amos had heard that Nick had beaten him half to death once for getting out of line, but apparently the thrashing hadn't curbed the young man's spirit. "Eddy in trouble with the law?" Amos asked quietly.

"Naw, I wish that was it." Nick allowed a brief smile to touch the corners of his thin lips. "I'd know how to handle that." He looked a little embarrassed. "Well . . . what it is, Amos, Eddy's got the same bug Owen's got. He's joining the army." He watched as shock ran over Amos, then nodded. "Surprises you, don't it? Yeah, me, too. And Mama's goin' crazy!"

"I bet she is. He always was very special to your mother," Amos replied. He sat there thinking about the wild young man, then said carefully, "Well, I guess the draft would've gotten him anyway. He'll just be going earlier."

"But the draft wouldn't have got him. Them things got Boards, ain't they? I can fix that . . . I can fix anything that money'll buy, and money'll buy about anything." It was the sum total, Amos knew, of Nick's philosophy. "I wanna ask you a favor, Amos."

"Sure, Nick, anything I can do. What is it?"

"Well I talked to the kid and he won't listen to reason. But what I did get out of him—and it cost me plenty!—was his promise to try to get in an outfit that would be good for him. You know, where somebody could look out for him."

Amos was doubtful and it showed in his eyes. "I don't think that can be arranged, Nick. You got connections, but not in the army. And anyway, when they get in the trenches, you're not going to be standing there ready to buy off some lieutenant to keep Eddy from going over the top."

"Yeah, sure, I know that. But what I got in mind is this," Nick said carefully, "what about if Eddy goes in the same outfit as Owen?" He began to speak rapidly, as if to convince Amos. "I mean . . . Owen, he's a preacher, right? And pretty well-known. He could look out after the kid."

Amos frowned. "No, I don't think so, Nick. If the kid won't listen to you, why should he listen to Owen?"

"I dunno," Nick said wearily. "All I know is I gotta try *somethin'*. Kid don't know nothin'. Here he's sittin' right on top of a gold mine—I'm makin' money all the time and the kid'll come in for his share of it someday. But what good's it gonna do him if he gets blown apart in France? No, it's the only thing I can come up with and I got the kid's promise—if I don't kick him outta the family completely—that he'll listen to Owen. What I wanna know is," he demanded, "will *you* talk to Owen? Tell him the situation, tell him to kinda look out for the kid?"

"Why, sure, Nick. I'll be glad to do that. Or you could do it yourself. Owen always thought a lot of you."

"Ah, I'm just a sinner to him, I guess. You do it, Amos. I know how much he looks up to you."

The food came and the two men settled down to their meal. As they ate, Amos's mind was racing. What Nick was asking would be an extra burden on Owen, for Eddy Castellano was a tough punk, unlikely to listen to anybody in authority.

But when they parted, Amos said, "I'll do what I can, Nick. . . ." He hesitated before adding, "But I don't mind telling you I'm worried about these guys. It's a rough show they're going into over there. Lots of boys aren't going to come back. Makes you think, doesn't it?"

Nick's dark eyes were shadowed with a vague regret and uncertainty. He was a man who had learned to take what he wanted—anything that caught his fancy. But this, he knew, was beyond him, and he could only say, "Yeah, I guess that's right, Amos. You tell Owen if he'll look after the kid, I'll make it right with him." Then he blinked and shrugged. "But that don't mean nothin' to him, does it? I mean, he don't care about money."

"No, but he cares about people, so I know he'll do the best he can. I hope so, anyway. So long, Nick."

As Castellano left to go talk to his brother, he was wondering if he had done the right thing. As head of his family, he had to do *something*—but he wasn't sure this was going to work at all. Riding toward his mother's apartment, he thought gloomily, *The kid's gotta learn to listen to somebody! Maybe this war will shake some sense into him!*

And who would lead these thousands, perhaps even millions, in their war? There was little question about that. The army of the richest nation on earth had only a few weapons. The Air Force was a joke, there was no heavy field artillery, flamethrowers, or tanks, and nobody knew this better than John J. Pershing, appointed Commander of the A.E.F.—Allied Expeditionary Force.

Pershing, a farm boy from Missouri and a graduate of West

Point, had served in the West, where he had fought the Sioux and the Apaches. During the Spanish-American War, he had served in Cuba with the Tenth Cavalry, an all-Negro regiment, which had earned him the nickname of "Blackjack." He liked the nickname and was proud of it.

Blackjack Pershing was a tough, hard-as-nails professional soldier. Completely fearless himself, he admired courage in others. The highest compliment he could give anyone was to say, "He's a fighter . . . a fighter . . . a fighter!"

Pershing had been serving in Texas in 1915 when word came that his wife and three young daughters had died in a fire, and only his son Warren, age seven, had survived. Although he remained outwardly calm, he never fully recovered from the loss of his family. Sometimes his pain was evident despite his self-control. Once, when a curly-haired girl handed him a bouquet of flowers, he found himself facing the welcoming crowd with tears streaming down his cheeks. A lonely man, he buried himself under a mountain of army work. The Service became everything to him—career, family, home. He was the ideal choice to command the AEF.

Pershing threw himself into his work and, under his leadership, thirty-eight training camps were built to hold not only these first volunteers but also the thousands of draftees in various parts of the country they soon began taking in.

Owen stepped off the train along with three hundred other newly enlisted soldiers and joined the three or four hundred others already milling around the train station. He glanced behind him and saw Eddy Castellano, who was looking a little strained, as were most of the men in his company. Eddy and Owen had gotten together only three days earlier, when they had met Amos and Nick Castellano for lunch. It had been a failure—that particular occasion—Owen remembered. Eddy Castellano had been sullen and uncommunicative, and although Owen had tried to put him at ease, the tall young Italian had only glared at him with a pair of hard brown eyes.

"It's not going to work," Amos had said to Owen when the two were alone. "Eddy's stubborn as a mule and rebellious as Cain!"

Owen had merely shrugged. "I don't blame him much. He's a grown man, and Nick's trying to treat him like a kid. But I'll do the best I can for him."

All the good-byes had been said and now, as the two joined the milling throng, Owen edged closer to Castellano. "Well, I've got the idea this isn't going to be much of a vacation, Eddy."

"I can handle it!" Castellano snapped. He'd always liked Owen, had been impressed by the fact that he had once been a successful prizefighter. But from the moment Nick had told him that he'd have to listen to Owen, Eddy had grown resentful. Now his lips thinned and he refused to say more. *Why should I listen to this man?* he was thinking. *A preacher! He don't know no more about soldierin' than I do! Nick musta been crazy to think of it, and I musta been crazy to agree to it. I won't do it!*

"All right, you birds! Come on!" A tall, wiry man they had met when they boarded the train made his way through the crowd, calling out the names of his squad members. "Come on, girls! It's time to get you into this man's army!"

Sergeant Mack Stone was regular army, from Texas. He had light blue eyes and prematurely white hair, and he even chewed tobacco in his sleep, it was told. Tough as boot leather, he was incredibly profane.

Stone led his group to a long low building. When they got inside, he ordered, "Okay now, strip!"

One young recruit named Tyler Ashland turned beet red. Owen, who had talked to Ashland on the train, took note. *He'll have to get over that, in this Army.*

Under Sergeant Stone's direction, they all stripped down to the buff and got in line. Running the gauntlet between two rows of bored medics, the men were jabbed, tapped, and injected. When Ashland saw the first needle, he shut his eyes, but when it came at him, he fainted dead away.

A hollow laugh went up and Eddy mocked, "What a sissy! They'll never make a soldier outta him!"

Sergeant Stone stared at him. "But you'll be one, won't you, Castellano? It's good to know I've got at least one tough guy in my squad. Go ahead, give him them shots," he said. "He won't feel 'em now." The others watched as the needles were plunged into the unconscious form of Ashland, then Owen helped get him on his feet.

"Don't feel bad," Owen whispered to him. "I'm just about to do the same thing myself."

Ashland, a fat, rosy-cheeked fellow, not much older than eighteen, was pale as dough. "I wish I'd never thought of this," he mumbled.

"You'll be okay. This is rough on everybody." Owen made a mental note to stick close to the boy and try to deflect some of the worst of the ribbing.

After the men had all received their injections, they were led to the barber shop. Castellano was the first to crawl up into the chair.

"And would you like to keep your hair, sir?" the barber, a corporal, asked politely.

Eddy ran his hand through his black curly locks. "Yeah, I would."

"Then you'd better get a sack!" A laugh went up from the other barbers at the old joke.

Eddy flushed but could do nothing more than sit helplessly while the barber ran a pair of clippers down the middle of his head, leaving two mountains of black hair on each side. Then the rest fell, covering the floor with black curls.

"There you go, soldier," the corporal said. "Them cooties won't have nothin' to hold onto now!"

Soon the squad, naked heads shining, arrived at the quartermaster's shed. They drew mess kits, blankets, a bed sack to stuff with straw, and a uniform. When they were dressing, Kayo Pulaski yelled, "Hey, this crummy thing's too tight!" Pulaski, a husky, foul-mouthed man of twenty-seven, had been a fighter, although not a very successful one as far as victories in the ring were concerned. But he was right about the uniforms, as Owen discovered when he pulled his on.

The tight-fitting blouse was made of scratchy wool of the dullest olive drab. The jacket's high collar came up under his chin, and he had an idea it would rub his neck raw immediately. The trousers were like riding breeches, roomy in the seat and tapered toward the knees. The "wraps"—six-foot lengths of woolen bandage that were wound around each leg from knee to ankle—came last. The trick, they were informed by Sergeant Stone, was to make the wraps look smart without cutting off circulation in the legs. Boots came in two sizes—Too Large and Too Small. The outfit was crowned by a high-peaked campaign hat with a wide brim.

"I'd like to meet the designer of this crummy uniform in the dark," Pulaski muttered. He stuck the hat on top of his shaved head. "I'd show him a thing or two!"

"Well," Owen said, "I guess we'll see a little worse than this when we get to France."

Sergeant Stone, standing nearby, scowled darkly. "You got that right. Now, you girls come on with me and we'll start makin' soldiers outta you."

All through May, June, and July, Sergeant Stone struggled to turn his green farm boys and the soft city boys into battle-ready soldiers. He had little to work with, for weapons of every kind were in short supply in the training camps. Many a dummy labeled "Kaiser Bill" had his stuffing torn out by the rookies, lunging with bayonets tied to the end of broomsticks.

Despite these shortages, Stone was gratified to see the men hardening up. They learned to speak a new language, including *M.P.* (military police), *AWOL* (absent without leave), *shavetail* (second lieutenant), and *doggie house* (guardhouse).

Nasty details like digging latrines and filling sandbags became somewhat easier by singing nonsense songs such as

"One Grasshopper Hopped Right on Another Grasshopper's Back," and "One Hundred Bottles of Beer on the Wall." But the song that was most familiar was written by a doughboy named Corporal Irving Berlin: "Oh, How I Hate to Get Up in the Morning!"

Training for Owen had been a snap. He'd been in good shape to begin with and was accustomed to discipline. Only once, when Kayo Pulaski had tried to bully Tyler Ashland—the fat-cheeked, baby-faced rookie—had Owen experienced a bad moment. Stepping between the two, Owen had gone outside with Pulaski and had toyed with the ex-prelim fighter, letting him tire himself, before knocking him out with one swift blow to the chin. Then he'd picked Pulaski up and made a friend out of the man, winning the undying gratitude of Ashland and other young recruits he had helped. And by the end of their training period, Owen Stuart was awarded his corporal's stripes.

But the one recruit he'd wanted most to befriend turned a cold shoulder to him. "I don't need none o' your preachin'," Eddy Castellano had said defiantly, "and I don't need you to fight no battles for me, Owen. I can take care o' myself! I know I promised Nick I'd listen to you, and I will—about soldierin'—but that's all, see?"

"Okay, Eddy," Owen said regretfully. "I know it's tough on a young guy like you to be put under wraps. But if I can be of any help, I'm always here."

By the end of August, it was time to ship out. Sergeant Stone came in one day, saying, "Okay, we're about ready to go over the Big Pond. There's gonna be one big review. Blackjack himself is gonna be here, so I want my outfit to look better than anybody else's. Now get all your equipment ready."

The big review took place in New York City. The first contingent of American soldiers to cross the Atlantic Ocean put on quite a show for the whole country. They marched down the main street under a storm of confetti, performed drills on some of the larger fields, and were given heroes' send-offs by the city.

After all the festivities, Owen stood at the dock, saying good-bye to Allie and to Amos and his family. Down the way he could see Nick and Anna Castellano telling Eddy good-bye. There was nothing ominous about the scene to most of them, but Amos was painfully aware that of all the thousands of men boarding these ships, not all would return.

"Don't worry," Owen whispered to Allie, "I'll be back."

Allie held him tightly. "Oh, Owen! I couldn't live without you—!"

Just down the wharf, Anna was clinging to her son Eddy. She had grown plump over the years, and she held him as if she couldn't bear to let him go. "Oh, Eddy, Eddy!" she moaned.

Eddy endured the embrace, then kissed her fondly on the cheek. "Aah, don't worry, Mama. I'll go over and teach those Huns a lesson, then I'll be back." He glanced at Nick and winked. "When I learn a few tricks over there, I'll be about ready to take over from you, big brother."

Nick forced a smile. "Sure, kid. That's the way it'll be."

The ship's horn gave three short blasts, and the sergeants and noncoms marched the soldiers on board the ships, and soon they were sailing out of the harbor.

These troop ships, really converted ocean liners, were unlike anything the men had ever imagined. No longer proud sea queens, they were painted in gray, black, and white stripes to confuse U-boat commanders. The vessel that Owen and his squad was on carried upward of nine thousand troops, three times their normal capacity. Living quarters were so cramped you couldn't move without stepping on someone. The sergeants would be forced to work overtime, breaking up fistfights, but most of the men remained too seasick to get out of bed.

The land started fading into the distance, and Owen shoved through the throng to stand beside the members of his squad at the rail. Silence fell over them as they stood waving to the crowds on the wharf.

"This is gonna be great!" Eddy said.

Owen thought about what lay ahead, then looked out to see Allie growing smaller as the ship cleared the harbor. "No," he said sadly, "it won't be great, Eddy."

16

Escape!

The small town of Villengen bordered the prison camp where Gavin Stuart was taken. Villengen was in Baden, a small section of Germany lying on the east bank of the upper Rhine River. Across the surface of Baden, the high plains and the mountains of the Black Forest rose up spectacularly. The camp itself, surrounded by barbed wire and considered to be escape-proof, was outside the village.

On the morning he was brought in, Gavin took one look around as the steel gates slammed behind him and vowed, *I'll get out of this place or die trying!* He was assigned to one of the barracks housing thirty other prisoners. But during the first two weeks, he found it was not as bad as he had expected. The food was plain, consisting mostly of potatoes with an occasional portion of pork, but the farmers round about were enjoying bumper crops, so prisoners were fed vegetables fairly regularly. The prisoners themselves were a mixed lot of French, Belgians, English, and a few other nationalities thrown in.

On his entrance into the barracks, Gavin met a young man of twenty-two by the name of Harry Douglas, whose distinct dialect gave him away at once.

"Take that bunk. It'll ha' fewer bedbugs than the rest, I think," said Douglas.

"Thanks," Gavin murmured and tossed the few items of clothing he had been issued on the bunk, then sat down. It was quiet in the barracks, most of the men being outside, and he turned to the young man. "You been here long?"

"Aboot three months," Douglas replied with a broad Scots accent. "What's your outfit?"

"Lafayette Escadrille."

Douglas lifted his eyebrows in surprise. "We've heard aboot ya. Got shot doon, I suppose?"

Gavin nodded. "That's it. But I got shot down with class. Baron von Richthofen himself did the honor."

"Aye, he's a real fighting mon, so I hear." Douglas nodded. "Weel, this is no' a bad place for sittin' oot the war. The food's not Scottish, but it's pretty good for the bloody Krauts."

"What about escape?" Gavin asked instantly. "I don't plan to spend the rest of my life in this place."

"Ah, weel now, that's a noble aspiration." Douglas grinned. "But it's no picnic, gettin' oot o' here. The place is guarded like the Bank o' Scotland. There've been three attempts in the last two months and no' a man o' them got ootside. All but one was shot doon just ootside the wire." He stared curiously at his young neighbor. "It'd take quite a magician for a mon to get oot o' this place."

Gavin shook his head stubbornly. "I'm not going to stay here," he said. "This war's going to go on for a long time, and I'm not going to rot in a prison camp." He walked to the window and looked outside where the barbed wire fences rose in the distance. "That piece of barbed wire was put there by a man. And anything a man can do, some other man can *un*do."

Douglas continued to study the young flyer. "Ah, I feel the same way, laddie, but a mon would have to be a bird to fly over that wire. Or a mole to tunnel under it. They check three times a day. We all line up, and if a mon's missing, they throw a cordon round the whole camp, thick as fleas." He dropped his head sadly. "If you think o' anythin', let me know. I'm the mon to go wi' you, if you find a way oot o' this place, that is."

The days stretched into weeks, and Gavin endured his captivity with an impatience he did his best to suppress. He got no letters, and he wrote none, but during the long days and even longer nights, he thought and dreamed of home . . . and of Heather Spencer. The possibilities of escape seemed to be diminishing, although he and Harry Douglas spent hours and hours making plans. Some of them were fantastic and totally unrealistic; all of them seemed impractical. He grew fond of the young Scot and the two formed an exclusive club, the focus of which was escape.

June, however, with all of its balmy breezes and warm sunlit days, seemed the ideal time to break out. They walked around and around the inside of the compound, gazing at the high mountains of the Black Forest.

"If we cud just get into those woods, I'd take my chances," Harry said one day. "But getting oot o' this place . . . I don't know, Gavin. Seems like it canna be done."

"It can be done, Harry!" Gavin retorted stoutly. "We've just got to find a way!"

Not long after that conversation, two prisoners constructed crude ladders, set them against the barbed wire, and had just reached the top when they were cut down by machine gun fire. Another group made a flimsy bridge of small pine boards from Red Cross boxes and tried to scale the high fences. They, too, were shot down. After both escape attempts, all prisoners were lined up into ranks and addressed by the Commandant, who informed them harshly that the guards had been instructed to shoot to kill any man who touched the fence in the future. In fact, he insisted, they would be better to stay at least ten feet away from the fence itself.

A month after the last escape attempt, Gavin lay in his bunk staring into the darkness, his brain fluttering like a bat as he reviewed the possibilities of breaking out of the camp. Getting over that fence had become the biggest goal of his life, and he knew that he would give twenty years of whatever time he had left just to be on the outside.

Wearily his mind turned over old schemes, rejecting them. Finally he tried to put it aside and lay in the darkness, thinking of other things—mostly of Heather—before reliving the instant he had been shot down by von Richthofen. He seemed to hear again the stutter of the German Spandau machine guns and the whistle of the slugs past his ear. Clenching his fists, he remembered the horror of going down, reliving the instant when his plane went completely out of control and plunged toward the earth and sudden death.

And then he remembered something he had evidently blocked out. *God . . . help me get out of this!* His frantic prayer came back with sudden clarity, and then he remembered that the plane had somehow, against all the laws of gravity, pulled out of the spin so that he was able to land.

That couldn't have been God! Gavin thought stubbornly. *It was just an accident.* Nevertheless, the more he thought about it, the more he was forced to question his own beliefs. Owen had said, *God's in everything, Gavin. What we think is a coincidence may be something he puts in our way to help us. The things we feel are bad might turn out to be good. Don't ever give up on God.*

All night long Gavin lay sleepless, thinking about his prayer—the first one he'd prayed in years—and his miraculous escape from death. Finally, almost in jest, he said silently, *Well, God, you've gotten me out of one mess. Let's see you get me out of this one!*

Then strangely, even though he had not been serious, a quietness seemed to settle over his spirit, and a sudden assurance came to him. If a voice had spoken, it would have said something like, *I will show you what I am able to do.* That was all. He heard nothing, and he felt almost foolish. Yet for several days he pondered those words: *I will show you what I am able to do.*

Finally, almost in desperation, lying again on his bunk with that phrase running through his mind, Gavin Stuart gave up. "All right, Lord," he whispered very quietly so no one could hear, not even Harry, snoring in the bunk next to his. "I can't do anything for myself, so I'm asking you to show me what you can do." He felt hypocritical as he prayed. He had not served God—in fact, he had run *away* from him—and now here he was asking God to do something for him. Nevertheless, he held his ground and whispered fiercely, "If you've spoken to me . . . then I want to see what you can do!"

Almost immediately an idea began forming in Gavin's brain. It came in small impulses of thought, but with such clarity that it was almost like watching one of those new motion pictures that had taken the country by storm. He lay there, his breathing short and choppy, as these "visions" flickered in his imagination. They did not last long and then they stopped, but he knew that it could not have been his own mind that had devised these things.

"Harry!" he whispered. "Harry, wake up!"

"Wh–What? What is it?"

Gavin waited until the Scotsman was awake, then he said, "I've got an idea." Feeling constrained to at least be honest, he added, "It's probably going to get me killed." He smiled thinly in the darkness. "I think God just spoke to me."

The Scotsman was a devout Presbyterian and did not laugh, as Gavin had half expected. "Weel, now," he said, "I canna think o' anyone I'd rather be hearin' from. What did the Guid Lord say?"

"Well, he said that he's going to get us out of this place. And here's the way it's going to be. . . ."

When Gavin had finished, Douglas nodded. "Only God himself could think up such a thing as that, so I think we'll ha' ta pay attention to the Guid Lord!"

It was 2:15 in the morning when the big arc lights that surrounded the camp, bathing the barbed wire fences in their harsh glare, suddenly went out. The instant they did, two men dressed in German uniforms dashed out of one of the barracks, both of them waving aloft what appeared to be pistols. In the darkness and confusion, as the guards began shouting at each other, the two men shouted back unintelligible German phrases. The gate that had been opened four minutes earlier to admit some trucks was shrouded in darkness for that one moment, and the two men joined the shuffling crowd of German guards, each of them carrying at his side a heavily laden canvas bag. The two threshed their way through the milling guards, slipped by the shadows of the convoy that was coming in, and quickly moved toward the edge of a wooded area, avoiding the glare of the truck's headlights.

The camp was filled with the shouts of the guards, and a siren went off, breaking the stillness of the night with its cacophonous scream. The two men crouched low and Gavin stumbled into a hole, sprawling on the ground. "Are ye all right, Gavin?" Harry whispered, pausing for a moment.

"Yeah, go on, let's get outta here!"

They scrambled madly and, with relief, entered a line of trees that apparently formed part of a second-growth forest. They plunged into the woods as the sounds faded and suddenly stopped. Glancing back, Gavin saw the lights go on. "We won't have much time. They'll have a head count right away after a thing like that."

"Right. Now, how do we get past the ring o' guards that'll form, Gavin?"

Gavin had already thought this out long ago. In talking to several of the men who worked outside, cutting the trees for firewood, he had learned of a creek that ran along a bluff. The area was so heavily timbered and overgrown with scrub bushes the guards usually avoided it. Gavin was not sure where it was, but as best he could, he followed the directions he had received.

Three hours later they paused, completely out of breath, faces and hands scratched by the tangled underbrush, and threw themselves onto the ground. "I think we got through," Gavin panted. They lay listening for what seemed an interminable time and heard faint shouts behind them. "They're forming a line," he added. "They think they've trapped us inside."

"It's only God's mercy we got this far," Harry gasped. "But

they'll be finding oot right soon that we're na in that ring, so we'll have to get oot o' here."

Getting to their feet, the two men plunged again into the darkness.

For a week the two men, wet, miserable, and cold at night, lay hidden under rocks or dripping trees, for the rains had come. They moved on only during the deep blackness of the night hours, for these woods were dotted with woodsmen and hunters. They slept fitfully during the day, one keeping watch while the other slept. By now their feet were torn and bleeding, and when their food supply ran out, they lived on raw vegetables filched from farmers' fields and gardens.

Once they had the good fortune to run upon a chicken that had wandered away from a farmyard. Harry pounced on it and wrung its neck. Risking a small fire deep in the woods, they used small sticks to roast the bird over the glowing coals and ate it ravenously. When they had finished, they washed it down with water from a nearby creek and lay back, bellies full for the first time since their escape.

"You know, Gavin," Harry began drowsily, "the more I think of it, the more I think God *did* speak to you. Tellin' us how to make the guns oot o' wood an' all o' that. And everything's gone just right."

"I guess so, Harry. I don't know about things like that." Gavin paused, his eyelids growing heavy. He was weary to the bone, they were still hundreds of miles from home, and he was discouraged. "I guess the Lord will have to do more than that, though, if we're going to get through. We've got a long way to go."

After dark, they continued their journey and finally found themselves on a high cliff overlooking a river. "If I'm rememberin' my geography, right over that river is Switzerland," Harry said. "Come on, let's go across."

They waded down a little brook that ran under a railroad bridge passing directly through town, and finally, half underwater, they were suddenly carried downstream, both men losing their provisions in the swirling current.

Gavin saw that Harry kept going under and realized the man couldn't swim. He threw himself into the fast stream, bloated with the rains of recent days, grabbed Harry by the jacket and hauled him out. Coughing and gagging, Harry lay on the bank for a minute, and then the two dragged themselves onto the shores of Switzerland. They lay there, panting, and Harry said, "Weel, the Guid Lord sent the right mon to get me oot o' prison. I would've drowned if it hadn't been for you, lad."

Gavin was exhausted, but he got up on his knees and strained to see ahead where the murky gray skies were surrendering to the dawn. It was time to move on. Taking a deep breath, he said, "Come on. Let's get out of here. I want to get Germany as far behind me as I can."

The two men got up and staggered into a village where at first they were received with suspicion, a result of the German uniforms they wore. Given a chance to explain, however, they were welcomed royally, fed a hearty meal, and bedded down for the night.

The next morning the Swiss Frontier Guards showed up with a change of clothing for both men and transportation to France.

They arrived in Paris, thin and worn. "Weel, we be parting, Gavin," Harry said, "but let's try to keep in touch." He paused and said quietly, "The Guid Lord was wi' us, Gavin. No other way o' explainin' it."

Gavin took a deep breath, then nodded. "I guess you're right, Harry. Now, let's get back to the war. We've been away too long!"

17

THE WOUNDED EAGLE

O n the last day of Bloody April, Baron Manfred von Richthofen was informed that he would be meeting with Kaiser Wilhelm II. This news, which once would have made the flyer's heart beat faster, now had little effect. He had been saturated by the admiration of the masses but was now convinced that the war could never be won by Germany. Nevertheless, at noon three days later, von Richthofen was presented to Kaiser Wilhelm II, who looked him over as though he were buying a horse.

Wilhelm was a rather good-looking man, with close-cropped gray hair. He was about von Richthofen's height and had a good physique, although he bulged in the middle. The Kaiser congratulated von Richthofen on his fifty-two kills and on his twenty-fifth birthday. "You are a great asset to the fatherland," he said warmly, "and I trust you will double both your kills and your birthdays!" Von Richthofen thanked the Kaiser, replying, "Nothing would make me happier than to return to the front and fight for the fatherland."

Von Richthofen returned to Douai and continued to pursue his goal of shooting down a record number of enemy planes. He was saddened by the deaths of his old flying companions, who were falling rather frequently now. Von Richthofen claimed his fifty-fourth airplane after a flight over the front lines near Ypres on the evening of June 26. It was that same day that he was informed that Jastas 4, 6, 10, and 11 would from that day on constitute *Jagdgeschwader 1*. That was the technical name, but to the world it was called "Richthofen's Flying Circus," partly because of the garish and exotic designs and painting patterns of the airplanes, partly because of their activity. Under von Richthofen's leadership, the squadron immediately became more and more deadly and the Allied pilots dreaded to meet Richthofen's Flying Circus.

On July 6 a report came in that six observation planes were circling German positions. Von Richthofen led Jasta 11 into a clear sky and found British aircraft quickly forming a circle. One of the British airplanes piloted by Captain D. C. Cunnell was about three hundred yards from the all-red Albatros when its gunner, Second Lieutenant A. E. Woodbridge, began shooting at the German plane. Von Richthofen saw that he was under fire but because he was well out of effective range, it didn't worry him. He kept probing for an opening. Woodbridge, who said later that flying observation planes against the Flying Circus was "like sending butterflies out to insult eagles," stood up in his cockpit and kept firing at the red Albatros.

The observation plane and the Albatros then came at one another head-on. Woodbridge continued his steady fire, but the German was now firing back. Woodbridge could see his tracer bullets striking the barrels of the German's machine guns, and knew that there was a person right behind them. Von Richthofen's bullets were also finding their target, however, tearing holes in the observation plane. Then Woodbridge saw the red Albatros suddenly nose down, pass under him, and slip into a spin. It turned over several times, apparently out of control, and fell screaming to earth. Neither Englishman knew that von Richthofen was in the falling plane, but as they circled and watched it drop out of sight, they knew for certain that its pilot was not faking. Woodbridge suspected that he'd hit the German in the head and he was right.

The searing pain that overtook Manfred was more intense than anything he'd ever known, and beyond the pain was a dark fog. When the nausea started, he panicked. *This is how it feels to be shot to your death.*

As the scarlet Albatros spun slowly downward like a dying autumn leaf, Manfred struggled with the controls. It was clear that he was badly hurt, but he did not know how badly. He knew only that he couldn't see. The nerves between his brain and his arms and legs seemed to be paralyzed. He could think, however, and he thought about the Albatros's wings and wondered if they would break off. If they did, the airplane would drop straight down and destruct in a pile of wood, wire, and red linen. The Albatros kept falling and falling, and, for the first time, von Richthofen felt absolutely alone in the air.

Knowing there was no one to come to his aid helped him to fight for his own life. Blindly he reached for the gasoline valve, eased it back, and heard the horrifying sound of silence. The engine had stopped! Tearing off his goggles, he looked toward the sun but saw nothing. His head was wet and sticky, and he guessed that it was blood. The Albatros came out of its spin more than once as it fluttered down, and slowly he was able to pick out black and white shapes. Now he could see the sun as if through dark glasses. The blur in front of him gradually sharpened until he could see the instrument panel and was shocked to find that the altimeter was registering 1,000 feet.

His arms and legs began to respond and he worked them frantically, as he looked for a place to land. He had to land quickly because he knew he was in shock. Hundreds of shell holes passed beneath him. He strained to see ahead, ignoring the blood that ran down his neck, soaking his scarf and the Blue Max at his throat.

Suddenly he made out the shape of a small forest and knew that he was on his own side of the line. And then, before he could react, his airplane tore through telephone wires and made a bounding but right-side-up landing beside a road. Von Richthofen climbed out of the cockpit and stumbled, half unconscious, into some thornbushes. The blinding pain again ricocheted through him as thorns bit into his face and skull. And then the fog that had floated around him settled into a deep ebony blackness, and he knew nothing.

"Did you hear the news? They got the Red Baron!"

Lylah Stuart's heart seemed to stop beating as the fearful words registered, and her legs and arms momentarily went numb. She turned slowly to face her maid, Eileen, who had entered her dressing room reading the headlines of a paper in her hand. "What did you say, Eileen?" she asked, although she had heard clearly enough.

Eileen handed her the paper. Across the top of the page, in bold black letters was the message: "RED BARON SHOT DOWN." "There it is, Miss Lylah," she cried triumphantly. A small, heavyset woman, Eileen had had aspirations to be a star once, but now was content to bask in the reflected glory of one who *did* have her name on the playbills. "They got him! The morning paper tells all about it!"

Lylah took the paper and sitting down at her dressing table, spread it out. The words she had *most* dreaded to see were not there, she thought with relief. The Baron had been shot down, the paper said, but he had only been wounded. She read quickly, noting that the Germans had not released the news immediately, but had waited until they were certain of his condition. Manfred had been slightly wounded in the head, the account read, but would soon be back in the air.

"Let me fix your hair, Miss Lylah," Eileen said, coming up behind her. "You got it all mussed up in that last act."

As Eileen brushed her hair, Lylah thought of the long days and nights she had endured since her last meeting with Manfred. Of all the things that had happened in her life, she least understood this love she had for the German ace. She had had affairs before, two of which she had thought could have become serious. But looking back, she knew they were nothing like what she felt for Manfred von Richthofen. It troubled her more than anything ever had, and she had lost so much weight that the manager had censured her, trying to force her to eat more. But that had not helped.

Eileen finished arranging her hair, and Lylah put on her street clothes. When she was almost ready, a knock came at the door.

"I'll get it, Miss Lylah." The plump maid went to the door and opened it, saying cheerfully, "Why, come in, Mr. Hackett."

When James Hackett entered a room, he seemed to fill it. Now he sat down, tilting his chair back against the wall. "Sorry performance tonight, wasn't it, Lylah?"

The man's dark handsomeness was as potent as ever. Lylah had been a raw teenager when she met him, and since that time when he had lured her into her first youthful affair, she knew he had lured many others. In fact, Lylah knew Hackett better than most and had learned to accept him as he was—a womanizer who would never be any different. He was, however, a competent actor, and she also knew he spoke the truth about the performance.

"I was pretty bad," she admitted ruefully. "I'm sorry, James."

He waved his well-kept hand airily. "Oh, I didn't mean *you*, Lylah. We were *all* terrible. The audience thought so, too." His smooth features fell into a frown and he shook his head. "We're going to have to close the play. But I'd rather close it at the top than let it run down, hadn't you?"

Lylah nodded. She was tired of the play, tired of acting for that matter, and would welcome a break. "Yes, I've been expecting you to say so before this. How long will we go?"

"I'll make the announcement tonight that we'll close in maybe a week." Hackett stood up and stretched wearily. "I'm ready to go home. I like England, but I'd like to see good old New York again. Besides, with this war on, things are getting pretty tight over here, and it's going to be hard to do a successful play with money like it is. Shall I get your ticket when I get mine?"

Lylah shook her head. "No, I think I'll stay on awhile, James. Maybe a few months. I want to rest and this is a good place for it."

"What will you do, Lylah? Look for another part?"

"Oh, no. I know of a little house just outside of London that can be had cheaply enough. I think I'll just go there and . . . plant a garden, maybe. Lean back and take a long rest."

A shrewd man, Hackett had seen the changes that had taken place in Lylah. Now he studied her carefully, thoughtfully. "If I didn't know you better, I'd think you'd fallen for some man. But I suppose I'm wrong."

"You know me pretty well, James," Lylah said quickly. "But I'm really just tired. You go home, and I'll be there as soon as I get rested up."

She knew he did not fully believe her, but he didn't question her, only shrugged. "Well, let's do the best we can this next week. We may want to come back to England someday and put on another play, you know."

After he had gone, Lylah felt a sense of relief. She had not lied about the house; there *was* a small cottage to be leased, and she had money enough saved to stay for a year, if necessary. Thinking about the possibilities, she applied her street makeup mechanically. It would be nice to smell the flowers, she thought. Maybe take long walks. But she knew she was fooling herself; it was not flowers or long walks she needed. It was thoughts of Manfred von Richthofen that had caused her to make the decision to remain in England.

The play closed. Lylah took her last bow, said good-bye to the company, and that same day took up residence in the cottage she had leased. She had not known how really exhausted she was, but for days she did nothing but sleep, take long walks, and let the tranquility of the British countryside calm her. In her solitude she analyzed herself, trying to decide who she was and what she had become. Her childhood seemed a million years in the dim past. She thought of other members of her family who had found God while she herself had found only worldly success . . . and a love that could never bring any real happiness or contentment.

The weeks went by and autumn came, with its cool winds and cold nights. She loved the change of the seasons, however, and had learned to endure and even enjoy the quietness. She read more than she had ever read in her life, finding great enjoyment in the entire works of Charles Dickens, something she had never expected to do. A neighbor who was an avid Shakespearean addict made several trips to Stratford with her, enjoying the performances of the Bard's works.

So the days passed uneventfully. Lylah kept in touch with her family at home, writing long letters but saying nothing about when she was coming home. Her letters to Gavin, however, were the most painful. To him alone did she ever mention von Richthofen and then only briefly. Gavin was as silent as she, but Lylah sensed his resentment since coming back from his stint in the prison camp. *He hates Manfred*, Lylah thought. *Not because he's a German, but because of me.* This thought troubled her deeply. She could not put it away; she had to learn to live with it.

On September 2, she received a letter in Helen's handwriting. She had gotten several letters from Helen—long, newsy, informative letters—and was always glad to hear from her old friend, who was now living back in Germany with her parents. Lylah fixed a cup of tea, put out a couple of biscuits, and sat down to read.

But as soon as she read the first paragraph, all thoughts of food were forgotten. She sat there, riveted, as the words seemed to leap off the page at her:

> I hesitate to put this into a letter, my dearest Lylah, but I must tell you something and there is no other way to get in touch with you. My cousin, who was recently injured, is at home now. I cannot use names, but you will understand who I mean.

I knew you would want to hear, seeing you always had great affection for him.

Lylah understood at once that Helen meant Manfred and that she was writing in code in case the letter might fall into the hands of a censor. With the antiwar fever, anyone suspected of German sympathies could be clapped into prison and kept for a long time until a trial. For one moment she could not seem to think, and then she continued reading:

He was not injured seriously, as you may have heard. Not physically, that is. Since his injury, he has been back at work, but he has not been able to shake off the effects of the accident and so has been sent home to rest and recover before returning.

My dearest Lylah, I have something to ask of you, and yet my heart tells me it would be wrong. Nevertheless, our hearts are often wrong, and we do that which we do not understand, even in ourselves.

My cousin is in a rather pitiful condition. Not only physically, but mentally. Everyone here has tried to help him, but he seems to have fallen into a state of depression—not merely the result of his accident, I think, but for other reasons. He is, as you know, a lonely man, and although he has a family that loves him, still he has not been able to make close friends. The last time I tried to comfort him, something came to me, and I blurted out, "Wouldn't you like to see Lylah, cousin?" His eyes, which had been dull and weary, brightened up, and a rare smile came to his lips. "Yes," he whispered. "If I could see her, I would be happy indeed."

So you know what I ask without my putting it into words. Indeed, I will not put it into words. The decision must be yours. It would be difficult for you to come to Germany now, but as an actress, there might be some justification for your travel, maybe an artistic reason—perhaps the possibility of doing a play. I don't know. In any case, I have, after long searching of my own heart, written this letter. And now, I will leave it to your own heart, my dearest Lylah.

The letter was signed simply, "Helen," and Lylah sat there reading and rereading it until darkness closed around the cottage. Still she sat there, all other thoughts far from her mind. She got up and began to pace, then built a small fire, and sat, gazing into it until long after midnight, seemingly trying to see in the flames some indication of what she should do.

At last she made up her mind. "I will go to Germany!" And the decision somehow banished the strain. She knew it would be difficult; she would have to find some way to cross an enemy border, to travel in an alien land. But she was resourceful, and she had friends who could help.

Early in the morning, she stepped outside in the frigid air and looked at the stars, which shone coldly, like pinpoints of frozen light. "I will probably regret it," she said aloud, "but then I've regretted most things I've done in my life. Still, I must see him!"

"Oh, it's good to be back in Schweidnitz again, Manfred!" Lylah was walking hand in hand with Manfred through the woods, and the crisp air and the seared leaves that had turned glorious shades of red, yellow and orange scored the gray September sky. She had arrived three days earlier, after great difficulties in passing through the German borders, and had caught the wounded flyer completely off guard.

He smiled at her now. "I'm glad you're here, Lylah."

Manfred was vastly different from the man Lylah remembered. He looked thirty-five instead of twenty-five, and had become much quieter. He was prone, she discovered, to fall into long silences and she could not enter that part of his life.

Nevertheless, she had managed to lift his spirits a little, for as Helen had said, "You will be better for him than any medicine those doctors from the hospital have given him."

Helen had also filled Lylah in on some of the details of Manfred's accident. "When he crashed," she had said, "he was thrown into a thornbush, and some of the thorns penetrated his scalp. When they shaved his head, they shaved off parts of the thorns, leaving smaller ones embedded. It was only after Manfred complained of violent headaches that they discovered what had happened and removed them."

"Look!" Lylah exclaimed, pointing suddenly at a stag who had stepped out from behind a thick stand of trees.

Von Richthofen glanced up, then shrugged indifferently. He had not brought his gun; indeed, since coming home, he had said nothing at all about hunting, which puzzled his family.

His father was troubled over the changes in his eldest son. "Something is wrong with Manfred," he told his wife. "He's lost his hunting edge."

Lylah had noticed this as well, but it did not displease her. She stood watching the stag, then reached for Manfred's hand again and squeezed it. "I'm so glad you're better," she said. "I was so worried when I heard you went down. I didn't sleep for days."

He turned to face her and put his arms around her in an unexpected gesture of affection. Lylah was surprised, for his lovemaking was usually confined to the privacy of her room. She was almost certain now that both his parents suspected that the two of them were lovers, though neither of them had ever said a word. Now she surrendered to his embrace, and held him tightly in return.

Always before, he had been the hunter and she, the quarry. But this visit had been different. Lylah had held Manfred in her arms for hours, as if he were a child, and it had been a surprisingly joyful experience for her. She had discovered that, as she suspected, he had given up all hope of winning the war, and now he spoke of losing everything, even Schweidnitz. His titles would mean nothing when Germany lost the war. "I'll probably be out digging potatoes with the rest of the serfs," he had said listlessly.

Now as she held him, she felt a fierce maternal emotion such as she had never known. *I want to protect him*, she thought. *I want to just hold him and keep him safe. He's sick, and tired, but I could make him young again.* She pulled his head down and kissed him with a lingering caress. "Come on. Let's walk some more. I want to see the pond where we saw the wolf last year."

This idyllic interlude lasted for two weeks, and then it ended, as she had known it must. They kissed good-bye at the same railroad station where he had brought her the last time. They had said their farewells in private. Somehow, as he gazed down at her, unable to make a public display, she felt a frightening sense of loss. "Good-bye, my dear," he said quietly. "God be with you."

Manfred had never mentioned God to her before; or at least, not with any certainty. Now she saw the doubt in his eyes. She wanted to hold him, to comfort him. She wanted to do anything except leave, but the conductor was there, waiting for her. She put out her hand, taking Manfred's, which felt very thin and weak. "Good-bye," she whispered. "Good-bye. Oh, God be with you!" Then she turned and stepped aboard the train as it moved slowly away from Germany and away from the only love she had ever known.

18

BLUE DEVILS

Owen Stuart marched through the streets of Paris, a thrill sweeping through him despite his premonitions. The 16th Infantry Regiment, First Division, was following a predetermined parade route through the City of Light, overflowing the sidewalks and leaving only a narrow lane for the marchers.

As the column threaded its way along, its progress was marked by crowds of shouting celebrants: *"Vivent les Americains! Vive Pershing! Vivent les Etats Unis!* Long Live the Americans! Long Live Pershing! Long Live the United States!"

Blizzards of colored paper drifted from the rooftops, and Owen glanced down the line and saw Eddy Castellano grinning broadly. He winked at Owen. "Wait'll I get a chance at some of these babes, Preacher! I'll show you something!"

Owen had noticed that many of the women who stood on the sidelines were weeping and dressed in black, mourning husbands and lovers who would not come home. Old graybeards bared their head as the marchers went by. Of course, many pretty young women forced their way into the ranks, placing wreaths around the necks of the doughboys or blowing kisses from a distance. Soon the column, flower petals covering their campaign hats and single stems poking out of their rifle barrels, began to look more like a moving flower garden than a military formation.

At last the column reached its destination, Picpus Cemetery, resting place of so many French heroes. As the doughboys stood at attention, Blackjack Pershing and his staff walked to the marble tomb of the Marquis de Lafayette. Pershing placed a wreath of pink and white roses on the tomb, mumbled a few words in halting French, and stepped back. Captain Charles Thanton, his friend, now moved forward. Groping for words, Thanton snapped a salute and cried, "*Nous voila Lafayette!*"—*Lafayette, we are here!*

After the speeches were made and the Yanks were marched back to a barracks just outside of Paris, Eddy began to pester Sergeant Mack Stone. "Hey, Sarge! What about leaves? I mean, after all, we're war heroes, aren't we?"

Stone glared at Eddy with a baleful eye. "Just you wait 'til you win a few medals, Castellano. Then we'll see about that leave."

"What comes next, Sergeant?" Owen asked. "Will we be going up pretty soon?"

Stone shook his head. "Naw," he said, "you boys ain't tough enough for that yet. First we make soldiers out of you."

"Aw, c'mon, Sarge," Kayo Pulaski said. "I can handle these Krauts right now. Just let me at 'em!"

An eager cry went up from most of the men around, but Stone was adamant. "You'll get your shot, don't worry. But first you're gonna have to learn a little something more about this here trench warfare. It ain't like huntin' pheasants in Texas!"

"Well," Owen said as Stone and the others moved away, "we better do something. The year 1917 has been a bad one for the Allies."

Owen was right about that. In the early spring, the revolution in Russia had broken out and the Communists had overthrown the government. In April, only days after the Congress had declared war, French General Robert Nivelle lost a massive attack which was crushed by German artillery and machine guns, costing Nivelle 120,000 men in five days. And the British had fared still worse. Late in July they began an all-out attack at Passchendaele Ridge, in Belgium. When the attack ground to a halt weeks later, they had gained fifty square miles, at a cost of 340,000 men. During the fall the Germans and the Austrians broke through the Italian lines at Caporetto, killing and wounding 600,000 men.

Mack Stone had become a close friend of Owen Stuart, and knew Stuart was a man to be relied upon. Often the two had had long talks. "Yeah, you're right, Owen. All these setbacks just about wiped out the fightin' spirit. You know, I heard the other day that sometimes the British troops march to battle now, braying like sheep: '*Baah . . . baah . . . baah.*' And the word is, the French troops have just downright mutinied. Tens of thousands of what they call *Poilus* just simply refuse to fight or to take orders."

"It's pretty bad," Owen agreed. The two of them had been walking around the barracks when they came upon civilians who had gotten into the camp. Some were young women who had come to view the soldiers. Owen watched carefully as Eddy had his arm draped around one young woman's waist and was talking to her in an animated fashion. "From what I hear everybody's counting on us to make a difference."

"I guess so," Stone said, and there was a mournful look in his light blue eyes. "These birds don't know what they're runnin' into. They squalled like babies over some of the training they got back home. When they see what's comin' over here, they'll do more than squall!"

"When do we pull out? Have you heard yet?"

"Tomorrow," Stone replied, then he left Owen to pull one of the recruits away from a young woman who was beginning to find his attentions a little embarrassing.

The next day the men were hustled into freight cars marked: "*Chevaux—8 Hommes 40*—Eight Horses or Forty Men." The cars stank of horse sweat and manure. Odd lumps of manure remained in the dark corners. During the next two days and nights, the smell got into everything—into the straw they slept on, into the food they ate, into their clothes and hair. Their destination was the Vosges, a low range of mountains in east central France near the Swiss border, an hour's drive from the war zone.

As soon as the men got there, they were thrown into a regimen of training that became a struggle for survival. Living conditions were deliberately made difficult to prepare them for the trenches. They lived not in barracks, but in barns, stables, haylofts, and unused buildings that dotted the countryside. Their quarters, damp and stinking, were impossible to keep clean. The food was awful. Lunch, the day's main meal, usually consisted of a strip of fatty bacon with hardtack biscuits, a boiled potato, and a mug full of weak coffee. Tyler Ashland lost some of his chubbiness, and once, staring down at his plate, said, "I'd like to put my head in my mama's garbage can for thirty minutes and get a square meal!"

The French were amazed at the doughboys, whose mouths always seemed to be full of a rubbery glob called "gum." And they watched in disbelief as the Yanks bathed daily in streams, no matter what the weather. Europeans—country folk—seldom bathed more than once a week. But astonishment soon gave way to affection. The Yanks, generally generous and kindhearted, made friends easily. They were like overgrown Boy Scouts, and it wasn't uncommon to see an off-duty soldier drawing water or carrying firewood for an aging peasant.

In the meantime they spent their time learning something about the art of war. One day Sergeant Stone lined them all up and barked, "Okay. You're gonna learn a little something. Got some French crack troops comin' to give you a little lesson in how this here war's got to be fought."

Kayo Pulaski said sullenly, "I don't need no Frogs tellin' me how to fight!"

"Yeah? Well, we'll just see how well you make out with these fellows." Stone smiled slightly.

Two days later a unit of French troops arrived to complete the training of the First Division. Dressed in light blue uniforms and helmets and known as "The Blue Devils," they were the best troops in the French Army. Many of the American boys were skeptical, but they soon found out that every man was as tough as piano wire, and each was a veteran of countless battles.

They discovered very quickly just how tough these French troops were, for on the very first forced march over rugged terrain, and weighed down by fifty-pound packs, the Frenchmen walked the legs off the strongest doughboy. By the time they had staggered back to camp, all the Americans were winded. Some of them, in fact, had fallen, and the trucks had to be sent out to bring them back.

Sergeant Stone stopped near where Kayo Pulaski had slumped down, without even enough strength to remove his pack. His face was pasty pale. "Well, these Frenchmen ain't much, are they, Kayo?" Stone said mildly. "Not tough like us, huh?" Pulaski gave him a glassy-eyed stare, dropped his eyes, and said nothing.

The French troops were amused at what they considered the softness of the American troops. The Frenchmen thought nothing of picking up a rifle by the bayonet tip, using only two fingers. A favorite trick was to juggle three hand grenades, nasty things, with a habit of exploding if bumped the wrong way.

The Blue Devils put the Americans through their paces until the doughboys could take a weapon apart, clean it, and reassemble it blindfolded. Trench warfare was made as realistic as possible without actually killing the other team. The Blue Devils and the American troops would start digging toward each other from opposite ends of a field, singing as they worked. The Yanks often sang a new song, soon to become the favorite of the AEF. There were countless verses of the song, which could be heard floating over the terrain:

Oh, mademoiselle from Armentieres, parlez-vous,
Oh, mademoiselle from Armentieres, parlez-vous,
The mademoiselle from Armentieres,
She hasn't been kissed in forty years,
Hinky-dinky, parlez-vous?

When the diggers met, the team that had covered the least territory was given a few hours of extra practice.

And there was no more drilling with wooden guns. The doughboys fired live ammunition and they fired it often. As heavy machine guns unloaded five hundred bullets a minute over their heads, they wiggled under barbed wire entanglements. Some of the men died during these exercises.

Training was difficult, but it hardened the Big Red One, as the First Division was called. Later on, they would look back with gratitude on those days in training with the Blue Devils. In a letter home, Owen wrote: *It was this period that made us tough. We got tough and stayed tough. By the time we were ready to go into the trenches we were so mean we would've fought our own grandmothers!*

Finally Owen's unit completed its training and was sent to the front. To condition them for being near the enemy, they were assigned to a quiet sector. Not every part of the western front was an active battlefield. Both sides, in certain regions, had a gentlemen's agreement to "live and let live." Trenches were deep and well drained, about as comfortable as trenches can be. If patrols met in the night, the men kept moving, pretending the other fellows didn't exist. Bombardments always came over at the same time each day, to give the enemy time to take cover. At least war was endurable here . . . until the Americans arrived.

But Owen's crowd saw things differently. As newcomers to the war, they had none of the caution of the European veterans. War was a novelty to them—an exciting game with deadly toys. They hadn't learned to appreciate the fighting skills of the German soldier.

At nightfall on November 1, 1917, Eddy Castellano and Kayo Pulaski were on night duty in the trench. They had been warned by the French sergeant not to shoot at everything, but at two o'clock in the morning, when Eddy saw movement, he whispered, "Hey, look, Kayo! There's a bunch of them Krauts!"

Pulaski peered through the darkness and grinned. "You're right! Let's give it to 'em, Eddy!" The two men immediately opened fire with their rifles, yelling and whooping when they saw at least two of the men go down.

The French sergeant appeared at once, cursing them soundly. But Eddy said rashly, "Shut up, Frog! I'm here to shoot Germans, and I'm shootin' 'em wherever I can find 'em!"

The two men wasted no time in boasting about the number of Germans they had killed. But at nightfall the next evening, a 250-man company of *Stosstruppen*—the German version of the Blue Devils—filed into the trenches near where the First lay crouched in its trench. At 3:00 A.M., gunflashes lit the eastern sky. Tons of explosives left fountains of earth and stone leaping skyward.

"Barrage! Barrage!" the noncoms shouted, and the shells began to fall in the pattern of a hollow square, or box. The box crept slowly forward, deliberately searching out its objective. At last it fell around Owen's platoon, and fifty-eight men were isolated within the walls of death. There was no escape. It was Pulaski who began screaming in fear.

Eddy, however, slapped him across the mouth. "Shut up, Stupid! You can dish it out, but you can't take it!"

Owen pulled Tyler Ashland into a small crevice when he found the boy just standing, paralyzed, staring blankly across the lines. The air was filled with the sound of bursting shells, and Owen was sure that the next volley would wipe out the whole platoon.

Suddenly the explosions on one side of the box stopped, and gray-uniformed men, wearing helmets that came down over their ears and necks came rushing in.

"There they are! The Krauts!" yelled Eddy Castellano, jumping to his feet. "C'mon, you guys! Let's get 'em!"

Most of the men leapt up and ran to meet the wave of German soldiers, who dashed toward them, bayonets extended. There was a clash as Eddy engaged the leader. He slipped the German's bayonet aside, reversed his own rifle, and smashed the face of the storm trooper with the butt. As the man fell helplessly, Eddy ran his bayonet through the man's body, screaming as he did so.

The rest of the men, seeing this, entered the fray. The Germans were amazed at their reception. Instead of panicking, as they had expected, the outnumbered Yanks fought back with everything that came to hand—rifles, grenades, knives, chunks of wood, fists.

Back at the edge of the box, Owen found he could not move. The screams of the dying smote his ears, and he knew his job was to join those who had already entered the fight. He tried to get to his feet, but for some reason discovered that he could not. He could not think clearly, but one thing was certain. He himself was not afraid of death, but for the first time Owen was actually seeing men die, and it shocked him in a way he had not expected. He knelt beside Ashland, who made no attempt to get up, but covered his head with his hands.

I've got to go! Owen thought. *I've got to help the men!* Yet still he could not seem to move. The idea of killing a man was one thing; he thought he had prepared himself for that. But as he watched Eddy cutting down the storm troopers, screaming and yelling, and the others joining in, he suddenly could not bear the thought of taking another human life. He thought he had settled this long ago, but thought, *An idea is one thing! But the reality of blood and death is something else again!*

Finally he forced himself to his feet and moved slowly toward the battle zone, the racket beginning to subside as the Germans retreated. Reaching one of the wounded German soldiers who looked up in fear, no doubt expecting to be bayoneted or shot, Owen moved by, leaving the man in shock that his life had been spared.

By this time the doughboys had reached a place of safety and were laying down heavy fire. "Okay, you guys!" Eddy shouted. "Let 'em go!"

As the last of the retreating Germans disappeared from sight, Eddy came back and found Owen standing in front of the wounded man. Seeing that the German was alive, he lifted his bayonet. Owen caught the barrel of the gun, and the two men struggled for a while.

Ripping his rifle out of Owen's grasp, Eddy spat out, "What's the matter with you? Kill that Kraut!"

"He's a prisoner," Owen said. "We can't kill him."

There was battle madness in Castellano's eyes. "Maybe *you* can't!" He stopped suddenly, regarding Owen with distrust. "Where were *you* when all the fightin' was goin' on? Last I saw, you were in a trench holdin' that baby's hand!"

Owen could not answer even though he could see that the others were waiting to see what he had to say. Eddy studied him, then a sneer curled his thin lips. "I knew you couldn't be any good . . . no preacher is!" He whirled away and said, "C'mon you guys! Let's get these prisoners back! And Tom's taken a pretty bad cut. He needs to get back to the field hospital."

As the men scurried around, moving out the wounded and rounding up the prisoners, Owen stood looking on helplessly. As they left, he found himself completely alone. His hands were trembling. In the eyes of his friends and fellow soldiers, he had just been labeled a coward. Even worse, perhaps, was the nagging doubt in his own mind. Was he a coward? He tried to tell himself that he had never really been afraid. As a fighter, he had fought some of the toughest men in the country, but he knew that wasn't the same thing.

Slowly he retraced his steps, and when he finally got back to headquarters, he noticed that even Sergeant Stone was studying him with a peculiar look in his light blue eyes. "Pretty rough out there, Owen?" he asked. When Owen did not answer, he said, "Well, sometimes the first gunfire gives a man buck fever. You just sort of freeze up." He slapped Owen on the back. "You'll be okay, Owen. Next time. Next time you'll show 'em!"

But as Owen turned away, he knew it wasn't over, and he was not at all sure that next time would be any different.

19

A BITTER CHRISTMAS

The year 1917 had been a bitter time for both the Allies and Germany. Now, as Christmas came, cold, hard weather fell over France.

Gavin walked the streets of Paris, the snow-laden skies overhead reflecting the mood that had controlled him for weeks. Walking past the Lycee Henri Quatre, the ancient church of Saint-Etienne-du-Mont, and the windswept Place du Pantadon, he cut in for shelter to the right and finally came out on Boulevard St. Michel. Hunching his shoulders against the wind, he pushed on until he came to a café he had visited before.

He entered, hung up his raincoat and his cap on the rack, and looked around eagerly. Seeing Heather seated in a booth beside the window, he rushed over to join her and put out his hand to grasp hers.

"Oh! Your hand's cold!" she said. "Sit down and thaw out."

Slipping into the booth, Gavin rested his elbows on the table, cupped his chin, and stared at her. She was so fresh-looking that he was reminded of the flowers he had seen in her garden the previous spring. Her lips were pink, her cheeks were aglow with good health, and her shiny ash-blond hair fell over her shoulders in a silken cascade. "You look beautiful," he said simply.

A flush came to her cheeks and she smiled. "You soldiers are all alike! Always trying to get next to a girl." And then, because she knew he was not that sort, she reached for him again. "Here, let me warm your hands." He extended them eagerly, and she enclosed them in her own, which were small with long tapering fingers.

As the feeling returned, he turned one of her hands over and stared down at it. "Blisters!" he said and grinned up at her, cocking his head to one side. "I didn't know royalty ever got blisters."

"I've told you a thousand times I'm not royalty! I'm not even nobility! When Father dies, the title will go, and we'll be just people again. That's all we are now, really."

Just then the waitress appeared and asked for their order. Gavin said, "You order for me. I still don't speak enough French to ask for a hamburger." He listened as Heather gave the order, and when the waitress was gone, he said, "I'm glad you've come back. It's been a cold, lonely place without you."

She had gone to England when winter had come, but a week earlier he had received a handwritten note from her, saying: *I'm back in Paris. Come to me when you can.* He had written her a note telling her to meet him here. Now he stared at her almost hungrily, and as the numbness in his body thawed, so did his spirit.

"Tell me about your family," he said at last. "I want to visit them if I ever get across to England."

"Father would love that," she said. "He's been practicing up to beat you at chess."

As Heather began to speak of her family, a feeling of nostalgia overcame Gavin—a longing for his own home and family. And when she had finished, he leaned back and sighed. "I wish there were no war. I wish the thing would end today." His tone was laced with bitterness. "I guess I'm fed up. A thing like this eats at a man."

"I know," Heather said softly. "I've seen it destroy some men . . . and some women, too."

"What are you doing here? Are you going back to nursing at the hospital?"

"Yes. I felt so useless at home with nothing to do but roll

bandages and be a night air raid warden. It's hard at the hospital, of course, seeing the young men . . . and the older ones, too . . . come in all shot to pieces. But at least it's something I can do."

They spoke of the war. Gavin told her what he had been doing, leaving out much of it. Finally the waitress brought the food, and both of them fell on it and ate hungrily. After the meal, they sat for a long time, drinking the strong black coffee.

It was getting late and Heather said, "We can't stay here forever. Let's go to my place."

He paid the bill, helped her on with her coat, then moved across the room and picked up his own. Fixing his hat firmly in place, he said, "We'd better take a cab. It's cold out there."

"No, let's walk. The exercise is good. Besides," she added, "I think it's going to snow." As they walked along she continued, "I hope it does snow. I love it!"

"So do I. Makes me think of wintertime back in Arkansas. Even though we didn't have warm enough clothes, all of us kids would get out and romp around in it. When it got deep enough, we'd make snowballs and build snowmen." He paused, a faraway look in his eye. "That was a good time."

"Do you hear from your people often?"

"Oh, sure," he said. "They were real worried while I was in prison camp." He grinned then and took her arm. "You know what they ask about most though? You. My younger brothers and sisters want to know if I'll be Lord Gavin when I come home . . . if I marry you." He had mentioned marriage almost unconsciously, and now that it was out, he was surprised himself.

But it was no surprise to Heather. Though she knew Gavin would likely go back to America after the war, and she, to England to care for her aging parents, Heather *had* thought about what it would be like to be married to Gavin. She shouldn't have, she knew. Gavin was a man who hadn't found

God, and she could never give herself to a man like that. But she had thought of it.

"The man I marry will definitely be a lord," she said, her eyes twinkling merrily. He turned to look at her and thought he had never seen anything more beautiful. "You know, the Bible says that Sarah called Abraham 'lord.' So if I married you, you'd be Lord Gavin to me."

"Sounds like a winner." Gavin grinned. "But I don't have a castle to put you in. Best I could offer would be a share-cropper's shack back in the woods of Arkansas."

"That would be fine," she said. "When you love some-one," she said softly, "wherever you are . . . wherever you live . . . is a castle."

They walked along in silence after that. Her words had caught his attention. Gavin had not had much experience with women. But this woman had worked her way into his spirit and, now that the word *marriage* had been mentioned, he was considering it seriously, though too shy to pursue the subject. Mirroring her thoughts, he pondered the obstacles that loomed as high as the Alps between them. Well, he would just have to be satisfied with the time they had together. No-body knew what tomorrow would bring anyway.

They arrived at Heather's room, which was not really an apartment, but had a small table and stove. She made tea while he stood at the window, looking down at the white stripes that were beginning to form on the street.

"It's snowing now," he said. "We'll go out later and have a snowball fight."

She moved efficiently, as she did everything, and when the tea was ready, they sat down at the tiny table in the two hard-backed chairs and talked for a long time.

Later they did go out. The snow was only an inch deep, but they managed to make a few snowballs which they tossed at each other. Soon they were laughing like children, and when Heather caught Gavin full in the mouth with a hard-packed snowball, it made his eyes blink with pain. She came running up to him, gasping, "Oh, Gavin, I'm sorry! I didn't mean to hurt you!" and she put her fingers on his lips.

"Back home when I got hurt," he said, "Mama would kiss the place and make it well."

She hesitated, then reached up, pulled his head down, and kissed him lightly on the lips. "There," she said, "it's all well now." She smiled and again touched his lips lightly with her fingertips. "Come now. No more snowballs. Let's go inside and have some more tea."

His time with Heather was an oasis of peace, for Gavin's work at the aerodrome had grown deadly serious. What he had not told her, and what he had tried to forget during their times together, was that as he fought the Germans, he was beginning to see in each face the enemy Baron Manfred von Richthofen.

He knew it was foolish, and that his fellow pilots thought he was going over the edge. "It won't do to hate these fellas too much, Gavin," Bill Thaw warned him. "A man who's full of hate can't think. And that's the sort of thing that gets a guy killed."

Gavin had agreed, but as the weeks went by and his score had increased to twenty-eight kills, he found himself more and more in the grip of a bitterness and a hatred he could not shake off. Part of this was due to the letters he received from his sister Lylah. Though they could not meet, she wrote regularly, and the last letter or two had been rather strange and even rather mysterious. He knew Lylah. He knew her speech, he knew how she thought, and those letters had been vague and obscure.

She's hiding something, he thought. He longed to go to her. *She'd never tell anything if she didn't want to; hot pincers couldn't drag it out of her. But she might tell me if I could just see her.* The dread continued to grow and he could not purge himself of it.

He knew that von Richthofen had apparently recovered from his wounds and was again knocking British and French planes out of the sky diligently. He knew also that, according to the papers, the Baron had been sent to visit Russia to fight on the eastern front; and with the knowledge that von Richthofen was out of his life, Gavin had calmed down and found some peace. But as soon as the Flying Circus received their leader back on the western front and von Richthofen began shooting down planes, the bitterness came upon him like a black cloud again.

Like Raoul Lufbery, Gavin now began taking off on his free hours and hunting Germans to shoot down on lone patrols. Several of the pilots tried to warn him. "Lufbery can do it, but he'll die sooner or later. And so will you when you're outnumbered someday."

But Gavin paid no heed. He took off one cold February morning, knowing he shouldn't. The weather was so cold that motor oil had to be heated over an open fire, poured hurriedly into the reservoir, and the motor started immediately to keep it from freezing again. On top of that, when Gavin climbed to an altitude of 15,000 feet, he began to stiffen up almost at once, the subzero temperature penetrating to the very marrow of his bones. Despite three or four pairs of gloves, his fingers coiled around the stick were almost paralyzed within five minutes. He had to force them open in order to restore circulation. His feet became twin lumps of ice, rigid and unfeeling. His body was wracked with shooting pain. Even his eyeballs and teeth smarted and burned, and his icy scalp contracted until it felt as if his skull would explode in a shower of bones. He flew for two hours but saw nothing, no sign of an enemy plane. Then he turned and headed back for his own lines.

But just as he leveled off on his turn, making a sharp wingover, three German Albatrosses dropped on him, all of them from slightly different directions and with all guns blazing. Gavin threw his Nieuport into a quick turn. For the next few minutes he exercised every bit of skill at his command trying to lose the three planes. Finally he succeeded in hid-

ing behind a cloud, but his hands were shaking—not entirely
from cold—as he realized how close he was to being killed.
His ancient Nieuport would have no chance at all against the
late-model Albatroses.

He stayed in the clouds as long as he could, then dropped
down to take a look around and saw nothing. But even as he
dropped lower, he heard the stutter of guns. Panic-stricken,
he turned and saw one of the German planes right behind
him, both machine guns flaming. Soon his whole tail assembly was torn to pieces, and two of the wires controlling his
elevator and rudder were hanging by one strand. There were
holes in the wings and the fuselage, and he knew that, short
of a miracle, he would not escape the German.

Once again he tried a half roll, a dive, a spin, but still the
German hung on. While Gavin was maneuvering to shake off
his enemy, an image was forming in Gavin's mind. He did not
have time to think about it; it just happened. The plane that
was shooting him to pieces was primarily painted black and
yellow. But as he fought, somehow in his mind, it began to
change color, and he began to see a scarlet Fokker triplane.
In his imagination, the pilot at the controls was Manfred
von Richthofen. The image filled him with hatred like a powerful drug and he wrenched his ancient plane around the skies
so violently that he almost tore the wings off. In doing so, the
pilot shot past him and suddenly Gavin saw his enemy ahead
of him. The Albatros was much faster so he had only time for
one burst and as soon as he fired it, he saw holes appear on
the cowling and at once the white fumes issued that indicated
a gas leak. When that happened, he knew it was the end. Either the plane would burst into flames, burning the pilot to
death, or all the gas would miraculously leak out, and the
plane would have to crash to the earth.

Gavin followed on the enemy's trail and finally observed
the crash-landing in a field far from the front lines. Circling
overhead, he saw the pilot struggle out and stumble away
from the downed plane. Gavin wheeled his Nieuport around

and dove straight at the figure of the pilot. When he was only a few hundred yards away, the German halted, turned, and lifted his hands in surrender.

To Gavin, it was the face of Manfred von Richthofen. His hands closed on the trigger, and as the Nieuport roared downward at full speed, the figure of the German loomed even larger. Hatred boiled over in Gavin's mind. As he thought of Lylah and the German who had defiled her, he squeezed the trigger.

The tracers plowed the ground in front of the Nieuport, raising the dust and stitching the German from stomach to chest. Driven backward, the pilot crashed to the ground and lay still. Then Gavin pulled the stick back sharply, sending the plane into a steep climb. Even as he did, revulsion for himself at what he had done swept over him. He knew, suddenly, that he had performed the most cowardly act of his life, one he had sworn he would never commit. Shaken and sick, he began to retch, and it was all he could do to keep the plane in the air.

Gavin never knew how he made it back to the base. When he got out of the plane, the mechanics came running over. "Where are you hit, Lieutenant?" one of them cried.

"Leave me alone," Gavin whispered. "Get away from me."

The mechanics watched as he walked stiffly away and then turned to inspect the plane. "They got him pretty good," one of them said. "But I don't see any holes around the cockpit."

"What's wrong with him, then? I never saw him like this before."

"Neither have I, but something's got into him. He looks just like Thompson did. Remember? He was a great pilot until he nearly got killed that time over Ypres. Never was any good after that." He looked at the retreating figure of Lieutenant Gavin Stuart and shook his head. "I hope the lieutenant don't turn yellow like he did. He's too good a man for that."

Gavin did not go to the barracks. He knew that with one look at his face, his fellow pilots would know something was wrong. Instead, he turned and walked toward a clump of trees that sheltered one side of the aerodrome. It had been left, probably through someone's mistake, for more than one pilot had nearly crashed into them.

He entered the grove and leaned with his back against a tree, and the trembling began. He shook all over. Finally he slumped down in the snow, and buried his face in his arms. There Gavin Stuart cried as he had not cried since he had been a very small boy.

Part 4

ACTION OF THE TIGER

20

THE LAST CHANCE

No one knew better than General Erich Ludendorff that, unless some miracle occurred, his country was doomed to defeat. Early on a cold day in 1918, he sat staring at the maps, a feeling of hopelessness apparent in the slump of his shoulders. Although the man standing beside him, Kaiser Wilhelm, did not have the military knowledge to understand the reasons why, he knew well that the war was not going as he had planned. The two men had been up for hours, exploring every possibility, and both of them were gloomy and unsmiling.

Finally Ludendorff smashed the map with his large fist. "It's the Americans! There's no way to stop them or slow them down! We'll be facing a million of them by year's end! They can't win the war by themselves, but they'll tip the odds against us."

Kaiser Wilhelm had no choice but to agree. He was a man who had been brought up to believe that Germany could never lose, but he was well aware of the staggering losses his nation had sustained. Still, he had a shred of the vision that had caused him to lead his country into the war. "Yes, that's true, General. But now that Communism is broken, we'll have all the valuable lands in the East! And we'll have many divisions to ship from the eastern front to the western front."

"Yes, sir." Ludendorff nodded. "But how do we play our hand?" He stared at the map and then began to speak in a professorial tone. "There are two choices—both very promising and both very dangerous. First, we can play it safe. We can dig into such strong positions that the Allies may lose hope and come to the conference table."

Kaiser Wilhelm shook his head. "We would have to return all of the territory we've won in France and Belgium. But," he added thoughtfully, "we might keep Alsace-Lorraine."

"Yes, we could do that. The only problem is that the Allies might decide to dig in and tie our armies down while Allied shipping does its work. The blockade," he said grimly, "has been more effective than we thought it might be. Hunger has Berlin gripped in an iron cage."

"What is our other choice?"

Ludendorff hesitated. He had thought long over this, agonized over it, and had counted well the cost. Still, there was no other way. "The other choice," he said slowly, "is to launch an all-out offensive to win the war before the Americans get here in power. And this, too, is dangerous—very dangerous!"

Kaiser Wilhelm stared at Ludendorff. "What would happen if the offensive failed?" the Kaiser asked, almost timidly.

Ludendorff stared at the map, then turned a pair of iron-gray eyes on his leader. "Then," he snapped, "Germany must perish!"

The result of that meeting was that Germany would throw the iron dice and gamble everything on a quick victory. Win or lose, the war would be over by the close of 1918.

The buildup of one of the largest and most secret operations in history went on throughout the winter, although Ludendorff kept his preparations under a tight lid of secrecy. Roads, railroad lines, and airfields were built all along the front so as not to arouse Allied suspicions about one area in particular. Troop trains and air convoys moved constantly, but only at night, with the lights out. Troops were marched along back roads in darkness, hiding in forests in the daylight when Allied patrols were most active. Artillery positions were dug in at night and camouflaged. Mountains of shells were accumulated and placed near the guns under camouflage nets.

Before dawn on Thursday, March 21, 1918, preparations were complete. Three and a half million Germans, many trained as storm troopers, crouched in their trenches, waiting. A ground fog, promising to hide the assault wave during their dash across no-man's-land, shrouded most of the western front.

Men stared tensely as the luminous dials of their wristwatches ticked off the minutes. Shells were slid into the firing chambers of cannons with a soft swish. Silently the long gun muzzles were raised, moved from side to side, then steadied. Artillerymen stuffed wads of cotton into their ears.

At exactly 4:40 A.M., Ludendorff unleashed the heaviest bombardment in the history of the world. Six thousand cannon opened fire at once along the Somme and continued firing for five hours without letup. The British replied with twenty-five hundred guns of their own.

The ground trembled as if in an earthquake, and the effect was paralyzing. Shells, hundreds of them at a time, landed in straight rows, five yards apart, the edges of their craters touching to form series of neat figure-eights. Command posts vanished into smoking shell holes. Trenches caved in on the inhabitants, becoming mass graves. Ammunition dumps roared and crackled like strings of firecrackers. Barbed-wire entanglements were shredded.

At 10:00 A.M., whistles blew and waves of storm troopers, led by flamethrowers, ran from their trenches. Minutes later, they were attacking the British in their trenches, shouting, shooting, slashing through the Somme defenses. Behind them, the regular infantry surged forward to mop up and destroy any remaining strong points. For the first time since the war began, an advance was measured not in yards, but in miles. Within three days the Germans had jabbed a salient— a wedge—forty miles into the Allied front.

Ludendorff and the High Command were jubilant. Their

gamble, so it seemed, had paid off, as the Allied line collapsed, and seemed almost at the point of being broken.

"Now we shall see!" General Ludendorff exclaimed exultantly. "We will teach them what the German soldier can do!"

The members of the Lafayette Escadrille had looked forward with eager anticipation to the time when they would be attached to an American Air Force in France. However, when that time finally came, it was a day of bitter disappointment for all of them.

Bill Thaw was enthusiastic about the news that at last the slow-moving brass hats were sending a delegation of high-rankers to examine the Lafayette Escadrille pilots. "Just a matter of time now, chaps!" he said, beaming. "We'll be flying under the Stars and Stripes before you know it!"

The examiners came, and all of the pilots took physical examinations, including urinalysis, blood tests, and a long series of rather ridiculous physical demonstrations. And the next day, when the men were called together, a chastened Bill Thaw stood up to say, "Bad news. The Board decided that most of us are not fit enough to make an aviator."

A cry of amazement went up from all the flyers, but it was Gavin who said, "Why, that's the craziest thing I ever heard! We shoot down Germans every day!"

"I know. All I'm doing is passing along what they said," Thaw explained mournfully. Then he mentioned Dud Hill's blind eye, his own bad vision and crippled arm, Lufbery's inability to walk a crack backwards, Dolan's tonsils, Hank Jones's flat feet.

"So we're just a bunch of broken-down, crippled misfits?" Genet exclaimed in disgust. "How do they think we score kills if we're in such bad shape?"

"I don't know," Thaw said. "But I'm afraid it's bad news. And I might as well be honest with you. It's the end of the Lafayette Escadrille."

In December, the Escadrille had been ordered to the field

of La Noblette, and all the pilots presented their applications to the French Army for release, expecting to receive immediate commissions into the American Army. Their releases were officially granted, but no commissions arrived.

From December 1, 1917, through February 18, 1918, the men flew as civilians in the uniform of the French Army, and during this time, Gavin Stuart had had his hardest struggle. He watched as the Escadrille was broken up. Thaw and Lufbery were given commissions in the American force. There was a sprinkling of captaincies, but most of the flyers received commissions as first and second lieutenants and were placed under the commands of newly arrived "ninety-day wonders," men who were full of ambition and disciplinary theories, but had never fired a gun at the enemy.

During this time, Gavin grew very close to Edmund Genet, the smallest and softest-speaking of all the Escadrille flyers, and a direct descendant of the Edmund Genet who was the ambassador the French Revolutionary Government sent to the United States in 1792. Genet did not have the appearance of a fighting man, but Gavin had come to know him very well. When the Lafayette Escadrille had begun breaking up, the two of them talked it over seriously.

"You're not happy about going into the American Army, are you Gavin?" Genet asked.

"No. None of us are going to get a fair break. They're gonna put their own guys in whatever planes are available."

Edmund, a chunky little figure, topped by a thatch of short-cropped blond hair above the round, pink-cheeked face of an infant, pondered this for a moment. He still didn't look a day over sixteen, with his peach-bloom complexion showing little traces of ever having met a razor, and his stubby little nose. There was always a constant expression of pleased surprise at the wonders of the world in the wide-set blue eyes. Now he said with some excitement, "Let's join the French Air Force, Gavin! They'll be glad to have us. I've already talked to some of the commanders. We can stay together."

Gavin made his decision at once. "Sure! That's the thing to do!"

And so it was that on February 18, when the Lafayette Escadrille passed out of existence as a French unit, lock, stock and barrel, and became the 103rd Pursuit Squadron of the American Air Service, Edmund Genet and Gavin Stuart were the only two members who did not join. Instead, they were attached to a French unit under the command of Lieutenant Claude Demond, a tall distinguished man with black eyes and hair to match.

The French unit was short of flyers, so the two young men were immediately thrown into the battle that was raging on the ground beneath—Ludendorff's last offensive—that was eating up men from both armies.

Every day was a life-and-death struggle, and Gavin grew very close to young Edmund, who became almost like a younger brother to him. They covered the bare walls of their room with corrugated cardboard strips, and Edmund painted vivid imaginative scenes of air combats between French and German planes all over the place.

"Don't we see enough fighting?" Gavin complained one day as he lay back on his bunk. He was staring at Edmund, who was busy painting a French Spad.

Edmund grinned at him and threw down his brush. "All right. Let's go see if we can find anything to eat. I'm hungry." He was always hungry, and it was a miracle to Gavin that such a small young fellow could stuff so many groceries down his throat and never gain an ounce.

"Thanks, but I don't want anything."

Edmund took one quick look at Gavin and came over and sat on his friend's bunk, facing him. "What's wrong? You haven't been yourself, not for a long time now." Edmund, young as he was, had lived under intense pressure and had come to recognize the symptoms of a pilot who was ready to crack under the strain. He had been concerned about his roommate, of whom he had grown genuinely fond. "Maybe it's time for you to ask for a leave."

Gavin leaned his head back against the wall and shut his eyes. He had never told anyone about the "vision" he had had, and it sat heavily on him, weighing him down. Night after night he had relived the scene. He was tempted to unload to his young friend. But he knew that Edmund would never understand such a thing, so he merely passed it off. "No, I'm okay. Just tired, I guess."

Frowning, Edmund decided not to push the matter. "Well," he said, "according to the word, one of us can have a leave day after tomorrow, and the other, next week. Tell you what. You take the first one, go scout out whatever can be found. I'll stay here and keep the war going." He smiled gently at his friend. "We'll be all right, Gavin. God hasn't brought us this far to let us be killed."

But he was wrong. The next day when Genet went up for the second probe of the day—he had already done an early two-hour morning show—he seemed so bushed that Gavin warned, "You've done enough, Edmund. Let someone else go."

Tired as he was, Genet's eyes were twinkling as he said, "No, I'll do it. You old fellows go take your nap, and let us youngsters take care of the fighting."

Gavin looked down at his young friend, desperately wishing that Genet would listen to him. He put his hand on the younger man's shoulder. "You're tired. That's when you make mistakes. Let Demond do it. You and I can take an early break."

But Genet only laughed. "You're a regular mother hen! Don't worry about me. I'll be all right." He hesitated for a moment, then clapped Gavin on the shoulder. "It's you and me. I never had a brother . . . until now. So we'll take care of each other. But this'll be easy . . . a piece of cake."

Genet turned and climbed into his plane and soon disappeared behind a cloud in the sky. Gavin slowly turned away, and for the rest of the afternoon walked around the field, idly killing time. But he became more agitated as the afternoon wore on, for Genet's mission was not supposed to have taken so long. When Lieutenant Demond came looking for him, Gavin knew at once that something was wrong. The lieutenant's face was fixed and his mouth was set in a bitter line.

"Is it Edmund?" Gavin asked, dreading the answer.

"Yes. I'm afraid so. An observer just got back and saw him go down not far from our lines. . . ." Demond hesitated. Knowing of the friendship between the two men, he said gently, "He's dead, Gavin . . . hit by a shell splinter, we think. He fell with his motor going full speed. The observers who got to the spot say he never had a chance." He shook his head sadly. "Poor little dreamer! And what a fine young man! He gave his life for his ideals."

Gavin felt as if the earth had been yanked out from under him. He had not realized until that moment how much it had meant to have such a friend, a dear friend. Now he had nobody. He was all alone.

He looked at Lieutenant Demond with eyes that were curiously empty. "They won't stop, will they?" he asked in a hollow voice. "Not until all of us are dead." Then he turned and walked away, his back stiff and rigid.

Demond stared after him with compassion in his eyes, but there was nothing he could say. Nothing anyone could say at a time like this. No matter how many times it happened, it was always the same. You lost a buddy and were filled with a great hollowness, and then you had to fill that void the best you could. He knew that he had a bitter and angry man on his hands in the figure of Gavin Stuart.

Gavin flew automatically, performing with unusual competence. He had shut everything out of his mind except flying, and nothing about his demeanor betrayed the bitterness that was clawing at him. His close friends were gone; he knew few of the French aviators beyond the surface meetings they had day by day. He became known as a man unapproachable, and soon his fellow pilots gave up all efforts at friendship.

Getting out of his aircraft one day, Gavin walked toward the barracks and was surprised to find his brother Amos waiting for him. "Why, Amos!" he said. "I didn't know you were in Europe!"

Amos hesitated, then said, "I just got here a week ago. I'll be here until the Armistice. Covering it all."

A bitter smile touched Gavin's lips. "That'll never come."

"Why, of course it will. It's just a matter of time. The German push is running down, and the war will soon be over." Amos was shocked at the coldness that seemed to freeze his brother's eyes. This was not the man he remembered. "You need time out from all of this," he said, waving toward the airfield. "You're getting stale. Come along."

"Where to?"

"Into Paris. I've wrangled you a short leave—two days. We've got things to talk about."

The two men left the airfield and later that evening found themselves sitting in a café in Paris. All afternoon Gavin had been aware that something was troubling Amos. Finally, after nibbling at his meal, he asked his brother, "What's wrong? Anything wrong at home, Amos? I haven't had a letter for a while."

Amos shook his head. "No, everything's fine at home. But," he paused and grew very still, studying Gavin's face before continuing, "I went to England first. I've been with Lylah for the past week."

Something in his expression alarmed Gavin. "What's wrong, Amos? Is she sick? I've been worried about her. Her letters, they're not the same as they used to be. She's not telling me something. What is it?" he demanded.

"I wish I had something good to report, but I don't." Amos hesitated, dropped his head, and tried to think of a gentle way to break the news. But there was no way to make what he had to say pleasant. He looked up. "She's pregnant. The child will be born sometime in June." He saw Gavin's face harden and said, "She told me who the father is. I guess you already know, though, don't you?"

"Von Richthofen."

The bare mention of the name dropped from the lips of Gavin Stuart like acid, and Amos realized how bitter his brother was. He sighed. "I can't understand it, Gavin. And she can't, either. It's not easy for her."

"It's easy enough for her to carry on an affair with him," Gavin said sarcastically. "And now this." His face looked drawn and old as he stared at Amos.

Amos began to speak. He told Gavin how shocked he had been, how much this had hurt him, how it had hurt everybody, but most of all he spoke of how much it had hurt Lylah, with no hope of happiness. "They could never marry, even if they wanted to," he said. "The war, despite what you think, is about over. Germany is going down. But even if it weren't, those two could never be happy together." He sat in grim silence, bonded with his brother by the enormity of what had happened.

Finally Gavin spoke up. "Nothing seems to work. Everything's falling to pieces. I just don't care anymore, Amos."

The weariness and pain in Gavin's voice prompted Amos to say, "You can't quit. God's still in heaven. He hasn't forgotten us."

But Gavin did not respond. He sat there quietly, and nothing Amos said could rouse him. Finally, in desperation, Amos said, "Look, I can't talk to you. But you need to talk to somebody. Owen, maybe. He knows you and loves you as much as I do. It would help if you'd talk to him. We can get him a leave."

"No, I don't want to talk to Owen." But even as Gavin spoke, an idea came to him, and he sat nursing the thought. "There *is* someone I want to see, though. Would you mind if I didn't spend the rest of my leave with you, Amos?"

Amos shook his head. He knew something of the young

woman Gavin had been seeing; he knew, at least, that she was a Christian, and he suspected that Gavin would go to her. "No, of course not. You go ahead."

"I will, then. Don't worry about me. I'm fine."

But as the two men left the café—Gavin to the right and Amos in the other direction—the older man thought, *He's in a bad way. He won't make it if something doesn't turn around for him.*

As Gavin trudged along, however, he found himself reluctant to see Heather. He walked for hours in the cold weather, unaware of how much time was passing.

It was quite late when he found himself standing in front of the rooming house where Heather lived. He hesitated briefly and then went inside and on up the stairs to her door. Lifting his hand, he knocked, and almost at once the door opened.

"Why, Gavin!" Heather said. "I had no idea . . . come in! You look half frozen!"

Gavin took the chair she indicated, and for a while the two chatted about trivial things. But Heather was sharply aware that Gavin was hurting, and eventually she drew it out of him. Once he began to open up, he told her more than he dreamed he would. He told her about the breaking up of the Lafayette Escadrille and finally, with great pain, he told her about the loss of Edmund Genet. Then he skirted around the subject of his sister, finally saying, "And Lylah's in terrible trouble."

Heather listened, looking into his haunted eyes, feeling his pain. She let him talk until he ran down. Then slowly she began to speak of peace. "Peace is only in Jesus," she said quietly. "This war . . . all the horrors, the death, the suffering—that's the world, Gavin. It will always be like that . . . on this earth. We all have our pain and our struggles, and we all must die. But in Jesus Christ, there's a world that's better than all of this."

Gavin listened as she spoke, and when she picked up a Bible and began to read verse after verse, strangely enough he did not rebel. His spirit had been dead and flat and empty for years. But somehow the words rang in his mind and in his heart. She talked on and on, and Gavin listened, occasionally asking a question.

Finally he said, "I don't know what to do. I just don't know."

Somehow Heather knew what to do. She put her hands on his and leaned forward, gazing into his face. "I know what it's like to be so shattered you can't even pray. So I'm going to pray for you, and I'm going to pray that you receive mercy . . ." She hesitated, adding in a whisper, "and that you will *grant* mercy."

As she began to pray, Gavin thought of his hatred for von Richthofen. *I can never forgive, never!* But on and on she prayed softly, never raising her voice. Sometimes she paused as though listening, and there was silence in the room. But there was healing in that silence for Gavin Stuart and there was healing in her soft words.

Finally she paused, looking at him intently. "You may not feel a thing, Gavin, but *I* feel something. I know God has heard, and you are going to be found by Jesus Christ . . . and you are going to find him. I know it, because God has told me in my spirit."

On his two-day leave, Gavin and Heather talked about many things, but avoided discussing what had happened in her room. But when Gavin was telling her good-bye, he said, "Something has happened to me, Heather. I don't know what, but I know it's something important."

Heather's eyes filled with tears. She reached up, put her arms around him and clung to him, her cheek resting against his. "I know, my dear, I know! And I know you'll come back to me. God has promised me that. Only be careful . . . be very careful."

He left and she went back to her room. All the way, she was praying, *God, he needs you so much and he's so confused. Give him the peace that only you can give.*

21

DEATH OF A KNIGHT

The streets of Berlin were filled with people who looked hungry and whose clothes were old and patched. The flying officer walking along the street attracted little attention, although now and then someone would cast a puzzled glance at him, wondering what a pilot of the German Air Force was doing in the city at this time. Most of them knew that the great push—Germany's one chance to win the war—had begun.

The officer turned into a shop at the corner of Linden and New Wilhelm and stared at a picture mounted on the wall. The caption beneath it read: "Baron von Richthofen—The Red Battle Flyer."

"Some people say I look like him," said the officer to the old man who came up to wait on him. He gave the proprietor an intense look. "Do you think I do?"

The man put on his glasses, studied the painting, then turned an appraising eye on the pilot. "Hardly!" he said angrily. "And how dare you presume to compare yourself to him! That's Baron von Richthofen, the Red Battle Flyer!" He gave Manfred a long contemptuous look and stalked off.

Turning away, von Richthofen made up his mind. He did not like the painting, had never liked it. Outside, he made his way to a cabstand and, after a quick trip to the airport, climbed into his crimson triplane and flew back to the airfield. He had taken time off to be interviewed by a few of the newspapers and magazines—something he did not like to do—and one particular interview had almost gotten out of control. One of the reporters had mentioned that Allied pilots were going after ground soldiers, strafing them, and had stated with some contempt, "That's the kind of thing that sort will do, isn't that right, Captain?"

Von Richthofen had almost blurted out, "That's what we're *all* doing!" Instead, he had merely shrugged the question aside. Actually, he found strafing ground troops terrifying, much more dangerous, in his mind, than a dogfight. He preferred the three dimensions of maneuvering room—not the two of low-level flying—and would rather have two or three pilots chasing him than have to fly through what seemed like a wall of rifle and machine gun fire.

When he arrived at the aerodrome, he made his way to his quarters, threw off his coat, and sat down wearily in the leather-covered chair where he did most of his work. The light was fading outside, and a gloominess had settled over the airfield that communicated itself to the pilot. Glancing up, he saw his reflection in a small mirror fastened over the washbasin. Carefully he examined the tired-looking features, the glazed, lifeless eyes. What would become of him? Of Germany?

He looked around the room at his trophies. He had a roomful of them at Schweidnitz, but here were his cavalry sabre, a stirrup cut nearly in half by shrapnel, Lanoe Hawker's machine gun, a bust of the Kaiser. Mounted on the wall was a box containing some of his decorations. Too many to display at one time. Besides the Blue Max, he held the Bulgarian Order of Military Valor, the Iron Cross (First Class), Hungarian Order of the Holy Crown, Order of the Royal House of Oldenburg, Turkish Star of Gallipoli, Order of the House of Saxony, Cross for the Faithful Services, Imperial Order of the Iron Cross, and many others.

Seeing these badges of distinguished service, Manfred knew he had achieved everything he had set out to do. It was gratifying to be considered a superb leader on the ground as well as in the air, an excellent judge of pilots. Yet despite all this recognition, he had no one to share his fame. He had never been a good mixer and certainly was not a partygoer. Indeed, he lived a solitary life, spending his time alone or playing with his dog, Moritz.

The time had long passed when he could think with delight of his medals and trophies. Now dark thoughts that had begun months ago closed in. He was a man who lived for action, and his philosophy was very simply to be a good soldier and a good son. This he felt he had done.

"Why isn't it working, then?" he asked himself aloud. The sound of his own voice startled him, and he got up and walked over to look out the window. On the ground a crew of mechanics serviced the planes, while a flight of Albatrosses came in for a landing, and another crew swarmed over them, inspecting for leaks or tears. Manfred watched as the weary pilots climbed out and walked stiff-legged into headquarters.

He went back, sat down at the desk, and began sorting through the mail that had backed up while he was in Berlin. A large part of it, he knew by sight, were fan letters from silly girls all over Germany. He tossed them to one side, knowing that he could delegate their reply to someone else. Those that contained official seals he opened, read through rapidly, made decisions, and placed them into a small stack to be answered.

There were several personal letters—a rare one from his father containing a message of congratulations on his latest kill. His father went on to ask if he planned to come home. The hunting was good, and he would be most welcome.

The letter from his mother was more personal. It was a long letter. The only strange thing about it was her frequent mention of the American girl. This seemed odd to von Richthofen, for his mother had never liked the girls he had seen socially. They had been few enough, in any case, and none of them had ever pleased her. But she seemed to know that Manfred had more than a casual interest in this woman. She mentioned several times how much she had enjoyed Lylah's last visit, and hoped that when the war was over, she could come back again. Puzzled, von Richthofen studied the letter and put it to one side.

The last one was from his cousin Helen. He recognized her handwriting on the envelope. But when he opened it, he was shocked to find only a brief scribbled note from Helen, saying:

> Manfred,
>   This letter came for you, sealed, and I have not opened it.
> There was a note with it, asking that it be forwarded, which
> I do now.

Manfred saw at a glance that the enclosed letter was from Lylah and wondered what this could mean. He had received many letters from her, but had replied only twice. Since he did not feel safe writing to her, he had not signed his name. In fact he had even asked a friend in Switzerland to mail them for him.

He picked up the sealed envelope, slit it open with his finger, and took out a single sheet of paper. Leaning back, he held the letter up to the fading light that came through the single window.

> My dear, I have been unable to make up my mind what to do.
> For weeks now I have kept my secret and no one is here that
> I can trust to go to for advice. Perhaps you may have guessed.
> I am expecting a child.

A sudden trembling overtook Manfred, and he had to put the letter down for a moment. He could not identify the emotion that came over him. He only knew that he had never had an affair with a woman like this one before, and what he felt for her was the closest thing to love he had ever known. But the idea of a child frightened him. He sat there as the gray light fell over his shoulder, trying desperately to put his thoughts in order. Then he lifted the letter and read the rest.

I have not known whether to tell you this or not. Your life is so hard, so dangerous! I would not add anything to your burden. Up until now, I had decided that you would never know about our child, that I would go back to America and never contact you again. We both know how impossible it is for us ever to be together, but for the last week I have felt such a thing would be unfair to you.

You understand I am not asking for help. I know you, better than anyone else, I think, and I understand how unlikely it is that you would be able or even want to have a family, especially an American wife. So I am not asking for that. But I finally have decided that you have the right to know that there will be a child. He will not have your name . . . that is impossible, of course.

There is nothing else I can say, except that you are the only man I have ever loved. And though I am not in any position to ask God for favors, every night I ask him to spare your life.

I love you,
Lylah

Von Richthofen rose abruptly, walked again to the window and stared blindly out. A child. He and Lylah would have a child! But what did that mean to his life? The difficulties yawned under his feet like a huge chasm. He was German; she was American. She was his enemy . . . at least in the eyes of the world. The war, he knew, was lost, and he did not think for one moment that they could live in a defeated Germany, where everything was falling to pieces already.

The gray light waned, and still he stood there as though fixed in place. When the sky gave up its last bit of reflected light, he turned and walked back to the table. He picked up the letter, folded it carefully, put it in his wallet, and left his quarters.

For long hours Manfred walked, avoiding friends and companions. When he finally came back and went to bed, he lay there all night, a bitterness and unhappiness such as he had never known, filling him.

Yet, he was amazed to find, in the middle of this unhappiness, a note of joy. He had longed to carry on the von Richthofen line, but there had been little chance of that. Now as he lay sleepless, he wondered when and how he could see Lylah again, and what he would say when he did see her.

Ludendorff's German advance plodded on. While down on the ground men were dying by the hundreds of thousands, the Richthofen wing swept the skies overhead. His men had noticed that their leader was pale and appeared to be ill, but it had not affected his flying. On March 24, he led twenty-five of his scouts into a fight with ten S.E. 5's of the 56th Squadron and shot one of them down for his group's only kill of the day. The following day he shot down a bomb-carrying Camel and claimed his sixty-ninth kill on the 26th. Later, on another patrol, he brought down his seventieth. To his squadron mates and certainly to the German public, which was following his exploits with avid interest, von Richthofen seemed like his old self. No one except his adjutant knew of the sealed envelope labeled: "Should I Not Return, Open."

On March 27, von Richthofen downed three airplanes, his best day since the previous April. Scores of British craft fell before the blazing guns of his wing; in fact, half of the R.A.F. squadron losses that month were claimed by von Richthofen's Circus. Kill number seventy-seven, a Camel, went down on April 6, and von Richthofen said to one of his squadron leaders, "Strange, the last ten I shot down all burned, and the one I got today also burned."

His squadron leader nodded. "If I had my choice, I'd leap to death on the ground rather than risk burning alive."

The German advance on Amiens kept the squadron in the center of action. Below, on the ground, the German army moved forward at a rapid pace, and General Haig, the British Field Marshal, entered what became a famous order of the day: "There is no other course open to us but to fight it out!

Every position must be held to the last man: there must be no retirement. With our backs to the wall, and believing in the justice of our cause, each one of us must fight on to the end. The safety of our homes and the freedom of mankind alike depend upon the conduct of each one of us at this critical moment."

The rain continued through Saturday morning, April 20. Later that evening, in only three minutes, von Richthofen shot down his seventy-ninth and eightieth kills—two Camels. He went to bed that night, having officially killed seventy-seven men in the air, wounding nineteen and making prisoners of ten.

On Sunday morning, April 21, a mist spilled off the Somme and draped itself around the base of Jasta 11. Von Richthofen slept until almost eight o'clock, which he always liked to do when possible. He then got up and ate a light breakfast. When he stepped out of his quarters, he was greeted by a military band, sent by a local division commander to serenade him in honor of his eightieth kill.

Von Richthofen shook his head and walked away. He was hardly in the mood for a celebration. Instead, he paced the aerodrome, watching the sky and thinking of the mission that was to come. He was thinking also of the letter from Lylah. He had never received news that had shaken him more. Over and over he had explored the possibilities, but had concluded that there was no way he would ever have the child in his arms.

Glancing up, he noticed Richard Wenzel, a young pilot who had come to Jasta 11 only a month before, playing with his dog Moritz. Von Richthofen whistled to the dog, and Moritz came walking slowly up to his master, dragging a heavy wooden field chock tied to his tail, which the pilot had put there. Manfred laughed, removed the wooden bar, and embraced the grateful dog.

At that moment, he heard a faint sound and whirled to see a man snapping a picture. At once von Richthofen's mood grew grim. He did not like having his picture taken before a flight. Always he thought of Boelcke, whose photograph had been taken before his last flight; and although von Richthofen was not especially superstitious, this had stayed with him.

He turned and took the dog back, telling Wenzel to make sure he was fed. "I'll take him for a walk as soon as I get back," he said.

Walking over to where his triplane was being warmed up, von Richthofen climbed inside and led the others into a westward climb. They were speeded on their way by a rare wind blowing toward the Allied lines. It would take them farther than they wanted to go.

Twenty-five miles from the German base was a Royal Air Force base at Bertangles. It was the same airfield where, less than a year and a half before, Lanoe Hawker had taken off to meet his death in his duel with Baron von Richthofen.

At 9:35 A.M., the flight of Squadron 209, led by Captain Roy Brown of Toronto, Canada, lifted off. One of its Camel pilots, Second Lieutenant Wilfred May, was on his first combat flight. May was an old friend and schoolmate of Brown's, so the flight leader advised him to avoid engaging the enemy until he could get some experience under his belt. May resolved to do as he was told, for he knew Brown was in no mood to be crossed.

Brown was not a particularly fine pilot. He had joined the Royal Naval Service in 1915 and had spent most of 1916 in the hospital. In 1917, he had been assigned to a naval squadron. When the Royal Air Force came into being, he joined 209 Royal Air Force Squadron and was given the army rank of Captain. He had joined the Navy, was now in the Air Force, and did not really like either. In fact, he hated war. He had seen many of his companions killed, had seen others' nerves shattered so that they had to be removed from active duty.

His flight was followed into the air five minutes after it left by a second flight of five Camels, and five minutes after that by a third flight of five. After the mission was accomplished, Brown waved some of his pilots back and kept eight of them for one more swing. He led them northeast toward the Somme, which was exactly where von Richthofen was headed on his westward patrol, but at a different altitude.

The Germans attacked an observation plane and in doing so, attracted antiaircraft fire which began exploding around them. Brown, alerted by the explosions, turned toward the triplanes and the Camels caught three Fokkers, sending one of them down at once. The controlled attack degenerated into a typical free-for-all with planes kiting all over the sky.

May tried hard to obey Brown's warning. He circled at 12,000 feet while the battle went on under him, and even let a triplane pass close by without chasing it. Then when a second triplane flew by, he could restrain himself no longer. He pushed the stick forward and followed the German right into the thick of the fight, firing all the while and finally hitting his target.

The German turned away and May did not chase him. Instead, he simply fired a long burst at another enemy plane who flew in front of him. Then both guns jammed, and he decided to get out as quickly as he could. Dropping out of the swarm, May leveled off and headed toward home. He did not see the red triplane that was following him.

But Brown saw it. He saw May streak for the aerodrome and he saw the red triplane go into a long dive behind the fleeing Camel.

Hearing the machine gun fire, May glanced back and saw the Fokker. He put his Camel into a shallow dive but could not shake off the red airplane. By that time, Brown was above the German and close enough for a burst of machine gun fire. All three airplanes were now within two hundred feet of the ground and following the Somme above a low ridge a half-mile east of Vaux-sur-Somme.

Brown fired a short burst close behind the triplane and saw its pilot turn as if wondering who had hit him and then slump as bullets ripped maroon linen. After he got off the burst, Brown's dive brought him behind and below the triplane and, when he pulled up, May and the German were gone.

Down below, on the ridge, Australian riflemen and machine gunners fired a volley of bullets at the Fokker as it passed, now a hundred yards behind May and still closing. They could see pieces breaking off as their bullets hit. The Fokker also came under fire from an antiaircraft battery controlled by Sergeant Alfred G. Franklyn.

A cheer went up from the ground crews as the red triplane swerved, seemed to hesitate, and then started down. Staggering and slipping, it glided a few hundred yards before crashing just north of the road, a mile and a half from the ridge.

The Fokker's landing gear was smashed and the gas tank had collapsed. But everything else was intact when the first soldiers reached the aircraft. Inside, they found the pilot, his nose and jaw smashed on impact with the machine gun butts in front of him, and they realized he was dead even before they unstrapped him and laid his body beside the airplane. The body was searched, and the sergeant who pulled out the identification papers stared wildly, then shouted, "We got 'im! We got the bloody Red Baron!"

Germans with telescopes had followed it all, and a telephone message describing the scene was relayed to the command post.

Half an hour later the triplane had been picked almost clean. Patches of maroon linen were distributed throughout the area. And the body of Baron Manfred von Richthofen was tied to a sheet of corrugated steel and dragged, as if on a sled, down the far side of the ridge. Eyes open, he stared up blindly into the sky where overhead, the air war continued. But it was over for him. The Red Baron, the Knight of Germany, was dead.

22

"HE'LL BE A STUART!"

C avin caught the gaily painted Albatros in his gun sight, waited until he was less than a hundred feet away, then squeezed the trigger. The tracers reached out and stitched a pattern of holes from the nose of the German aircraft all the way to the tail. The Albatros shuddered, and a trail of white vapor began to pour out of the engine.

He followed closely as the plane nosed downward, but was aware that enemy pilots often pretended to be disabled, only to drop to ground level and slip away. This time, however, Gavin could see the aviator climbing out of the cockpit. Carefully he pulled back on the stick so that the body of the struggling man was in the cross hairs of his sight. His finger touched the trigger.

I can't do it, he thought suddenly. *What would it prove? He's going out of it.*

The German crawled over the side of the falling Albatros and threw himself into space. At first Gavin thought he was doing what many others had done—leaving a doomed airplane before it burst into flames or destroyed itself by crashing into the ground. Then he saw the envelope of white silk fluttering open and knew that his enemy was wearing a parachute.

Gavin made a graceful turn, glanced over his shoulder, and saw that the rest of the Germans were fleeing for home, pursued by members of his own flight. He was alone in the sky. He made another turn, watching the Albatros as it plummeted downward.

Circling the parachute closely, Gavin could see the pilot's features. He was a young man, Gavin saw, no more than eighteen or so, and terror was written on his face.

He expects me to shoot him as he goes down, Gavin thought.

He circled again and this time, just to test himself, made a run straight at the pilot. The parachutist held up his hands as if to ward off the bullets he knew were to follow. Unexpectedly, Gavin banked his plane, waved at the young German, and climbed into the sky. In the last moments of his turn, Gavin had time to see the amazed look on the face of the downed pilot and then the wild waving of both hands as the young man signaled his gratitude.

Gavin flew back to the aerodrome, pondering what had just happened, knowing that if this had occurred before the time of prayer he'd had with Heather, he would have killed the pilot without compunction. Ever since that evening in Paris, though, he had known something was different. He still flew, of course, and had downed two more planes since that time. But both times he had seen the pilots crash-land and struggle free. He felt free from the fierce desire to kill that had consumed him before.

As he approached the landing field, another thought came to him. *What if that had been von Richthofen?* he thought. *Would that have been different? Would I have filled him full of bullets for what he did to my sister?* His wheels touched down and he glided to a stop, performing his movements automatically, still lost in his thoughts.

When Gavin got out of the airplane, he saw the mechanics and some of the pilots milling around, talking excitedly among themselves. As he approached, Luf came running toward him. "Gavin! Gavin! He iss down!"

Gavin stared at the stocky pilot. "Who's down?"

"Von Richthofen! He hass been shot down!" Luf exclaimed. "Jus' got da news!"

Gavin felt as he had once when he had fallen into a river of icy water in the dead of winter. The shock of that plunge had taken his breath away. Again the world seemed to stop. His head was filled with confused thoughts and there was a lightness in his chest. "Is he . . . finished?" He was not aware that he had whispered the question.

"Vat? Oh, yess, he vas dead, vee heerd. No more Ret Baron!"

Gavin knew then that he was a changed man. For there was in his heart no thrill, none of the vicious feelings of revenge that had driven him a few weeks earlier. Now he could think of Baron von Richthofen as merely a human being of great talent whose life had been tragically cut short. True, he had been an enemy, but Gavin could no longer hate the enemy. He had seen too many of their young men die, just as his own friends had died. He had come to understand that it was not their wills, but the wills of generals and politicians and civilizations that pitted men against each other in battle, and wasted lives. Von Richthofen had simply obeyed his country's call and now he was dead like so many others.

"Come on, ve vill go hear all de news," Luf was saying.

But Gavin shook his head. "No, I've got something to do." He walked off, ignoring Luf's wondering gaze, and went at once to his superior officer, requesting a leave.

"A leave?" Demond stared at him blankly. "What do you mean, a leave? The Germans are sweeping ahead faster than we can hold them! We need every pilot we can get!"

"I know that, sir. But I have a personal problem. If I don't get some time off, I'm afraid I may have some sort of breakdown."

Demond still stared blankly, uncertain if Gavin was serious. The flyers were always pulling his leg, although Stuart had never been guilty of such. He considered Gavin and tried to assemble in his mind the number of pilots, the number of planes, the missions, and also tried to assess whether Gavin was telling the truth. He *had* seen men go almost insane under the pressures of combat, and he tried to keep a close watch on his pilots to relieve them when the strain grew too great.

Finally he asked, "How long do you need?"

Gavin sighed, relieved that the lieutenant was willing to grant his request. "I don't know. I need to go to England."

"England, eh? Well, that might work out," Demond said, his eyes brightening. "There's a wing of new fighters ready at the factory, and we've worked out an arrangement with the British that they furnish us with some of their planes. Perhaps you could bring one of them back. Could you do that? And would a week be enough?"

"Oh, yes, sir! Fine, sir!" Gavin said quickly.

Demond nodded. "I will make out your orders and give you clearance. One week! Be sure to be back by then."

The French decided to hold a grand funeral for the Red Baron, and having made plans to honor the dead German flyer, they overdid the thing somewhat. The entire burial was like some ritual scene from a Gilbert and Sullivan operetta.

The body was shrouded and laid on the back of a military truck bedded deep with flowers. A stiff, correct escort of six officers from the R.A.F.'s 209th Squadron walked in solemn parade step behind the slow-paced lorry. Then the body was removed to a hangar and prepared for burial. The Red Baron lay in state during the day, and hundreds of British officers and rank-and-file ground crews filed past their dead enemy.

He lay untouched, or so it seemed, for the bullet that killed him had not marred his features. A post-mortem showed a slug had entered one chest wall, banged against the spine, gone through the heart, and moved on to the other chest wall.

Actual burial took place in French soil with full military protocol, the coffin carried by six air captains wearing black armbands. Wreaths were piled on the coffin. One was lettered "To Our Gallant And Worthy Foe."

At the cemetery gate, riflemen formed two lines facing each other, and the captains carried the flower-draped coffin past the riflemen standing at salute position. The entire procession was led by a well-fed, neatly-robed chaplain of the Church of England, prayer book in hand. An orderly crowd of soldiers and a few townspeople gathered around the best surviving hemlock tree, where the chaplain recited the Church of England ritual for the dead. A eulogy was said. Then the coffin was lowered into the fresh grave. A crisp officer's bark stiffened the firing party into position and three times, in paced order, volleys were pressed off. Finally, a bugler stepped forward, wet his lips, and blew "The Last Post."

A cross cut from a four-bladed propeller was banged into the soil above von Richthofen's head. At the center of the propeller was a round plate, with the inscription: CAVALRY CAPTAIN MANFRED BARON VON RICHTHOFEN, AGE 26, KILLED IN ACTION, AERIAL COMBAT, 21ST APRIL 1918.

On the evening of April 22, a Royal Air Force pilot risked being shot down to drop a photograph of von Richthofen's grave into the German aerodrome at Capi. Accompanying the photograph was this note:

To The German Flying Corps Rittmeister:
    Baron Manfred von Richthofen was killed in aerial combat on April 21, 1918. He was buried with full military honors.

The Richthofen wing felt an overwhelming loss at the death of their leader. When the letter he had given to his adjutant weeks before was opened, it turned out to be, as expected, his aeronautical Last Will and Testament:

Should I not return from a flight, Lieutenant Rhinehart, Jasta 6, is to command the Geschwader.
                                        Richthofen, Rittmeister

Rhinehart was killed not too long afterward, and the new commander of the von Richthofen wing was a pilot named Goering. He was a mediocre pilot, to be sure, but one who was a gifted orator. This would not be the last Germany, or the world, would hear of Hermann Goering.

★   ★   ★

The tap at the door was so light that Lylah scarcely heard it. She had been dozing in her chair, the book she had been reading having dropped to the floor. The tap came again, louder, more insistent, and she gave a start, blinked her eyes, then rose heavily from her chair. Even beneath the loose-fitting blue dressing gown, her pregnancy was evident as she moved awkwardly across the floor. She put her hand on the knob and hesitated, wondering who could be coming at this time of night. It was after midnight, she saw by the clock. "Yes? Who is it?"

"It's me . . . Gavin."

"Gavin!" Lylah slipped the bolt and opened the door. "What are you doing here?"

Gavin put his arms around his sister, hugging her carefully. "I came to see *you*, of course." Holding her at arm's length, he studied Lylah's face, seeing the circles under her eyes, the lines of fatigue bracketing her mouth. "Aren't you going to invite me in?"

"Of course, come on in," she said. "I was just so surprised." She pulled him inside, shut the door, then went over to turn on the lamp. "Can I get you something to eat?"

"No, I just got off the ship and came here as soon as I could. I could use some coffee, though." He didn't really want anything, but he did hope to break the stiffness that existed between them.

He sat down on a chair in the small kitchen and watched while she measured the coffee and put the water on to boil. As she did so, he said, "I came over to take a plane back. We've ordered a whole flight of new English fighter planes and somebody has to fly them over. The last bunch was flown by amateurs, and two of them landed in the drink."

"I'm so glad you came," Lylah said. She set out two cups,

a bowl of sugar, and some fresh cream, and then poured the steaming coffee into the cups and sat down across from him.

Gavin stirred two spoonfuls of sugar into his coffee and a large dollop of cream. Lifting the cup to his lips, he took a sip of the steaming brew. "This is really good. The French don't know how to make coffee, not like we do."

For a few moments, they sat in companionable silence.

"I have several letters from home," Lylah said at last. "You'll want to read them."

"Are things all right?"

"It seems so. Logan got married." She allowed a slight smile to curve her full lips. "A widow with three children."

Gavin blinked, then laughed out loud and slapped the table. "What's he going to do with them? Logan never could stand kids! How old are they?"

"Three, six, and eight, I think. Two girls and a boy. And he's wild about them—or so he says in his letter—and I think he got a good wife, too. At least Dad says so."

She went on, filling him in on news of home, reading him excerpts from letters, and the time went by. But both of them spoke guardedly, with none of the ease they had always known before, and finally Lylah said abruptly, "Just why did you come, Gavin?" Her eyes were filled with apprehension and her lips were drawn tight. She was as beautiful as always, but there was a tense, wary look in her face now. For weeks she had wondered how she would face any of her family, and now one of them was here and she expected a sermon, at the very least, about her wicked ways.

"I came to get an airplane. . . ." Gavin said, then broke off sharply. "Well, that's part of the reason. But that was just an excuse to come and see you." He put out his hand and grabbed hers, stroking it tenderly. When he looked up, she could see the care and the concern in his expression. "I'm worried about you, Sis. I just had to come."

Tears stung Lylah's eyes. She squeezed his hand, then lifted it to her lips and kissed it. He felt her hot tears falling on the back of it. "Oh, Gavin, Gavin!" she whispered brokenly, but she could say no more because her heart was too full. Here was one of her own blood, and he had not come to convict her.

"I want to tell you something," he said quietly. "Then you can tell me what you want to, or nothing at all. . . ."

He began his story, explaining that, when he had found out about her affair with von Richthofen, he had been blind with rage, and consumed with hatred and bitterness. Her eyes were fixed on him, and his own gaze did not waver as he confessed, "I would've killed him in a minute. In fact, it would have been a joy!"

And then Gavin went on to tell her about the young English nurse. "I've written you about Heather in my letters, but you'll have to meet her. There's nobody like her. . . ." He told her how Heather had prayed with him, and that, since that moment, he had not felt hatred for anybody. Then he described his last mission when he had refused to shoot down the parachutist. "On my way home, I wondered, 'What if that had been von Richthofen? Would I have let him go?'" Gavin smiled. "That's when I knew for sure that something had really happened in my heart. I've found God is the only way to say it, I guess. Owen's always talking about it, and now I know what it's like."

Gavin stared down at his hands for a moment, then looked up in wonderment. "I had no hatred for the man. When I heard he was dead, Lylah . . . as God is my witness . . . I felt nothing but grief."

Lylah sat looking at him, mulling over his words. She got up suddenly and took a few cumbersome steps around the room, then came over to him, and he stood to meet her, cradling her in his arms until she began to weep.

She was a strong woman, Gavin knew, always had been. Strong to the point of rebellion at times. A woman who had to have her own way and would do whatever she must to get the desires of her heart. All his life Gavin had seen this in his sister, and now he saw that she had become entangled in something she could not handle.

"Gavin, what will I do?" she whispered, trembling. She was sobbing convulsively, and he held her until the spell of weeping was over and she took a handkerchief from her pocket and wiped her eyes. Then she looked up at him. "They tried to get me to get rid of it . . . my baby," she said. A fierce light came into her eyes and she lifted her chin defiantly. "But I wouldn't do it. I could never do a thing like that . . . never!"

"I'm glad," Gavin said simply. "You did the right thing."

"But what comes now?" she asked. She bit her lip and with a piteous look in her eyes, she said, "He'll be no one's child. I can't give him his father's name. The von Richthofens wouldn't want him. He'll be no one's child."

And then Gavin Stuart proved that he was a man of understanding and compassion.

Putting his hand on his sister's slight shoulders, Gavin smiled broadly. "He'll be a Stuart, Lylah," he said.

His words were like a lifeline to her. It had been as if she were drowning, going down, down, with no hope. Suddenly her brother's statement brought life, and hope, and joy.

Lylah smiled back at him. "Yes. Yes, Gavin, that's what he'll be." She whispered again the phrase he had used. "He'll be a Stuart."

23

BATTLE CRY

Lieutenant Colonel Theodore Roosevelt, Jr. was sitting down with his back to a tree, eating beans out of a tin plate. He hadn't shaved for several days, and his tin hat was pulled down almost over his eyes. But when he looked up and smiled at his visitor, he looked very much like his famous father, the former president.

"Mr. Stuart, my father's told me a great deal about you." Colonel Roosevelt nodded. "Sit down and have some beans."

Amos Stuart sat down, accepted a plate, and began to eat hungrily. "Thank you, Colonel," he said, talking over a mouthful of beans. "I hate to be a hog, but I haven't had anything to eat all day."

Amos had come to find Owen and had been pleased to find that the battalion commander was none other than the son of his old friend, Theodore Roosevelt. All around them, soldiers were busy checking their gear, eating as they worked.

Colonel Roosevelt gave Amos an odd look. "You came at a pretty bad time, Mr. Stuart. Maybe you don't know what's happening."

"Only vaguely, Colonel," Amos admitted. "I did hear that General Pershing is sending General Bullard with the First Division to plug the gap here."

"That's right." Roosevelt took a swallow of water from a canteen, then spat it out. "Bad stuff! No wonder they drink wine over here!" Then he looked across the field where a line of trees filled a low-lying ridge and nodded. "That's our next objective over there—Cantigny. We've got to take it, General Bullard says."

"Must make you feel pretty good, Colonel, being picked to lead the first Americans in France into action. Your father will be proud of you."

The reference to his father seemed to embarrass Roosevelt, and Amos was sorry he'd mentioned it. "I don't know about proud," Roosevelt said briefly. "I know it's going to be quite a chore. The Germans are holed up pretty thick in there, our scouts say."

The two men chatted while they ate. At length Amos put down his empty plate. "I hate to ask favors, Colonel, but I've got a brother in your command. . . ."

"You'll want to see him, then," Roosevelt interjected. "He's not an officer, I take it?"

"No, he's a corporal. His name is Owen Stuart."

"I don't know him, but I'll have my adjutant locate him and escort you to him. You'd better see him pretty quickly, though," he added hurriedly. "We'll be pulling out early in the morning to take that town over there."

"Thank you, Colonel. And God be with you."

Amos followed a lieutenant appointed by the colonel and soon found himself weaving his way through the clusters of soldiers. Walking up to a tall officer, his escort said, "Lieutenant Masters, this is Amos Stuart, war correspondent from New York. His brother's in your company, isn't he?"

Masters nodded. "Yes." He put out his hand, "Glad to see you, Mr. Stuart. Come along and we'll see if we can find your brother."

Amos thanked the officer who had brought him over and followed Masters past a spot where a small group of men was busy assembling a machine gun. "How's my brother doing, Lieutenant Masters?" Amos asked as they made their way along.

Masters hesitated, scanning the groups of men around them. "Uh . . . not too well," he said finally. He stopped and turned to face Amos. "He's the best shot in the battalion and as tough as any . . . but we had a little action a while back, and some of the men got the idea that your brother is a little bit . . . well, timid. Nothing to it, probably," he said hurriedly, "but I thought you ought to know. Sergeant Stone and I are keeping an eye on him, and I'm sure he'll be all right."

Masters moved on, and as they walked over to the group of men, Amos felt a keen disappointment. He could not understand it, for he knew Owen was as brave as any man. But there was no time to question the lieutenant any further, for the officer had called out, "Corporal Stuart! Visitor here to see you! Drop back by the headquarters if you like, Mr. Stuart. Like to get my name in those New York papers." He grinned broadly then went back along the lines.

"Amos! What in the world are you doing here?" Owen exclaimed. *He looks trim and brown and fit*, Amos thought. *But then, he always did.*

"I just came for a visit. And to get a story, maybe." He looked across the line toward Cantigny. "Understand you're going to take a little walk over that way tomorrow."

Owen nodded. "Looks like it. C'mon and meet the fellas."

"All right. But tell me first, is everything okay? With you, I mean."

Owen looked up suddenly, his bright blue eyes steady. "Been hearing things, Amos?" he asked quietly. Noticing his brother's hesitation, he shrugged. "Eddy got the idea that I was a little slow getting into the fight we had a while back." He stopped, gazing out into the distance. "He may be right. I *was* slow. Don't know yet if it's something permanent or if it'll go away."

Amos knew his brother very well. He saw that this thing was troubling him greatly, although he was trying hard not to let it show. He slapped Owen on the shoulder. "You'll be all right. We Stuarts are slow starters, that's all."

Owen's face was very sober and serious. "I don't know, Amos. A man never knows what he is 'til he's tried. And when the bombs started going off and the bullets started flying, something seemed to happen to me. They say some men just don't have it. I hope I don't turn out to be one of those." Before Amos could speak, Owen said, "C'mon, let's go see some of the guys."

Sergeant Stone caught Amos's eye at once. This man, Amos knew, was a fighter, despite the prematurely white hair. He shook his hand warmly. "Glad to know you, Sergeant. You're a regular, I bet."

"That's right, Mr. Stuart. Growed up as a cowboy in Texas and turned out to be a soldier." He nodded slowly. "These here youngsters seem like babies to me."

Tyler Ashland, whom Amos met next, did look like a baby—plump and rosy-cheeked, with innocent blue eyes. He was very eager to meet Amos. "Your brother and I are real good friends. We've been together ever since we came across the Pond."

Kayo Pulaski grinned at Amos. "Get my name right, Mr. Stuart. When I get back, I'm gonna become heavyweight champion of the world, and I want the folks to get ready for me." He spelled his name carefully and Amos nodded, promising with a smile that he would be in the story.

As they were talking, another man joined the group and Amos looked up to see Eddy Castellano staring at him. "Hello, Eddy. I saw your brother a few days before I left."

"He still sore about my joinin' the army?" Eddy grinned. With a cocky look he added, "Tell him when you go back I'm learnin' how to shoot straight. That oughta help in the family business."

Amos blinked in surprise at the casual reference to the gangster activities of the Castellano family. When he hesitated, Eddy laughed. "Don't worry. Tell Nick that when I get back, I'll be able to take over all the heavy-duty stuff."

Amos stood there listening, making mental notes for the story he would write. He knew the real story would be here, with these foot soldiers, not with the generals. Intuitively, he also knew that most of them were afraid. All except Eddy, at least, and maybe Pulaski, for some of the younger men went a little bit pale when Eddy said, "I wish we could go after them Krauts right now! Can't wait to blast 'em outta that place!"

"May be a little bit tough." Stone shrugged. "They've had plenty of time to get nestled in."

"Won't be no trouble for us, Sarge." Eddy grinned, his gaze falling on Owen. He started to say something, then glanced at Amos and thought better of it.

Amos chatted with the young men for a while. Later on, when he was ready to leave, he had a chance to talk to Eddy. "I'll tell your brother I saw you. Any word you want to send home?"

Eddy shook his head. "Naw, this thing'll be over pretty soon and I'll be back." Then he narrowed his eyes and glared at Amos. "Nick says you're a pretty straight guy. But Owen, that brother of yours, he's a phony! I never had any use for preachers anyhow. And he's showed he's got a yellow streak a mile wide. If I was you, I'd take him outta here if you can work it. Old man Hearst ought to have some pull." He glanced over where Owen was talking with Tyler Ashland and shrugged. "Them two sissies . . . I ain't worried about *them*, but they could get the rest of us killed. The guy beside you is real important out here."

Amos hesitated, then said, "You're wrong about Owen, Eddy. I never saw a man with any more nerve than my brother."

"Yeah, he was a fighter, I know, but facin' a fist is different from facin' bullets. He just ain't got it, Amos. Try to get him outta here if you can, 'fore he gets the rest of us hurt."

Amos saw that the young man's mind was made up and left him with a brief salute. Walking back toward the waiting car with Owen, Amos talked of home, carefully avoiding mentioning the fight to come. Finally he said, "Well, good-bye, Owen. I've got to get back. I'll see you in a few days, I hope. I'll be right behind the troops here . . . along with the generals." He grinned and clapped his brother on the shoulder. "God wouldn't have brought you here unless he had a purpose behind it. So you just watch out for yourself, Owen. It'd be a pretty grim world for me without you. I've always been proud of you. You know that?"

"Guess it's really the other way around," Owen muttered. "I've always been proud of you and looked up to you, Amos. Don't worry about me. I'll be all right. And thanks for reminding me why I'm here."

Something about the harsh tone of his voice caused Amos to search his brother's face carefully. "Now wait a minute. Don't go getting yourself killed just to prove you're not a coward."

Owen shook his head. "Tell Dad and the others I'm missing them. And you take care of yourself. And," he hesitated, uncertainty clouding his eyes, "if anything does happen, watch out for Allie and Joey for me, will you, Amos?"

"Well, sure, I'd do that, but . . ."

Owen turned away. "Thanks a lot," he said over his shoulder and walked back to the group.

Amos got into the car and drove slowly to a position behind the lines. All the time he was thinking, *Owen's just the kind of guy who would do something crazy to prove a point. I hope he doesn't try it this time.*

At dawn on May 28, four thousand Americans of the First received their orders: "Come on, boys!" A deadly artillery barrage, striking about twenty-five yards ahead of their front ranks, supported the advance. Across the chewed-up ground they moved, infantry and machine gun companies spraying lead and spewing rifle fire.

The fight was bitter and sharp, but brief, and the Eighteenth Infantry did not really get into it. When the battle let up, there was time to rest and regroup, and that night there was cheer in the camp.

Sergeant Stone remained cautious, however. "Tomorrow morning," he said to his squad, "we'll catch it."

"Ah, the Jerries are finished," Eddy said airily. "They're still runnin'."

Sergeant Stone knew better. His mouth tightened into a firm line. "That kind of thinking will get you killed, Castellano."

Mack Stone proved to be a prophet, for on the next day, May 29, every German gun within range began pounding Cantigny. Owen and the rest of the squad took shelter where they could; avoiding the buildings, for fear of being buried alive. The barrage continued. Then Lieutenant Sam Masters came running along the line, screaming, "Come on! They're coming in!"

Stone whipped around, checked his rifle, and shouted an order. "Get set, you guys! This is where you earn your money!"

As the Eighteenth Battalion rushed forward they saw wave after wave of German soldiers, a gray tide coming against them, in the heaviest counterblow of all. Owen had no time to consider whether he would fight or run, for there was nowhere to run. Stone led the men forward, moving from point to point, throwing a deadly fire on the German troopers in the front lines. Men were dropping on both sides of Owen, and he saw one of his good friends—J. T. Donaldson, whom everybody called "The Professor"—suddenly stand up, sigh, and fall to the ground, the front of his uniform a mass of blood. His glasses fell beside him. He had taught English in college, and his wife and son had died with the flu. And now he was dead.

Tyler Ashland ran up to pull at Donaldson's tunic, but Owen called him back. "He's dead, Tyler. C'mon, nothing we can do for him now."

The fight raged on, and Owen and Tyler found themselves separated from the squad for a time. "Where are they?" Tyler cried out, his mild blue eyes glassy with fear. "I don't see them, Owen! We've gotta get out of here! We're going to be surrounded!"

"Take it easy, Tyler," Owen said calmly. "They've gone around the point. We'll just move forward and find them later on."

Over to the left, Sergeant Stone and the rest of the squad had found themselves commandeered by Lieutenant Sam Masters, who barked, "Stone, take as many men as you can and get to that point over by those rocks! Look! The Germans are throwing their full weight there! We've got to stop them!"

Obeying the order instantly, Stone yelled, "Machine guns! Get the machine gun!"

Eddy and the others began to advance, throwing themselves behind rocks and trees, firing steadily as the Germans continued to pour across the field. It was a bloody, violent fight, and it went on for over an hour.

Suddenly Eddy heard Sam Masters say, "We've gotten cut off!"

As Masters stood up to look, a bullet took him in the throat. He fell to the ground, gasping for air, but it was too late. He bled to death in a few seconds and lay still. Down the line, Stone hollered, "Lieutenant! Lieutenant!"

Eddy kept his head down, but yelled back, "He's dead, Sarge! Nothing we could do for him!"

Stone wiggled along the trench. He had almost reached the squad when a bullet raked him across the back, right above the beltline. When he discovered he could not move he cried out.

Eddy jumped up and dragged him to safety, calling to the others, "Keep firing! They're still comin'!" Then he leaned over and examined the wound in Stone's back. "Sarge, I don't think it's too bad."

Stone gasped, "Well, it hurts bad!" Stone tried to move and found that his legs and arms would still work. "Get this shirt off me!"

Somebody said, "Hold still so we can bandage that wound."

But Stone waved him off. "Never mind that now!" Looking up, he saw the Germans charging across the field. There were hundreds of them, it seemed, and he pulled his pistol from the holster. "We gotta hold 'em! If they break through here, they'll flank the whole battalion!"

Eddy's face was pale. "We ain't got much ammunition, Sarge."

"Then don't miss!" Stone said. "Let 'em get thirty feet away before you shoot! We gotta keep 'em outta here!" He rolled over on his stomach, held the pistol with both hands, and waited.

Others along the line waited, too, a small group at the point of the salient. Every man there knew that the Germans would be throwing their full weight against this one point.

"Kayo, I don't know if we can do it!" Eddy whispered to Pulaski. "There ain't many of us, and we ain't got much ammunition! And those guys have got flamethrowers!"

Pulaski swallowed hard and stared at the advancing gray wave. "It looks pretty bad. Too late to send somebody to the rear for help."

The men stood their ground. The Germans were massing for another attack. There were over two hundred of them, maybe more, at this particular point.

"That's more men than we got bullets!" Pulaski said.

An ominous silence seemed to fall across the field as the Germans massed. All of a sudden they rose up and began charging across, bayonets gleaming in the sunlight, and calling a wild battle cry as they advanced.

"Here they come, Kayo!" Eddy Castellano felt an uncharacteristic sense of despair. But at that moment a sudden movement caught his eye. He swiveled his head to see two men approaching from the rear with a machine gun. "Look! There's two of our guys and they've got a machine gun! They can hold them, if they can just get here!"

Every member of the squad turned to watch as the two soldiers, crouched low—one carrying the machine gun and the other several rounds of ammunition—stumbled and dodged as they headed for the salient where the squad was pinned down. A cheer went up from the squad.

But Pulaski flinched as bullets dusted the ground around the two struggling men. "They'll never make it," he groaned.

At that same moment an artillery shell exploded fifty feet behind the two soldiers. A second one came a few seconds later, no more than fifty feet in front.

"They got 'em straddled!" Eddy growled. "Them guys ain't gonna make it! And if they don't, we're dead meat!"

Taking another look, he saw that the shell had hit very close to the runners and that both of them were down. Eddy groaned and said wearily, "Well, that's it. It's over. We'll take as many of them as we can!" He lifted his gun and took aim, knowing his rifle would be impotent against the oncoming masses of Germans.

At that moment he heard Stone holler, "Look at that!"

Turning, Eddy saw that the two men were up on their feet again. This time he recognized them. Gasping incredulously, he said, "That's Stuart! That's the preacher! And the kid! It's the preacher and the kid!" which were his usual names for Owen and Tyler Ashland.

"They got Owen!" Pulaski strained to see. "Look at that arm! It's all bloody! I don't see how he can hang on!"

But the two men staggered forward for another twenty-five yards, and they heard Owen say, "Here, Ash—" The two men fell, Ashland fumbled with the machine gun, setting it in place, while Owen set the belt into the machine.

By now the Germans were no more than a hundred yards away, firing as they advanced. Bullets struck all around the machine gun, and Eddy yelled, "Give 'em cover! Give 'em everything you've got!" All up and down the line, a blistering fire from the Eighteenth Battalion began to open up. There were not many of them, but enough to discourage the front line of German soldiers, who began to take cover. And yet the wave came on.

"Why don't he fire!" Eddy yelled. "Why don't he shoot?" His voice was panicky.

And then there was the welcome stutter of the machine gun. Ashland was firing, holding on with both hands, as Owen fed the belt into it.

"That's it! Give it to 'em!" Eddy shouted, and the men began cheering again and redoubled their fire. The German line that had been advancing at a half run halted as though it had run into a concrete wall. Men began to drop everywhere. "Give it to 'em!" Eddy fired the last bullet he had, then picked up Donaldson's rifle and began firing again. "We got 'em!" he exulted. "We got 'em! Look, they're runnin'!"

It was true! The German advance had been halted in their tracks, and now those soldiers who were not down had turned and were desperately seeking shelter.

"C'mon!" Eddy called. "We gotta see about those two guys!" He threw down his empty rifle, pulled his pistol, and ran toward the machine gun. It was silent now, and the Germans were firing in a random, desultory fashion as they pulled back.

Eddy and Pulaski reached the two men at the same time. "Hey, you guys pulled our bacon outta the fire!" Eddy said.

"Yeah, it's great! A knockout!" Pulaski added.

But then they stopped, seeing Owen's face, as pale as paper. Looking down, they gasped in horror. Owen's right hand was missing. A crude tourniquet was tied around the stump, but blood still oozed from the wound.

"Hey!" Eddy cried. "Hey, Owen . . ."

Tyler Ashland reached over and grabbed Owen as he sagged. "We gotta get him to a doctor, or he's gonna bleed to death!"

Eddy at once said, "Tighten that tourniquet! Here, Kayo, help me carry him! Kid, you help too!" He stopped abruptly, eyeing Tyler with new respect. "Hey, Kid!"

Ashland looked at him, his pale face quivering, and Eddy grinned. "I take back everything I ever said about you. And I ain't never gonna call you 'Kid' again. You're a true man!"

"Yeah," he said. "Now let's get Owen to a medic."

They carried Owen back and found a stretcher. There was no lack of willing hands to take him to the field hospital. When they got there, the doctors were ready for a private who had had a finger shot off. But they were shocked when a tough-looking soldier elbowed the man aside and said, "You'll hafta wait. We got a real case for the docs."

The doctor was incensed. "Get out of here and wait your turn!" he said. "Out!"

And then he halted, for the tall, black-haired soldier with a pair of steely black eyes had lifted his pistol and was aiming at his heart. "Shut your mouth, Doc. Or I'll make it so *you* need a doctor. Now, fix up my buddy here."

The surgeon glanced down at the pale-faced form on the stretcher and glared at Eddy. "We'll talk about this later, after I take care of your friend."

"You can do anything you want to . . . *afterwards*," Eddy Castellano said. "And I'm tellin' you this: If he dies, I'll put a bullet through you."

The doctor, a heavyset gray-haired man, directed the men to lift Owen onto the operating table. Then he put his mask on, glanced at Eddy, pulled out his own pistol, and laid it on the operating table. "You stand right there, soldier. 'Cause I'll tell you something else: If this man dies, I'll know it five seconds before you do!"

Castellano appreciated the doctor's grim humor. He holstered his pistol. "You're okay, Doc. Don't let me stand in your way."

The doctor grunted, then turned to see what he could do for Owen. "Doesn't look good," he muttered. "He's lost too much blood. It'll take an act of God to save him!"

Castellano nodded. "That's okay. God's his partner. You just do your part and let God take care of his."

24

A BIT OF RIBBON

W here's Lylah Stuart's room?"

Nurse Alice Bendell, who had been reading one of the charts, looked up with a startled expression at the three men who had appeared out of nowhere. "I'm sorry. Visiting hours are over," she said primly.

A slight woman, Alice Bendell was conscious of her lack of stature and drew herself up to her full height. But that didn't help much. The three men standing before her were all tall. One of them was in civilian clothes, the second wore the uniform of the French Air Force, and the third was an American soldier, and she saw with a start that the sleeve of his right arm was pinned up.

The civilian spoke first. "Yes, we know that. But we really need to see her. We're worried about her. I don't think your supervisor would mind if we saw her."

"Has the baby come yet?" the flyer asked.

"Why, yes, but the mother's had a very difficult time. I'm sure the doctor wouldn't want her to be disturbed."

"My fiancée, Lady Heather Spencer, is with her," said the flyer. He used the title purposely, hoping it would impress the nurse as it had impressed him. "I think Lady Spencer might like for us to be admitted."

Nurse Bendell was taken aback. She had not realized that the woman who had come into the hospital the previous day with the American actress was a titled Englishwoman. Nevertheless, despite her size, the nurse was used to having her own way. "I'm afraid it's impossible!" she snapped.

The largest of the three men—the American soldier with the missing right arm—said rather gently, "I really wish you would ask the doctor, Nurse. We're very concerned about our sister."

"Your sister?"

"Yes. I'm Amos Stuart. This is Gavin Stuart, and this is Owen Stuart."

"Well . . ." the nurse relented, impressed by their rugged good looks and their courtesy. "I'll ask, but I can't make any promises."

"That's fine," Amos said quickly. "We'll wait right here." She left and he winked at Owen. "You should have shown her your Medal of Honor."

Owen grinned with embarrassment. "I don't think that would cut any ice with that one," he said. "Anyway, I'm a little bit shaky right now."

Almost at once the nurse was back with a short, rumpled-looking doctor with a shock of wild gray hair. "I'm Dr. Stevens," he said. He peered at the three men and inquired, "You're Miss Stuart's brothers?"

"That's right, doctor," Amos answered. "How is she?"

"Oh, very well." He shrugged slightly. "The first child is always difficult, and she's older than most first-time mothers, but she's fine."

"And the baby?" Gavin asked eagerly.

"A perfect specimen."

"Well, is it a boy or a girl?" Owen burst out.

Doctor Stevens grinned at him, suddenly amused. "It would have to be, wouldn't it?"

The three men stared at him, then all three burst into laughter. "I didn't know you English had a sense of humor," Amos said. "Well, which *one* is it?"

"A fine boy." The doctor nodded. "Nurse, go along and take these men to see their sister."

The diminutive nurse led the way down the hall, came to a door and opened it, standing back to allow them to precede her.

"Thank you, nurse," Amos said and led the way into the room. His quick eye found Heather, who rose at once and came to stand beside Gavin. *He picked a winner this time, that brother of mine,* Amos thought.

Then he went to the bed and stared down at Lylah, who was holding the baby to her breast. "Well, Sis," he said, "we missed the main event." He grinned and lightly put his hand on her head. "But it looks as if you did all right without us."

Surrounded by her three strong brothers, Lylah felt very small. "You're quite a committee. Did you come to conduct an inspection?"

"Right," Gavin said. "Let's see the little varmint."

Lylah pulled the blanket back. Gavin leaned over and looked at the child. "Why, he's all red and wrinkled!"

"You idiot!" Heather gasped and struck him a light blow on the shoulder. "He's a beautiful child! I hope you have a little more sense later on!"

Owen shouldered his way closer and looked down. "Can I hold him?" Lylah nodded and held up the little one. Owen reached out with his left hand, gathered the baby close, and held him awkwardly, gazing down into the tiny face. For a long time, he didn't say anything. Lylah watched his eyes carefully. Finally he smiled and said, "You know what? He looks like Pa!"

Amos came and stood behind Owen to stare down at the baby. "You know, I think you might be right? He does look like Pa!"

"Do you really think so?" Lylah whispered.

Gavin squinted and looked closer. "That he does!" Then he held out his hand and Lylah took it. "You did fine, Sis. Real fine."

Amos looked around at the family gathered here. "There sure are a lot of us Stuarts in this room." Then he glanced at Heather. "And some honorary Stuarts, almost. When are you two getting married?"

"As soon as Father can take his shotgun to Gavin." Heather smiled and linked her hand with his, leaning against him.

"Then the fight will begin—whether we'll live in England or in America."

Gavin grinned. "Got to win *this* war first." He looked at her adoringly. "But any place will suit me as long as you're there."

Lylah lay quietly, listening to the conversation swirling around her. She was very tired, but the pain and the difficulty of the birth now seemed magically gone.

Amos leaned down and kissed her on the cheek. "What are you going to name him?"

Lylah took the baby from Owen and nestled him close. She ran her finger across his forehead, and the tiny face wrinkled up at her touch. "He looks like a little old man when he does that, doesn't he?" Then she looked up at Amos and said, "His name is Adam."

"Adam Stuart . . . Adam Stuart . . ." Amos murmured. "Has a nice ring to it."

"Sounds good to me," Gavin said. "How about Adam Gavin Stuart, just to give him a little class?"

"It'd probably be confusing. We're going to name our first one Gavin. That'd be too many Gavins around for even me," Heather said, smiling slightly.

Owen stood looking down at Lylah and her son. Then he glanced over at his brothers. "Seems like a long time ago, doesn't it, when we were all kids back in Arkansas? We've come a long way together." His face grew cloudy. "We've still got a long way to go."

"The war will be over soon," Amos said quickly. "Our troops are pouring in by the hundreds of thousands. Germany's already making peace offers. It'll be over before the year's out."

Gavin reached out and touched the ribbon on Owen's chest. "There'll be a big to-do over you when we get back home, Brother. Not many men win the Medal of Honor and live to tell about it."

Owen was again embarrassed. "It's just a bit of ribbon, that's all."

"It's more than that," Amos said quietly, "and everybody knows it. But I can see you'd rather not talk about it." He leaned down and whispered to Lylah, "We don't want to tire you. But we'll be back."

"Stay a while, Amos," Lylah pleaded. Knowing that these two were especially close, the others prepared to leave the room.

"We'll see you later, Sis," Owen said, "and I'll hold that little scudder some more."

Gavin grinned at Heather. "Come on, woman. You can cook us something to eat."

When they were gone, Amos pulled up a chair and sat down beside Lylah's bed. Reaching over, he took the baby from Lylah and held him. Pulling back the blanket, he stared at the infant and murmured, "Adam Stuart. He's a fine boy, Lylah. I know you're very proud of him."

"But he'll never have a father, Amos. Never."

Amos looked across at his sister, his fine eyes quiet and watchful. Then a smile came to his lips and he shook his head in denial. "Yes, he will, Lylah. Didn't you know that God is the father of the fatherless?" He held the child up and looked at him, and many thoughts ran through his mind. Then he simply reached over, giving the child back to Lylah, and kissed her on the cheek and sat back saying, "God will be the father of your child, Lylah."

The two sat there in silence, and Amos watched as his words soothed the worried wrinkles from Lylah's brow. Her lips grew soft, and she leaned over and kissed the baby's cheek. Her thoughts were far away, he knew, in a world that none of them could ever enter—the world she had known with the German. Then he looked at the baby again. "He has a goodly heritage, Lylah. A goodly heritage."

Again silence flowed over the room and they sat in the quietness, watching as the baby beat the air with his fists and wondering what sort of world Adam Stuart would know.

A Time to Laugh

After the Great War, it seems that America has gone wild. In book three of the Odyssey Series, members of the Stuart family struggle with a changing society. Their experiences during the Roaring Twenties and prohibition do not leave them unscathed.